WAITING FOR THE VIOLINS

Acclaim for Justine Saracen's Novels

"*Mephisto Aria* could well stand as a classic among gay and lesbian readers."—*ForeWord Reviews*

"Justine Saracen's *Sistine Heresy* is a well-written and surprisingly poignant romp through Renaissance Rome in the age of Michelangelo. …The novel entertains and titillates while it challenges, warning of the mortal dangers of trespass in any theocracy (past or present) that polices same-sex desire."—Professor Frederick Roden, University of Connecticut, Author, *Same-Sex Desire in Victorian Religious Culture*

"…the lesbian equivalent of Indiana Jones. …Saracen has sprinkled cliffhangers throughout this tale…If you enjoy the History Channel presentations about ancient Egypt, you will love this book. If you haven't ever indulged, it will be a wonderful introduction to the land of the Pharaohs. If you're a *Raiders of the Lost Ark*-type adventure fan, you'll love reading a woman in the hero's role."—*Just About Write*

"Saracen's wonderfully descriptive writing is a joy to the eye and the ear, as scenes play out on the page, and almost audibly as well. The characters are extremely well drawn, with suave villains, and lovely heroines. There are also wonderful romances, a heart-stopping plot, and wonderful love scenes. *Mephisto Aria* is a great read."—*Just About Write*

Sarah, Son of God can lightly be described as the "'The Lesbian's *Da Vinci Code*' because of the somewhat common themes. At its roots, it's part mystery and part thriller. *Sarah, Son of God* is an engaging and exciting story about searching for the truth within each of us. Ms. Saracen considers the sacrifices of those who came before us, challenges us to open ourselves to a different reality than what we've been told we can have, and reminds us to be true to ourselves. Her prose and pacing rhythmically rise and fall like the tides in Venice; and her reimagined life and death of Jesus allows thoughtful readers to consider 'what if?'"—*Rainbow Reader*

"*Mephisto Aria*, brims with delights for every sort of reader...at each level of Saracen's deliciously complicated plot, the characters who are capable of self-knowledge and of love evaded their contracts with the devil, rescued by each other's feats of queerly gendered derring-do done in the name of love. Brava! Brava! Brava!"—Suzanne Cusick, Professor of Music, New York University

In *Beloved Gomorrah*..."Saracen's prose is efficient and purposeful; it's straightforward enough to get the point across and just showy enough to make you grin while reading. She also has a great ear for dialogue that sounds spoken instead of written. Even if you're not interested in Sodom and Gomorrah as paradise or seeing avenging angels as terrorists, you'll love being sucked underwater by Saracen's characters in this addictingly readable novel. Highly recommended."
—Jerry Wheeler, *Out In Print*

Visit us at www.boldstrokesbooks.com

By the Author

WAITING FOR THE VIOLINS

by

Justine Saracen

2014

ISBN 13: 978-1-62639-046-1

This Trade Paperback Original Is Published By
Bold Strokes Books, Inc.
P.O. Box 249
Valley Falls, NY 12185

First Edition: March 2014

CREDITS
EDITOR: SHELLEY THRASHER
PRODUCTION DESIGN: SUSAN RAMUNDO
COVER DESIGN BY SHERI (GRAPHICARTIST2020@HOTMAIL.COM)

Acknowledgments

Historical novels, whatever their fictional content, require research, and sometimes you need more than a few books or an afternoon of Googling. Sometimes the memories and experience of a living person are invaluable, and several such people have assisted me. I am therefore most grateful: to Celine Bissen, for offering information, documents and a visit to the gravesite of her heroic aunt; to Shirah Goldman, for sharing intimate family history and guiding me through a concentration camp; to Leon Van Audenhaege and Laci Meert, for supplying historical facts about Woluwe St. Lambert; to Julie Tizard for the nomenclature of flying; and to Laurence Schram for providing details on the Dossin Caserne under the German Occupation.

On the business end, not just for this novel, but for all its predecessors as well, I owe enormous gratitude to Shelley Thrasher for constant patient editing, to Sheri for a great cover drawn from the deep pool of her imagination, and to Radclyffe for making the whole endeavor possible in the first place.

Acknowledgments

[faded, illegible text]

Dedication

To Celine Collin, killed while courier for the Ardenne Maquis, Aisik and Rywka Goldman, who perished at Auschwitz, and to all those who resisted the German occupation of Belgium.

CHAPTER ONE

Dunkirk
June 1940

Antonia Forrester brought the ambulance to a sudden halt at the top of a bluff. The sounds from the beach that had been muffled as she came up the hill now assaulted her with full force: the shouts of men, the thunder of artillery, the *rat-a-tat* of strafing shot all along the beach, the wind scattering sand against her windshield.

She jumped from the driver's seat onto the ground and gawked for a moment at the terrifying panorama of a fleeing army. Lines of men in the hundreds of thousands striated the gray sand like swarms of insects crawling along the beach into the surf. The wind rising from the sea carried the sooty metallic stench of explosives.

In the distance, the heavy troop carriers and hospital ships waited, unable to approach for risk of beaching. Above them, Stukas swooped low and strafed the water, striking some of the craft.

"Move it, move it, for Chrissake. Get the hell down!" A cluster of men ran toward her and yanked open the rear doors of the ambulance. The walking wounded staggered out onto the sandy ground, and a medic guided them away toward a path leading to the beach.

She ran to the rear of the ambulance and grabbed one end of a stretcher. It slid out and dropped between her and another soldier, suddenly tugging on her shoulders.

"This way," the medic barked. "Wounded have priority, over here to the right." Staggering slightly under the load, she followed him along the same sandy path to the shoreline, where boats were loading on stretchers in small numbers.

"How're you doing?" she knelt and shouted over the din at the man she'd just carried down. He'd been hit in the lower back and was paralyzed.

"Okay," he said mechanically. "Just stay close by, please."

"Sure thing. Promise." It was all she could offer, and she meant it.

A tiny fishing boat came in fighting the waves, and the fishermen jumped from it into the frothing surf. "Come on, load 'em in. We got room for six, and a few standing." He took hold of the stretcher poles.

Antonia waded into the water and felt the shock of cold, but focused on lifting the stretcher up onto the rocking skiff. A moment later, someone heaved her up over the gunwale as well. Then, alarmingly low in the water, they pushed back away from shore.

No one spoke over the wind, the gunfire, and the sound of the outboard motor. Antonia gripped the soldier's hand, though both his and hers were ice cold.

Motoring against the wind under low-swooping fighter planes, they arrived at the hospital ship. *Paris*, it said on the bow. Experienced hands threw down ropes and hoisted the wounded on board, and the exhausted stretcher-bearers struggled up the ladder.

The deck was covered with wounded lying on stretchers or huddled together. "You're the last," one of the officers called out to the group. "You'll have to stay topside till we get across."

The ship turned laboriously in the waves and headed out to sea.

"We've made it." Antonia leaned over her patient. "You're gonna be okay. We're on our way home."

"Thank God for—"

The explosion stunned her for a moment. Then, through the smoke, she saw the hole in the stern deck. Heavy bombers had arrived, backing up the Stuka fighters.

"It's okay. The explosion was above the waterline. We're still sailing." She squeezed his hand, though her own trembled.

The second bomb crashed perpendicular through the deck deafening her with the sound of ripping steel. A third bomb struck; she felt the ship shudder with it. Within minutes, the stern was under water. All was chaos, smoke, coughing, screaming, and a hellish pain in her neck. The clothing on her back was on fire and so was her hair.

Something crashed against her and sent her toppling over the side. The frigid water momentarily stopped the scorching pain but she struggled to stay afloat. She still held her patient's sleeve, and he slid off the stretcher into the water next to her. Paralyzed from the waist down, he flailed with his arms, imploring her with his eyes to save him. He clutched at her as water covered his face and pulled her under with him. She thrashed, trying to regain the surface, but her own chest hurt with every movement, and the drowning soldier pulled her ever deeper.

Desperate and choking, she pried off his rigid fingers, and as he fell away from her, she kicked with all her force. But even without him, the weight of her shoes and sodden clothing was too great, and she sank, her lungs screaming for air. Reflexively, she gulped salty water, and her last faint sensation before she blacked out was of something yanking hard on her hair.

CHAPTER TWO

June 1940

Sandrine Toussaint stood at the window of the Château Malou gazing out over the verdant grounds. How unjust that the estate was still so lovely when she herself, and all of Belgium, had suffered catastrophe. The surrender of the king a month before after an eighteen-day struggle against the Germans was devastating, but she grieved more for her own loss. She turned away from the window and took up the photo of her brother Laurent, killed by one of Rommel's troops. Rommel, the only military name she knew other than Hitler, and she hated him.

She'd spent all the tears she had for Laurent, and life had gone on. But today she'd come across his violin among the long-neglected items in his wardrobe, and the pain of his absence had swelled up once again.

He was dashingly handsome in his uniform, and she was struck again by the extraordinary resemblance between them. Both were Nordic pale, with prominent strong chins, long straight noses, and intense eyes, though his were blue and hers green. They had passed as twins in spite of his being two years younger. Only their temperaments were different, he being the quiet musician and she the truculent tomboy.

The door from the entry hall opened, and Gaston, her gardener, carpenter, and house repairman, thrust his head through the opening. "Madam, they've arrived, as you expected."

She nodded and prepared for the charade she and her household had prepared. The Germans had occupied Château Malou once before, during the Great War, so it was inevitable they would lay claim to it again. But this time, it wouldn't be so easy.

The disappointment on the face of the officer when he came into the entry hall and glanced around amused her. "Could use a little maintenance," he said, pointing his baton at the cracked ceiling. "Does it leak?"

"Yes, unfortunately," she replied, glancing down at the puddle at her feet. Then she led him into the main room. Another man, of some lower rank, followed him in.

"How long have those been broken?" He pointed with his chin at the half-dozen cracked or missing glass panes. The rain-chilled air wafted through the openings.

"Since before the fighting. Political vandals, we think."

He nodded. "Communists. They don't much like mansions."

"A shame." She sighed. "The glass has to be specially cut, so it will take weeks to replace."

He wrinkled his nose. "What is that odor?"

"It's probably the mold. From the cracks between the walls and the ceiling. Or do you mean the plumbing problem?"

The officer looked alarmed. "You have a plumbing problem?"

"Unfortunately. The pipes are a hundred years old and they've just burst. We've had to turn off the system and bring water from the fountain outside. It's very inconvenient for the toilets."

The officer scribbled something in a notebook, and she knew her case was made.

The rest of the tour of the decrepit château would hardly be necessary: the smoke-filled kitchen downstairs from the coal-burning stove, the rotten and stinking carpet in the upstairs corridor, and the pools of water on the floors of several of the upstairs rooms would simply cement the conclusion he had already drawn. The château was a wreck and not worth requisitioning.

"The Belgian aristocracy has come down in the world," the officer remarked upon leaving.

The ruse would have amused her if she hadn't been so embittered. As soon as it was clear the house didn't interest the occupiers, they would turn the plumbing and the water boiler back on and get rid of the stinking carpet. She even knew a glazier who could replace the windowpanes. But she couldn't undo her leaden sense of defeat and violation.

She had to do something. She had no idea what, but surely someone would resist, somewhere. She would join them, and she would take revenge.

"For you, Laurent," she said, placing the violin next to his picture on the mantelpiece. "And for my conscience."

CHAPTER THREE

Orpington Hospital
August 1940

Antonia lay stupefied by morphine, cordoned off from the all-male population of the hut. How long had she been in hospital? A few weeks, a month? She'd lost count.

Her shoulder was in a cast, and the unremitting ache with every breath told her she had broken ribs. The doctors had informed her that a severe concussion had caused her headaches and distorted vision. The worst had been the second- and third-degree burns on her back and neck, and she had lain in purgatory for weeks before the pain subsided.

Memory of the attack lingered dully, but she was safe now, and the moans of the more seriously wounded soldiers on the other side of the partition kept her from self-pity. The long, green-painted ward held some forty wounded soldiers, and a dozen other huts spread out over the grounds held hundreds more. Cripples, amputees, respiratory cases, shell-shocked soldiers—all comrades from those terrible days in France and Belgium.

She'd asked where the other women were, her nursing comrades from Dunkirk, and got no answer, but her solitude in the Orpington ward made it clear no other women had survived the destruction of the *Paris*.

She glanced up as the curtains at the foot of her bed parted and a gray-uniformed nurse swept in with quiet efficiency. Three stripes on her sleeve, an assistant matron. Her white muslin cap with MPNS embroidered on it was tilted carelessly over short gray hair.

"How are we feeling this morning?" She came to the side of the bed.

"About the same." Antonia twisted sideways, and the nurse lifted her nightgown away from the back of her neck. The cool air of the room felt good on the sensitive skin.

"It's looking better." We should be ready to release you to a rehab facility soon. Can you walk without help?"

"Yes, but I'm a bit wobbly."

"Well, come along then. A gentleman's here to see you, and he's requested the privacy of the Sisters' Room. Here, I'll help you put on your dressing gown."

"Gentleman?" Antonia slid her arm into the sleeve, puzzled. She didn't have any gentlemen in her life. Not since the death of her father a year before. Her superiors in the Queen Alexandra's Imperial Military Nursing Service were all women. "Did he say what it was about?"

"No, only that it was confidential." She took Antonia's right arm and guided her past the curtain and into the small room at the end of the hospital hut. A military officer stood by the window smoking a cigarette, as if deep in thought. He turned around at the sound of their entrance.

"Thank you very much, Sister," he said. The nurse left, closing the door quietly behind her.

"Please, sit down, for heaven's sake." He motioned toward the chair in front of the desk and took up position behind it.

"Forgive me, I'm Major Atkins," he said, reaching across the desk to offer his hand. She took it, though extending her arm hurt both her ribs and the new skin on her back. She waited for him to explain the cause of his visit.

He studied her for a moment, holding his cigarette delicately between his index and middle fingers, then tapped it once over the glass ashtray. "The doctors inform me you're healing very well and that after a few months of rehabilitation, you'll be able to resume normal activity. May I ask what your plans are?"

"My plans? I don't know. I don't think it'll be nursing. I hate the helplessness."

"Do you?" His tone seemed to hold a certain satisfaction.

"Umm. Eventually, I thought I might apply for the Wrens, or even the Women's Air Force."

"You're ready to go back to the front? In spite of all that?" He gestured with his chin toward her shoulder cast.

The memory of the scorching flames struck her briefly, as did the image of a soldier, paralyzed and drowning. "Yes. I'd go tomorrow if it didn't still hurt to move."

He opened the file that lay on the desk, which she hadn't noticed. Her photo was clipped to the upper corner. "I see you lived for a few years in Brussels."

"Yes. My parents moved there when I was four. My father was a chemist involved in the Solvay Institute, which met in Brussels. We returned to England when the Germans occupied the city."

"Yes, in 1914, when you were eight. Your record also indicates that you spent two years studying in Paris, starting in 1924. Your French should be pretty good, then."

"I like to think so. One of the advantages of learning a language at a young age."

"What about German and Dutch?" He took up his cigarette again and puffed between questions.

"A little of both, but nothing useful. Why are you asking?"

He blew smoke out of the side of his mouth. "Are you afraid of guns, or flying, or…say…parachuting in the dark?"

"No to all of those. Why do you want to know?"

"The prime minister has just approved a new organization that can use your talents and zeal, and you'll have a much greater effect on the war than you would ministering to the wounded, or even flying auxiliary aircraft. It has the very dull name of Special Operations Executive."

"That doesn't tell me much. What does it do?"

"*Will* do. We hope. Espionage, sabotage, reconnaissance, fomenting unrest, resistance. Mr. Churchill wants to send some of our people back to 'set Europe ablaze.'"

Antonia winced at the word *ablaze.* "And what, specifically, would I do?"

"Whatever you prove to be most skillful at, after your training." He closed her file. "So, what do you think? Are you interested?" He finished his cigarette and stubbed it out in the large square of cut glass.

"Oh, I'm definitely interested. But as you can see, I'm handicapped at the moment."

"You can take as long as you need to recover. A year, two years even. We'll wait. When you're ready, we'll escort you to the training location. Until then, you'll be sworn to secrecy. You understand that."

He removed a piece of paper from the middle of the file and slid it toward her. "This specifies what I've just told you. Do you want some time to consider our offer?"

She glanced through the agreement while he took a fountain pen from his breast pocket and unscrewed the cap.

"No." She held out her hand for the pen. "I accept."

Chapter Four

June 1941

Heinz Büttner patrolled the Rue des Bouchers along with three others in his detachment, though he gradually fell behind. His boots were giving him blisters, and his bladder had begun to act up again.

Why the hell were they patrolling anyhow? The damned Belgians should have been their allies, and some of them, the Rexists and the Flemish nationalists, already knew that. Like the Dutch, they were of good racial stock, and some of the women were real lookers. Almost Aryan, though he wasn't really sure what that was.

But you never knew when you passed these people on the street. You could look a man right in the eye, and he might be thinking about putting a bullet in your head.

Damn, his feet were killing him. And he had to piss.

"Keep an eye out, will you?" he said to one of his comrades, then stepped into an alleyway and relieved himself with a sigh. His hot urine gave off a sharp odor that mixed with the smells of the trashcans along the wall.

Rebuttoning his trousers, he pivoted back toward the entrance to the alley where his companion stood watch, but he stepped into something slippery-soft. "Ah, shit." The irony of his expletive made him even angrier. At that moment he spied the culprit, a piebald dachshund squatting beside the trashcan, and he kicked it in irritation.

The kick caught the animal just at the hip, causing it to spin around facing him. With a low growl, it bit his ankle. His heavy boots protected him from any harm, but the double insult of attack and a shit-stained boot enraged him. He shook his foot briefly, throwing the cur off, then drew his sidearm and shot it. The bullet pierced the tiny hip and slammed against the plaster wall behind it. Shrieking, the dog retreated on three legs, blood pouring from the wound.

At the sound of the gunshot, one of the doors on the alley opened and girl of about fourteen stared at him, then rushed to the wounded and yelping animal.

"Heinz, you idiot! You can't go around doing that," his comrade shouted at him.

"Büttner! What the hell are you doing?" His superior appeared at the entrance of the alley.

"The cur attacked me, sir."

"Get back to your work or I'll put you on report. The last thing we need is this kind of crap stirring up the locals."

"Yes sir." He saluted and strode angrily back onto the main street.

"My apologies, mademoiselle." The senior officer tipped his head slightly toward the sobbing girl, who held the dog in her arms, then followed the delinquent gendarme.

❖

Sandrine Toussaint was sitting inside the Café Suèdoise, looking out onto the Rue de Bouchers, when she heard the gunshot. Laura Collin turned in alarm, and as she rushed through the stockroom to the rear door, Sandrine followed.

Laura's younger sister, Celine, knelt on the ground clutching the injured dog to her chest. "They've shot Suzi." She sobbed, struggling to her feet.

Speechless, Sandrine held the door open while Laura helped Celine inside. Crouching beside one of the café tables, Laura pressed a linen napkin against the wound to staunch the bleeding, then inspected the dog's hindquarters.

"Look, there are two holes, a little one here and a larger one in the back. The bullet passed all the way through." The dog curled up and shrieked at her touch.

Francis Brasseur, Laura's husband, came from behind his counter and stood over them. A handsome man, his size and mane of black hair gave him a commanding presence, which belied a passive personality. A weak back had kept him from military service, but both he and the army seemed to agree he was not soldier material. "They shoot our dogs to remind us they can shoot us."

"The bastards," Laura snarled. "I'd like to shoot a few of them, and the damned Belgian police along with them." Half the size of her husband, Laura seemed to contain all the aggression he lacked. She helped Celine carry the dog to a chair at the side of the café.

"Don't be ridiculous," Francis said. "You'll just get us all in trouble with that kind of talk."

Sandrine followed Laura and Celine across the café. "It's not ridiculous, Francis. Resistance is developing everywhere in Belgium. The Germans just call it terrorism."

"Well, I'm not keen on that kind of thing. Anyone who resists is going to end up in a Gestapo jail." He went back to his counter and resumed drying glassware. "Besides, not all Belgians want to. Your own neighbors, you don't know whether they hate the Nazis or welcome them. Not to mention the Rexists and the collaborators and the Belgian SS. The dog's still alive, so it's best to forget what happened."

Sandrine crossed her arms. "I don't think she should forget, Francis. I don't think any of us should forget that Belgian men died less than a year ago trying to stop this occupation." She addressed Laura. "If you're really serious about resistance, I know people who are already doing something, and they need help."

Laura took a step toward her, pale eyes squinting slightly. "You want us to assassinate Germans? At this point, you could convince me."

"No. Nothing direct like that. But I know an organization of Belgian patriots who are smuggling people down to Spain and then to England, soldiers who couldn't escape at Dunkirk and men who want to fight with the free Belgian Army. A young woman started it, all by herself, with just a couple of guides to cross the mountains."

"Who are you talking about?"

"Andrée de Jongh. Her father is headmaster at one of the schools near here, and I'm sure they'd be grateful for some assistance."

Celine still held the bloodstained napkin to the rump of her whimpering dog. "Count me in," she said hoarsely. "Just tell me what to do."

Staring into the distance, Laura seemed to jump ahead. "They'll need new identity cards, ration stamps, people to hide them along the route…"

"Clothing, medical attention, communications systems," Sandrine added. "Some of that already exists. And we're working on the rest."

"We?" Francis remarked. "Does that mean you're one of them?"

Laura still stared into space, nodding to herself. "I know someone who works in the town registry and I bet—"

All heads turned as the door swung open and a German officer entered, followed by a subaltern carrying a briefcase. Sandrine recognized him from the newspapers and unconsciously took a step back. He marched halfway into the café and clicked his heels with a sharp military bow in front of her.

"Alexander von Falkenhausen at your service. Are you the owner of the dog?"

"No, Herr Baron. That is the young lady." She pointed toward Celine, who still sat with the wounded dog in her arms.

His eyebrows rose and he smiled faintly. "Recognition by a lovely lady. What a compliment." He turned and approached Celine, who glowered up at him.

"Mademoiselle, please accept my apologies for the unpleasant incident."

"His name was Büttner. Heinz Büttner. He's a criminal," Celine said defiantly.

"It's not just an 'unpleasant incident,' Herr Baron," Sandrine said with a more conciliatory tone. "The dog is a beloved family member, an innocent creature."

"Yes, quite so, madam. I've had a few dogs and understand your concern. I will see to it that the division veterinarian tends to the creature and that the gendarme responsible is disciplined." He bent slightly at the waist as if asking her to dance. "And might I ask to whom I am speaking?"

"Sandrine Toussaint," she said coolly.

"Ah, yes. Owner of the Château Malou. As I recall, my officers inspected it last year as a possible headquarters but reported it as unsuitable." He paused, apparently for effect. "Had I known the owner of the Château Malou was so charming, I would have insisted on making the inspection myself. Perhaps you will invite me to visit one day." He held her glance longer than she liked, and she looked away.

"Of course. You are always welcome," she replied mechanically.

Francis came out from behind the counter. "Herr Baron. Can we offer you a glass of wine or beer?" Sandrine looked at him with surprise, Laura with horror.

"Thank you, but I have other duties to perform today. Perhaps another time." He swept his gaze around the café. "Nice ambiance. I shall make a point of recommending this place to my colleagues."

"We would be honored to provide a little sanctuary to the Wehrmacht," Francis replied with a slightly servile tilt of the head.

Von Falkenhausen returned his attention to Sandrine. "I hope we can continue our chat on a less sorrowful occasion." He took a step toward the sullen Celine. "Once again, mademoiselle, my sincerest regrets. I will send the divisional veterinarian as soon as possible." He snapped another quick soldier's bow and left, his adjutant following him silently.

"What in God's name did you just do?" Laura hissed at her husband. "You're going to make us into a club for the Wehrmacht?"

Francis held up both of his hands. "My dear, if we're going to engage in smuggling Allied soldiers, we'd better have a few Nazi friends to protect us from scrutiny, don't you think?"

He turned to Sandrine. "Would you be so kind as to inform Monsieur de Jongh that we are at his disposal?"

CHAPTER FIVE

June 1941

Sandrine rode her bicycle through the strip of woods toward the Château Malou. Even from a distance, it was at once majestic and pathetic, reminiscent of class privilege and testimony to its passing.

In spite of the crisis with Celine's dog, the trip into Brussels had proved productive. The de Jonghs would be glad. Now two new people were on board, three if she counted Celine, who was barely fifteen.

She dismounted at the entrance of the château and stared up at it nostalgically. With its two stories and seven bays of tall shuttered windows it had a certain sad splendor, even in the rain.

The housemaster came out at the sound of her arrival to take her bike to the carriage house. "Thank you, Gaston." She climbed the stone steps to the entrance and slipped through the still-open oak doors.

The high-ceiling entryway with its wall niche and marble Greek vase might have been imposing a century earlier, but now the vase was empty, and it all seemed cold. Warmth and welcome came toward her in the form of her rambunctious wolfhounds. "Hello, Baudie, Vercie." She scratched energetically under their ears.

As she hung up her coat and exchanged her wet shoes for dry slippers, her housekeeper appeared.

"Hello, Mathilde. Everyone fed and watered?"

"Yes, madam. Would you like to eat something too?"

"That sounds lovely. I'm famished." With the dogs pattering happily behind her, she followed Mathilde down the stairs to the kitchen. The pleasing smell of fried onions met her in the doorway, but she hesitated.

"Let me first go check on our guests," she said, and continued down the narrow corridor leading to the coal room. At the end of the corridor, the cupboard that concealed the hidden "apartment" was slightly ajar.

"It's me, lads," she called out, and swung the cupboard out toward her. A cloud of warm air, thick with the odor of men, wafted toward her.

A young man of about thirty, wearing corduroy trousers and a pullover sweater that had seen better days, stood up to meet her. Behind him, a younger man, blond and boyish, hiked up trousers that were obviously a size too large. Both were pale from weeks of hiding.

"Hello, Jack, Teddy. Listen. I've talked to a few friends in Brussels. It's going to take awhile, but they're putting together a plan to move you south, through France to Spain."

"Crikey, I'm ready. Tomorrow's not too soon."

"We're not that far yet. Could be a couple of weeks. We need to make identification papers and travel permits for you. Then we have to find safe houses where you can rest and eat, guides through the mountains, all that sort of thing. I just wanted to let you know we're working on it."

"Weeks, eh?" The one called Teddy sighed.

She nodded sympathetically. "Do you want to go for a walk?"

"Thanks. Gaston already took us out for an hour, with the dogs. I think the big one likes me. The one with the name I can't pronounce."

"Vercingetorix. A Gallic hero in ancient war. We call him Vercie."

"Vercie, right. Anyhow, I think I'll simply take another nap," Teddy said. "Like the one I just had."

"Be patient, lads. We're doing the best we can." She turned away, hating to leave them in their dark hideaway, hating the sense of helplessness, theirs and her own.

❖

Adding another log to the fire, Sandrine buttoned her sweater against the chill.

Well, that was the price one paid to be heir to a three-hundred-year-old estate. She stood close to the flames while the log caught, enjoying the warmth on her legs, and glanced again at the pictures on the mantelpiece, of her parents, her husband Guy, and her brother.

She was proud of her family and their mansion, but maintaining it was a financial nightmare, even with the income from Guy's investments in the Congo plantations. Laurent's last big expenditure outside of house repairs had been in 1939, his beloved Mercedes Benz 230, but he'd been able to drive it for only a year before the war started. And now the juggling act had fallen to her, the sole surviving member of the family. She brushed dust off the picture of Laurent.

She missed him terribly. Her husband and father less so. Politically they had been conservative and she could not forgive them for the right-wing Rexist party they belonged to.

The 1930s had decimated the two families of the Château Malou. One death after another followed—her mother of pneumonia and her husband after only four years of marriage, of yellow fever.

Her father had lived on, still inviting his dreadful guests to the house where they ranted about the "moral renewal" of Belgian society through a more powerful Catholic church. She ceased to argue with them, seeing that their anticommunism, anti-Semitism, and anti-masonry were nearly identical to German fascism. But it was all rather naïve, as it turned out.

Her father's death in 1937 had spared him the irony and the sorrow of seeing German fascists kill his own son when they seized Belgium.

How things had changed. The four people who had made up her family were gone, the house was cold and empty, and she harbored two British soldiers in her basement.

"Baudie! Vercie, come here!" she called, retreating to the sofa, and in a moment the clattering of their claws sounded on the hardwood floor. The door was already ajar, and the two Russian wolfhounds leapt onto the sofa scrambling for places over and under her legs. Awkward as the tangle was, the warmth of the dogs was a great comfort, and she slowly slipped from brooding into napping.

The ringing phone woke her and she sat up, shooing away the dogs. It took a moment for her head to clear and for her to recognize the voice, and she cringed.

"Oh, Baron von Falkenhausen. What an unexpected...pleasure. I'm fine, thank you." She finished the conversation mechanically, providing the only allowable answers to the most powerful man in Belgium.

Yes, she did like classical music. No, she hadn't heard about the new Bulgarian violinist playing with the National Orchestra. Yes, she'd be delighted to attend a concert at the Palais des Beaux-Arts. In the company of the famous General Rommel? What an honor that would be.

An evening with the biggest Nazi in Belgium and with the general whose soldiers had killed her brother. When she hung up, her fingers were white.

❖

The château Baron von Falkenhausen had chosen as an alternative was vastly more imposing than her own, but just as hard to heat, and at the post-concert reception, she found herself once again trying to warm herself by a huge and ineffective fireplace. This time two Wehrmacht generals in full dress uniform flanked her.

She stood between two monsters, and only the comedy of their competing displays of military prowess alleviated the intimidation she felt. Both stood erect, impeccable, in gray-green tunics with gold, braided shoulder boards and the arabesque collar patches of a general. Both had the embroidered swastika over the right pocket and hugely impressive medal arrays across their chests.

Rommel wore the Knight's Cross with diamonds, swords, and oak leaves, putting him at the highest level of decorated soldiers. But von Falkenhausen's Knight's Cross of the Württemberg Crown was bestowed primarily on the aristocracy, and the sparkling star at his throat advertised that he was a baron.

Dining with the devil, she'd thought all evening, though in spite of her appalling escort, she had greatly enjoyed the Tchaikovsky violin concerto. Only the invitation to the private reception at the château afterward had come as an unpleasant surprise. At least they weren't alone. Half a dozen other officers, some with wives or female companions, made small talk throughout the drawing room.

While a waiter filled her champagne glass for the second time, von Falkenhausen said, "I've always found Tchaikovsky a bit too emotional. Like all the Russians. What do you think, Herr General?"

Erwin Rommel downed his champagne and held the glass out to be refilled. "Emotional? Why not? I tried learning just the first movement of that concerto when I was young. Never got it off the ground."

"You played violin, Herr General?" Her astonishment was sincere. A common bond between her brother and the general whose troops had...she shook her head. Trying to reconcile his musical aspirations with his role as enemy general made her dizzy.

"Yes, I did. Though perhaps it was the soldier part of me that played it so badly."

"I find the violin a bit depressing." Von Falkenhausen looked into the air, apparently trying to recall something. "Don't the French have a poem about the languorous sobs of the violin?"

Sandrine nodded. "Yes. Verlaine's 'Violins of Autumn.' It's true, they can be poignant, but if you know the passage is coming, you wait for it with pleasure. Violins can be deeply affecting." She thought of Laurent and hated herself for drinking champagne with his killers.

"Rommel chortled. Well, well. It appears we've established who in this company has a soul and who does not."

Von Falkenhausen hadn't taken his eyes off Sandrine. "I venture that Madame Toussaint's soul is beautiful indeed."

Sandrine stood by while Gaston closed the double doors of the carriage house, protecting the Mercedes Benz 230 Laurent had bought in 1939. When the Germans had arrived and begun requisitioning, she and Gaston had hidden it in the woods under a tarp and a mound of dirt and brush. Deceit had saved the Château Malou from their grasp, and simple concealment had saved the car. She wasn't sure what good it did, though.

"A dilemma, isn't it, madam?" Gaston seemed to read her thoughts. "If you drive it, the Germans will take it. If you don't drive it, it's the same as if the Germans had taken it."

Their feet crunched on the gravel as they marched back to the house. "That's it, precisely. But I'm still hoping that friends in the local administration can counterfeit papers registering it as an official, or even medical, vehicle. Then we could use it to transport the men."

"Not very far, though. They would still stop you at the border, even if you were in a tank." He hiked up his overalls. "And getting enough petrol on the black market? Well, that's another issue altogether."

"Ever the optimist, eh, Gaston?"

They'd just reached the door when the sleek black car of the military governor swung around the curve toward them. Without a word, Gaston hurried into the house, she knew, to warn the hidden Englishmen and remove all signs of them.

As the car pulled up in front of her, she noted with irony that it was also a Mercedes, though of a grander design than hers. When the door opened on the driver's side and Baron von Falkenhausen stepped out, he was alone. Her fear gave way to dread.

She remained composed. "Good afternoon, Herr Baron. To what do I owe the pleasure?"

He stepped toward her and took her hand, executing a military bow with a hinted heel-tap and a quick nod. "Madame Toussaint. How lovely to find you at home. The other day at the Café Suèdoise, you were so kind as to invite me to your château, and I confess, the idea intrigued me. Have I disturbed you?"

"No, not at all." The bastard. He'd invited himself. And now she had to keep him far away from her Tommies.

"Won't you come inside?" Forcing calm on herself, she ascended the stone steps ahead of him.

Gaston stood in the entryway, and his calm manner told her that her two Englishmen were carefully hidden.

"Would you please bring up a bottle of wine, Gaston?" she said as they passed into the sitting room. The fire he'd laid before they went to the carriage house now burned brightly.

She gestured toward the long leather sofa. "Please make yourself comfortable."

Von Falkenhausen held out his own hand, waiting for her to sit first. Then he sat down a discreet distance from her and glanced around the sparsely furnished room. "Elegant simplicity. Excellent taste, though rather understated, for someone who loves Tchaikovsky," he said.

"Now you're teasing me."

"Yes, I am. Forgive me, dear lady. I thought we were friends enough for me to indulge in a bit of playfulness."

Gaston returned with one of her good bottles of wine and two glasses on a tray, which he set on the table in front of them. He leaned forward in his best butler manner and announced quietly, "A Bordeaux, Monsieur Baron. From 1933."

"Ah, yes. A fateful year," von Falkenhausen murmured, watching the wine trickle into both glasses. He held out her wineglass to her and she accepted it, tapped its rim against his, and drank.

"I see you have retained your automobile," he said casually.

Sandrine almost choked. She set down her glass to conceal the trembling in her hand.

"Don't be alarmed, my dear lady. I'm not here to cause you any trouble. Though you were naughty to not register it as ordered."

"How did you…?"

"My dear. As military governor of all Belgium, I do have to take note of inconsistencies, such as a château that hasn't registered a motor vehicle. It was easy to send over someone to peek into your carriage house."

"Does this mean you'll requisition it?"

He touched her wrist with feathery lightness. "Perhaps we can arrange for it to be an exception. As an official vehicle, for example." His smile, too subtle to be lewd, was just as alarming in its discretion. The cards were laid out.

Shaken by the hold he now had over her, Sandrine took another sip of wine. In spite of its nine years aging, it suddenly tasted bitter. Von Falkenhausen also drank and stared for a moment into the glow of the fireplace.

"You will be pleased to know that I've ordered the division veterinarian to tend to your friend's dog. He usually works with horses, but I'm sure he can dress the wound on a dog as well." He smiled with a beneficence that looked out of place on the rest of his rigid military person.

"That was very kind. It's only a pity that such brutal men have to patrol the streets. Or that anyone has to patrol them. Surely we're civilized enough…"

He raised his hand to silence her. "Please, dear lady. Do not taint those lovely lips with political talk. Not now, in front of this glorious fire and with this magnificent wine. Let us enjoy the moment, as a man and a woman."

He set his glass down and shifted sideways to face her. She dropped her eyes, focusing on his dress boot, so polished it reflected the firelight.

"We are not monsters. We are soldiers doing our duty, far from our homes, our wives and children. Can you for a moment forget the uniform I wear and just see me as a man?"

She knew what was coming and it sickened her. "Herr Baron, we have different national loyalties."

"Oh, but it is mere fate that I was born in Prussia and you in Belgium. There is a far older, one might say, primitive element that unites us. We are human, with human needs. You are a widow. You've known your husband's desires. Surely you miss the touch and protection of a man." His hand brushed her thigh as he leaned toward her.

"Your hair is so lovely. Rather like my wife's. Autumn-leaf yellow, she calls it, though yours is more tawny. Lioness, perhaps." He ran his fingers down a few strands of it.

She flinched at the unwelcome flattery of the molester, all the more because it seemed sincere.

"Thank you for the compliment, Herr Baron, though I'm afraid your attentions would count as illegal fraternization." She tried to back away from him but found no place left on the sofa

His hand was creeping along her shoulder. "My dear, I make the rules for this country, and I exempt us from them. I can assure your car and a petrol ration. Come, dear lady, and comfort a lonely man." He slid closer, enfolding her in an embrace. His dry lips were already on her neck, and the double scents of wool and French cologne filled her nostrils.

She thought of the two desperate pilots in her cellar and of the string of others that would come, week after week. The house was critical for their safety, as the car was for transporting them. Lives, scores of them, depended on her overcoming her disgust.

Though her skin crawled, she forced herself to say, "Just a moment, Baron. Let me lock the door."

CHAPTER SIX

Beaulieu, Hampshire, England
January 1942

The mix of gravel and ice crunched loudly as the car pulled up in front of a stately stone building.

"Nice house," Antonia remarked. "Gothic, isn't it?"

Major Atkins opened the door on his side. "Yes. Apparently it used to be the gatehouse of an abbey. Thirteenth century, they tell me. He stepped out onto the hard-packed snow and came around to her side. "Don't much care for the style myself. A bit too Knights of the Roundtable for me." He held the car door open for her.

"Is that where I'll be training?" she asked, drawing her coat collar up around her neck and surveying the vast snow-covered estate. "It seems such an anachronism, teaching modern warfare in a medieval building." She gazed up at the gables and turrets, all with a cap of white. "We should be learning Gregorian chants or how to roast boar."

"Wouldn't that be lovely? But this is just administration, and I'm to deposit you here for check-in. The courses you'll be taking will be scattered throughout other locations."

"Just what *are* all those courses?" she asked, then chuckled. "I suppose I ought to have asked that sooner, eh?"

"Well, if you had, I wouldn't have been able to tell you. It's all top secret, you know. Some of the groups training here don't know about all the others. It's to prevent anyone revealing the whole operation if they're captured."

He leaned in front of her to open the front door, and they both stepped into a warm vestibule. She wiped her snow-damp shoes on a mat as an officer in his early fifties approached.

"Miss Forrester. Pleased to meet you. I'm Major Woolrich." She took his proffered hand and liked the brief firm grip he offered.

"Thank you, Major Atkins. That will be all." After a casual salute he led her down a corridor to his office. Once inside, he motioned her toward one of two armchairs and sat down in the other, then drew a pipe from his shirt pocket. He fished a matchbox up from the same pocket, lit the already-full bowl, and puffed a few times to get it going. Relaxing back into his chair, he crossed his legs.

"I understand you were injured at Dunkirk," he said. "I trust by now you are fully recovered. It was burns, wasn't it?"

"Burns, ribs, broken shoulder, and a concussion. And yes, I'm fully recovered. Thank you for asking, Major."

"I'm glad to hear it because some of what we will be doing here is very taxing. But let me start at the beginning."

He puffed a few times on his pipe. "Beaulieu is part of eleven schools on or near this estate, each one teaching a different skill, and you will have a superficial experience of all of them. The point, of course, is to determine your strengths, and the sort of mission we might send you on will depend on your performance."

"Can you tell me what some of those subjects are?"

"We'll start off teaching you to recognize the uniforms and ranks in the German military. Then you'll review the geography of France and Belgium. We don't want you getting lost, now, do we?" He smiled, though his teeth still clenched his pipe.

"And the physical training?"

"A bit of running about, shooting, self-defense, parachuting. That's usually the way we get you there."

"So I have to learn to jump from an airplane."

"Afraid so. Though the planes fly below radar, so the drop isn't so great."

"So, jumping. That's it? In the physical department, I mean."

"Uh, no. You'll also be trained to kill. Silently."

"Ah."

He puffed again, letting the thought sink in. "We'll also teach you how to stay hidden and keep warm sleeping in the woods, how to operate a radio, that sort of thing. And…that's about it. Do you have any questions?"

Antonia slowly shook her head, then took a long breath. "All right, then. When do we start?"

"Tomorrow, if that suits you, after you've had a good night's rest. I'll send a man out to collect your luggage and take you around to your quarters." He stood up and tapped out the cinders from the bowl of his pipe into a glass ashtray, signaling the end of the conversation. Amidst the charred tobacco, a few cinders still burned, like a minute landscape of ruin. She blinked away the grim image and turned toward the door.

"Ready when you are, Major."

As the car that had deposited her drove away, Antonia unlocked the cottage door and let herself in.

"Oh, sorry!" She halted in the doorway.

The woman in bra and panties who, judging by her towel-turban, had apparently just shampooed, waved a dismissive hand. "Quite all right. You must be my new housemate." She held out her hand. "Dora Springfield."

Antonia set down her suitcase and handbag and gripped the damp palm. "Antonia Forrester. You been here long?"

"No, just started yesterday. Looks like we're both beginners." She unwrapped the towel from her head and used the dry corner to rub at reddish-brown hair. "Do you suppose we'll be training together?"

"Dunno. All I've been told is that they're going to send us around all these schools to learn things they don't teach you back home." Antonia hefted her suitcase onto the only other cot in the room and began transferring her clothing into a set of drawers at the foot of it.

"Yes, skulky things like living in the woods, breaking a fellow's neck, jumping from airplanes. Well, if it knocks off a few Jerries, I'm all for it." Dora slid long legs into a pair of dark-green slacks and slipped on a gray turtleneck. Against her tousled hair, it looked quite attractive, and Antonia was a bit surprised she was beginning to notice things like that again. Perhaps she was finally shaking off the trauma of Dunkirk.

"The airplane part, for sure. But we may not be doing anything as dramatic as neck-breaking."

"Well, I hope we do. The Jerries banged up my fiancé over in France, so I figure they've got it coming. Anyhow, I've got water on. Would'ja like some tea?"

"Sounds lovely. 'Banged up?' I'm sorry to hear it. Is he all right now?"

"No, he's not. He's paralyzed, see? Got him in the legs, the bastards. So the first Jerry I run across, you know where I'm going to shoot him. What about you? You got a beau?" Dora spooned black tea into a teapot and poured the boiling water over it. The fragrance reminded Antonia that she was hungry.

"Uh, no. I was a nurse. You know, one of the Queen Alexandras. I was injured at Dunkirk, so I've only just now got back into the battle, so to speak. No time for a beau."

"Dunkirk! Oh, my, you're a real veteran, then. Me, I'm just a simple secretary they called up because my mum's from Marseille and I speak French."

"I do too, though in my case it's because I lived over there." Antonia saw no reason to give details.

Dora poured the steaming tea into two mugs and brought one over to her. "No beau? That's a crying shame. And now they'll have us running around in the dirt in khakis. The lads like that." She blew into her cup and squinted in an attempt at lewdness. "And if things happen in our off time, who's to find out, eh?"

Antonia forced a smile. The thought of meeting a man romantically in training hadn't crossed her mind. "Somebody's been reading romance novels."

"Hey, a girl's got to fill up the lonely hours, especially when her fiancé's incapacitated. If you know what I mean." She strode across the room to her night table and picked up a battered paperback.

"I've just finished this one. Take it. It's on me. You'll need something to relax your brain after all the stuff they're going to pack into it during the day."

Antonia glanced at the title. *The Grenadier and the Widow.* She settled back on her cot. Well, why not? It was hours before the canteen would open for supper. She opened to the second chapter and read the opening line.

"Oh, Pierre, how I've missed you," the widow murmured, as he sat down on her bed and slid his hand under the covers.

Ah, it was going to be *that* kind of romance novel.

❖

Antonia flipped through the pages of her notebook to review the lessons of the last few days. Across the room, smoking a military-issue cigarette, Dora did the same.

"I had no idea there was so much to know about German uniforms," Dora complained. "There's no bloody end to it." She took a drag and blew smoke sideways. "But I got to tell you, much as I hate the buggers, I like some of the uniforms. The black ones with the high boots are really smashing. Our Tommies, well, I love 'em to pieces, but they're kind of drab in comparison."

"You think so?" Antonia studied the pages of SS officers. "Yeah, but according to this, those are only fancy-dress uniforms. In the occupied countries, they're all wearing gray-green field uniforms like the Wehrmacht."

"Pity. Have you learned the SS ranks yet?"

"I think so." She stared up at the ceiling. "Let's see, there's *Sturmmann, Rottenführer, Unterscharführer, Scharführer, Oberscharführer, Hauptscharführer*—Boy, they really like the sound of 'Führer,' don't they? Then there's *Sturmscharführer, Untersturmführer, Hauptsturmführer.*"

"And the Wehrmacht?"

"Yeah, but don't make me name them. They're all so repetitive."

"Would you recognize them by their uniforms?"

"Not jolly likely. It took me six months to recognize our *own* men by their insignias."

"Well, somebody's got more homework to do, doesn't she?" Dora smirked. "Okay, then let's move on to Belgian geography?"

"Easy. Flanders up, Wallonia and the Ardenne down, Brussels in the middle."

"Who's the king?"

"Leopold III. Surrendered to the Germans against the advice of his cabinet, for which some condemn him as a traitor, but others hail him for saving the lives of his defeated army. Technically a prisoner of war."

"What happened to the Belgian army?"

Antonia dropped back onto her pillow and emitted a long sigh. "Oh, please. Can we stop now? My brain's turned to porridge."

"Yeah, I'm burnt out myself." She glanced at her watch. "Crikey, it's ten o'clock, and we've got to be up at six tomorrow. Fifteen minutes and it's lights out for us."

"Good. I've got just enough eyesight for a few pages of your trashy novel. Let's see, where was I?" She opened at her bookmark and began to read out loud.

He stood in the doorway of her room. His blue tunic was dusty from the ride, his white jodhpurs stained by the saddle. Belinda pulled her blanket up to her chin. "Dear lady, do not fear," he said. "No man shall lay a hand on you while you are under my protection." She was glad for his protection, but the bulge in his white trousers told her she would have to pay for it.

"See? That's the way to win a war." Dora rubbed out the butt of her cigarette. "Hero rescues heroine, shags her, and in the morning he drives away the enemy."

Antonia dropped the book on the floor. "Yeah, but what about us? Who do we get to shag?"

Antonia took her seat in the classroom, little units of dots and dashes buzzing through her head. After two months of memorizing Morse code, she was finally ready for real wireless transmitters.

"Welcome to our new 'pianists,'" the instructor said. "As you are aware, every team sent into the war zone will have a radio operator to maintain contact with headquarters. However, all agents are required to have some knowledge of the skill.

"Please make up groups of two and put on the earphones," he said. "We'll start with you, Miss Forrester. You are to transmit this message, and you, Mr. Devon, will receive and transcribe it. Then you will reverse roles. Are you ready?"

Thus began an entire morning of back-and-forth transmitting, at first awkward and error-filled and broken by moments of frustration, then increasingly with ease. At the lunch break, the instructor signaled for them to remove the headphones.

"Very good, both of you. Miss Forrester, you are obviously a bit nervous. Everyone has a distinct 'fist,' but for the moment, yours is a bit jittery. We'll smooth that out in the coming days. We'll also work on speed. Remember, while you're transmitting, the enemy's directional finders can detect you. You'll want to send your message in less than three minutes and then shut down."

"Will we be carrying a radio like this?" Antonia gestured toward the black box on the table that they'd been using.

"We hope not. We've got our men working on developing smaller versions that can fit into a valise."

"What about encrypting?" Antonia asked. "Surely we're not going to transmit open messages."

"No, of course not. We use what we call 'poem codes.' To be precise, the sender and receiver have a pre-arranged poem, like a Shakespeare sonnet. The sender chooses some phrases from the poem and gives each of their letters a number. The numbers make up the key for some cypher that is then used to transmit the message."

Antonia frowned. "What happens if the agent is captured and forced to reveal the poem?"

"Well, that's the weakness, of course. Obviously, the idea is to not be captured."

Obviously.

❖

"Sabotage," the instructor said, pausing with upraised chalk, "is a fine art."

A soft chuckle went through the room of a dozen students.

One of the men in the front row spoke, a well-muscled soldier whose posture, even when he sat, projected confrontation. "I don't see what's so fine art about jammin' a few sticks of dynamite under a railway track and runnin' like hell."

The rest of the class laughed, and the soldier glanced over his shoulder at his admirers.

The instructor was unperturbed. "On lucky days, lads like you can do that, and get away with it. But the tracks are patrolled, and you could get caught. And if you just blow up tracks, the enemy can replace them in a day." He turned to the blackboard.

"So let's look at some other tools," he said, and chalked a list onto the board, naming them as he wrote: "plastic explosives, shaped charges, time fuses, incendiaries in coal piles, abrasive lubricants, land mines disguised as cow dung, and…" he wrote in large letters at the bottom, "especially for you, Mr. Rhydderch, sledge hammers."

He turned to face the class again. "Imagine, if you will, the advantage of paralyzing a train full of German troops and supplies halfway to the front. If you strike the locomotive rather than the track, you have an enormous obstacle frozen on that track, an obstacle that has to be moved before the entire line is operational again."

He set his chalk on the rim of the board. "Good sabotage is not always dramatic and is most effective if it undermines a large system."

"Such as blowing up power stations," the Welshman added.

"Ah, I see you have a penchant for explosives, Mr. Rhydderch. I grant you, a big explosion is very satisfying, but if you can achieve a similar amount of disorder to the enemy while remaining invisible, your life may be longer."

"What about guns? Will we be supplying weapons?" The Welshman seemed to enjoy being the center of attention.

"Yes. After a preliminary reconnaissance with local movements, we'll drop containers of rifles, ammunition, other material." He strode over to a cabinet and unlocked the padlock on its doors. "And since you've brought up the subject of weapons, Mr. Rhydderch, we will move on to that now," he said over his shoulder while he drew something long and metallic from a high shelf.

"This is our weapon of choice for the resisters we hope to inspire." He laid the object on the desk in front of him. "The Sten gun."

Antonia leaned forward from her second row seat for a better look.

"Called the MkI Sten T-40/1, it has just rolled off the Enfield factory line. You will note how light it is. Also simple to operate, with a minimum of maintenance. It has a flash-hider, so the enemy can't target you by the flash, and a forward handle to hold it securely. The stock is a simple double tube that can be rotated forward for stowing. It has a horizontal magazine with a thirty-two-round capacity, and its barrel is just a steel cylinder. Ideal for your average Frenchman to use on the street."

"And what about us?"

"You'll be issued side arms. In addition, special missions will also include one of these."

He laid a variety of knives on his desk. "Obviously the smaller blades are designed for concealment, in these cases in a coat lapel or a shoe."

"But this is my personal favorite," he said, reaching again into the cabinet. "The wire shoelace." He opened his hand, revealing a black cord. "Totally innocuous in your shoe, but once you take it out, you merely walk up behind the target and loop it around his throat. Then, before he can react, you place your knee in his back and pull. He will instinctively grasp the wire and not you. Of course success depends completely on the element of surprise."

The Welshman interrupted. "When I were a lad, a good fist were all I needed in a scrap."

"That's a good point, Mr. Rhydderch. We will give you instruction at another time on physical self-defense, though against armed Gestapo, it will be of limited use. And this brings me to our last point. The ultimate 'escape,' so to speak."

Reaching this time into the breast pocket of his uniform, he produced two items: a lipstick tube and what looked like the cork of a wine bottle. He unscrewed them both, revealing capsules at the bottom, and set them on his desk.

"Suicide ampules. Two of them. We can also conceal them inside coat buttons. I will not dwell on the subject, but the fact is, if you are captured, you can be certain of harsh interrogation."

One of the students interpreted. "Torture."

"Yes, torture. So, these contain potassium cyanide. Keep them on your person for critical moments when other escape is impossible and it's likely you'll be tortured. If you bite down on them and then swallow, you'll pass out within a minute or two. Your brain is affected quite quickly, so you feel nothing when your heart stops a few minutes later."

He returned the capsules to a box. "Agents do get captured. That's a reality you must be aware of. And no one here expects you to stand up long under interrogation."

Torture. She hadn't much thought about that. She wondered if the SOE had a course on that, but the subject had changed, and the others were already standing, ready to view the model locomotive and the display of explosive devices. Nothing like imagining explosions to take your mind off suffering.

She gathered her notes and pens and followed the class out the door.

Chapter Seven

February 1942

"Welcome to RAF Ringway parachute training school, ladies and gentlemen. I hope you're all ready for some excitement." The instructor, who—perhaps deliberately—bore a significant resemblance to General Montgomery, paced as he spoke.

Antonia looked around her for familiar faces and spotted the mouthy young Welshman. What was his name again? Oh, right. Rhydderch. He stood with his hands in his pockets, his chest thrown out, stalwart and a bit smug, while she shivered in her oversized RAF overalls.

She turned her attention back to the instructor and to the giant slides built up against the rear wall of the hangar. They began at a height of about twenty feet and ended abruptly at about eight feet. Directly below the drop were mattresses that seemed far too small.

"First of all, we'll practice landing. As soon as your feet strike the ground, you must throw yourself sideways to distribute the impact to your calf, your thigh, your hip, and finally the side of your back. Keep your legs slightly bent at the knee, your chin tucked in, and your hands linked behind your neck."

He paused, as if to give them time to reconsider, then pointed toward the ladders. "All right, you lot. Up you go. Try not to break anything, will you?"

Antonia dutifully executed the slides and tumbles, finding the first drop painful but each consecutive one more tolerable. By the tenth, she was more fatigued from climbing the ladder than from taking the fall.

"Good show, chaps. No smashed bones yet," the faux Montgomery announced. "Go get yourselves some sandwiches and tea, and in an hour, we'll move on to the pulleys."

As the group migrated toward a table with the promised lunch, Antonia sensed someone at her side.

"A right harsh way to treat a lady, innit?" a voice said.

"Mr. Rhydderch," she said, guessing, and looked over her shoulder at him. "Thank you for your concern."

"Please, it's Llewellyn. Me mates call me Lew. And you're Antonia, right? Toni." They reached the food table and he handed her a tin mug of tea. "I was just looking after ya."

"No need for that, Lew. I'm doing just fine. What about you? How are you coping?

"Smashing. I seem to have the knack, you know?" He handed her a spam sandwich but she raised her hand. "Thanks, I'll take the cheese." She reached across him and helped herself. "Do a lot of falling, do you?"

He looked puzzled for a moment, then chuckled. "Aye, that I do. Rugby, see? When eight blokes at a time thrash you on the field, falling's the easy part. Say, if you're free this evening and fancy a bit of company, maybe we could have a pint at the village pub."

"Thank you, Llewellyn, but I don't think we're supposed to draw attention to ourselves in the village."

"Well, we can skip the pub and have us a beer at my place. Me flat-mate dropped out of the school, so I've got the place all to meself." He bit into his sandwich.

"Thanks again, but I think I'm going to be pretty knackered by tonight. Most nights, in fact." She sipped her tea.

"Pity," he said through a full mouth, then chewed a bit more and swallowed before adding. "I could teach you how to fall."

She ignored the innuendo and looked to the side where the only other woman in the class was conversing with the instructor. "Why don't you ask her? She might need help falling."

He scrutinized the other woman. "Quite a lot of nose, that one. Not me type."

"I don't think I am either, Lew. Here, have another sandwich." She slapped a spam-on-whole-wheat onto his open hand and walked away.

❖

At ten in the evening Antonia stood on the field with the others who had made the first cut and stamped her feet to keep warm.

"Don't be nervous, Toni. You'll be *fane*," someone said. Fane? She turned to see Llewellyn smiling down at her. "Thanks for the encouragement, but I told you not to call me Toni."

"Sure thing. But look, I watched you doing the balloon jumps and yer doin' great. You know it's the time before the jump that's difficult. Once you're out in the air and your chute opens, it's like a baby's bottom. Come on, they're calling us up now."

They clambered into the Armstrong Whitley along with four other candidates and took off. To her surprise, she was less nervous than she'd been on the ground. The noise of the plane engine seemed to lend a sense of drama and excitement, and made the jump seem heroic. She checked all the fittings on her jumpsuit, the buckles and straps on her parachute, the laces on her boots. She adjusted the Bungey training helmet and put on her goggles.

"Over target area!" The jump-officer shouted, although, amidst the roar of the engine, Antonia could only read his lips. She stood up, second in line, behind Lew, and they shuffled together toward the bomb bay of the plane.

When Lew reached the edge, just before jumping, he twisted around, puckered his lips and mimed a kiss. Then he stepped into the hole.

Behind him, Antonia shivered in her jumpsuit as she reached the edge. Below stretched a terrifying, dark emptiness. The clouds had moved away, revealing the full moon upon which the RAF so much depended. It was all the light she was going to get.

The green jump light flashed on, and before the jumpmaster touched her shoulder, she dropped.

Terror. Wind blew her out of the vertical and caused her to tumble. She couldn't orient herself because she had nothing to look at, nothing to grab on to.

Whoomp! A violent jerk from the straps under her crotch told her the ripcord attached to the plane had opened her chute. It was suddenly quiet.

How fast was she falling? She had no way of measuring, and the memory of all the damage done to her body at Dunkirk shot through her. At least there'd be no fire this time.

She glanced downward and saw the glim lamps, four on each side, and though the wind was blowing her at a diagonal across the landing strip, she finally had a sense of approach.

Suddenly the ground filled her entire view. She bent her knees and pressed her elbows to her sides. The moment her feet touched earth, she threw herself sideways into a roll. *Ooof.* A quick, sharp pain in her shoulder told her she'd been ambushed by a rock. A small one apparently, but she felt cheated, for the jump had otherwise been perfect.

For the first time during the entire training period, she felt exhilarated.

A figure approached in the moonlight, one of the other jumpers still dragging his chute. When he came within shouting distance, he called out. "Tidy jump, eh, Toni?"

She scrambled to her feet and gathered up her own silk, rolling it into a bundle. "I told you not to call me Toni."

"Ah, shush yer noise, girl," he called back amiably while he rolled up his chute. "You proved you could keep up with the lads, so come have a pint with me."

"Sorry, Lew. I'm still not interested." With the entire silken mass rolled up and slung over her shoulder, she began the hike across the field toward the waiting troop carrier.

When the team was present and accounted for, the instructor joined them and they made the drive back. "Good job, all of you. And when we get to the hangar, you'll meet somebody who cares about your success as much as you do."

"Who's that?" one of the men called out. "Me mother?"

"No. You'll find out when we get there. But make sure your chutes are tied up neatly and your gear is in proper order. I want you to look good."

"Ooo, must be someone important."

Twenty minutes later the group filed into the drop-off room and stowed their chutes for the repacking women. Antonia was one of the last, and when she stepped through the inner door into the hangar, a semicircle had already formed around the guest.

She had to walk all the way around the mass of bodies to the end, and when she finally stood in place, she was slightly disappointed to see a portly, balding man in a rumpled three-piece suit and a black overcoat. He held his bowler hat and a cigar in one hand while he shook hands with the other. Ah, she thought. So that's Winston Churchill. Britain's most powerful man looked a bit seedy, like a slightly disreputable banker.

Chapter Eight

Brussels March 1942

Standing in the tiny corridor, Moishe Goldman pinched out the tip of his cigarette and dropped the remaining butt into his pocket. Then he knocked and let himself be scrutinized through a crack in the door. He heard the safety chain being undone, and when the door opened, his brother Aisik leaned toward him and spoke over the din. "Come, sit down. You're the last." In the room behind him where the others were gathered, people were arguing in their mixed versions of French, Polish, and Belorussian Yiddish.

Aisik had packed almost a dozen people into the tiny flat, and, for lack of furniture, most sat on the floor or leaned against the wall. A pity they couldn't have met in Aisik's old place, a comfortable three-room apartment with its own toilet. What luxury it seemed, now that most of them were living clandestine lives in whatever cramped housing sympathetic Belgians would offer them.

Moishe stepped over the legs of the men on the floor and squeezed himself into a corner. Glancing around the room, he realized he knew almost everyone. He was especially pleased to see the muscular Jakob Gutfrajnd, whom they all called Kuba, and the young medical student Youra Livschitz.

In the far corner, his sister-in-law Rywka stood holding her baby.

Kuba shouted over the general noise. "All right everyone, calm down. We're all here now, so let's get started." In a moment, the sound subsided, and Moishe heard only the dry coughing of smokers and the simpering of the two-year-old.

"You all know why we're here," Kuba said, and everyone seemed to listen. "Most of us are old comrades who fought together in Spain, and if we're not all good Communists, we're still brothers in arms. And we all know about what's going on in Germany—the burning of the synagogues, the smashing of Jewish shops, the deportations. Belgium was safe, but the Germans are here now, and things are going to get worse."

"They're already worse. Tell them about the labor camps," Aisik said.

Someone lit up a cigarette, took a long inhalation, and passed it to the man next to him. "They've built a big new one now at Oświęcim. The Germans call it Auschwitz. We've got to let people know."

Moishe snorted. "We report it all the time in the Jewish newspapers. But everybody thinks they're immune because they work in important jobs or have influential friends."

"What about the Christians?" The boyish Youra called from the back. "The ones who can't read Yiddish. All they hear and read is the crap coming from the Germans."

"That's right." It was Rywka, who spoke over the head of her baby. "Christians got us this apartment. If they knew, maybe they could prevent the deportations."

Aisik put his arm around her. "That may be too optimistic, Rywka. Why should they care about us? Who here is a Belgian citizen? Raise your hands."

Not a single hand went up. "No one? Okay, then, who here even speaks good French?" Three hands went up.

"So where are the Belgian Jews? Leaders in business, banking, the diamond industry?" It was Youra again. Unlike most of the others, he'd had a university education and seemed to understand about things like banking and business.

"I'll tell you where they are," Moishe said. "The ones who could afford to get away are in London. The rest are hoping it will all disappear. And the worst of them are collaborating. Not to mention the Judenrat."

The baby began to whimper and Rywka held him close. "Well, they did open some schools and clinics for Jews."

"It's true. They do good things too," Aisik said. "They've set up a whole new business employing lots of Jews to make winter clothing for the Wehrmacht. A lot of men are supporting their families that way."

"Don't fool yourself, Aisik. Anyone who works for the Germans is collaborating," Moishe said. "All that crap about the social welfare of the community. I piss on their social welfare. They'll do what the Germans want. And you know what that is? To round us up and get us out. It's only a matter of time before we'll have the yellow star and the roundups."

Grunts of agreement came from the others.

"So where does that leave us?" Aisik rubbed his forehead, a nervous habit he'd developed since the occupation began.

"It leaves us in shit," Moishe muttered.

After a moment of angry silence Kuba spoke up again. "Well, now that you've got that out of your system, we can begin to get organized."

"To do what?" Youra asked the obvious, and the room buzzed again.

Kuba raised a hand. "Listen, everyone." He wasn't a tall man, but the breadth of his chest and his strong baritone voice made him seem large. The murmuring stopped. "As I see it, we can work in three areas." He held up a finger. "One. Find ways to hide anyone who can't fight. The old, the children." He looked at Rywka and her baby.

"Two. Collect money."

"No one's got any money to give," Moishe said. "We can hardly feed our families as it is."

"I was talking about robbery."

"Ah." Moishe scowled for a moment. "Doesn't that require guns?"

"Yes, it does. And that brings us to number three. Fight. I mean really *fight*. You've heard the rumors of partisans fighting here and there. We can do that too."

"How do we get guns, Kuba?"

"People are hiding weapons left over from the retreat, from the English and the Belgians. We just have to track them down."

"I don't know if I could kill a man," someone said.

Moishe relit the last bit of his cigarette and puffed on it, then crushed the centimeter of stub into the saucer beside him. "I could. I've got nothing to lose."

"I've got a lot to lose." Aisik Goldman glanced over at his wife and son and rubbed his forehead again. "But Moishe's right. Things are going to get worse, and if you can fight back, you should."

"So, who's willing to fight rather than hide?" Kuba laid down the challenge.

Two hands went up hesitantly. Then two more. Slowly the rest of the hands rose as well. Even Rywka nodded agreement, holding her cheek against her son's head.

"All right, then. Let's put some organization into this," Kuba said, and in the remaining half hour, he assigned tasks, outlined policies, and described the means to gain adherents. After a final emphasis on the critical need for secrecy, he called an end to the meeting.

When all had filed out of the tiny apartment, Moishe embraced Aisik. "So, here we are, brother, the Armed Jewish Resistance."

Rywka set down her toddler on newly cleared floor space. "I know we have to do this, but I wonder how many of us will pay with our lives."

"At this point, darling, it doesn't matter," Aisik said, kneeling by their child. "The Germans are coming for us anyhow. We're fighting back so a few can live and tell the story." He caressed the hair on his son's head with his fingertips. "We're doing it for Jackie."

Moishe felt an odd sensation. A feeling so long forgotten he almost didn't recognize it.

Hope.

CHAPTER NINE

March 1942

Sandrine strode along the Rue Marché au Charbon, developed, so she'd learned in school, in the thirteenth century, as a center where coal merchants and investors did business. But the coal marketeers had disappeared centuries ago and left rows of small shops, which had thrived until the Germans had occupied the city. Now some of the feet that trod its cobblestones were shod in jackboots.

She crossed the intersection into the curved end of the street and located the shop she wanted. Broader than most of the other houses on the street, it was rather attractive, with a wide window on each side of a high oval doorway. Three stories, four if you counted the tiny mansard.

She was about to reach for the door handle when it opened from within and eight men filed out. Swarthy, Eastern-looking. They nodded courteously to her as they passed and dispersed in both directions.

Christine Mathys sat at her counter and looked up as she entered. A tall, energetic woman in her late fifties, she gave the impression of utter competence in whatever she did. "Sandrine Toussaint, what a pleasant surprise. Come in, come in! Don't tell me you want to buy any of my old trash for your château."

"No, nothing like that. Something more…delicate, in fact. Is it safe to talk?" She glanced around for any listeners.

"Yes, we're alone. What's on your mind?" Christine pulled a second stool up next to her and signaled her to sit down.

Sandrine slid off her heavy coat and draped it over the counter, then perched on the stool. She thought for a moment, then blurted out,

"I know you're sympathetic to resisting the occupation, so I'll speak directly and trust that I'm not endangering myself."

Christine crossed her arms to add vehemence to her declaration. "Anyone who stands up to the Germans has nothing to fear from me. How can I help you?"

She took a deep breath. "Well, in the simplest terms, I work with an escape line that helps people flee south to Spain. We call it the Comet Line. Andrée de Jongh set it up, but the Gestapo arrested her father and is on the lookout for her, so she operates from the Spanish end of it. We evacuate Allied pilots, Belgians who want to fight with the Free Belgian Forces, occasionally a Jew or an escapee from the labor drafts."

Christine slapped her hand on the counter. "Bravo. I knew such organizations existed, and it's just like you to be in the thick of it. So what do you need from me?"

"Anything you can offer. But most urgently, we need more safe houses, both in Brussels and outside. We've been taking the men south in twos and threes, but the operation is disorganized. Worse, we've got more men than we can handle. At the very least, someone has to house them while we set up the machinery to move them faster."

"Machinery?"

"You know, forged identification, clothing, medical assistance. And before we even start, we have to interrogate them to be sure they aren't Gestapo plants. Obviously, we need more people. I always thought I could trust your abilities, and your loyalties."

"You *can* trust them. My loyalties, at least. Do you mean you want me to hide some of them here? I've already got a Jewish family living clandestinely upstairs, so all that's left is the garret."

"I was hoping you could work actively with us, contacting other trusted people. For housing, of course, but can you can think of anyone good at forging documents, or stealing them?"

Christine thought for a moment. "I may know one or two. I'm not sure how they would be able to feed new mouths, though. So much is rationed."

"We're working on getting counterfeit ration coupons, but we have only one forger so it's slow going."

"I'm beginning to appreciate the difficulties. But sure. I'll pay a little visit to my friends this evening to see what's possible. I won't bring up *your* name, but you mustn't bring up mine either. And no mention of my Jews upstairs."

Sandrine patted her on the arm. "I see you're getting the knack of this already."

"Don't worry about—" Someone was shouting in the street, and they both went to the shop window.

Outside a double line of boys was marching past in formation, shouting in unison.

"Look at them," Christine muttered. "Belgian boys stomping around like Hitlerjugend. In their little brown shirts, black shorts, and neckerchiefs. Every single one of them with his sleeves rolled up to the exact same spot above their elbows. What's going on in those foolish heads?"

"The same thing that's going on in the heads of their Rexist parents. A vicious mix of fascism and Catholicism."

"Not even that much. I remember when my son was that age. All he cared about was whether his friends admired him. They love the uniforms and the swaggering. A lot of good it did him, joining the military with his pals when he was twenty and getting killed when he was twenty-one."

"What are they doing here?" Sandrine asked. "Don't they usually parade down the Boulevard Anspach?"

"Yes, but they end up here at the pilgrim's church down the street. Makes them feel like God's on their side."

Sandrine retreated to her stool. "Fortunately not all the young ones feel that way. A friend of mine, about eighteen herself, who lives in the Ardenne, says that young people are coming together to resist the German labor roundups."

"You mean Celine? Laura's sister? The one with the dachshund? Yes, she's a brave one. By the way, how's the dog?"

"Last I heard she was fine. A little furry war hero. She has a bald patch on her rump, though."

The chanting from the street was suddenly loud as the door opened and two uniformed men burst in. Belgian auxiliary gendarme.

"How can I help you?" Christine asked, unperturbed.

The higher-ranking one stepped forward. "We've had reports of people living in this street without papers. Who resides in this building?"

During a moment of tense silence Christine shifted objects on the counter, clearly buying time.

Sandrine stepped forward. "Excuse me, Captain," she said with extreme courtesy. She couldn't determine his actual rank but was certain it was far below captain. "I am Madame Toussaint, a personal friend of General von Falkenhausen. These premises are under my, and therefore under *his*, protection. Please contact Herr von Falkenhausen's office before you storm in here looking for criminals where there are none." She pointed to the telephone at the rear of the shop. "Be sure to identify yourself by name as well." She glared at him, as they stood almost chest to chest.

She could see the confusion in his eyes and his conflicting urges—to slap her out of the way or to back off from danger. Obviously, no woman had ever spoken to him in such fashion, and if she was who she said she was, he risked damage to his career. She fervently hoped he wouldn't call her bluff.

The senior gendarme glanced upward, as if to detect movement on the floor above, then capitulated. His only problem seemed finding the right words to climb down from his original order. "You may take this visit as a warning, madam. The punishment for housing unregistered persons is severe."

With that, he gave the faintest flick of his head in a sort of condescending salute and did an about-face. The parade of young Rexists was just finishing as the door closed behind the two gendarmes.

Christine exhaled slowly. "Well. You won, but obviously you can't pull that trick very often. They'll probably leave me alone for a while, but still, this isn't a good location for housing your escapees. I've got enough going on already. I'll ask around for other places though, and let you know."

"Thanks, Christine. I'm sorry about your son."

"I'm sorry about your brother."

"Yeah." Sandrine shrugged. Two young men had died for a defeated country, and there was nothing comforting to say about it.

She let herself out and made her way along the now-quiet street deep in thought. What did Christine make of her claim of association with the Nazi governor general? Did she think it was a lie, a stunning bluff, or did she sense the truth in it?

How cruel war was. She couldn't even feel the satisfaction of heroic behavior when the tool she'd used was her own collaboration. The power she exercised was flimsy, the fleeting influence of the master's favorite whore.

She felt soiled and suddenly desperately lonely.

CHAPTER TEN

June 1942

Three months later and two hundred miles away, Antonia waited on an airfield at RAF Tempsford. *Christ, it's cold.* Standing next to the Armstrong Whitney that would carry them across the channel, Antonia swore to herself in language she rarely used out loud. Was it fear or simply the night wind over the tarmac? It was supposed to be spring, but you'd never know it.

The wide money belt around her midriff itched but was the most important thing she carried, with money and papers identifying her as Sophie Lajeune, nurse's assistant from Etterbeek. In a tiny pocket at one end of it were her cyanide capsules. Over that she wore a skirt, blouse, and sweater that were specially tailored to look Belgian, though as far as she could judge, that meant drab.

The camouflaged jump overalls weighed a ton. They were the smallest size made for men and still too long in the torso, so the material bloused everywhere. The long zippers, two running from ankle cuff to mid-chest and the third from neck to crotch, made them easy to get in and out of, even with bulky clothing, but once they were zipped up, every object she'd need was tacked on outside.

The tube-pocket on her left shoulder held the switchblade knife, attached to a length of paracord in case it slipped out of her hand. It could come in handy if her chute got hung up in a tree. A leg pouch ran almost the length of her left calf. Secured by snaps, it held four small inner pockets for maps, radio codes, documents, files, hooks, anti-drowsy pills, a compass, and a vial of morphine.

The triangular pocket on her left thigh held her pistol, an Enfield Mk1 .38 caliber revolver in a canvas holster attached to a lanyard. She wondered, idly, if they ever fired upon impact. If it did, it would blow off her kneecap.

The weight on her right side was greater, since it held the pouch with her shovel and its detachable handle, and two double pockets above that contained a flask of water, a torch, survival rations, and a first-aid kit.

And that didn't count the double parachute pack and harness and the empty rucksack rolled up as a cushion in the small of her back.

She did like the canvas jump helmet, with its ring of cushioning around the forehead and mica glasses attached by an elastic band. It made her look like an aviator and not like a walking hardware store.

She shifted her weight to her other leg and jumped slightly to settle her bulky load into a more comfortable position. She then did a mental rundown of everything they had packed for her that wasn't on her body. In addition to what she wore under her overalls, the dispatcher would drop a suitcase containing a Belgian-style coat, three sets of underwear, more emergency rations, and additional bandages.

Next to her, Llewellyn Rhydderch looked just as cluttered, though less bothered by the weight. Their separate tasks were clear. He was in charge of the mission and would make the day-to-day decisions of what to do on the ground—gathering Resistance forces, setting up communication lines, collecting intelligence to pass back to London.

Antonia was the "pianist" who would transmit all communications on the wireless radio that would go with them on this trip, and she curled her fingers inside her gloves, itching to telegraph her current misery. *Di di dit, dah dah dah, di di dit. Get me off this damned airfield.*

"Here ya go, Toni," Lew said, smearing her cheeks with two fingers covered with camouflage cream the color of cooked spinach. She tolerated it because he was in charge. His own fully greased face made him look like a swamp demon.

A figure strode toward her in the dark, though the moonlight lit his white hair and revealed it was the squadron leader, arrived for the final briefing. He shook all their hands first, then unfolded a map onto the tarmac.

"Here's your dropping point, on this field." He tapped an area at the top left. "It's bounded by woods, so that should give you some cover. This stream is just north of you, so once you get your bearings, you should move on eastward toward Brussels. Remember, it's going to be a very short jump, only around 300-400 feet to avoid radar detection, so after your chute opens, you'll hit the ground within about fifteen seconds."

"Yes sir. We'll be ready," Antonia said.

"Good. And once you're down, remember to bury your chutes and overalls. You're to make your way into Brussels and try to locate Andrée or Frédéric de Jongh. I wish we had more information about them, but all we know is that Andrée walked into the British Consulate in Bilbao with three escapees she had brought down from Belgium. Your task is to find her and help integrate her network with us. As soon as you've connected with her, contact us on the wireless. You've got plenty of Belgian money between you, but obviously your contacts are going to have to find you lodgings to start off with. After we've gotten your message, we'll prepare the next phase of operations."

"Yes, sir. They've explained all that to us," Lew said, fidgeting under the weight of his equipment.

"Remember, if you're captured with your wireless and the enemy forces you to radio us, you must include this in your message: *We're fine, both of us. Don't worry.* In any normal transmission, no one will ask how you are, so you should wire those words *only* if you have, in fact, fallen into their hands."

Two men emerged from the hangar wheeling a handcart that held their suitcases and wireless kit. With a brief salute to the squadron leader, they slid the three items into the tail section of the aircraft, attaching them to a static line that would open their shared parachute.

The flight crew of pilot, navigator, and radio operator saluted as well before climbing aboard to prepare the flight.

"Off you go now, chaps." The squadron leader shook both their hands again and clapped them once on their shoulders. "Godspeed."

Antonia gripped the sides of the entry hatch and threaded herself inside, along with her bulky parachute. Once inside, she moved in a crouch to the center of the refitted bomber. She sat down and drew up her knees to make room for Lew to squat next to her. Directly behind him came the dispatcher, who would accompany them as far as the landing zone before returning with the flight crew.

The plane engines began, preventing any talk between them. They squatted in a compartment separated by a wall from the cockpit. Only the dispatcher had a headset for communication with the crew. While they taxied to the runway, he hooked her parachute to the automatic rip-cord system in the plane.

The dispatcher said something into his headset, and a minute later, with a roar of the engines, the plane lifted off the runway.

They had no porthole to look through at the night sky or the ground below, but Antonia found the isolation a sort of comfort. She didn't want to be reminded of the darkness she would have to leap into over an unknown place.

It was cold inside the fuselage, and she shivered in spite of the woolen clothing she wore underneath. When the dispatcher handed her a sleeping bag and gestured that she should try to sleep, she slid awkwardly but gratefully into it. She was far too nervous to sleep, but welcomed the extra layer of warmth.

Slouched over her parachute pack amidst the roar and with nothing to do but wait, she was left prey to her wandering thoughts. How had she ended up here?

What would her parents have thought if they were still alive? Her father would certainly have been proud, but dear sweet Mum would've been in a panic. After all, in a few hours, her life would be on the line. At least that had been Dora's argument as she'd slipped into bed with Antonia the night before. Dora herself was scheduled to be shipped out the same evening as Antonia, somewhere into France.

"This could be our last night alive. Don't you want to make it a sweet one?" she'd cajoled, sliding a warm hand inside Antonia's pajama pants.

The insinuating touch was like a charge of electricity that spread immediately upward to her sex. She would never have considered Dora or anyone at the school as a lover, but that night, the chasm of uncertainty that lay before both of them and Dora's warm lips on her throat made an irresistible argument.

Dora was certainly skillful. Or perhaps, after the long dry spell since Dunkirk, Antonia was just unusually receptive. Whatever the reason, she returned Dora's kisses ardently as the delinquent hand moved quickly from caresses to invasion. After the first shock of penetration, Antonia had been awash in simple lust. Within moments, she climaxed, and before the heat of orgasm had subsided, she slid halfway over Dora and returned the favor.

Afterward, they had both simply said "Good night," and Dora had returned to her bed. Curiously, or perhaps obviously, Antonia had fallen asleep immediately, quietly resigned to her fate, whatever it was.

But now sleep was nowhere near. She did a rundown of what she needed to know to stay alive and undetected after leaving the plane: how to maneuver the chute to avoid treetops or water, how to tuck and roll upon landing, and how to bury her chute and overalls.

Under the roar of the airplane engine she detected a softer sound, and she smiled. Lew was snoring as if by a cozy winter fire. The big lug. She was confident that if they were captured, he'd hold out against the enemy and would be an inspiration.

She wiggled her fingers, practicing the codes for the reports she would be sending back. Her code name, Sophie Lajeune, was amusing, and gave no information about her except that she liked the opera *Rosenkavalier*.

A soft tap on her shoulder startled her. It was the dispatcher with a tin cup of tea.

She took off her gloves, warming her hands on the cup while she sipped, and tasted a good shot of rum in the tea. Rum that had been calming British sailors since the days of the tall ships comforted her now.

Lew was awake too, and when they handed back their mugs to the dispatcher, he signaled that they were almost at the drop zone. Slated to jump first, she checked all the buckles on her chute, tightened the strap on her jump helmet, and clambered toward the open hatch.

Her chute-release cord slid along the pipe over her head, and she stood with legs wide apart over the hatch opening, watching with dread as the dull-gray patches of ground slid by. The dispatcher tapped her again on the shoulder, pointing to the rip cord attached to the static line, reassuring her that all was well. She turned her attention to the signal box, waiting for the red light to turn green.

Tiny white lights sparkled on the ground below; a fraction of a second later she heard the detonation. Flak cannons. Her heart thudded with fear. They'd been spotted. In that instant the light turned green and the dispatcher shoved her out of the plane.

Scarcely two seconds after she plunged into darkness, the rip cord yanked her to a virtual standstill, and she began floating downward with a wild lateral sway. She tried to tilt her head upward and search the sky for Lew's parachute, but the wind whipped her around and she had to look down to prepare for the landing.

As she struck ground and rolled over on her back, she saw one of the flak shells strike the fuselage. It belched out a spray of fire from its engine, then spiraled downward with a metallic scream and crashed into a distant field.

Dear God. Five men dead in an instant. Or had any gotten out? She saw no other chutes, only the distant red glow of the burning aircraft.

Not enough time to wonder. She was alone. No mission leader, no wireless radio, nothing but a compass, a side arm, and the contents in the pockets of her overalls.

She had surely been seen jumping from the plane, so there was no point wasting time burying her chute. She unhooked the straps, stepped out of them, and with the sound of men shouting in the distance, she ran full out for the nearest line of trees.

The spade proved useful after all, as she made her way to the center of a copse of trees where the soil was damp and loose. Sheer terror gave her strength and she frantically dug a shallow pit, just deep enough for her in her bulky jumpsuit. Lying on her back, she swept loose soil and underbrush back over herself, covering her face with the jump helmet. In her free hand, she held her revolver over her chest. If they found her, she would take at least one of them out with her.

The dirt and brush muffled all sound so she could hear nothing until they were literally on top of her. She felt the pressure of someone walk right over her legs and then back again. She held her breath, and even when the dull buzz of voices was gone, she remained under the dirt, breathing slowly into her helmet.

But however slowly she breathed, the oxygen was soon depleted and she began to feel drowsy. Fearing asphyxiation, she lifted her head and gasped in air, holding her pistol at chin level.

She tensed, fearing a boot or a bullet, but she felt only the dirt trickle from her collar down her back. The men were still within hearing range, but they were apparently headed away from her. She took a deep breath and tried to see around her.

The full moon shone through the branches with deceptive serenity. She knew the men had seen her come down, and her abandoned parachute made it clear she was alive and in the vicinity. They wouldn't give up until they'd captured her.

Crawling toward the edge of the thicket, she surveyed the field in front of her. In the bright moonlight every protuberance was clearly visible in silvery blue and black shadow. Behind another row of trees an orange glow showed where the plane was still burning. On the south and west, dark patches of woods.

How many men were searching for her? If only two or three, she had a chance to evade them, as long as she kept to the shadows. Brushing the soil from her overalls, she made her way along the line of trees in the opposite direction from the voices. She kept her pistol in one hand and grappled with the underbrush with the other.

She forced herself onward, in spite of aching muscles and the accumulation of dirt inside her clothing. At the corner of the field was a barn, but she dared not hide in it. It would be the first place they'd search in the morning. She staggered onward, moving from copse to copse, and tree to tree, never stepping out into the moonlight.

After what seemed like the entire night, she took the risk of crouching over her wrist and flashing her torch on her watch for the briefest second. It was four in the morning. She'd been running for over two hours and didn't have much strength left.

She chose another secluded place in a wooded patch and dug a second pit, deep enough to reach to her shoulders when she crouched in it. For her head, she gathered loose branches and leaves and wove them into each other to create a primitive roof. Satisfied with her cover, she set it aside and climbed into the pit. While every part of her hurt, her strongest sensation now was thirst.

She took a long pull on her water flask and, risking the brief use of her torch once again, she studied the other emergency rations. Besides the "compo-meal" for which she had no appetite, she found packets of salt, matches, service chocolates, powdered tea, a tiny block of soap, and toilet paper.

Ah, yes. That reminded her. That one last thing.

She struggled out of her hidey-hole and found a spot some ten paces away. Using her spade, she dug another hole. Then she undid her overalls, discovering in the process how filthy they were, and relieved herself with a quiet sigh. The toilet paper was rough but she was grateful it had been included, and when the business was done, she carefully covered the pit again, pressing the dirt down flat with her boot.

With that taken care of, she returned to her hiding pit. She gathered the branches and brush over her and settled into something approximating the fetal position, holding her holstered pistol to her chest like a lethal teddy bear.

She brooded for a while on her plight, with a mixture of fear, sorrow for Lew and the other good men who'd just lost their lives to the war, and an unfocused anger at the Nazis who'd caused it all.

Bastards, she thought. Murderous bastards. Then, in spite of the damp and the discomfort, and the sensation of being filthy, she succumbed to her exhaustion and fell asleep.

CHAPTER ELEVEN

Antonia was jolted awake by the bleating of a goat. She held her breath, gripping her gun to her chest. Agonizing minutes passed until she heard the bleating a second time, this time right over her head, and a moment later, a hand pulled away her brush cover. Pointing her gun out in front of her, she looked up into the face of a terrified woman.

"Please! Don't shoot! I have babies at home." The woman cowered, holding a kid goat to her chest as if it were one of them.

"No, of course I won't. I'm sorry." Antonia returned the gun to its holster and climbed out of her hole. The woman looked to be about thirty, had mousy brown hair drawn back into a single braid, and wore a tattered blue-patterned dress and jacket.

They stood as if paralyzed, facing each other, and the sound of the pattering rain all around them seemed suddenly loud.

"Is anyone else on the road with you?" Antonia asked.

"No. I just bought two goats and was bringing them home. One got out." She pointed with her head toward the road, and Antonia stepped forward to look. In fact, a mule-drawn cart waited on the shoulder of the road holding straw and another goat.

"English?" the woman asked.

Given that she was hiding in a hole in jump overalls and with her face painted green, asserting she was Belgian would be ludicrous. "Yes. Can you help me? At least a better place to hide." Antonia clutched her own shivering shoulders. "Out of the rain."

The woman looked around nervously and hesitated, it seemed, for an eternity. "All right. Come on. Under the straw, but hurry."

"Yes, yes. Of course." She dropped her jump helmet into the damp hole and spread the loose underbrush over it. The woman was back on the road now, urging the errant goat into the cart, and Antonia hurried toward her.

She climbed in next to the kid, and the woman covered her with armloads of straw. After bleating a brief protest, the goats resumed nibbling on it, and, a moment later, the cart jerked into motion. She pressed her eyes shut against the dust of the straw and the foul-smelling grit on the cart floor, but all of it adhered to her damp hair and skin.

The ride over the pitted road was a test of endurance, but after what seemed like an hour, the cart stopped. A gate creaked, and then they moved again, this time rocking violently from side to side. A yard, she guessed, with even bigger potholes.

The gate creaked closed again, and the goat hooves thumped lightly as the woman untied them and led them off the cart. Then the straw over Antonia's head parted to reveal daylight.

"Please, wait for me by the door."

"Gladly." Antonia climbed over the side of the cart onto the thick mud of the yard. She glanced around while her rescuer unhitched the mule and led it into a stall. The yard was open to the rain, but on one side a covered area protected half a dozen chickens, and on the other, an elevated hutch presumably housed several rabbits.

The woman opened a door leading from the barn area to the house and frowned as she studied Antonia's squalid state. "Please wait outside. I'll bring you something to put on."

Antonia stood obediently in a sort of vestibule, but the smell of boiled potatoes suggested she was right outside the kitchen. She unlaced her boots and yanked them off, along with the wet wool socks inside. Grateful for the warmth surrounding her, she also peeled off her filthy overalls and stood in equally wet but at least unmuddied women's clothing. But she stank, and the rucksack she'd unrolled from her back was damp and malodorous as well.

The woman returned carrying a man's coat. "My husband says you can come in. So, umm, I guess you should tell us your name."

"Sophie." Antonia gave her code name.

"I'm Berta. And this is my husband, Albert." Antonia stepped into the kitchen to confront a man sitting at the table. Like his wife, he was hard to place in age. His face was gaunt, with beard stubble, though he had the full head of hair of a young man. When he didn't get up, she moved toward him and offered her hand. "Thank you for taking me in. I'll try not to be a lot of trouble."

He bent forward and shook her hand, and when he righted himself, she could see why he stayed seated. His right leg ended just below the knee. And on the floor under the table, just within reach, was a set of crutches. He glanced up at her matted hair. "Perhaps you would like to wash."

"Oh, yes. I would love to. I'm afraid I smell like goats." She touched her cheek and remembered that her face was still covered with camouflage grease. "And look like a monster."

He smiled weakly. "We have no bathroom, only that." He pointed toward a wide square sink that presumably served for all washing and laundry needs. "There's hot water in the kettle. I'll leave you to your privacy so you can bathe, and my wife will give you something dry to wear. Then you have to hide in the basement. The Germans come every day to requisition our eggs."

"You are very kind."

"Not kind. Just vengeful. I lost this leg last year to German shrapnel." He groped under the table for his crutches and struggled to a standing position. "I wish we could do more for you, but we have the children to protect. It makes a man timid." He hobbled toward the door of the other room.

Berta was already pumping cold water into a pitcher in the sink. She added boiling water from the kettle and tested the temperature of the mix. Satisfied, she drew a bottle of brown liquid from a shelf over the sink. "This is soap I make myself. Nothing like they have in Brussels, but it will clean."

"Thank you. I'll try not to use too much."

Antonia unfolded her jumpsuit, transferring all the survival equipment from the pockets into the rucksack. "I need to destroy this." She stood with the suit hanging over her arm. "Can you burn it, or should I bury it?"

"Give it here." Berta laid the jumpsuit over the kitchen table and fetched a large pair of scissors from a drawer. "It won't fit into the stove except in pieces," she said, and began cutting it apart. When she'd reduced the garment to a pile of rags, she lifted the iron lid from the stovetop and fed the pieces one by one into the hole. Each section of the thick damp fabric smoked for a moment, then caught fire.

While it burned, Antonia tested the water in the pitcher and found it pleasantly hot. Leaning over the sink, she poured a portion of it over her head, then lathered her scalp thoroughly, stopping to pick out particles of leaf or straw. Probably worse things, she thought, recalling the goats. After the first rinse, she used the same soap to scrub the camouflage paint from her face and neck and then to scratch out the soil from under her fingernails.

She considered staying clothed, but she had never felt so dirty and couldn't bear another moment of it. She unsnapped her money belt from around her midriff and then her brassiere, and with the remaining warm water, she scrubbed the grit from every place she could reach. Her nether regions would have to wait for more favorable conditions.

"Give me your clothes," Berta said, and strung the articles on a line in front of the stove. "In the meantime, you can put on my husband's coat."

Antonia snapped on the money belt again and drew on the coat. It smelled of a man, though not unpleasantly.

"Can I come back in now?" Albert called through the door.

"Yes, please do." Antonia buttoned the coat closed, then added her wet socks to the line of clothing over the stove.

Albert hobbled back into the room with a girl of about two next to him. One of her hands grasped the side of his trousers, while the other seemed attached to her mouth. "This is Elsbeth. The baby is with her grandmother."

Antonia smiled at the child, who seemed baffled to see a complete stranger wearing her father's coat.

"She's precious. I'll try not to endanger you and her very long. I just need to rest a bit and then get to Brussels, to the Rue des Bouchers. If I remember correctly, it's close to the Grand Place, isn't it?"

Berta hefted the child into a highchair while Albert, in spite of his handicap, insisted on pulling out a chair for Antonia. "Well, you'll have no trouble finding the Grand Place. But Brussels is about five kilometers from here and nobody has a car."

He paused and broke off a morsel of bread for his daughter. "You can get to the first tram stop in maybe half an hour by bicycle. But we have only one and can't give it to you."

"Albert, the parish curé has a bicycle. Two of them, in fact." Berta brought the steaming pot of soup to the table. "And he's sympathetic to anyone fighting the Germans."

Albert nodded. "That might be a solution. I'll talk to him. In the meantime, eat your soup and then go rest downstairs." He began to slice bread as Berta ladled out the soup. Bean soup, Antonia noted and, after only a single meal of cold field rations since yesterday, it smelled heavenly.

❖

Lighting her way with a lantern, Antonia descended the stairs to the cellar in her underwear and overcoat. The walls on all four sides were stone, joined by crumbling mortar. On the one side, shelves held preserves and empty jars; on the other side, a carpenter's worktable stood looking neglected. In the corner, a broken easy chair, with a ragged blanket thrown over it, offered the only accommodation for sitting. Everything smelled of mold.

She slid her hand inside the coat to check that the money belt was secure. It was not only the money that she had to guard, but also her counterfeit ration cards and identification and baptismal certificates, artificially aged, all under the name of Sophie Lejeune. She'd soon find out how convincing they were.

The gloom around her reawakened the shock of the plane crash. The mission had seemed so brave, so promising. But now the lives of all those men were snuffed out, just like that, and she was crouching in a cellar at the mercy of strangers.

Turning the lantern flame low to save fuel, she waited. An hour, hour and a half, two hours. The inactivity caused her to doze.

She dreamed fitfully, of running to catch a train, which, upon her entering, proved to be a plane. She leapt from an open door and flew blissfully, high over what appeared to be the Paris of her youth, then awoke with a start at the sound of a woman's voice.

A figure was silhouetted against the light. "I'm sorry if I frightened you. I've brought your clothes. The curé is here now too."

Berta handed over a pile of neatly folded garments that still retained a bit of warmth. "Clothes and daylight. That would be good. Thank you."

She slipped on the skirt and sweater, feeling the pleasure of clean cloth against her skin.

"Your boots don't really go with the clothing," Berta said. "Didn't they give you anything better?"

"No, these will have to do. Do you think I'll attract attention?"

"Probably not. But take this. Sometimes they do just a quick search, so they feel like they're doing their job and they don't look any further." She handed over an old purse, small, with a frayed strap and soiled leather. "It was my mother's. She's dead a long time now, but I'm sure she'd like you to use it."

Antonia accepted it gratefully. She hadn't thought about being searched, but now that she did, she drew her holster from her backpack and strapped it to her thigh under her skirt.

They were on the stairs now, and as she emerged into the light of the kitchen, the curé stood up to meet her. A slender, almost gaunt man, he wore a black cassock with an unbroken row of buttons from collar to hem. A biretta with a rather ragged pom lay on the table, and the white collar under the soutane was discolored. "Madam," he said, taking her hand. His grip was firm.

"We are new at this, I mean in dealing with…um…visitors such as yourself," he said without preliminary courtesies.

"First time for me too," she replied weakly

"Yes, I suppose it is. Well, here's the plan. You'll travel on one of the bicycles to the first tram stop, which is at the end of the highway outside the village. I and a young lad from the parish will follow some distance behind you on the other one, but if you're stopped we will turn away and leave you."

"Yes, I understand."

"Ah, there he is now. Come in, Johann," The priest stepped back as a boy of about fourteen came in and stood shyly near the kitchen door. "You must lock the bicycle near the tram stop," he continued. "After the tram pulls away, we'll fetch it and return. You should arrive in Brussels close to sunset but long before curfew."

He scribbled something on a piece of paper. "If you need a place to stay, go to this address. It's not far from the Rue des Bouchers, which I understand is your destination. It's owned by Christine Mathys, who lost her son in the fighting and has no love for the Germans. When last

I heard, she had rooms available. If you're able to pay some rent, I'm sure she'd appreciate it."

"I'll be happy to pay it. I have Belgian francs."

"All the better."

The priest donned his biretta. "Are you ready to leave?"

"Yes, I suppose I am." She took hold of her pack. "All I have is this."

"That will be—"

"Shit!" Albert sputtered suddenly, peering through the window. "The Germans are here. For the eggs. Come this way." He snatched up his crutch and hobbled toward the door to another room.

Antonia lurched after him, though behind her the priest and his boy remained unperturbed.

He led her through the adjacent sitting room into a bedroom and threw open the window. "Wait until they're in the kitchen. The curé will delay them a few minutes so you can get to the goat stall. Stay there until someone comes for you." Without waiting for a reply, he limped back to the kitchen. He closed the bedroom door behind him, but as she slid one leg over the windowsill she could already hear German voices.

She scurried across the same yard she had arrived in that morning and saw the German motorcycle and sidecar. For the briefest moment she wondered if she could steal it, then realized it would mean a death sentence for her rescuers. She continued past the vehicle into the goat stall, which was as rank as the cart had been.

"Hi, kids," she whispered to the two young animals, and snickered in spite of her fear. She stood pressed against the wall breathing through her mouth and hoped the egg transaction would be brief; she didn't want to arrive in Brussels smelling of goat.

Finally she heard the two Germans emerge laughing from the house and start their motor. She waited for the sound to fade away, then crept from the stall. To her relief, the priest and the boy waited before the house, holding the handlebars of two bicycles.

CHAPTER TWELVE

On the same morning as Antonia's goat-cart rescue, Sandrine hurried toward the Café Suèdoise for an early meeting. Sixteen-year-old Celine kept pace beside her, leading her limping dachshund.

Sandrine still had misgivings about involving so young a girl in the operation. "Laura thinks you should stay in Marcouray where it's safer, and I'm inclined to agree."

"Look, I know what I'm getting into, so please don't treat me like a child. Besides, I was already a courier for the maquis, so—"

She stopped abruptly, bringing Sandrine to a halt. Directly ahead of them were two of the countless German gendarmes that swept along the streets at all hours, making random identity checks.

One of the two gendarmes also halted. He stood with his feet wide apart, one thumb hooked in his belt, the other one cupping the sleek holster of his Lugar.

"You again," he said, his face darkening. "I recognize that shitty little dog. It was you that got me demoted, you little bitch."

Sandrine didn't recognize him, but she remembered the incident. Was that all the punishment he got? Demotion? She took a step closer to confront him. "She didn't get you in trouble. It was the governor general of Belgium who thought what you did was cowardly."

His scowl ratcheted up a degree in intensity. "Who the hell are you to talk about cowardice? Your whole shit-country and its army is one big shithole of cowardice. Eighteen days, and you were on your knees."

Sandrine's voice turned to ice. "Our soldiers fought and died defending their own homes, and all you did was shoot a tiny dog."

The gendarme's eyes widened in rage.

"Come on, Heinz." His companion took hold of his arm. "Don't get yourself worked up again. It's not worth it."

Sandrine and Celine tried to pass around him, but he stepped sideward and blocked them again. "You're going to pay for that, you bitch. Just wait…"

"Leave them, Heinz. Anything happens to them, you'll just be in more trouble."

"Oh, I won't have to do anything." He glowered at her. "But everyone breaks the rules some time, and you'll break them too. Maybe you'll steal a little fuel or buy on the black market. Maybe help someone avoid labor conscription. I'll find out about it, and you'll go down."

He stepped back, to let them pass, then called after them, "I'll be watching you."

Sandrine took Celine's arm and led her and Suzi down the alleyway to the service door of the café. "Don't let him rattle you, dear. He's just a blowhard. We just have to be a little more careful." She didn't sound terribly convincing, even to herself.

In the back room of the Café Suèdoise, Laura and Francis sat at the table that served as their business desk and turned at the sound of the door opening.

"Oh, good, you're here." Laura waved them over. "Francis has just been telling me how dire our finances are."

Sandrine and Celine hung up their coats and unleashed the dog, who bounded over to be petted. Laura obliged her while Francis remained focused glumly on his account book.

"I don't know how much longer we can keep this up," he said. The escape line is spending all the money we earn, and now we're not even earning very much."

"Why not? The place is always full." Sandrine pulled over a chair and joined them.

"Yes, but it's full of Germans, and they won't settle for the stew we concoct with whatever meat's available that week. That might be good enough for the Belgians, with their food coupons, but the Germans want good wine, champagne, pork sausage, and real butter. I have to buy all those things on the black market, but they don't pay me the black-market prices at the table."

"At least they provide a good cover for us," Celine offered hopefully.

"Yes, but I can't keep up the juggling act—feeding the Germans, financing the Comet Line, and hoping the Communists don't shoot me as a collaborator."

"We need to contact someone in the partisans to get them to back off," Sandrine said. "But we have another problem. We just ran into that German who shot Suzi, and he threatened us. He said he was going to be watching us all the time, to catch us doing something illegal. And that includes buying on the black market."

Francis frowned. "Well, he won't catch us doing that here in Brussels. I purchase everything through an intermediary who trucks it in from the countryside along with the legal foodstuffs. A bigger problem is the money."

"How much have we got left?"

He turned a few pages in his ledger, made a brief calculation on a scrap of paper, and blew out a little puff of air. "Maybe enough for a couple of train tickets, another food allowance for the safe houses around Brussels, but not enough to pay off the guides."

The sound of the door opening again startled all of them, but it was one of their own. Quiet, bespectacled, and with soft, prematurely gray hair swept across his forehead, Philippe Ledoux looked professorial, if not monkish. With a demeanor that aroused immediate trust, he seemed the last person anyone would suspect of militant resistance. Christine had brought him into the organization, and from the first day he had proved his worth. He had a barn and a horse that had escaped requisitioning, and he had quickly learned the escape route and its strategies.

He limped painfully over to the table where the others sat.

Sandrine looked down anxiously at his leg. "What happened to you? Did our 'parcels' make it to Spain or did you have trouble along the way?"

"Yes to both questions. We got the pilots through to Bilbao without incident, but on the way back, a disaster occurred. I'm sorry to tell you that Andrée was captured. Last night at Bayonne. I was afraid to risk a telephone call and just came home."

Sandrine felt as if she'd been struck. "Dear God, first Frédéric and now Andrée. What happened? How did you get away?"

"We kept a distance from each other, as always, and when she arrived at the customs station, a security policeman simply stopped her. Obviously they were waiting. I couldn't do anything for her, so I went to the men's toilet and jumped from the window onto the street. I sprained my ankle pretty badly, but I don't think I broke anything. Anyhow, our local people in Bayonne are trying to find out where they've taken her."

Sandrine laid her forehead in her hands, and for several minutes no one spoke.

Francis broke the silence. "Do you think the Gestapo can break her?"

Sandrine shook her head. "It's hard to imagine. The Comet Line is her creation. She'll die before giving anything away."

Francis brushed his knuckles under his chin. "Don't be so sure. If the torture is really bad, who knows? She might give *something* away. Something that could lead back to us. She's only human, after all."

"To some extent we're protected, aren't we?" Laura asked. "We've got half the German officers' corps in the café all the time, and we're always quite careful. She was rarely here, as far as I can remember, so unless she talks…"

"No, she stayed away from the café," Philippe said. "Only the people working on the line know her. More likely the Gestapo will simply snoop around everyone she knows and every place she's been, to try to pick up a trail."

"You can be sure that this Heinz Büttner will also be sniffing around for anything unusual," Laura added.

Francis winced at the reminder of the new danger. "Let's just agree, if anyone comes around asking about Andrée, it's probably the Gestapo putting out feelers. And we simply shrug and know nothing."

"Okay, so, assuming we can fend off any questions about her, *and* keep this Büttner idiot away from us, we should be able to continue the line." Sandrine was businesslike.

Philippe looked doubtful. "You want to send off another group even now?"

"We have to. Pilots and evaders are piling up all around Brussels, and we don't have any more places to hide them. I've got a new batch at my place now. They have a better chance moving than they do hiding in cellars and attics. You know that's exactly what Andrée wants us to do."

"Yes, but we need more of everything—money, couriers, blank forms for the forgers to print the identifications." Francis stared into the air as if reading from a list.

Philippe massaged his swollen ankle. "Yes, but who's going to take the evaders down the line? I'm no good until my foot heals."

After another long silence, Francis spoke. "I'm sorry, Sandrine. It's got to be you. You're the only one left."

CHAPTER THIRTEEN

Papers, please." The German gendarme held out his hand.

Antonia remained calm, perhaps because the physical exertion of pedaling the old bicycle for several miles had simply depleted the energy needed to panic. At least she didn't have to worry about her Brussels accent not being right. The man's French was a horror.

"Yes, Officer." She opened her purse and drew out the battered leather folder with her identification papers. He inspected her handbag, and she sent up a thought of gratitude to Berta, for its contents were flawless. Yesterday's paper, a set of keys to presumably long-forgotten locks, a bit of food, a coin purse, and a half-used lipstick. Her money belt was deep inside her sweater, and her revolver was strapped to the inside of her thigh. She was in danger only if he rifled through the rucksack strapped to the rear of the bicycle.

"Where are you going in such a hurry?" He swept his glance over the papers. She was ready for him, adding a wistful note to the expression she held.

"Into Brussels to buy shoes. Just look at these old things." She pointed down to her mud-encrusted boots. "Would you want to wear these? My father gave me money and coupons to buy new ones for my birthday. Which is very soon." She indicated the date on the identification.

"Ah, well then, off you go." Now he was smiling too as he handed the papers back with a snap. "Happy Birthday." He bumped his fellow gendarme with his elbow and they strolled together across the street.

Stalling for time, Antonia tucked the papers back into her purse, alongside the bread and cheese Berta had packed for her. She waited until the two men were out of sight before riding the last few streets to the tram stop.

As arranged, she locked the bike directly across the street from the stop, and when the tram rattled up in front of her, she caught sight of the boy. She took a seat, and as she watched from the tram window, he unlocked the bike and rode off in the direction she had come from.

She glanced around the tram car and realized to her surprise it had not emptied out, even though this was the final stop on the line and the tram was about to reverse direction. Then she saw the reason.

Men stood by the two doors with clubs, and a third one guarded the driver of the tram with a pistol. They must have leaped onto the tram just as she was boarding. What was going on?

"Ladies and gentlemen," the one in front was shouting. "We are sorry to disturb you this way. But we are taking the day's receipts from the tram, as well as a small contribution from each of you." He spoke French with a strong accent, though unlike that of the gendarme. Something Eastern European, probably Polish or Russian. "We will not hurt any of you if you remain calm. We are all resisting the occupation as best we can. But for that we need money, to buy food for those who are hiding." He yanked open the fare box, and a shower of coins and small bills flowed into his cloth bag. "Remember, we are fighting for Belgium, and for freedom. So please give generously. If not, we may have to help ourselves to more than you'd like. Do we have an understanding?" A few passengers grumbled their assent.

A simple robbery. For the Resistance, supposedly. She was glad she'd moved a few Belgian francs from her money belt into her coin purse. She could allow herself to be robbed, and she certainly had no need to reach for her pistol.

One of the men was standing in front of her now. She stared at him, struck by how unlike a robber he was. His high forehead and horn-rimmed glasses gave him the look of an intellectual. He seemed both patient and nervous as he waited for her to react, occasionally glancing to the side to assure himself no one was moving.

She opened her handbag and emptied her coin purse into his sack, Though it couldn't have amounted to much, he seemed satisfied and moved on to the next passenger.

"Thank you all for your generosity, my friends," the leader said. "Now, if you will wait a few moments while we make our escape, we wish you a good evening. Long live freedom!" And with that, the three of them leapt from the tram and ran off into one of the dim evening streets.

The fifteen or so other passengers remained seated, whether out of fear or sympathy wasn't clear. But after some two or three minutes of murmuring among themselves, most of them descended the tram, leaving only four to make the return trip into Brussels.

The driver looked at the broken and empty fare box, cursed under his breath, and then started the motor. With a clang, the car lurched forward and rattled along its track.

❖

It was dark when Antonia exited the tram at the stop the priest had suggested. She hurried to find the correct building, to avoid another confrontation. It might not be so easy to fool a Belgian policeman, who could hear her imperfect French.

But there it was, just off the Boulevard Anspach, in the Rue Marché au Charbon. To her surprise, it wasn't a residence, but a shop with display windows on both sides. Above it were two more floors and an attic. Out of keeping with its stately façade, the shop windows displayed a mixture of secondhand shoes and clothing, and a variety of household goods, all of it a bit shabby.

She entered and seemed to surprise the lone shopkeeper, a tall fifty-something woman with graying once-red hair that covered her head like a mushroom cap. "Can I help you, madam?"

"Are you Madame Mathys?"

"Yes? What can I do for you?" Her tone was cordial but cool, full of suspicion.

"I have a note for you from Father Vandenhoven. In the village of Zobroek." She slipped it from inside her sweater and laid it on the shop counter.

The shopkeeper's expression softened immediately. "I see. You are in need of accommodations. Unfortunately, Father Vandenhoven doesn't know that I've already rented the apartment. I can offer you only the attic room. It's much smaller, but has a bed and a sink. The toilet and bathroom are on the floor below." She named a modest sum for the monthly rental.

"That's fine," Antonia replied, she hoped not too quickly. "If possible, I'd like to move in immediately."

"Yes, of course. I'll take you upstairs right now." She locked the front door, though the empty street outside suggested she had little business in any case. At the back of the shop a spiral staircase with an iron railing led to the upper floors.

"This is my apartment," she said, pointing with her head toward the door on the first floor. On the second floor she explained, "The new tenants are here. Over there on the right is the bathroom you share with them. Your room is on the top floor."

Antonia followed her host silently to the last floor, where she opened a narrow door, and turned on an overhead light. It was a room out of a Kafka novel—a single bed with an iron bedstead, a sink, and a tiny table with two open shelves above it. The room would have functioned perfectly as a prison cell.

The proprietor led her to the window, and she looked down onto the Rue Marché au Charbon. It was now full night, with a single streetlamp and a few windows lit across the way providing the only light. She dropped her rucksack onto the bed. "It suits me fine, Madame Mathys. If you will give me a moment to unpack my belongings, I'll come down to pay you the first month's rent."

"Take your time." The shopkeeper withdrew, leaving the key in the door lock.

Antonia examined the shelf over the small table. It contained two porcelain plates, a pitcher, and an immersion heater for boiling water. At least she'd be able to make the tea from her emergency rations in the morning. In a cardboard box she found a set of cutlery—two sets of knives, forks and spoons, once silver-plated but now tarnished and lacking most of their plating. An electric hot plate and a battered pot on the bottom shelf hinted that she would have a steady diet of soups.

The apartment provided sheets and a blanket for the bed, but no towel. She would see to that, as well as to the question of laundry and additional clothing. She made a mental note to purchase soap, bread, and whatever fresh produce was available. At least she didn't have to worry about cost, as long as her money lasted. But the thought of having to live alone for very long in such a grim place made her slightly nauseous.

Well, she was as safe as could be expected now and needed to bathe and sleep. She drew the required amount of Belgian francs from her money belt, along with counterfeit ration coupons, and went downstairs to take care of business.

As she approached the floor directly below, a woman stood in the doorway with a baby of about two in her arms. As a first social encounter, it seemed unthreatening.

"Hello. I'm your new neighbor upstairs," Antonia said. "I hope my tromping around over your head isn't a problem."

The woman shook her head without smiling. "No. No, I'm sure it's not," she replied with a thick Slavic accent and closed the door. Rebuffed, Antonia continued down the stairs.

Mme Mathys was opening the shop again, though there seemed no hope of business. A horse-drawn wagon passed by, the clopping of the horse's hooves resonating on the cobblestones. Children ran after it, their sabots giving off a softer, higher-pitched clopping.

Antonia glanced around at the sad racks and shelves of used merchandise.

"Can I purchase a towel and pajamas from you? Actually, I could use some underwear too. And perhaps some soap?"

The shopkeeper looked faintly amused at the long list. "I have some Marseille soap. She reached under the counter and retrieved a block of something greenish brown and named a price. "As for the towel and clothing, look around for whatever you need. The prices are all attached."

She perused the rack and found several items that would suit. She wasn't happy to have to buy used underwear, but it was certainly cleaner than what she wore. The men's pajamas and socks would be enormous, but that made no real difference. She wouldn't be entertaining.

"I guess that's all for now." She counted out the Belgian francs to cover both the rent and the purchases. "Good evening, then," she said, bundling everything up under her arm and starting back up the stairs. She wondered if there was a Monsieur Mathys and whether she could depend on either of them for assistance. Or was their resistance simply passive and unspoken? She began to appreciate the difficulty of determining who she could or could not trust.

As she reached the second-floor landing, a man emerged from the bathroom. His head was down as he set on his glasses, presumably after washing his face. When he raised it to glance at her, both of them recoiled at the same time.

It was the robber from the tram.

Her first instinct was to flee. But before she could move, he hurried past her, into the second-floor apartment.

Nonplussed, she climbed the last flight to her own room, entered, and locked the door behind her. Thoughts crowded in on one another. Was he a bandit or a patriot? Did he have a gun and would he try to enter her room? Well, she had hers too, though the last thing she needed was a gunfight. It was surreal.

Crap. As a battlefield nurse, she'd known who the enemy was and, from hour to hour, what her job was. Now every hour seemed to bring a new danger from an unexpected quarter. She felt as if she were in a maelstrom simply trying to stay afloat.

Extinguishing the harsh overhead light, she clicked on the reading lamp and undressed. She'd planned to bathe downstairs but was too rattled now. Instead, she washed standing before her pathetic little sink. Using the harsh soap she'd just purchased, she scrubbed the parts of her body she'd neglected in Berta's kitchen until she finally felt clean. The pajamas, for all their enormous size, felt luxurious, and so did the thick new socks.

That task taken care of, she prepared for supper, which was the "compo meal" tin in her emergency rations. She pried the top off with the tiny opener taped to the outside and, using one of the once-silver spoons, shoveled portions of the mixture into her mouth. While the lumps had a strange texture, she recognized the taste of stewed lamb and vegetables.

More or less clean, and more or less full, she took to her bed. Sad and cold though it was, it was better than the hole in the ground of the previous night. In fact, it was a major accomplishment to have climbed out of that hole and made her way to the target city.

All things considered, the mission was still on. She would look for the mysterious Andrée de Jongh early the next morning and carry on from there.

CHAPTER FOURTEEN

A ntonia awoke the next morning to sunlight. Her watch indicated nearly eight. Obviously, in spite of her anxiety and the new surroundings, she'd slept well. She hurried to dress and ate the now-dry bread and cheese Berta had given her. It was time to start work, whatever that turned out to be.

Too many years had passed since childhood for her to have any clear memory of Brussels, so she consulted the city map they'd given her at Ringway. She confirmed that the Rue des Bouchers was just on the other side of the Grand Place, and she could get there easily without asking directions.

By eight thirty she was on her way down the stairs, though she hesitated a moment before the door of the second-floor apartment. Who were they, she wondered. A woman with a baby, and a robber. Were others behind the door? All questions she would answer later.

The shop was still closed when Antonia reached the ground floor, and she wondered what kind of customers came in anyhow. Then she was out on the street.

A walk of a few blocks, a turn to the left, then to the right, and she halted, awestruck. She'd seen the Grand Place as a small child but had been too young to appreciate its splendor. Now she walked to the center of the square and turned slowly, studying all four sides.

On the south side, the stunning Town Hall, with its enormous tower and filigreed façade, dominated the square, and she knew vaguely that it was built in the Middle Ages and had undergone many restorations. Directly across from it was an equally ornate building she'd learned was from the sixteenth century and called the King's House. The east and west sides of the square held the old guildhalls and mansions of rich merchants of the time. Impossible to tell when the various Gothic, Baroque, and Louis XIV ornamentations were added, but the overall image was of a Grimm's fairy-tale setting, like a picture on a tea tin.

Uniformed Wehrmacht soldiers were already passing through the square, so she hurried toward one of the narrow streets leading away from it. It wasn't until she had crossed the Grasmarkt that she saw the sign PETITE RUE DES BOUCHERS. Tiny shops, some boarded up or derelict, but many, like the Mathys shop, still displaying wares for the few francs the Belgians had to spend.

There it was, finally, the Café Suèdoise. She halted, rehearsing in her mind what she intended to say.

She entered, and several heads turned, so she sat down at the closest table to avoid prolonged attention. A few moments later, a woman, presumably the proprietor, came to take her order.

"Just a coffee, please. Or the closest thing." She had no idea what foods were currently available and how cafés dealt with rationing restrictions or coupons. But several of the other customers had coffee cups in front of them.

While she waited, she glanced casually, indifferently, around the café. Attractive. Lots of old wood, good lighting, a homey feel. All but the clientele. A few men in slightly rumpled suits sat here and there, but another half dozen were German officers, and she smiled to herself, thinking she could actually read their ranks. All those hours of study had paid off.

But what the hell was she doing in a den of German officers? What if one of them came over and tried to talk to her? She kept her eyes lowered, pretending to study her train schedule. No, this was not good. The SOE information from the Bilbao consulate must have been wrong, or outdated.

Still, she couldn't leave without a try, however weak. She finished her coffee and went to the counter where a tall, black-haired man was drying glasses. "Excuse me."

He looked at her with open courtesy, his raised eyebrows a signal he was listening carefully.

She leaned forward and spoke sotto voce. "I'm looking for an old friend and understand she might have been a regular here. Andrée de Jongh."

The courteous warmth disappeared instantly, and he replied too quickly, "I don't know any such person."

Antonia might have believed him but for the fact that he too had dropped his voice. The name, apparently, was a dangerous one.

"Are you sure? Do you know anyone of the de Jongh family?"

"No, nobody of that name. So sorry." He glanced nervously past her toward the seated Germans.

Further dialogue seemed pointless, but just then a woman appeared from a room at the back and Antonia shifted her attention. A woman in her late thirties, elegant. Her amber hair, like that of someone who had been a blond child, was done up in a loose roll in the back, and careless strands of it hung in front of her ears. She joined the bartender, apparently sensing his distress.

"Can we do something for you, madam?" she asked gently, obviously studying her. Where the man's face had registered alarm, this woman seemed suspicious but intrigued, and her glance swept quickly down Antonia's body and back to her face.

Antonia repeated her question and met the same sudden hardening of expression. The woman's voice became soft. Too soft. "We can make inquiries, if you'd like. Who is looking for her?"

"It's just an old friend. From Bilbao."

Their expressions became even colder. She would have to take another tack. "If you can give me the name of anyone who might know her, I would be most grateful. I'll…uh…stop by again in a day or so."

"Would you like to leave your name?" The voice was still velvet, ominous.

Antonia felt the chess piece go down that checkmated her. How could she refuse to leave a name? Well, she did have a false identity, and this, she supposed, was what it was for.

"Sophie. She'll remember." She was bluffing. "Well, thank you for your time." She began to back away.

"Excuse me, madam," a new baritone voice said at her shoulder. "Might I have the honor of inviting you to a cup of coffee?"

Antonia turned to face a German officer and swept her eyes over his insignias. Two stars on his shoulder board but no braid. On his sleeve three green bars and one oak leaf spread. Double lightning bolts on his collar bar.

"Thank you, Hauptsturmführer. You are most kind, but my husband would not allow me to accept your invitation." She turned back to the two proprietors. "Thank you for your time, and good day."

She hurried from the café, not daring to look back until she was out the door. The officer was returning, rebuffed, to his table, but the woman still stared after her. What was going on?

❖

Antonia let herself back into the shop in the Rue Marché au Charbon. Mme Mathys was in the process of selling a used overcoat to someone, so she passed with a brief greeting and climbed the stairs to her attic room.

She dropped down onto her bed, frustrated by the failure of her one purposeful act since she'd arrived in Belgium. What now? The imperative to contact London still remained, but otherwise, aside from her ability to speak French, she was in roughly the same position as the pilots she'd been sent to rescue.

All that training at Beaulieu, and they hadn't told her what to do if she found herself alone and incommunicado.

Brooding in the silence of her tiny room, she became conscious of the sounds coming from the apartment below her. First the crying of a baby, then a woman speaking. By his own assertion, at least one of the people below was a Resistance fighter. It might be useful to listen in. She rose from the bed and lay down on the floor, pressing her ear to the wood.

However closely she listened she couldn't make out a single word, and then she remembered, the men on the tram had spoken some other language to each other. Polish, or Russian, or Yiddish. Another dead end. Crap. She was getting tired of those. A man spoke angrily, and then another man, and the woman responded. Apparently three adults were downstairs, as well as the baby, and they were quarreling. The apartment door below slammed.

Then suddenly, bang! Something pounded on her door, and before she could rise from the floor, it flew open. The tram robber from the day before stood before her once again, and this time he held a gun.

Still squatting on the ground, she put her hands up. He stood in the doorway for a moment, then came inside, scowling, and closed the door behind him. He stood over her, as if trying to decide what to do, then waved her to stand up.

He stepped back to allow her room to stand, and in that unguarded moment, she seized his leg and yanked it forward, causing him to fall back against the wall. She leapt on him, pressing her knee onto his wrist, and wrenched the gun from his hand.

Now she stood over him and gave the same order to stand up. He glared at her without moving.

"Do you speak French?" she asked. He nodded.

"Why did you come up here with a gun? For more money, or to attack me? I could shoot you and the police would support me." She was bluffing again.

"The police would support you anyhow. No one's going to take the side of a Jew who robbed a tram."

"I know why you robbed the tram. Your friend explained all that. But you still haven't told me why you came up here."

"I'm not sure myself." He stood up slowly and she backed away, still holding the gun on him.

With surprising fearlessness, he brushed the dust from his trousers and sat down on one of her chairs. "It's not loaded. You can check. Not only that, it doesn't even shoot. The first time I ever tried to shoot a gun, and it jammed."

She opened the magazine and saw he was right. "So why did you come up here with it?"

"I wanted to scare you so you wouldn't denounce me. The gun was an afterthought. Not a very good one. You can see what an amateur I am."

"You're right about that." Her fear dissipating, she handed the gun back to him. "Here, for your next robbery." He slid it, shamefaced, into his pocket, where it hung, bulky and obvious.

"So why didn't you report me yesterday?" he asked.

Antonia studied his earnest schoolteacher face, debating with herself, calculating the dangers and benefits of revealing herself. It seemed, in the end, that if he and his group weren't exactly the people she'd been sent to help, they were close enough.

"Because I'm on a Resistance mission myself, in a way. From Britain."

His face lit up. "Britain! Well, I thought I heard a faint accent, although my own French isn't always so good either." He offered his hand. "Sorry about the gun. And the robbery. What's your name?"

She shook his hand nervously. "Sophie. Let's leave it at that, all right?"

"Sophie it is. Mine's Moishe Goldman."

"And you live downstairs? Or is it just a hideout."

"Hideout. After we robbed your tram, my friends and I got a little over-confident, so we hit another line. That one didn't turn out so well. The police chased us and I ran here to hide. The people downstairs are my brother and his wife. Maybe you'd like to meet them."

❖

"Moishe, why did you bring this stranger into our house?" The woman stood up from a table where she'd been feeding a child of about two.

"She's not a stranger, Rywka, not any more. Her name is Sophie and she's from England."

A man who had been assembling—or disassembling—a lamp on the other side of the room approached them still holding a screwdriver. "What good is an English girl to us? Their soldiers have all run away and gone home."

"Aisik, you know very well the British are bombing the Germans all the time. Anyway, she's on our side and wants to join our Resistance."

Antonia frowned slightly. That wasn't at all what she'd said upstairs, though she declined to correct him.

"This is Aisik." Moishe held his hand out toward the balding man with pale gray-blue eyes and a more benign expression than Moishe himself cultivated. He was better dressed than his brother, with well-tailored trousers held up by suspenders and a blue dress shirt with the sleeves rolled up.

"And this is Rywka, my wife," Aisik said. Slender, with a somewhat pretty oval face, dark-brown eyes, and a small puckered mouth that tilted slightly to the side, Rywka nodded a distrustful greeting.

The baby began to fret and she soothed him. He had the same round, slightly crooked mouth as his mother, the same eyes that looked up anxiously at the newcomer.

Aisik was apparently more curious than threatened. He motioned her to a chair. "What brings you to Brussels, then?"

Sitting again with her child on her lap, Rywka was not so easily reassured. "How do we know you're not getting information for the Gestapo?"

"I suppose you can't be sure. Although I already know where you live, and if I were with the Gestapo, it would already be too late. But you could have me arrested as well now. I'd be shot even sooner than you."

Moishe lit a cigarette, took a puff, and blew out disagreeable-smelling smoke. "She's right about that."

Aisik got to the point. "So why did you come? What are you doing here? How can you help us?" His French was thickly accented, but it would have been rude to ask his country of origin. Her first guess was still Poland.

She shrugged. "Unfortunately I've only just arrived and have little to offer at the moment. I came with another agent, but our plane was shot down, along with the wireless I was supposed to use. I need to contact London for instructions."

"So you're as helpless as we are," Aisik said glumly, and rubbed his forehead.

"For the moment, yes. But as soon as I can contact London, our forces will be able to help in lots of ways. The critical thing is the wireless. Does your organization have one?"

"We never thought about needing one," Moishe said. "No one's ever discussed getting help from outside. But of course we could always use money."

"Can you tell me more about your group, and others too? What kind of resistance is there right now? The more I know, the more I can report back to London. For example, is Christine Mathys part of the Resistance? Can I trust her with information?"

"You can trust her not to denounce you, but you shouldn't give her information. She provides shelter, maybe a connection or two, but I'm sure she doesn't want to know what other people are doing. It keeps everyone safer."

"But what about the groups that *are* active? Where are they, what are they? Who's running them?"

Moishe stared up at the ceiling and scratched his chin. "I don't know that much myself. Only what I read in some of the underground papers. Our group is the *Partisans Armés*, and we're under the *Front de l'Independence*, but the Zionists, the Socialists, and the Communists are all active one way or another. The political parties have their resistance groups too, and then there's *Solidarité*, which produces false identity papers and steals ration tickets for people living clandestine, like us. I've also heard people are hiding from the labor conscriptions in the Ardenne. *Maquisards*, they call themselves."

"Who's in charge? Who can I make contact with?"

"I can't really tell you. The groups are always changing, merging or breaking up. I only know who I take orders from, but none of the others. We want to keep it that way. When the Germans capture and torture you, you can't tell them much."

Antonia grumbled. "Uh. Everyone's always talking about torture."

"It's a reality." Moishe shrugged. "And the chances are good they'll get you."

"Yes…well…" She changed the subject. "Have you heard the name de Jongh? Andrée or Frédéric?"

"No. As I told you, we don't exchange much information, least of all, names."

"So, what does your group do? Other than rob trams?" Antonia asked.

"Well, we do rescue operations. Recently we got one of our own out of the hospital at Etterbeek." He chuckled, obviously recalling the incident. "You can't just walk in, you know, so one of our women faked an illness. Two of the men carried her in, and while she was being examined, they locked up the policeman on guard. When our guys found Kuba, the patient, they got him out while the doctor was still examining the woman."

"Tell her how it ended, Moishe." Aisik was snickering now too.

"So, our guys walk past the exam room where Sarah is sitting with her shirt off. While the doctor stands there, his mouth wide open, she puts the shirt on and comes out to join them. Then the whole gang marches to a back door and out they go. And all the while, the hospital staff is calling out, "Bravo." Outside, they grab a Red Cross ambulance, tie the friendly driver up so he doesn't get in trouble, and take off."

Antonia nodded, amused. "Rescue operations are good, but what else do you do against the Germans?"

"Whatever the leaders order us to. Fires, sabotage, eliminating informers and collaborators. We're also pretty good at stealing things. Why are you asking? Do you want to join?"

"Can you get me a wireless?"

"Not right away, but eventually. We have to put the word out that we need one and see what happens. Could take a few weeks."

Antonia considered the alternative. To do nothing and hope a wireless would magically appear in her room, or fight alongside the armed partisans in exchange for their finding her one. Eventually. Maybe.

"All right, then. I'll join you. And I already have a gun. One that works."

Moishe smiled. "That would be a great improvement. Could you teach me how to shoot it?"

CHAPTER FIFTEEN

On an early morning not long after, Sandrine Toussaint was threading her way along the narrow walkways of Spilliaert's fish market holding her breath at the smell of rotten fish that seemed to emanate from the very cobblestones. She marched past a row of carts that were particularly pungent and slipped into the back room of one of the market merchants. Repugnant as the smell was during the interrogations, it kept passersby at a distance.

She called out the code greeting, "Have you any sardines today," and a second door opened up. Christine Mathys was on duty and waved her into the erstwhile storeroom. At the center of the room stood an old worktable, and behind it a British pilot sat looking dazed and disheveled. A thin file lay in front of him.

"The other one's with Philippe," Christine said. "A farmer found them hiding in his barn outside of Mechelen and called us last night. They speak only English, of course."

"Of course," Sandrine said, resigned. The soft-spoken Philippe was Christine's addition to the line, a clever, courageous man, but like most of the others, he spoke no English. It was going to be up to her to do the interrogations, and she dreaded it. Two years of English at university supplementing a woeful preparation in secondary school was scarcely adequate for her to detect lies or falsehoods in the testimonies. All she could do was ask the pilots to talk about themselves and study their handwritten accounts to see if they were reasonable and consistent.

She glanced up from the dossier. "You're Harry Chapman?'

"That's me, Miss." The beefy redhead with a shadow of red stubble on his chin nodded like a schoolboy anxious to please. "And my mate is Eddie Boyle. I'm glad they got someone who could talk to us. It was getting kinda frustrating out there."

"Yes, I can imagine. Now can you tell me about your mission and a little bit about yourself?"

Sandrine drilled him on details, names of family members, flight instructors, places, but she was unable to verify his answers. If the Gestapo had trained him to infiltrate their operation, she could do nothing about it but see if Eddie Boyle, being held in the other room, confirmed his story.

So much was at stake—her own life and that of all the other good people on the line—but her knowledge of life in England was based on the one visit she'd made with Laurent before his death. She feared they would one day pay for that deficiency.

Having accepted the pilots' stories, Sandrine passed them along to the photographer for their false identification papers. Three head shots for each man, six flashes of light, and the job was done. "We'll get these to you as soon as possible, but you know how it is," the photographer said to Sandrine, packing his camera and lights into his valise. Without further conversation, he slipped out again.

The door had scarcely closed when they heard another knock and a repetition of the code greeting. Philippe opened the door to Celine holding the bundle of clothing.

"I'm sorry. Laura couldn't get away from the café so she sent this with me."

"Well, come in, dear." Sandrine took the bundle out of her arms. Across the room, Christine shook her head with maternal concern. "Francis shouldn't have sent you. Now you're in the same danger as the rest of us."

"Don't worry. I got here by all the back ways without passing a single German," she said with youthful certainty.

Sandrine carried the bundle to the table where the pilots sat and examined all the articles. Two sets of pants, two shirts, two jackets, all worn and mended. Just what they'd ordered.

"Here, try these on between you."

The men retreated to the adjacent room and made the change. A few minutes later they returned.

"Not a bad fit," Sandrine said. "Trousers are a bit short on you, Eddie, but no one looks very fashionable these days." She handed each one a beret. "Make sure you wear them pulled down over your forehead to cover your British haircuts. We'll also teach you to walk right. You Brits arrive here strutting like roosters and would be spotted in a minute. You've got to learn not to walk with your hands in your pockets, jingling your change, and don't stare at the women."

"That last one's gonna be hard." Harry winked.

Christine turned on him. "Yeah, well, force yourself. It's not a joke. Your lives depend on this charade, and so do ours. If you're caught, you'll go to a prison camp, but we'll all be shot. So no more wisecracks, eh?"

After a sideward glance of admiration at Christine for the verbal knuckle-rap, Sandrine continued. "A car will come by for you this afternoon. You'll be in among bundles of firewood, so don't worry if it's a bit stuffy. The trip will only take about half an hour."

"Where are they taking us?" Eddie, the more slender man who spoke little, asked anxiously.

"To my place," Sandrine said.

❖

It was still early afternoon when the delivery wagon pulled up to the entrance and Philippe drew the snorting horse to a halt. With Gaston's help, he quickly unloaded the firewood, and the two Englishmen clambered over the side. They gawked at the château façade until Gaston prodded them up the steps into the entryway.

"Are you sure you don't want to stop and have a warm bite, Philippe?" Sandrine touched him on the arm.

"Thank you, but I have to return the cart to the farmer before he gets anxious. Besides, I'm having dinner with Christine."

"All right, then." Smiling inwardly at the thought of her two good friends spending an evening together, she waved him off and followed the men into the entryway.

Harry stepped toward the main room where the tall fireplace was burning impotently against the chill. Glancing around, he whistled softly. "Is this a famous mansion or something?"

Sandrine drew him back by the arm and led him toward the stairs. "It's better you don't know any names. Come on downstairs to meet the others and see where the facilities are. Mathilde will bring you some hot food in a while, and after that, you can settle in."

"How long are we going to be here?" Eddie asked.

"I don't know." She marched toward the stairwell and glanced back at them to let them know they were to follow.

At the bottom of the stairs, she led them along the corridor to a wall that was supposed to be deceptive but, under any real scrutiny, could be seen as false. The cupboard in front of it slid to the side and opened to a small room. Inside, lantern light revealed two pale faces.

"It's all right, men. I'm just bringing you two more comrades. I'll let you show them around and explain the rules."

Harry grumbled. "Jaysus, it's like a prison cell down here."

"You think so? Guess you haven't been in a German prison," one of the others replied.

"Look, I'll let you all get acquainted. Mathilde will have lunch in a while, and then, if everything's quiet, we'll bring you up for some exercise in the woods. You know the rules. If you hear anything outside, like a car arriving, extinguish the light and be quiet."

Once upstairs, Sandrine allowed herself to drop onto the sofa in front of the useless fire. It barely raised the room temperature, but if she drew the sofa up close to it, she could stay warm enough to sleep.

Almost soundlessly, Mathilde appeared at her side.

"Oh, thank you, Mathilde. A glass of wine is exactly what I need right now." Tell Gaston not to worry about bringing the wood inside. When I take the men out tonight, I'll have them bring some of it in. They could use the exercise."

"Yes, ma'am." Mathilde returned downstairs to her kitchen to conjure a meal out of the foodstuffs Gaston had procured on the black market.

Sandrine drew up her knees and stared at the flames, suddenly filled with doubt. Had she accepted the stories of any of the men too easily? The interrogation was a farce, and any person who could speak English without a German accent could pass. If the Gestapo could infiltrate someone in Brussels, who could travel down the entire line, it would mean the capture of the airmen and a death sentence to all the patriots who had helped them.

Infiltration or betrayal could come from anywhere. And what of that woman who came to the café the other day? The one called Sophie? Surely not her real name. Had she sent her away only because of the possibility she was Gestapo? Or was it something more personal? Seeing her had been a jolt. With her narrow, intense face, she was the image of Isabelle. Isabelle, who had stirred her so strangely, for years, until she married and moved to Liege.

There seemed a parallel between her own integrity and that of the Comet Line, though she wasn't sure which of them had sent up an alarm when she saw Sophie's face. Was she protecting the line or her peace of mind?

In any case, who *was* the stranger? Was she still lurking outside the café, like Büttner, keeping an eye on them? For the briefest moment, Sandrine wondered if she should have sent someone to follow and, if necessary, kill her.

Sandrine had scarcely drunk her wine when she heard the car pulling up in front of the house. Gaston would have alerted the soldiers downstairs to go dark and so she waited, filled more with dread than fear. A few moments later, Mathilde came into the room again, her eyes averted, and Sandrine guessed who the visitor was.

"General von Falkenhausen is waiting in the entryway, madam. Should I bring him into the library? He is alone," she added unnecessarily. He was always alone.

Sandrine took a deep breath. "Yes, bring him in."

❖

The business was quickly done, though the fire in the fireplace had burned down when General von Falkenhausen buttoned his uniform trousers and drew on his tunic. He set another log on the embers and returned to the sofa, pouring two more glasses of wine.

"To your beauty," he said, offering one glass to Sandrine.

She smoothed her skirt into place, suppressing the desire to rush upstairs and bathe. She drank and was silent. What possible remark could either of them make after their coupling? Should he thank her for her cooperation? Or should she admit the act was in fact no worse than most of those she'd experienced with her husband?

Von Falkenhausen seemed concerned only with the proper fit of his uniform. He stood up again, tugged on his tunic, and brushed invisible dust from the front of his trousers. Then he took her hand and kissed the back of it.

"With your permission, Madame Toussaint. Duty summons me."

Wordlessly, she unlocked the door and guided him to the end of the entryway, where Gaston already held his greatcoat. The general slipped both arms into the sleeves and buttoned it closed. He withdrew leather gloves from the pockets but shook her hand briefly again before pulling them on. "I thank you for your kindness and look forward to seeing you again. Good evening."

He stepped toward the open door but then swung around to face her again. "Oh, yes, I forgot to mention. I will send around a man tomorrow with a few liters of petrol. And some ration tickets to buy more. You will be needing that, I believe, for your lovely car."

He touched his cap and stepped through the doorway. Within moments, his Mercedes rumbled over the gravel and down the road away from the house.

"Wait a few more minutes, then go and tell the men it's all right to turn the light on again," she said woodenly.

Relief and disgust settled over her in equal measure. She was safe, obviously, and so were the men she was hiding. She trudged up the staircase to the bathroom at the end of the corridor. Mathilde, bless her, had already run a bath. Shivering, she stepped into the tub and scrubbed herself raw.

Von Falkenhausen's whore. The words rang in her head. Did submitting to a high-ranking Nazi in order to continue the Comet Line mark her as a martyr or a collaborator? Was she different from any woman who gave herself to any Nazi in order to feed her family?

The bathwater was cooling, so she climbed out and dried. It was at least pleasant to put on fresh clothing. The evening wasn't far along so she returned to the fireplace, added more wood, and curled up on the sofa. Mathilde had cleared away the glasses, removing all traces of the act that had just taken place.

The phone rang. Mathilde took the call in the entryway and then appeared in the doorway. "Madam, it's the Delivery Service calling. From Bayonne."

Delivery Service, the code name for the network of people who linked the safe houses along the line. If it was from Bayonne, it would have to be about Andrée. She took the call at the corner desk she never used.

The voice on the other end was familiar and, as always, gave no names. It was also somber. "I am sorry to report that we've had no luck obtaining the product you ordered. Every time our men followed a lead, the competitors were there before us. I'm afraid the trail has run cold."

"Thank you." She hung up slowly, benumbed, and dropped back onto the sofa. The coded message was of disaster. The Comet line had been halted while good men and women risked their lives trying to save Andrée. Dangerous, audacious attempts, each one just short of success. But each one had failed, and now she was on her on her way to a German concentration camp. Buchenwald? Ravensbrück? Sandrine didn't even know which one.

She was certain of only one thing. Even if they could beat Andrée down to the point she would cease to care about the foreign pilots, she would never betray the good Belgian, French, and Basque people who had put themselves at mortal risk. Sandrine was as certain as she was of her own heartbeat that they could not make Andrée talk. She would sacrifice her life first.

Sandrine stared into the dying embers of the fire. *Her* only sacrifice was her "honor." How trivial it was in comparison.

She called her two dogs to her and scratched them both for a while as she brooded. Conditions would only get worse, not better, both in Brussels and everywhere in the occupied zones. She did a mental inventory of the safe houses, the supplies, and the remaining resistants. It was time to begin another trip along the line.

She stood up and went to the stairs leading to the cellar.

"Come on, all of you," Sandrine said to the men. "We've got just a little daylight left. Let's go for a walk and talk about how we'll get you to Spain."

"Jolly good," Eddie said. "Anything to get out of this cave." Then the rest of the message registered. "Spain? Oh, yes, let's do discuss that."

She led the four of them upstairs and through the front portal into the woods. Having just made a "payment" to the governor general, she had little fear of official patrols anywhere near the château. Going out with the men would physically invigorate her, and doing actual planning for the escape would remind her the humiliation had a purpose.

"Our forgers should have your identifications papers soon, but then we have to teach you how to behave."

"For sure we can't speak any French, so we'll bloody well have to keep our mouths shut," Harry said.

"You could practice some of that right now, old chap," Eddie joked. "He's been talking me ear off."

"You've done your share, mate—"

A gunshot sounded, and the four men threw themselves onto the ground. Sandrine remained standing, torn between fear and annoyance that someone was shooting on her land. But who *had* shot?

It couldn't have been a patrol since there would have been no point in striking them down simply because they were there. Moreover, no one was shot. Then who? Most likely a poacher after one of the small boars in her woods.

Leaving the men behind and under cover, she pressed forward toward the sound. A second shot rang out and told her she was closer.

She continued, hearing a third and fourth shot, and now was certain it was poachers. But when she stepped out into a clearing she halted, astonished.

❖

"I can't believe I've agreed to do this," Antonia said as they strode together to toward the Tram 28 stop. Moishe sucked on one of his Russian cigarettes, which he seemed unable to do without.

"We'll be at the far end of a woods that's already at the edge of Brussels. No one's going to hear us except some cows in the distance."

"Maybe so, but getting there carrying a loaded gun on a public tram is the real risk." She glanced around nervously.

"I told you, no one will bother us. Not with me in a uniform of the *Service d'Ordre Publique*. The Germans recognize us as fellow fascists, and the Belgians are afraid of us. Them, I mean."

"Where did you get that thing, anyhow?" She stepped back for a full view of him.

"On our last raid. We broke into their office for the money. Didn't get much, but this was just hanging there, so we took it. We knew it would come in handy."

The tram pulled up as they arrived, and they fell silent. Antonia tried to look like a stalwart Rexist woman, but no one seemed to glance their way anyhow.

In forty-five minutes they were at the last stop, at the Place St. Lambert, and they descended. "It's this way," he said, pointing eastward. She could see the woods already, behind a stately white eighteenth-century mansion.

"What about people in that house? Are they going to hear us?"

"Maybe they'll hear a little pop, but they'll think it's hunters. There's small game in the woods, and some of the farmers still have hunting rifles."

With her fears only partly assuaged, she followed along away from the plaza across a wide country road and into the woods. The path ran circuitously, across footbridges over shallow streams, and it took another fifteen minutes to reach the place Moishe deemed safe.

It was late afternoon, and the foliage admitted only a soft dappled light, not the best for precise targeting, but Antonia decided that teaching stance and a steady hand was just as important as marksmanship. She pinned up four targets of folded newspaper and came back to him.

"All right. Let's see what you can do." She handed him the revolver. "Note that unlike *your* useless gun, which has a magazine, this one has a rotating cylinder with only six cartridges. Here's the safety. See? On…off. Be sure to use it. You don't want it to go off in your pocket."

He opened and closed the cylinder, hefted the gun's weight. "Very light."

"Yes. But you still need to hold it with two hands and keep both thumbs on the same side. Stand with your legs and your elbows apart. If you have time to aim, center the front post in the rear groove, place the front sight where you want to hit, and slowly squeeze the trigger."

She let him insert the six bullets into the barrel, click it shut, and take aim at the first target. *Bang!* He twitched at the sound of the gunshot and the bullet went wild.

"Okay, you're going to have to expect the sound. Just caress the trigger while keeping the front sight on the target."

Bang! He tried again, and this time a black spot appeared at the bottom right side of the target.

"Ah, *that's* how you do it," he said, pleased with himself, and took aim again. The crack of the gunshot no longer startled him, and the third bullet struck at the bottom left side.

"Hey, I like this." He took aim yet again, toward the fourth target.

At that moment, a woman stepped out from among the trees and halted.

Moishe turned toward her and dropped his hand.

All three stood as if paralyzed, forming a bizarre triangle of mutual fear.

"What are you doing in my woods?" the woman called out. "You're not allowed to hunt here." She glanced over at the row of paper targets, then at the uniform. "Don't they let you target practice at the shooting range?"

Antonia now realized it was the resident of the château they'd passed. Strangely, her voice seemed familiar. The stranger approached to confront the delinquent shooter, and her face became clear.

It was the woman from the Café Suèdoise.

In rapid sequence Antonia felt surprise, then pleasure, then an internal slapping of her forehead. Christ. It was another disaster. This was the woman she had to win over to contact the Comet Line. But now, standing next to a man dressed as a Belgian fascist, she had no hope of doing that.

"Apologies, madam," Moishe said in his best cavalier voice. "We're sorry to have trespassed on your woods." He holstered the gun and handed it back to Antonia, who stood holding it foolishly.

"We'll go now, and wish you a good evening," he added, and after an unnecessary and slightly theatrical bow, he stepped around her onto the path.

Antonia followed, speechless. No remark, apology, or compliment could remedy the situation. As she passed, she looked directly into the woman's face. In the graying light, her expression was impossible to discern, but her eyes were still green.

CHAPTER SIXTEEN

S andrine Toussaint. So that was the name of the woman who owned the white mansion called the Château Malou, and who had some mysterious connection to the Café Suèdoise. The information did Antonia little good, but knowing the name gave her a handle. On what, she wasn't sure.

But now, a few days after the target-practice encounter, she strode from the Marolles rummage market, Brussels's black market for food. She'd paid a king's ransom for a thin slice of ham and a kilo of potatoes, which, due to a parasite-destroyed harvest, were now rare all over Belgium. It was risky business walking around the Marolles since patrols often swept through, but the alternative, standing for hours in a line in the street, was no less dangerous. She'd already done that once for butter, counterfeit food coupons in hand, but the others in line, mostly women, wanted to chat, and she feared her accent would eventually give her away.

At least lookouts were posted, to warn of approaching German soldiers or Belgian police. A graver problem was that her money was running out. And that was another reason to join the partisans; they provided an income, however modest.

She walked with her head down, hoping not to attract any attention. Passersby were simply vague shapes on the periphery of her vision, until she reached her own street, and then the sight brought her up short. A man came toward her, in a dark jacket, and on the left side a bright yellow image stood out like a scream. A six-pointed star with a cursive "J" in the middle.

How soon before the next step? For surely, a next step was inevitable. It wasn't only Moishe's partisans who whispered about the deportations. Labor roundups had been ongoing for a year now, first with cajoling and a promise of benefits, and then with coercion. One would have to be blind not to see the brutality or deaf not to hear the rumors.

No, in the absence of instructions from the SOE, she would stay connected with the Jewish partisans, in spite of the ad-hoc way in which they seemed to operate.

In the weeks since she'd joined them, she'd acted only as a courier with messages and documents, and had occasionally lent her Enfield .38 for robberies. The "armed" partisans were curiously unarmed, and Moishe's ineptness seemed typical. Fortunately, they always returned the gun to her by the next day, usually without using it.

She understood that they didn't quite trust her. She wasn't one of them, after all, except in sympathy, but if she was going to use them to gain access to a wireless, she had to be more engaged.

With her black-market potatoes slung over her shoulder, she passed through the downstairs shop in her building and mounted the stairs. As she reached the first floor she heard Moishe's voice behind the closed door. His visits were intermittent, usually on "business," and she wanted to talk to him. She knocked and called her name through the door.

Aisik opened, and though he seemed preoccupied, he invited her in. Moishe stood behind him smoking his eternal cigarette, and Rywka sat at the table, the young Jackie standing between her knees. The toddler played with a dishtowel, chewing on one corner of it, but the adults' faces showed more than the usual dread.

"What is it?" she asked.

Moishe blew smoke out of the side of his mouth. "The Judenrat has sent out letters ordering people to assemble at Mechelen, for work in the East. They say those who report immediately and arrive first in the work camps will get the best jobs."

"Nobody believes them, of course," Aisik added. "We've heard too many stories."

"People do send back postcards," Rywka said hopefully, but her tone revealed she didn't believe it herself.

"Postcards," Moishe said contemptuously. "They mean nothing. Anyone will scribble a postcard if someone is pointing a gun at them. And Kuba got a postcard that said 'Uncle Yitzak sends his love.' Yitzak has been dead for two years." He leaned on the windowsill. "And if it's for work, why are they taking children?"

"What will you do?"

Moishe stared out the window, smoke curling around his head. "At some point they'll have to go into hiding. Outside of the city some place where fewer Germans are poking around. I'm already living that way, in a room half the size of this."

"Can you get false identity papers? And food coupons if you're not registered?"

"Of course we can, the same way you do, but all that takes time. Everyone wants them now."

Aisik picked up his son and nuzzled his hair. "The noose keeps getting tighter and tighter."

"I'm sorry. I wish I could do something," Antonia said, but her remark sounded hollow. She edged toward the door. "Let me know if there's anything…" She fell silent before the magnitude of their dread and her impotence, and let herself out.

Antonia sliced the ham into strips and boiled them with two potatoes in her single pot on her single hot plate. She added the limp remains of her leek greens and stirred, staring down at the pathetic meal. She ate slowly but was still hungry when she finished.

She'd adjusted to the modest rationing at home that had started as soon as the war did and learned to live with little bacon, butter, and sugar, then meat and almost every other dairy product as well.

But in Belgium under occupation, things were much worse, and it was a mark of how miserable her diet had become that she missed the spare meals provided to her in the hospital. The British rationing had kept her trim, but in Belgium, she was slowly starving.

She cleared off the table and was about to change into pajamas when a quick rap on the door caused her to jump slightly. The voice outside said, "It's Moishe, with a friend."

She opened the door to him and another man. Stocky, wide-faced, faintly Slavic.

"This is Jakub. Kuba for short. He's in charge of the cell I'm in. Kuba, this is Sophie. She's the owner of the gun you used the other day."

Kuba nodded a greeting and she nodded back. She didn't offer them anything. In their shared privation, that social nicety had disappeared completely. She pulled the only two chairs in the room toward her bed and perched on the edge of it, making a little discussion space.

The two men sat down in front of her and Kuba began. "Welcome to our cause, Sophie, and thank you for your gun. We can't trust the ones we get here. Too many of them sabotaged in the factories. Ironic, isn't it?" He spoke with the same strong accent as Rywka. Polish, she decided.

"In our actions, we work in three-man detachments on orders from one person above. We collect funds, finance hidden families, move people around, and eliminate collaborators."

"Mouchards?" she asked. She'd learned the term from Aisik.

"Not only those. The mouchards are Jews who inform on other Jews to curry favor with the Nazis. They deserve immediate execution. But whole factories of Jews also serve the Nazis. We put them out of business when we can."

"I told Moishe I'm willing to help out, but I don't know whether I'm ready to kill someone for you. I also answer to orders from a superior. I just can't reach him without my wireless radio."

"What happened to your wireless? And how did you end up here in the first place?"

"I parachuted in with it and a colleague. Unfortunately the plane was shot down, so I don't even think the crew had time to drop it or even the other man. Judging by what I could see from the ground, everyone and everything was lost. After that, I was on the run."

"Is there any chance they might have dropped it before crashing?"

"I don't think so. The patrol that brought down the plane had to have seen any other parachutes. I gave it up as a lost cause."

"Where did you land? Do you have the coordinates?"

"I can show them to you. It was near the village of Oudenaken."

Kuba scratched his cheek. "That's not far from Breedhout, where we have contacts. I can at least put out an inquiry."

"We can clutch at that straw if you wish, but I'd also like to find out where other wireless radios might be. There's got to be more than one in Brussels."

"It's more than a straw. If it dropped from the plane, or even if it crashed inside the plane, someone will know. And wherever it is, we might get our hands on it. In the meantime…"

"Yes?" She realized this was the reason for the visit.

"I need your pistol again," Kuba announced. "You'll have it back tomorrow, of course."

"Yes, of course. Moishe knows I'm always willing to lend it."

"I know. But this time we may have to use it to execute someone. We just want you to know."

Lying in her bed that night, she ran the scene through her mind. "Execute," Kuba had said. It was wartime, and she'd seen hundreds, if not thousands of men die, so the mention of death hadn't kept her awake. She had just always thought of her own gun as a means of self-defense, and it troubled her to know it would be the instrument of an outright murder.

She thought of Major Woolrich and the teams back at Beaulieu. What would they think of her involvement in such a group? Was she doing the right thing, or was she endangering both herself and the SOE, in the event of her capture? What was Dora doing in France? Hobnobbing with handsome resistants in Paris, or was she too struggling alongside desperate men?

And the Comet Line? Was the mysterious de Jongh family a fiction the SOE had fallen for? She couldn't even be sure the people in the Café Suèdoise were resisters, and seeing the café full of German officers, she now thought it unlikely. They were all ordinary Belgians— with the exception, perhaps, of a commanding woman with green eyes who lived in a château.

High summer seemed to slow events down and lend an air of lazy normality to the occupied city. But one night, a noise from the street below roused Antonia from sleep. Drawing her blanket around her shoulders, she stood by her open window and looked down onto the Rue Marché au Charbon. In the predawn grayness, she saw little but the occasional flash of an electric torch. Obviously the people downstairs wanted to escape notice.

She first thought it was thieves, but the truck she could just make out suggested otherwise. She opened her window a crack and heard sharp commands that she didn't understand. *"Einsteigen, schnell."* Her eyes slowly grew accustomed to the darkness, and she could see individual forms now. Two people climbing into the rear of the truck. Others were already there, but the image was too blurry for her to count. Something heavy—a suitcase perhaps—was thrown onto the truck bed with a thud, and then two people climbed up after it. The truck motor started and the truck pulled away, the quiet of the empty street belying that anything ominous had ever happened.

But she knew what had happened. She simply had no words for it. She crawled back into the cold bed, sick to her stomach, and couldn't sleep. When she finally dozed, hours later, she dreamt of heaping sandbags against a rising flood. But for every sack she hefted onto the wall, another one washed away and the water kept rising.

She awoke in the morning to the sound of more quarreling and footsteps on the stairs on the floor below. Dressing hurriedly, she opened her door a crack and listened, but the language was unintelligible. Yiddish, she now realized, was the language most of the partisan group spoke among themselves, when they didn't need French. She crept out onto the landing and saw the back of a familiar head. Moishe stood outside his brother Aisik's door, and a strange woman was in the doorway just in front of him.

Antonia ventured a step farther, trying to make sense of the scene.

A baby blanket under his arm, Moishe backed up a pace to make room for the woman to pass him. As the stranger stepped out onto the landing, Antonia could see she held the two-year-old Jacques in her arms.

Antonia understood now and was appalled.

The woman began down the stairs, and Rywka, sobbing, tried to follow her, but Aisik gripped her by both shoulders and held her back.

The baby writhed and thrashed in the strange woman's arms, screaming, "Maman! Maman!" His face was red, and his face glistened with tears and mucous. "Mamaaann!" He stretched out the last syllable, reaching out over the stranger's shoulder and clenching his little fists. "Mamaaaann."

Finally Moishe went after her and threw a small blanket over the baby to calm him. But the cries continued, muffled and heart-wrenching, as the woman disappeared down the stairs.

Antonia watched, aghast, as Aisik dragged the hysterical Rywka back into the apartment and closed the door. Moishe remained outside leaning against the opposite wall, panting.

"Good God, Moishe. What was that?"

He wiped his face on his sleeve as he came up the stairs. "Please, can I have a glass of water?"

She opened the door to her apartment and motioned him toward a chair. While he dropped down on it, she drew water from the tap and handed it to him.

He emptied the glass and took a long breath. "They had to do it. He'll have a better chance now."

"What do you mean, 'a better chance'?" she asked, though she'd already pieced it together.

He laid his face in his hands for a moment. "There is a group. Belgians, of course. They hide the children…some place. I don't know where. Later, a week or a month, they find someone who'll keep them. It's hard on the kids, some of them. They cry for days, but…" He didn't finish.

"Who takes them?"

"Sometimes families, sometimes just an orphanage or convent. We have to pay them. A lot. But they make new birth certificates, baptize them, give them new names. Aisik and Rywka hope that after the war they can find him again."

He went to the window and pressed his forehead against the glass. Behind him, Antonia muttered, half to herself, "He's two and a half years old. He knows who he is, who his parents are."

"He'll forget. Eventually."

"I suppose so." She imagined the days and nights of desperate longing until his infant brain blurred the brutal separation with forgetfulness. She could think of nothing comforting to say, so she joined him at the window, looking down on the street.

The car was gone and so was the child, the light of Aisik and Rywka's life. A Belgian policeman pedaled by on a bicycle. The street held all the signs of normalcy. But behind the windows of some of the houses people cowered, hungry and desperate. She looked directly at Moishe.

"So it's started, then. The raids. I saw them taking people away last night."

"Yes. Not enough Jews are volunteering for those 'work places in the East.'" She could hear the quotation marks in his voice.

"How do they decide who to take? I mean, why only those two families?"

"That's the decision of the Judenrat. Apparently they have a registry of all Jewish families, the ones who haven't gone into hiding. A man named Holtzinger makes up a list every day of those who should go. He gives the addresses to the Gestapo, and they come around with their truck. Usually at night."

"God, what a dilemma. Registering means they can come and get you any time, and not registering is a crime, so they can round you up for that too." She glanced down at the floor, as if it were transparent and she could see them. "Aisik and Rywka, are they registered?"

"Of course not. Their ration books are from another street. But people in this street know about them. They could show up on the list too, tomorrow, or next week, or next month."

"Can't they go into hiding?"

"They're already in hiding, the same as you. But you mean like move to a basement and never come out? Yes, I suppose that'll be the next step, if they can find someone with a place for them." He shook his head. "It just gets worse and worse."

He took hold of the door handle. "This moves the schedule up a little. Are you ready to go with us on an action?"

Antonia could still hear the baby's screams and Rywka's sobs. "Yes, I am. Just tell me when."

CHAPTER SEVENTEEN

At the same time, in the far south of France, Sandrine and her five passengers were awakening. The woodshed in which they'd slept was only slightly more hospitable than the woods surrounding it, and at first light, all six of them began to stir. Rubbing sleep from her face, Sandrine did an inventory of her Englishmen.

Harry and Eddie laced up their boots stoically, Arthur and Nigel inspected their rucksacks, and Thomas curled into a tighter ball, trying to delay getting up. All, she knew, were sullen, stiff from sleeping on the ground, and hungry. And it was going to get worse.

She had interrogated all of them, but superficially, and still didn't fully trust them. Nonetheless, she had a great deal of pressure to move the "parcels" out of Brussels and down the line, for aviators were arriving every day. They had to take some risks.

She did trust Florentino, their Basque guide, for he'd proved himself journey after journey, as a vital cog in the escape machinery in the Pyrenees. Fortunately, that's where they found themselves now, in his trustworthy hands.

Wordlessly, they went out, and she gathered them around her for the day's instructions.

"We'll head southeast until we're near the Spanish frontier, when Florentino will decide which route to use."

"What's the difference? Is one tougher but safer, or what?" Arthur asked.

Sandrine shrugged dismissively. "Lots of factors. Patrols, weather. You don't need to know. Florentino is familiar with the terrain, so we follow his directions from here on out."

Florentino had already started off, uphill and on a route perpendicular to the path. After three hours of hard climbing, he called a halt. None of the five evaders would admit to fatigue, but clearly they were all greatly relieved.

Harry unlaced one of his boots and massaged his foot. "Hey, can we make this a lunch stop? I'm famished."

"Why not?" Sandrine signaled Florentino, who grudgingly agreed. Squatting down in front of the group, he opened the rucksack of food and distributed a portion of dry brown bread to each one. Harry stared at the dark lump in his hand. "My kingdom for a slice of cheese."

"I thought your lot preferred haggis." Thomas snickered.

"Never touch the stuff. Though at a time like this, I'd reconsider."

Nigel tore off segments from his bread and chewed each one thoughtfully. "I used to complain about the RAF escape pack, but it'd make a fine lunch right now." He closed his eyes and leaned back on one elbow. "Horlicks tablets. Who've thought you could get nostalgic about those, eh, Arthur?"

The faintest hint of a squint passed over Arthur's face. "I never cared much for those either. Don't like swallowing medication. I miss the biscuits, though."

Nigel didn't respond but chewed on his bread.

Florentino glanced up at the sky. "Rain soon. We have to move. Five minutes." His Basque accent was thick, and he'd used up half of his English in that single declaration.

"Crikey, you're a hard man, Florentino." Harry laced up his boot.

"Courage, Harry," Sandrine said. "Sore dry feet are better than sore wet ones."

As a cold mist settled over the hillside they traversed, they slogged onward. Florentino took the lead and Sandrine stayed at the rear, though gradually Nigel fell back and trudged alongside her. When the gap between them and the others widened, he leaned in close and spoke under his breath. "Something's not right about Arthur."

With a subtle turn of her head, she gave him her full attention. "Why do you say that?"

"The Horlicks tablets. He thought they were medicine, but they're just malt and sugar lumps. Candy. How can he not know that? They're in every escape pack. And while we were holed up in Brussels, he was asking a lot of questions."

Sandrine fought the instinct to halt and question him further. "Why didn't you mention that earlier?"

"Well, they weren't strategic questions, about our raids or anything. He just wanted to know the location of things and everyone's name. It seemed natural at the time."

"For God's sake, man," she hissed. "You should have told me. He could be a plant, and if he is, it could be the end of us all."

"I'm sorry. I wasn't thinking about that. His English is as good as mine, and he has an RAF uniform. I might still be wrong about him."

"Well, we have one more night before Bilbao. I'm going to find out."

❖

Florentino unlatched the barn door and swung it back toward them. As guide, he stepped in first, lit the lantern that hung on a hook by the door, and held it out in front of him. A cow swung her head toward them, then resumed chewing her cud.

"Well, this is an improvement," Arthur said, setting his pack on the straw-littered floor. "Where are we, exactly?"

"We're in a barn," Sandrine pulled over a milking stool and sat down. "And tomorrow we'll be out of it. That's all you need to know."

Thomas slid his backpack off and let it drop at his feet. "I could fall asleep in twenty seconds flat, but first I've got to go spend a penny. Back in a min."

"Good idea," Arthur said, hefting his rucksack onto his shoulder again.

"Why are you taking your pack?" Harry asked. "You think someone's going to steal your knickers while you're gone?"

"Yeah, I do. Can't trust you blokes." He chortled. "Besides, I'm carrying a bit of loo paper. Comes in handy." He glanced over at Sandrine. "Don't worry, I'll bury it. Won't leave a trace." He slipped out through the still-open door.

Sandrine and Harry exchanged glances. "We'll take a look tonight," she said softly.

But Arthur gave them no opportunity. As soon as he returned, he curled up in a corner of the barn with his rucksack under his head and an arm threaded through one of the straps.

Sandrine was furious with herself for not being suspicious sooner and, in spite of exhaustion, wouldn't allow herself to fall asleep. They were within sight of Bilbao, and if Arthur was in fact working for the Gestapo, he could slip out during the night and make his way into the city alone. And that would mean the capture and execution of all of them. Was she always going to be a fool? She'd almost trusted that "Sophie" woman, and she'd turned out to be a Belgian fascist. If meeting the woman in her own woods had taught her anything, it was to be suspicious. She would act tonight.

She quietly woke Nigel, Harry, Eddie, and Thomas. "Draw your guns," she whispered. "We have to disarm Arthur."

The five of them crept toward the suspect and made a loose circle around him while Sandrine held the lantern over his head and woke him.

"What? What the hell's going on?" Arthur blinked up at the light.

"Hand over your pistol and rucksack," she ordered him, taking hold of the grip to prevent him from snatching it out.

He sat up, clearly bewildered, letting her slide the weapon from its holster. She pulled the strap off his shoulder and dragged the rucksack away from him.

"Are you crazy?" He looked around at the four pistols pointed at him. "Why are you doing this? You think I'm a Nazi plant? I told you, I'm Arthur Talbot, tail gunner, 52nd Squadron."

"We just have a few questions," Sandrine said, unbuckling the straps on his rucksack. She rifled through it, pulling out dirty socks and underwear, a filthy towel, a canteen, an ammunition belt, and a wallet. She examined it, noting the lack of money and the photo of a woman and baby.

"That's my wife and son. Her name is Angela. The baby is Andrew. He's two and a half. Are you satisfied now?"

Assailed by doubt, Sandrine tossed the wallet back to him wordlessly. She had to admit, she had no idea what to look for that could establish his guilt or innocence. She felt crushed under the burden of responsibility, for either sacrificing his life if he was innocent or the lives of all the others if he wasn't.

Doggedly, she opened each pouch on the ammunition belt. All held cartridges but the last one. Instead, a soiled handkerchief had been stuffed inside. She pulled it out.

"What's this?"

"Isn't it obvious? I'm sure I'm not the only pilot who carries something to blow his nose on."

"Yes, but not usually made of silk." She held up the wad of soiled material. It crackled as she pulled it apart, separating the folds held together by dried mucous.

"You're disgusting," he said. "Do you like snot? You want to pick through my dirty knickers too? Help yourself. How about the ones I've got on?" He started to unzip his trousers.

Ignoring him, Sandrine held the crusty silk to the lantern light, peering at the lines and spots that could have been mucous or soil or blood. She grimaced as she scraped at some of the crust with her nail and held the cloth again toward the lantern. Something caught her eye that didn't belong on a silk handkerchief. If she squinted, she could just make out tiny lines of writing.

"Raise the wick, will you, Harry? Thanks." In the brighter light, she could read some of the lines. Names, compass coordinates, and, next to them, the word "Malou."

"Tie him up and take him outside," she ordered grimly.

"No. Wait!" He held out his hands. "You've got it wrong. I swear to God, I'm Arthur Talbot." He was obviously panicking.

Harry fished some cord from his own sack and tied the prisoner's hands and ankles together. Then the other men lifted him up and set him down outside at the foot of a tree. Sandrine drew her own pistol.

"NO! I swear! I'm RAF. I'm on your side. You're shooting an innocent man. For God's sake! I've got a baby at home. Don't do this!"

Sandrine wrapped the soiled towel around the muzzle of her gun to muffle the sound and pressed it against his sternum. Without pausing, she pulled the trigger twice. He jerked once and toppled sideways onto the ground.

"Come on, we've got to bury him quickly," she said coldly, but her hands were shaking.

CHAPTER EIGHTEEN

Antonia paced back and forth across her tiny room, haunted by the image of Rywka giving up her baby. Pure emotion was the worst motivation for action, she knew, but how could she not respond to such cruelty? And where would *that* lead? Damn. She had to find a way to contact the SOE and get back on track.

In the meantime, she would act according to her conscience. It was all she had to go by at the moment.

Kuba and Moishe were on time, and, hearing them on the stairs, she opened the door before they knocked.

"Are you ready?" Kuba asked.

"Yes, I said I would be. And I said you could use this." She handed him her holster, and he hooked it on his belt under his coat.

She snatched up her own coat from its hook and closed the apartment door behind them. "So, where are we going?"

"To the Boulevard du Midi. The Judenrat." Kuba led the way down the stairs. "They're the ones responsible for the raid on the families across the street the other night, and you can be sure Aisik and Rywka are on the list too.

"They sacrifice the foreign Jews, saving themselves from the Nazi murderers by handing over their brothers. They even sell 'protection papers,' which are supposed to keep you from deportation, but don't."

"How are we going to get in?" She had no idea how to undertake a raid of this sort.

"We've got a man who's infiltrated the office and will let us inside. After that, we decide as we go."

Antonia shuddered at the lack of planning. "What's my job?"

"You'll stay behind us. Once we're inside, you'll watch from the window. If someone manages to call the police, you'll see them coming."

"That sounds reasonable. How do we get there?"

"We walk. It's only a few streets from here. But after it's done, we'll have a car waiting outside for a quick escape."

While they marched along the Boulevard Anspach, Antonia marveled at the men's sangfroid. They glanced calmly around them, like workers on their way home from a long day's labor, though Moishe kept moistening his lips.

"We're here." Kuba halted suddenly next to a parked car. The driver emerged silently, opened the car trunk, and handed Moishe a jerrican. The faint odor it gave off told her it was filled with gasoline. He closed the trunk and returned to his place behind the wheel.

Five more paces brought them to the door of the building. Kuba rapped twice and twice again. The door opened, and the three of them slipped in past a man Antonia didn't know.

As soon as they were inside, Kuba drew the revolver and led them down the hall to the only office that was lit. Without stopping, he pushed open the door and they filed in, though Antonia stayed in the doorway.

Half a dozen men sat at a table at the back of the room. Two were bearded and looked rabbinical, but the majority had the appearance of regular Belgian businessmen. They looked up, obviously surprised, even annoyed at the interruption. It seemed to take a moment for them all to focus on the gun Kuba held.

He spoke calmly, his tone almost conciliatory, and while he explained what a betrayal it was for Jews to deport other Jews when none ever came back, Moishe and the third man swept all the papers from the tables onto the floor.

When they'd cleared the tables, they yanked open the drawers of the file cases behind them and emptied their contents onto the same spot.

One of their captives stepped forward. Slight of build, with eyes rendered enormous by thick eyeglass lenses, he managed to cower and threaten at the same time. "What are you doing? Get out! We are protected. You'll go to jail."

Kuba grabbed the man by his shirt with his free hand, and, shoving him up against a wall, he unleashed a tirade in Yiddish. Antonia didn't need to understand it to know the gist of it, that they all had become agents of evil.

Meanwhile, Moishe gathered the papers into a heap at the center of the room, and the other man emptied the jerrican of gasoline over it. The vile smell filled the room, and Antonia covered her mouth and nose.

Kuba finally let loose of the man and turned to the rest of the staff that hadn't moved. "I suggest you all back away, gentlemen," he said in French. Antonia took a step back herself.

Moishe dropped a single burning match onto the pile, and it caught with a sudden, explosive *whooooop*. Heat filled the room immediately, and everyone recoiled, falling back against their chairs and desks.

"Tell your Nazi masters that the Jews of Belgium are better than this, that we won't go without fighting," Kuba shouted against the crackling and the heat of the fire, then signaled his men to leave.

In the corridor, a bulky gray-haired man in glasses charged toward them, either indifferent to or unaware of the revolver. "Terrorists. Bolsheviks! I've summoned the police."

"Robert Holzinger. That's him!" the nameless partisan shouted, pointing with his whole arm.

"Mouchard!" Kuba shouted, and fired at him twice point-blank. With a look of outrage and confusion, Holzinger glanced down at his chest, then fell back onto the floor. Kuba stood over him and fired a third time at his chest, as red dots blossomed on his shirt.

Then they fled, followed by the Judenrat staff escaping the smoke and fire. One man knelt nonplussed by the body for just a moment, then followed the partisans out onto the street.

The car waited with its motor running, and the four of them leapt in. They pulled away from the curb and sped away while the Judenrat staff stood watching mutely in the street.

Once away from the scene, Kuba handed over the holstered gun with a muttered thank you, and Antonia tucked it under her coat.

She felt no triumph. The rush of exhilaration she expected never came. Just the memory of red blossoms on a white shirt.

Within minutes, the car pulled up at the corner of the Rue Marché au Charbon and Antonia jumped out. She broke into a jog, covering the short distance to the storefront, and admitted herself with her key. Relieved to finally be invisible, she proceeded through the dark shop and climbed the staircase, brooding.

What was the benefit of what they'd just done? A delay in the deportations perhaps, until the occupying authorities could find another way to round up Jews? Had she actually saved any lives or just helped to take one? It was despicable to make deportation lists. But Jews executing Jews for any reason seemed to play into the hands of the Nazis. And watching it unfold in a language she couldn't understand had made her feel detached. This wasn't what she'd signed on for.

Reaching the tiny apartment at the top of the stairs, she was forced to turn on the hall light to find her key. After fumbling for a few moments, she unlocked the door, pushed it inward, and flicked the light switch. The overhead light went on, illuminating something lying in the middle of the floor. She blinked for a moment, trying to make sense of it.

A bundle of soiled and foul-smelling newspapers was wrapped around something hard and square.

❖

"What do you think? Can you make use of it?"

She spun around to see Christine Mathys standing in her doorway with her fingers pressed against her nose. "God, I hope so," she continued. "It's stinking up the whole building."

Perplexed, Antonia took hold of a corner of the newspaper and delicately peeled it back. Through the mud, straw, and excrement, she identified it immediately.

The valise with her wireless radio.

With equal measure of hope and revulsion, she knelt and gingerly inspected the aluminum case, trying not to touch the vile-smelling sludge that caked it.

"It's pig shit, I think," Mme Mathys remarked. "Wipe off as much of it as you can with the newspaper, and I'll burn it in the stove downstairs."

"Good idea." Antonia began scraping off the disgusting crust. Wrapping the entire mess in an outer layer of clean newspaper, she handed it over.

"Thank you. While you burn that, I'll try to wash the rest." Reluctantly she took her only towel and soaked it in water, then set about cleaning the apparatus, focusing on the clip that held the casing closed. The stench had scarcely faded, but now she was excited enough to ignore it.

She snapped open the catch and pried open the valise. Her heart sank. All three components inside—receiver, transmitter, and power source—were wet and malodorous. They were theoretically waterproofed, but only against rain, not two months in a pigsty.

Tenderly, she drew out each component and wiped it down, rinsing the filthy towel repeatedly. When all three were clean, she noted with dismay that the one part that seemed damaged was the power unit. Even after adapting its cable to the electrical outlet in the room, she couldn't cause it to light. The radio was useless.

Mme Mathys had returned, wiping her hands on a clean towel. "Does it work?"

"Unfortunately not. How did it get here?"

"Two men brought it by. I didn't ask their names, of course. They said a farmer saw it drop into his pigsty. He detached the parachute and covered everything with mud before the gendarmes reached his farm. Judging by the condition of the case, I'd say he left it hidden for some time." She took a step closer and peered down at the three units. "What do you think? Can those things stand being submerged?"

"For a limited time. The units are sealed, but in this case, the power source seems damaged, possibly from a leak. I can't test the other parts until I have power. Or get another battery."

"Hmm. I don't know where you can get a radio battery without getting in trouble. Maybe Mr. Goldman can help you."

"Mr. Goldman? Aisik Goldman? How can he help?"

"He's an electrician. Didn't he tell you? First in Belorussia and then here. Until the new laws. Now he works clandestinely."

"You think he could repair this?"

"I don't know. But you might want to clean it off a little more before you ask him. Pig shit isn't exactly kosher."

CHAPTER NINETEEN

Francis bent over the bar counter reading *Le Soir*, glancing up periodically to monitor his customers. Only a few tables were occupied, and only one of them by Wehrmacht officers. Celine had served them and they seemed content, so he returned to his reading. Laura came to the counter with a tray of dirty dishes.

"What lies are they printing today?" she muttered, looking down at the paper.

He snorted agreement. "Aside from the usual reports of Germany's struggle against Bolshevism, there's been another arson. In the Boulevard du Midi at the Judenrat office. Someone was killed too. An assassination."

"Really? You think partisans did it?"

"I'm sure they did. The authorities are offering a reward for information."

"Anything about the RAF? The BBC announced last night that they'd bombed Essen."

"Well, they're not going to admit that, are they? The only articles I see here are about the German courage in the East. And the usual news about shortages."

The sound of the café door opening drew their attention.

Baron von Falkenhausen stood for a moment, as if waiting for acknowledgement. His pale eyes squinted behind wire-rimmed glasses toward his usual table.

"Ah, Herr Baron." Francis folded his paper and stepped out from behind the counter. "So nice to see you this morning. Will you have your usual?" He extended his arm toward the corner table the officer usually favored.

Von Falkenhausen took a seat and removed his peaked cap, revealing the severe military tonsure of the officer class. In an ironic reversal of a monk's patch, his head was shaved high above his ears, and only a narrow cap of graying hair remained at the top.

"How are you, today, Herr Baron?" Francis was at his affable best.

"Quite well, thank you." He smiled up at Laura as she set down a steaming cup of coffee. She gave him real coffee, obtainable only on the black market, though for lower-ranking customers, the Café Suèdoise made a special mixture of black-market beans and legally obtained chicory that satisfied most palates. Knowing his habit, she'd also brought him a glass of cognac.

"We've got our hands full, of course. The terrorists and thugs keep us busy."

"Yes. I see there's been another arson in the Boulevard du Midi. At the Jewish administration."

Von Falkenhausen took a mouthful of his cognac, savoring the taste for a moment, then followed it with a sip of coffee. "Yes, you have to admit, it was a clever strategy, setting up the Judenrat. They do the work of choosing who'll go on the work trains, and when there's resistance, they fight it out among themselves. Saves us a lot of trouble."

Francis nodded ambiguously.

Von Falkenhausen swirled the cognac in his glass. "That will all change soon enough. You'll see, my friend. Brussels will settle down into quite a nice city."

"I hope so. All these shortages are very hard on business." Francis dried his hands mechanically on his apron.

The phone rang in the office behind the bar, and Laura disappeared through the door to answer it. "If you'll excuse me," Francis said, and turned to follow her, leaving Celine to keep an eye on the tables.

On the floor next to his desk, Celine's dog Suzi raised her head as he came in, then seemed to recognize that he carried no food scraps and let it drop again.

Laura handed him the phone, and her expression told him it was escapee business. Always aware of the possibility of being overheard, he fell into code language. "Hello, Francis here. What's the news? Ah, the parcels arrived. Yes, that's good to know. One damaged? Oh, dear, which one? The tea? Well, thank you for calling. What's that? Oh, yes, I understand. Don't worry. We'll take care of that. I'll see to payment right away."

He hung up and turned to Laura. "Bayonne," he said quietly, ensuring his voice couldn't carry into the café. "One fatality."

Laura looked alarmed. "Who?"

"One of the Brits. We'll find out more when Sandrine is back."

"It sounded like there was some other problem too." She knelt down and scratched behind the dog's head.

"Yes. The guide, Florentino, wants to be paid. So do the farmers. They won't take any more people over until they are. You can't blame them, really." He knelt in front of the safe under his desk. With a few turns of the dial, he unlocked the steel box and pulled the door open.

"How much have we got left?" Laura asked, standing above him, though she already knew the answer."

"Nothing. Just a few francs to purchase food for the restaurant, and barely enough for that." He closed the door gently, as if to protect the little cash left inside, and stood up. "I don't know what to do at this point. I'm at my wit's end."

Celine poked her head through the doorway to the café. "New customers, and the general is leaving."

Francis returned to the dining room. Von Falkenhausen was on his feet, just setting on his cap. The tiny silver death's-head over the visor caught the light for a brief second, like a signal light.

"Good day to you." The general twitched a military greeting and stepped out onto the street. Francis glanced down at the money left on the table. A token payment. Less than he'd paid for the black-market coffee.

"Bastard," he muttered under his breath.

❖

A few streets away, on the Rue Marché au Charbon, Aisik Goldman wiped his hands on the already-filthy towel. "Well, I've done the best I can. It seems to be a basic AC adapter, and it looks like one of the wires was broken off the terminal. I've replaced it and cleaned the terminal so…we'll see." He laid the lid back on the unit and screwed it tightly shut.

"What about the current?" Moishe asked. Belgian current is 230 volts. But the numbers here show 110 or 220."

"That shouldn't be a problem." Antonia examined the newly repaired adapter. "It's designed with a 20-volt variance on both sides, so the 220 current should still work at 230. Did you find any problems in the transmitter or receiver?"

"They seemed intact, so I didn't open them."

"Well, let's see what happens." She plugged the wire from the power source into the wall socket, then sat down at the table and flicked on the switch. Nothing happened. The two men grunted disappointment.

"Wait. Wait. The switch is still on 110. Let me just move it over to 220. She flicked the upper switch to the right, then toggled the lower switch onto "on." The power light glowed.

She let out a long exhalation. So far so good, she thought, but it seemed unlucky to say it out loud.

"Do you want me to stay while you try the transmitter?" Aisik asked.

Antonia shook her head. "No. It'll take me a while to create a message in code. If I can't send it, I'll ask you to come back and we'll take the other units apart. For now, thank you."

She walked with them to the door and shook Aisik's hand, looking directly into his eyes for the first time. She saw kindness and deep humility and turned away, embarrassed.

If her wireless worked, she was going to abandon him.

Half an hour later, Antonia laid her pencil aside and read the message she'd coded, first in the SOE poem-based code and then in Morse. She'd asked for it to be based on Robert Burns's "Address to a Haggis," which she'd read a dozen times and still found largely unintelligible. It served nicely as a code source, however.

She connected up the power box and plugged the transmitter cable into the five-holed socket on the left side. As she'd been taught, she also attached the receiver by its cable to the transmitter. The plastic-coated antenna wire, all twenty feet of it, was carefully rolled up within the receiver box. She needed only to wipe it clean, tack it high along two walls of the apartment, and connect it to the transmitter.

She pinpointed the receiver on a frequency of ten point two megacycles and the dial on sixty, as they'd shown her in training, then set on the headphones and turned on the power supply. A hum sounded in her ears. She was perspiring now as she adjusted the volume to a comfortable level.

The crystal that came with the set seemed undamaged, so she inserted it into the correct socket in the transmitter and turned the dial to 8-14 megacycles. She adjusted the antenna coupling switch until the antenna resonance light glowed with a satisfying brightness, suggesting a strong signal.

Holding her breath, she began to send. Her hand trembled slightly trying to keep up the rhythm of transmission on the transmitter's tiny sending key. It was impossible to correct mistakes, and she couldn't broadcast more than a few minutes, or she risked being traced.

She tapped in code, a pattern of dots and dashes that a third person would have found gibberish, but as she sent, the actual words ran through her head.

Sophie here stp mission failed stp plane shot down all dead but me stp planned contacts don't trust me stp working with Jewish partisans stp need money weapons please advise end.

She ended with the code *RTST. Respond tomorrow, same time* and added the security code letters confirming she was who she said she was. Twenty-four hours should give the SOE enough time to decipher the message and take it to the relevant authority to verify its authenticity and formulate a response.

Then she disconnected everything, dismounted the antenna, and slid the set and accessories in its valise under her bed. It was a paltry protection, and the simplest search would uncover it, but she couldn't do anything else.

She lay on her bed, at once excited and relieved. After weeks of trailing along with partisan fighters, supporting acts that many called terrorism, she was ready to do the job she'd been sent to do. No more groveling before the mysterious Toussaint woman in the Café Suèdoise.

Now she could return and confront her with the offer of aid from London. She snorted. That would melt some of the ice in those cold green eyes, wouldn't it? She allowed herself the most delicious fantasy of grasping the woman's shirtfront and taunting her. "You want some help from the Big Boys? Then come down off your high horse and talk to me."

Ah, the reversal of power was sweet. So was the thought of laying hands on Sandrine Toussaint.

❖

Twenty-four hours later, she sat at her table again with the same array of transmitter, receiver, and power box in front of her. She repeated the steps of the previous day and set on the headphones, but sent only her agent's code and then waited.

The minutes ticked past, and she bit her lips. She checked her watch. What was the problem? Was her receiver not functioning? Or had headquarters not even gotten her message? She drummed her fingers and softly ground her teeth.

Then, a signal. She seized her pad and pencil, as the encoded dots and dashes came in. The message was no longer than hers had been, and when it stopped, she signed off again and killed the power. Then she set about deciphering what she'd received. In just a few moments, she had it.

Glad yur alive stp bilbao reports andrée arrested but comet line in operation at same location stp imperative you join them stp mission still urgent stp specify time and place for next drop of money and guns stp rtst end.

She could have wept for relief. The battle, her battle, was on again.

CHAPTER TWENTY

The Café Suèdoise had just opened and served only one other customer when Antonia entered. She decided not to approach the counter but sat down again, at the maximum distance from the other person.

To her immense disappointment, the male proprietor came to speak to her, clearly disconcerted. "What can I do for you, madam?" he asked coldly.

Antonia dropped her voice, forcing him lean in to hear. "Look, I know that Andrée has been arrested. That fact has reached London now too. So right now, I must speak with someone with regard to the escape line," she muttered under her breath. "Don't cut me out again. I have something important to offer." Out loud she said, "I'll have whatever soup is on offer today, please."

The man was taken aback, though more perplexed than anxious, as he'd been on their previous meeting. "Yes, madam," he said, and retreated to the counter and his partner.

A few moments later, he returned with the steaming soup and set it down in front of her. Potato-and-leek soup. On the plate beside the bowl lay a thick slice of dark bread. In spite of the importance of her mission, Antonia was too hungry to ignore the food. She dipped the bread into the hot liquid and bit off a piece. It was the most delicious soup she could ever remember eating. "Superb. My compliments to the cook."

The man dried his hands mechanically on his apron. "*I'm* the cook. My name is Francis." He dropped his voice. "What do you have to say?"

Antonia took a mouthful of soup, letting a lump of heavenly potato lie for a moment on her tongue. "I was told to contact your organization. We can offer you money and assistance."

"I'm afraid I don't know what you're talking about."

"Oh, please, don't go on with that game. Joseph McGee at the Consulate in Bilbao has apparently contacted London and reported that Andrée was arrested and has been replaced by someone else. No name, of course. Too dangerous over open airways, even in code. Is that you?"

"McGee? Bilbao?" The two words seemed to be the key. "You can talk to me, madam. I'll relay what you've said to the relevant persons."

Her annoyance at his evasiveness diminished the triumph she felt at his partial concession. She'd really had enough.

"No, I want to talk to the woman I spoke to last time." She savored the power of pronouncing the name, like a wizard, conjuring up the being with the word. "Sandrine Toussaint."

Francis studied her for a moment, obviously nonplussed. "Enjoy your soup, madam," he said finally, and retreated to a room behind the bar. Things were beyond her control now. She'd said the magic names, and now she had to wait. But in the meantime, she would finish the heavenly meal.

She finished the entire bowl and wiped it clean with the last morsel of bread, but still Francis didn't return. She pushed the empty bowl and saucer away from her and fidgeted with her napkin. She had no money to pay for the soup, so if Francis, or Sandrine Toussaint herself, didn't accept her claims, she feared an unpleasant scene.

Finally Francis reappeared. He bent over the table in a posture that could be taken as a courteous bow and said under his breath, "Please leave now."

"What?" Antonia was aghast. She remained seated, searching for a more convincing argument. She had none. She knew too little.

"Come back this afternoon at four," he added. "To the door in the alley. Madame Toussaint will be there."

"Yes, of course." Antonia dropped her napkin next to her plate, gathered her coat and bag, and left the cafe. To her relief, he hadn't mentioned payment.

She hurried back to her room in the Rue Marché au Charbon. She disliked waiting, but at least this time her stomach was full and the outcome looked promising.

Too nervous to wait any longer, she left at 3:30. At a leisurely pace, she made a circle around the Grand Place, stopping at the windows of the lace maker and the candle shop, both of which were empty. At 3:50 she crossed the last few streets to the alley beside the café. She knocked once and the door opened immediately. It led to a storage room, but a table covered with papers and a telephone revealed that it also served as an office.

Standing in front of a shelf of canned goods was the same blondish woman who'd rebuffed her weeks earlier and just recently thrown her off her property. She appeared more worn, her face more strained than before, but curiously more attractive. Perhaps because Antonia herself was no longer the desperate supplicant, they were on equal terms now.

She offered her hand. "Madame Toussaint, so pleased to meet you." The name was like a spice on her tongue.

The handshake was perfunctory, nervous. "Tell me about Bilbao," the woman said.

"So you finally want to listen. That's good. May I sit down?"

Sandrine ignored the question and kept them both standing, like duelists. "What about Bilbao?"

"Mr. McGee at the British consulate in Bilbao is our source, our only source of information about what you're doing to help our pilots escape. We understand that Andrée de Jongh was arrested and someone else is in charge, and that's the person I want to talk to."

"Our source. Who is 'our'?"

"The SOE. Special Operations Executive. They sent me two months ago, along with another agent. We were to locate you and offer guidance and assistance, but our plane was shot down and I was the only survivor. I had thought the wireless radio was also lost, but the people I'm now working with managed to salvage it and I could finally contact headquarters. They updated me on your situation, and now I've come back to make the same offer."

"Of guidance? We don't need guidance."

"I understand that. But perhaps you could use weapons or money."

Sandrine's expression changed subtly. "Money, certainly. Are you offering some?"

Damn. The woman was a hard sell. "Yes, I am. But you're going to have to be open with me as well. First of all, are you the one in charge?"

The woman frowned, still obviously conflicted.

Antonia felt a sudden unexpected sympathy. "I know it's a risk for you to trust me. But please, look at this." She pulled away the collar of her blouse and turned sideways to display the waxen skin of a burn scar at the back of her neck. "I got this at Dunkirk nursing soldiers, and it reaches halfway down my back. I nearly died, and thousands of good English, and Irish, and Welshmen *were* killed that day for you. For all of Europe. We're on the same side, so please don't shut me out any longer."

The woman winced at the sight, then appeared to relax her guard. "No one's really in charge. We're not a military organization. No one gives or takes orders, although I decide when the men go down the line, so I suppose I'm responsible if they're captured or if anyone is arrested."

"So it really *is* you. Well, London wants to work with you."

"Is that so?" Sandrine finally gestured toward the chairs by the storage-room table, and they both took a seat. "Tell me about the money."

Antonia also relaxed. "We have to set it up. Now that I have radio contact, I'll tell my people I've connected with you and ask them to make a drop at a time and location you designate. I need money too. I couldn't even pay for my soup today."

"We'll put it on your bill." For the first time Sandrine's expression hinted at a smile. "You said your name is Sophie. Is that your real name?"

"That's what's on my identification papers."

"Sophie it is, then. What have you been doing all this time since you arrived?"

"Since you brushed me off, you mean? I've been working with Jewish partisans. Not part of my orders, but we share a common enemy."

"I see. Well, if all it takes is a message to London…" She opened a drawer on the side of the desk and drew out a pad of paper. "Let's compose one."

What a relief. For two months, Antonia had been the spy that nobody wanted. And now, with a single conversation, she was once again an active agent in the British war effort. Her words, her presence now carried weight, and the promise of material assistance revitalized both the Comet Line and the partisans. Even Moishe came out of his secret world to join the Comet people for the first drop.

Now, a few days after the message to the SOE, while the early autumn night was still warm, Antonia stood with Moishe, Sandrine, Francis, and Philippe on the moonlit field they'd chosen. She explained the SOE flight strategy and the shape they had to present with their lanterns so the pilot could pinpoint the drop spot.

They'd paced out the 600 meters of unobstructed ground, walking into the wind and setting out beacon A after 100 meters, beacon B after the next 150 meters, and beacon C at a right angle from beacon B, thus marking out a reversed L. The arriving pilot could discern the pattern from afar and know that the recipients would be waiting at beacon A.

Antonia and Sandrine stood together near lamp A, imbedded in the ground so it would be visible only from above. Francis and Moishe dug holes for the other two beacons, then returned to wait with them. Philippe stood at the edge of the field holding the horse and wagon.

Sandrine drew up the collar of her sweater. "It's almost one."

"We have to be patient. I sent them the exact coordinates and a description of the natural landmarks on all four sides. But the plane has to deal with weather over the channel, then trace a slalom over land all the while flying below radar."

She was more nervous than they. If the drop failed, for whatever reason, her role as provider for both groups would disintegrate. She hadn't even mentioned the possibility of flak keeping the planes from arriving at all.

Moishe rubbed his arms for warmth. "All this standing around in the dark. You should have told them to include cognac in the drop."

Sandrine chuckled. "You mean we could order things? Damn, I would have asked for new boots."

Antonia shone her own torch on her watch. It was ominously late. If the plane didn't come at all, they'd have to go home empty-handed, evading the various patrols for bloody nothing, and she wouldn't even know why until she risked another radio transmission. The thought made her chest hurt.

Then she heard it, the growl of a low-flying small-engine plane. The others heard it too and peered upward, trying to spot it.

"There it is," Sandrine said, and Antonia watched the shadow emerge from the horizon, like an enormous metal bat. It swept between the two bottom beacons and came within 400 feet, where it seemed to defecate an object. A black chute opened over it, slowing its descent. Then the aircraft pulled up short and just cleared the row of trees behind them.

First shutting off the guide lamps, all five ran toward the container, an aluminum cylinder some eight feet long and with the girth of a horse. Antonia detached the parachute and rolled it into a ball before stuffing it into a bag. The others were already kneeling by the cylinder itself.

It was heavier than expected, and the mud it had dropped into added a suction effect. Grunting, the two men hefted it onto their shoulders, then fast-marched it to the hay wagon where Philippe waited on the road. Sliding it onto the wagon, they covered it with straw and climbed onto the front bench. Philippe urged the horse into motion and they rumbled away.

Behind them, Antonia and Sandrine collected the beacons and returned to Sandrine's car, and half an hour later they were in Philippe's barn tearing open the seals.

"Let's see what goodies London has sent us," Antonia said, undoing the bolts and raising the metal cover. Lying across two of the numerous boxes was a large padded envelope, and she grasped it reverently. "This is our primary cargo," she said, "but I'll count it later under better security."

"I can provide security." Moishe chuckled and held out his hand.

"Honor among thieves, eh?" Sandrine glanced at him playfully.

Antonia pawed through the items, doing a cursory inventory. "Plastic explosives, ammunition. These are for you, Moishe. Sten guns. There should be eight of them, but two of them are for the Comet."

"Excellent." Moishe lifted one out from the belly of the cylinder. "I've heard of them before but never laid hands on one. Do we have to train to use them?"

"Very little. They're designed for simplicity. Besides, look here. They've included instruction manuals in French." She tossed him a couple.

"What's this?" Sandrine lifted out a soft bundle wrapped in brown paper.

"Extra clothes for me, I think. And this…" She lifted up a string-tied cardboard box and balanced it on the end of the cylinder. "This should be the food I asked for. Field rations, probably, but at least I won't go hungry in my room."

"Don't worry, Antonia. We'll always feed you," Francis said. "We should save the field rations for when we take the men down the line."

She lifted out another box. "Even better. Corned beef, ten cans. And here, bless their hearts, they've added cigarettes and chocolate. Worth their weight in gold these days."

"It's almost dawn," Philippe announced, looking out through the barn door. "We'd better get moving."

"He's right." Sandrine took charge. "Moishe, why don't you take a couple of the Sten guns and explosives for your partisans? I've got a hidden space under the backseat in my car, so we can carry your material along with ours. As soon as the curfew is lifted, I'll drop you and Sophie off in Brussels and take the others to the café."

"What about the rest?" Moishe eyed the Sten guns that still lay in the cylinder.

"Don't worry," Sandrine said. "I'll drive back tomorrow to fetch another load and see that it gets to the right people. In the meantime, the cylinder should be safe here in Philippe's barn. You can trust us," she added. "Honor among thieves, right? If we find a bottle of cognac anywhere at the bottom, I'll make sure you get it."

From where she sat, with the lantern between them, Antonia watched the two of them bantering and felt a twinge of jealousy. She liked both of them, but she wasn't sure if she wanted them to like each other so much. Perhaps it was the radiance of Sandrine's hair next to the lantern and the way Moishe gazed at it.

Radiant hair? Where the hell had that thought come from? Antonia stood up and tucked the cash envelope inside her shirt.

Philippe dragged the barn door open. "Curfew's over. You can get on the road now." They filed out of the barn toward Sandrine's car, and Philippe padlocked the door behind them.

As car owner, Sandrine assigned Francis and Moishe to the rear seat and Antonia to the front next to her. There's at least that, Antonia thought.

Once they were on the road, Moishe leaned forward and spoke over the noise of the motor. "How lucky that you have your Mercedes. I thought the Germans confiscated all the non-essential civilian cars."

"Yes, lucky," Sandrine answered, noncommittal, letting the subject drop.

"So, have I finally earned your trust?" Antonia turned toward Sandrine, keeping her voice low.

With half her attention on the rough dirt roads, Sandrine replied as softly. "I'm sorry I ever doubted you. You've proved yourself very valuable."

"I suppose I have." Antonia patted the envelope inside her shirt. "That was the whole point."

"I don't just mean the money, though we need that, desperately. I was thinking more about your being British. We need to interrogate every pilot we find to keep the Gestapo from planting one of their agents. You'll know things about daily life in Britain that we don't, so you can help us ask questions."

"I can do better than that. I can ask headquarters to check each pilot's background and see if it corresponds to what he tells us."

"Oh, that will help enormously." Sandrine laid her hand on Antonia's forearm, sending a wave of pleasure through her. "I'm sorry for sending you back out on the street when you first arrived, Sophie. You're a real gem."

Antonia glanced over at her in the warm orange light of dawn. "I bet you say that to all your spies."

CHAPTER TWENTY-ONE

November 1942

The first successful supply drop led to another, two weeks later, and then to a third, in November, by which time the team was adept at collecting and distributing the material. After the November delivery arrived late, and Antonia had waited most of the night in an open field, she allowed herself a long restful sleep.

The next morning, she treated herself to a morsel of the precious chocolate, nibbling at its corners while she sent off her latest transmission.

Latest drop received stp two new pilots found luxembourg area stp pls confirm missing aircraft flight details and pilots in preparation for interrogation end.

Then she dismantled the parts of the radio and concealed them again inside their valise. It was a rather pathetic disguise, which would protect the radio only until someone opened the case, but it was all she had. The room had no false wall, no hidden cavities, and only the flimsiest wardrobe. She slid it under the bed simply because that was where a suitcase would be kept.

She was startled, as always, by a knock at the door but calmed upon hearing Moishe's voice. He slipped quickly inside with one of the Sten guns in hand.

"I like this gun." He inspected its simple barrel and wire shoulder stock. "Unlike the ones we usually get, these should actually shoot."

"Well, loyal British workers, not forced labor, made them. Cuts down on the sabotage. You haven't shot any of them yet?"

"No. Haven't needed to. For the last two months we've been mostly robbing people, with the handguns. Easier to conceal. So I think it's about time you showed me how to actually fire this thing."

"It's fairly simple." She took the weapon from his hands. "See how the bolt cocks to the rear and springs forward when you pull the trigger? It grabs the cartridge from the magazine much faster than a bolt-action rifle, but unfortunately, it has an effective range of only about 100 meters." She inserted the foot-long magazine and it gave a click. "Be careful when you grasp the magazine to support the gun. It'll wear the magazine catch and alter the angle of feed."

She detached it again and held it up in front of him. "This is nearly identical to the German 9mm magazines, so if you can steal any of them, you can increase your ammunition supply."

"Uh, hunh." He squinted at the chamber through his glasses. "I'll pass on the information." He set the gun down and gazed at her for a moment.

"You've been generous with material like this, but you haven't been around for any of our actions. Does this mean you're not working with us any more?"

"I'm afraid so. I was always only on the fringe of your group, anyhow. The Comet people are the ones London assigned me to in the first place."

"I'm sorry to hear it, but I understand. We all have our jobs."

At the door he said, "You're going to miss our next action. Kuba thinks we should hit the main downtown garage and get ourselves a car. We'll definitely use one of these." He held up the Sten.

She accompanied him to the Goldman apartment and met Aisik coming up the stairs from below. Rywka opened to the sound of their voices and beckoned them all in. Aisik set down his tool bag and marched toward the window.

"What's troubling you, Aisik?" Moishe asked.

"I just rewired an apartment in the Wolvengracht. I don't get much work so the job was welcome. But someone on the street saw me go in." He rubbed his forehead.

"It's the middle of the day. Lots of people must have seen you go in."

"Yes, but when I came out two hours later, he was still there. I recognized him because he had a red mark on his cheek, like a birthmark. It made him look a little like a clown. But then he followed me home. He thought I couldn't see him, but I'm like a rabbit. I circled around and saw that he was behind me. And he's still outside now, checking the address of this building."

Both Moishe and Antonia went to the window. "Yeah, someone's down there," she said. "A man in a brown suit jacket and a cap. He's looking through the window into the shop."

"That's him," Aisik said. "What should we do? I'm sure he's trouble."

"Two can play that game," Antonia said. "Let's find out where *he* lives."

"You think I should try to follow him home?" Moishe said. "How can I do that?"

"Let me do it. Keep an eye on him while I go up and get my coat. What was the address where you were working?"

"Wolvengracht 98."

"All right. I'll wait inside the shop. As soon as he leaves the street, someone call down the staircase and I'll follow him."

In two minutes she was back on the stairs buttoning her jacket. Moishe stood in the doorway. "He's just left and turned right at the corner."

The man was gone when she reached the street, but she quickened her pace, and on the other side of the Grand Place, on the Rue des Harengs, she caught sight of him. She kept him at a distance, with other people between them. In the brief times he disappeared around a corner, she always located him again and easily trailed him past the Kiekenmarkt and across the Place de la Monnaie.

As she expected, he turned on the Wolvengracht, and now she hurried to see where he would stop. She was within twenty paces of him when he turned into a bakery shop, and she stepped into an alley out of his line of sight. Some five minutes later, he emerged again with a loaf of bread wrapped in newspaper, and marched the last half block to an apartment building. Slowing her own step, she passed the door indifferently, and the briefest glance sideways gave her the address. Wolvengracht 100. Easy to remember.

But how to find out his name? At the bakery, perhaps? Presumably he was registered there to use his bread coupons.

She went in to look around, wondering how direct she could be without raising suspicions. "Good day," she said brightly to the man behind the counter.

"Good day, dear," he replied, the greeting ending on a questioning note. She was, after all, not part of his usual clientele. He was old and stooped, and he sat perched on a stool near the register, as if he stood guard over it. But the display case held only a sorry assortment of hard biscuits and a few loaves of grayish bread that she knew were full of potato flour and God knows what else.

On the floor at the end of the counter, a dog was sleeping on a cushion. A mongrel of some kind, and when he opened his eyes at her entrance, they were as weary and bloodshot as his master's.

Her mind raced, wondering how to win his trust. "The man who was just here, the one with the red birthmark on his face," she said. "I saw him beating a dog and I want to report him. Do you know his name? I hate cruelty to animals."

The baker scowled. "Corot, beating a dog? Well, that fits him. He probably beats his wife too," he grumbled.

"Oh, then you know him personally?" She knelt down and held out her hand for the dog to sniff. He licked it once and gazed up with baleful dog's eyes.

"No, he's just a customer, but he comes in most days. "His name is Jean Corot and he's a piece of work. Sometimes he shoots his mouth off, about the immigrants and the Jews. Says the Germans are the best thing that ever happened to Belgium, that they're going to clean the place out."

"Really? He supports the deportations?" She scratched behind the slightly mangy ears, keeping her voice neutral.

"Sure he does. Wouldn't be surprised if he called some of them in. Men like him, anything for a few extra francs." Suddenly he squinted, suspicious. "So who's asking? Who are you, anyhow?"

She stood up again, offering as warm an expression as she could manage. "Just someone who loves dogs. I lost mine last year. Nearly broke my heart."

He looked tenderly down at the cur at his feet. "Yeah, people don't keep 'em any more. Too hard to feed. Prince there, he won't eat anything but meat. I have to swap my best bread every morning with the butcher to get enough for him. Don't know how long I can keep that up."

She nodded. "I understand. You do the best you can. They give so much in return, don't they?" Without waiting for an answer, she stepped away from the counter. "Well, thank you for helping and maybe saving some dog from being beaten again." With a hand raised in farewell, she slipped out the door before he noticed she hadn't purchased anything.

Ten minutes later she was back at the Rue Marché au Charbon in the Goldman apartment. "He's a collaborator," she announced. "Probably not Gestapo, since the local baker knew his name. Probably just an amateur, trying to curry favor. Still, it might be wise for Aisik and Rywka to stay away from the apartment for a while. Can you keep them with you?"

Moishe closed his eyes in evident despair. "I just have a space under a roof with a mattress on the floor. No place to cook. That's why I come here."

"Maybe just for a week," Aisik suggested. "If nobody shows up at the apartment, we can move back."

"Yes, you should do that, Moishe. I'll give you a few tins of corned beef and some other rations that came from London. You can eat them without cooking."

Rywka looked completely beaten. She knelt by the sofa and pulled out a battered suitcase, muttering something in Yiddish. They had all agreed on a mere week of hiding, but Rywka's morbid tone had an air of finality about it.

Another month passed with ever more German advances in the East, ever more arrests, deportations, executions, and ever more downed aviators, escaped prisoners, despairing Belgians seeking to escape. In Belgium, the Armed Jewish Partisans nipped at the victor's ankles, the clandestine press reported the depressing truth in shabby one-page fliers, while the cellars and barns of Belgium filled up with the desperate and the doomed.

This was Antonia's fourth interrogation. She pulled up her collar and ducked her head against the pounding rain while Sandrine marched on ahead of her, seemingly oblivious. A few moments later they arrived at the fish market and turned into the alley where they gave the password at the rear door.

Inside they shook the water off their coats and made their way to the inner storage room, where Christine had brought the next group of men to be interrogated.

The two airmen stood up as they entered. One was short and gave the impression of plumpness, though closer scrutiny revealed that only his cheeks were pudgy. Under his rumpled RAF uniform, he was, in fact, rather thin. The other one was wiry as well, and though the bandage over his cheek concealed some of his face, the visible half was handsome.

"You are…?" Sandrine leaned toward the round-faced one.

"Ian Montcrief, miss, 602 Squadron." He offered an informal salute.

"I'm Nick Patterson," the other added, without waiting for the question. "Same squadron, miss."

"Sit down, gentlemen," She pointed toward the table. "We have a few simple questions, and then we can move on to getting you out of here."

Antonia took one of the chairs at the table across from the men. "Where did you come down? Can you tell us about that?"

Nick seemed the more talkative one, in spite of his bandage. "We were shot down just over Hasselt, returning from a bombing run. We'd dropped our load and were traveling light and thought we were home free, but then the flak caught us. I got this jumping from the plane." He pointed to his cheek. "Piece of metal flew off the fuselage."

"What were you flying?" Antonia only knew the Whitleys and Lysanders she'd trained with at Ringley, but the SOE had told her what aircraft were missing.

"A Halifax Mk I, miss. And a beauty too."

It was the correct answer but could have been a lucky guess. "What kind of fire power were you carrying?"

"We had the usual load in the bomb bay, of course, but also six bomb cells in the wings. We also had two 7.7mm Browning machine guns in the nose turret and four in the tail turret." He obviously knew his airplane.

"How big was your crew?" She directed the question to Ian, who had been silent throughout.

"Seven, ma'am. Pilot, navigator, flight engineer, wireless operator, bomb aimer, and two gunners. I was the wireless operator."

"Wireless operator?" She brightened. "Can you spell your name in Morse?"

"Sure can. *Di-dit di-dah da-dit. Dah-dah dah-dah-dah da-dit dah dah-di-dah-dit di-dah-dit di-dit dit di-di-dah-dit*"

She laughed, certain that no Gestapo plant could have mastered the code well enough to deliver the name with such speed. He was the real thing.

"And you?" She turned to Nick.

"Flight engineer. The tail gunner was killed right away, but the rest of us bailed out. I counted five other chutes, but four were shot as they came down. You know, you're just hanging there, an easy target."

It all sounded eerily familiar.

"Where did you learn to fly, and who was your commanding officer in flight school?"

"I learned to fly at the Central Flying School at Upavon, Wiltshire, mostly with Captain Harold Down, though they put in substitutes sometimes."

The lost aircraft and commander names corresponded to those sent to her by the SOE, and that was all she needed.

"Thank you, gentlemen. I think we've heard enough." She nodded approval toward Sandrine.

"Good." Sandrine took charge. "Are those your packs?" She pointed with her chin toward the military rucksacks leaning against the wall.

"Yes, miss. But we've eaten the escape rations. All that's left is the first-aid kit and the maps."

"Obviously you can't carry them when you travel. They're British military issue. But we'll give you a replacement along with a change of clothes. Oh, and you can have your side arms back now. We'll take your photos and then have a doctor stop by to look at that wound, but you'll have to sleep here tonight. In a couple of days we hope to have papers with your new names. Once we've got those, we'll move you to another shelter until we can set up the line. Is everything clear?"

"Yes, miss. We'll stand by," Ian said, looking around glumly at the storage room. "Um, will we be getting anything to eat?" He winced slightly.

"Yes, we'll send over some sandwiches. Maybe we can stir up some beer for you too."

"Thank you, miss. That would be very welcome."

Antonia turned away, weary on their behalf, and weary for herself. How many more men would come through those doors, hungry and hurt and depending on her? Lurking at the edge of her consciousness was her own hunger for something and someone, but against the needs of the battered young aviators, it seemed a luxury.

On the street outside the fish market the rain had stopped and they walked shoulder to shoulder. "It's such a relief having you do the interrogations," Sandrine said. "You and your wireless are invaluable."

They turned the corner onto a broad avenue and the sun came out, brightening everything. Sandrine halted and closed her eyes, savoring the sudden warmth.

Antonia glanced sideways at the sharp Nordic profile and smiled at the irony. One of Hitler's enemies was more Aryan than most of his soldiers. Beautiful too. Internally, she prodded herself back to the present. "On the subject of the radio…"

"Please don't tell me there's a problem. I was just beginning to have hope again."

"Don't worry. The link with London won't go away. I'm only concerned because I've been transmitting for two months from my room. We know the Gestapo has vehicles patrolling the streets with direction finders looking for radio transmissions. So far, I've banked on the unlikelihood that they'll be near my street during the few minutes I transmit, but some day, the odds are going to catch up. And to make things worse, a few weeks ago someone was spying on the Jews who lived below me so I suspect the security police has the building in its sights by now."

"Spying? How do you know?" Sandrine's green eyes clouded with anxiety.

"Someone followed the husband home from where he was working. Anyhow, I managed to follow the weasel back to his place and find out his name, Jean Corot, and even his address, Wolvengracht 100."

"Jean Corot," Sandrine said. "Like the painter? Hmmm. I don't know the name, but I do know that street. I used a tailor shop close by. So what did you do?"

"Well, there wasn't much anyone could do. The family has gone into hiding in a tiny room away from here so they're safe, even if they're miserable. I'm only worried that if the security service goons one day decide to raid the building, they won't find their Jews, but they will find my wireless. I don't have any place to conceal it. I'm sorry. I suppose I should have told you earlier."

Sandrine halted. "You should have. I'd have made you leave a long time ago. For all you know, the security police might even be watching you. Why don't you transmit from the Château Malou?"

Spend time with Sandrine Toussaint in her château? Antonia tried to sound deliberative, professional. "Well, that *would* protect the transmissions. But I'd have to come out to Woluwe each time I send a message. I'd need to get a bicycle, at least."

"Hmm. That's not practical at all. Why don't you just move out there?"

"You mean with the pilots?" The fantasy was evaporating.

"No, in my brother's room upstairs. It may not be as cozy as your room in Brussels. The whole place is always cold these days, but you'll be safe."

Oh, thank God. "When can I move in?"

"Tomorrow, if you like. I'll come by in the morning with my car. We can hide the wireless under the rear seat, although we shouldn't be stopped anyhow. I have all the proper permits and am thoroughly legal."

"What luck that you've been able to keep your car. With the shortage of petrol, it must be very costly, though."

Sandrine glanced away. "More than you might imagine."

CHAPTER TWENTY-TWO

Already in her coat, Antonia watched from her window, and when the car pulled up, she slid on her rucksack, grabbed the wireless valise, and started down the stairs.

At the landing just below her, she glanced mournfully at the door to the empty apartment. The Goldmans were now huddled together in Moishe's tiny room, wherever it was. Would they ever dare to come back? Or would the suffocation of living together in a garret devoid of cooking facilities drive them back in spite of the danger? She bit her lip in helplessness and descended farther.

When she reached the ground floor, Christine was behind the counter of her always-empty shop.

"Moving up in the world, I see. Good for you."

"I wish we could all move out there and operate the Comet Line from the château. Wouldn't that be great?"

"Nice dream, but in the real world, we've got to be in town, near the Café Suèdoise, the fish market, the counterfeiter, the photographer, all the others."

"You're right. Anyhow, now you'll have a room available for the next escapee. Assuming the security service doesn't come around." She laid the keys on the counter.

"I've been doing this for a while. I know what to say if anyone comes around asking." Christine held the door open and gave her a peck on the cheek as she passed. "Give my regards to our aviators."

Antonia found herself on the sidewalk, and the closing door behind her seemed a sign. She hoped it was for the beginning of better times.

The overcast morning gave little color to the street, but standing by her black Mercedes in a soft yellow sweater, Sandrine was like a beacon of light and warmth. Antonia had a sudden urge to embrace her but instead said, "Hi."

"Hi." Sandrine echoed the greeting and opened the rear door. "Let's put your things under the seat first."

"Good idea." Antonia handed over both the radio case and the rucksack containing her clothes and pistol. Sandrine deftly lifted the rear seat and deposited the case into the cavity beneath. The whole procedure took only seconds, and the seat was down again.

With a final glance around the street, Antonia climbed into the front of the car, and a moment later, they were on the Boulevard Anspach. She relaxed briefly, enjoying the comfort of being driven. The last time she recalled being chauffeured to something new was when Major Atkins had taken her to Beaulieu. A lifetime ago.

Delivery trucks passed them here and there, but no other private vehicles. She wondered again what the "special arrangement" was that permitted them to drive when others were reduced to horse carts and bicycles.

"I've never lived in a château," Antonia said. "You'll have to tell me the rules, about where I'm allowed and not allowed."

"You're allowed most every place around the house and the grounds, even when I'm not there. Just try not to be seen if anyone comes around. Since you'll be staying in my brother's room, you'll be able to hear if anyone arrives outside. If you do, you must be completely silent until someone comes and tells you it's safe to come out. Understand?"

"Whatever you say. Do you have dangerous visitors very often?"

"Sometimes," she answered vaguely." Gaston and Mathilde will take care of you when I'm away."

"'Away.' You mean taking the men to Bilbao."

"Yes, of course. As soon as we get the new identification papers for them."

"I want to go with you this time. I know I'll be an extra mouth to feed, but I'm carrying the funds, after all. We can distribute them as you see fit. That was always the plan. But I know London would like me to have more involvement in the line."

She paused a moment, then added, "I don't want to just sit in your house waiting while you risk your life. I've spent far too much time on this mission simply waiting."

Sandrine focused on the road but nodded faintly. "Yes, I suppose it's all right, as long as you let me make all the decisions."

"Of course you'll make the decisions. There was never any doubt about that."

They pulled up in front of the Château Malou and Antonia tried not to gawk. She'd seen the building from a distance, the day she'd taken Moishe shooting, but hadn't paid much attention. "Eighteenth century?" she asked, looking up at the entry façade.

"The estate itself is from the seventeenth, actually. Originally a rural residence surrounded by a park and lake, it passed through several hands to a banker named Lambert. He tore down the original house and built this one in the Louis XVI style. You can see for yourself." She gestured upward with her hand.

"Seven bays of shuttered windows with a triangular pediment. Pure classicism. The estate passed through several more owners, was embellished, and the park was developed. Finally it reached Jules Malou, after whom it's named. He was a big financier and finally minister of state. He had five children, one of whom was my mother. The others entered the church or died, and she ended up with the house. She married into Belgian business and so did I, so we managed to have heating and modern plumbing installed, before the male members of the house died off."

Antonia listened to the long historical narrative, concealing her surprise at hearing about a husband. She surveyed the enormous white edifice. "It must be a handful to maintain."

"It's a monster, impossible to really heat and requires a large staff to keep it going. I struggle along with Gaston and Mathilde and the occasional groundskeeper." She tilted her head toward the wall of split logs that rose along the side of the entryway. "You'll see. We just rattle around in the place." She glanced up as the portal opened. "Ah, here comes help."

A man of about sixty appeared, short and muscular, with a ring of close-cut white hair.

"Can you give us a hand, Gaston?" Sandrine called as she opened the rear car door. "There's some luggage under the seat. The rucksack goes to Laurent's room and the valise up to the attic."

"Yes, ma'am. But the attic's quite dusty. I'm sure Mathilde will want to do a little cleaning." He flipped up the seat with the same expertise Sandrine had shown. Clearly the compartment was used often. He pulled out both items and hurried up the stone steps to the wide oak door. Setting one of them down, he held the door open for them.

In keeping with the château's proportions, the entryway was immense. A tall oak wardrobe stood on one side, a narrow table and two potted palms on the other. Over the table, a niche in the wall held an enormous marble vase, though it contained no flowers. There was no other furniture, and the eye was drawn immediately to the finely carved double door leading into the main living space. Two huge wolfhounds ambled toward them when the doors opened. One of them sniffed Antonia's hand.

Sandrine patted the other one on the head as he looked up adoringly at her. "This is Vercie. Short for Vercingetorix, and the one who's fallen in love with you is Baudouin." She scratched the throat of Vercie and he panted happily. "We've taught them not to bark at guests, since that would make hiding soldiers difficult. Unfortunately, they don't bark at anyone. So actually, they're quite useless."

"They're beautiful, though." Antonia stroked both of them on the head, endeavoring to be fair.

"Let me show you first to the main hall, which also functions as the library. It's got a nice fireplace and is the best place to stay warm during the day."

The main hall, too, was majestic rather than inviting. Directly across from the vast fireplace, a sofa and low table stood in front of a wall of books. Farther away, near the tall windows, a few stuffed chairs were arranged around a small table far away from the fireplace. The chill in the room suggested they were used only in summer.

"The only other room on this floor is the banquet hall on the south side, which hasn't seen a banquet for twenty years. This spot right here, in front of the fire, is the only space on the ground floor we use. Essentially, it's a big, empty house."

Antonia hovered close to the fireplace, though no fire burned in it. The rather spare mantelpiece held only a violin and three framed photos. One of them, grainy and in sepia, was a wedding picture of a couple posing stiffly in an artist's studio, she on a brocade chair in a lacy dress and he in a dark suit. His full handlebar moustache concealed his age, though his wife appeared in her twenties.

"Your parents?"

"Yes. They were less stuffy than the photo suggests, though my father was rather authoritarian. Typical of his generation."

"And this man? He's a bit younger than your father, but too old to be your husband."

Sandrine chuckled. "You think so? So did I, actually. But he *was* my husband, Guy. He had a cocoa plantation in the Congo, where he caught yellow fever."

"Oh, I'm sorry," Antonia said vaguely, meaning it to cover both the yellow fever and the faux pas of saying her husband was too old for her. She set the photo back on the mantel and took up the third, a portrait of a strikingly handsome young man in military uniform. Blond hair was cut short over his ears but lay in a rakish wave over his forehead, and though the picture was in black and white, the pale glow of his irises suggested his eyes were bright blue. A real heartbreaker, he appeared in his mid thirties and bore an extraordinary resemblance to Sandrine.

"Your brother?"

"Yes. Laurent. He was killed at the beginning of the war."

"I'm sorry," she said again. This one was more sincere, though she knew it sounded trite.

Sandrine led her back through the wide door to the stairwell next to one of the potted palms. "Let me show you your room before it gets too late."

Antonia followed, slightly intimidated by the palatial scope of the house. Even the stairwell led past windows that extended up three stories.

Sandrine stopped at the top of the stairs. "We have six rooms up here, but the only one we heat is my bedroom. Over there at the far corner was my father's bedroom, and the three rooms on the east side are empty. I've put you in my brother's room."

She led her into a wide room brightly lit by the late-afternoon sun that shone through a window nearly as tall as the room. The furniture was sparse and dwarfed by the height of the ceiling, a touch of modesty that Antonia rather liked. The double bed was oak, carved in a pattern similar to the table that stood along the opposite wall and the wardrobe next to it. A chair, bedside table, and lamp made up the rest of the furnishing. Her rucksack lay beside the bed.

Sandrine opened one wardrobe door, revealing a display of men's shirts and trousers impeccably pressed. "I've left most of my brother's clothes in the wardrobe. I just couldn't bear to part with them yet, but you'll find room for your few things."

"Yes, I have only two outfits. I kept meaning to buy more things from Christine's shop, but, well, the skirts all looked hideous."

"I know what you mean. I have my skirts tailored. You know, for the 'lady of the manor' look, but I rather like trousers when I'm home. Here…" She pulled a pale-blue shirt out from the row that hung in the wardrobe. "This one is smaller than the others. A favorite of his that he outgrew. You can have it if you like. I'm afraid his trousers won't fit, though."

"Oh, thank you. I'd love to have a new shirt. It looks beautifully tailored." She rubbed the material between her fingers. "Nice thick cotton, too."

"We'll make sure you have enough blankets, Sandrine said. "But with those windows, it's quite cold in winter. We have a coal-burning central-heating system in place, but it warms the house just enough to keep the pipes from freezing, not you. You might want to dress in the bathroom down the hall. It has a hot-water heater that warms the room. A little."

Antonia sat down on the bed. "I love it, and the lack of heat will be nothing new. I was cold all the time in the apartment. The only warmth was from the tiny electric burner I used to make soup."

"Soup, yes. That reminds me. Mathilde makes us all dinner every evening, out of whatever she can buy legally and illegally. If there's no sign of visitors, we all eat together in the kitchen—Gaston, Mathilde, myself, and the pilots. In fact, she should be preparing it now. Do you want to unpack or wash before you come down to eat?"

Antonia lifted her rucksack onto the bed. "I'd really like to look in on the wireless. Why did you decide on the attic? I wouldn't have minded having it here in my room."

"As I mentioned, we occasionally have visitors. In the unlikely chance anyone inspects the rooms on this floor, they will discover you, and I can invent an explanation for you but not for the wireless. No one's going to look in the attic unless they know what they're after."

"Very reasonable. Do you have a power source up there?"

"Yes, one outlet at each end. We can go up if you'd like, though everything will be covered with dust and God knows what else. I'm sure there's some wildlife up there too."

"I'll brace myself. Let's go have a look."

The attic at the top of a narrow staircase was all that Sandrine had warned about and more. Gaston had set the radio case on a small table against a pillar at one end of the attic. The single overhead light held an outlet where the power box could be connected, so that problem was solved. But the dust, grit, and other refuse that had filtered down from the roof were intolerable. Noises in the far recesses of the space attested to the presence of mice, and a brief flutter of wings suggested birds or bats. It was also freezing.

"Do you have any rags? I'll clean this spot up myself. Mathilde shouldn't have to help set up a radio room *and* cook for us."

"If you insist. You'll find any number of rags in here." Sandrine opened a leather trunk that held a bundle of cloth items. Closer inspection revealed it to contain mostly single socks and shirts that had been worn to rags, and torn cotton underclothes. "Mathilde throws away nothing. She's probably wise, but I think we can sacrifice a couple of my socks. I'll bring up a bucket of water and help you do the wipe-down. Then you can make this your radio room. I'm curious to see how that thing works, anyhow."

Antonia set the radio case on the floor and examined the electrical outlet. When Sandrine returned with a bucket of soapy water, they started work, swabbing down the table, a chair, and nearby walls. An hour's labor was sufficient to clear away a tolerable workspace, and Antonia set about connecting the receiver and transmitter and stringing out the antenna along the rafters.

She spoke over her shoulder. "While I was waiting for you today, I scribbled out a coded note to let London know what's happening. I'll transmit that right now, if that's all right."

"Of course it is. Could you also ask them to check if an Arthur Talbot has gone missing from the 52nd Squadron?"

"Certainly. I'll add that to the message."

She set on earphones and tuned to the correct frequency. When the antenna resonance light finally lit, she exhaled in relief. She was connected.

Sandrine patted her shoulder, sharing her small victory. "I'm quite in awe of your ability to do this. Talking to London, here in the dark. It's a bit of magic, isn't it?" The hand lingered, and in an impetuous moment, perhaps out of the overall excitement of the day, Antonia tilted her head and brushed her cheek against it.

Was that a mistake? Had she overstepped?

But Sandrine's only reaction was to say, "Please go ahead and send the message. I'd like to watch."

Antonia took a breath to still the trembling in her fingers and began. Short taps, long taps, the rhythm came utterly naturally to her. The part of her brain that "thought" in dots and dashes came into operation, and as she sent, the long and short clicks turned back into words in her mind.

Last delivery in good hands stp have relocated to more secure spot stp nick and david verified stp waiting for new ids stp expect to start south in next days stp will contact upon arrival stp please confirm arthur talbot 52 squadron end.

Then she signed off with her code name and flicked off the power switch.

"That's it? That's all? I somehow expected it to last longer."

Antonia chuckled. "It's not an oration, just an update. And I don't want to expose us to detection."

"Ah yes. There's always that, isn't there? Well, let's celebrate our first transmission and go downstairs for lunch."

Our transmission. Antonia liked that.

The pile of burning logs gave off more light than heat, but that didn't detract from its comfort. The dogs lay like eyebrows in front of it, warming their bellies. Curled up at one end of the sofa, with Sandrine at the other end, Antonia couldn't remember being so tranquil. All around them was fear, misery, and injustice, and she was pledged to oppose it. But for the moment, the struggle was suspended.

A twinge of guilt struck. "A pity Gaston and Mathilde can't enjoy the warmth too."

"Don't worry. They have a stove in the kitchen that warms them much better than our picturesque fire. There's a reason Mathilde's always cooking something. The fireplace, like the house in general, is mostly display."

"Well, I love it. I don't think I've felt so cozy since...oh, since I was a child in Brussels."

"You were raised in Brussels? That explains why your French is so good."

"No, not raised. Just lived there from eight to fourteen. My father was a physicist who took part in the first Solvay conference here. It was such a happy time. He was a big success, he and my mother were in love, and I was their pampered daughter. When I think of all the chocolate I stuffed in my face, I'm amazed I never got pudgy."

"Why did they leave?" Sandrine drew up her knees and looked suddenly like a schoolgirl on holiday with a chum.

"The war, of course, and the German occupation. We returned to England, where my mother died in the influenza epidemic in 1918. My father wanted me to be a physicist, but I didn't have his affection for cold calculations, so I studied nursing."

"What got you into the spying business?" Sandrine's green eyes seemed to reflect the fire.

"Dunkirk. I was injured when the hospital ship I was on was sunk. While I was recovering, the War Office invited me to serve in a way that was even more dangerous." She snickered. "Couldn't stay away, I guess."

"No husband or beau waiting for you at home?"

Antonia's heartbeat quickened. "No, not much time for romance. Not with all the schooling in telegraphy and parachuting and killing people. Leaves a girl tired out at the end of the day."

Sandrine smiled, warming her more than the fire.

"What about you?" she ventured.

Sandrine shrugged and stared into the flames as if composing an answer.

"I'm a widow, as you know." She glanced up at the photo on the mantelpiece.

"When was that?" The question might have been impertinent; Antonia wasn't sure.

"September, 1933."

"Eight years. You're still in mourning?" That was definitely impertinent.

"No, but romance seems irresponsible in wartime. Oh, one always meets interested men, though I suspect half the time it's the money and the house that attract them. But that fire has gone out in me."

"So there's also no 'gentleman' in your life."

"No. Not the way you mean it."

"Does it have more than one meaning?"

The sound of a car arriving before the house prevented her answer. Sandrine lunged from the sofa toward the door. "You'd better go upstairs."

They were both in the entry hall now, where Mathilde was at the front window. "It's him," she said over her shoulder.

Sandrine seized Antonia by the arm. "Go up to your room, please, as quietly as you can. Don't come down until Mathilde tells you it's all right. And hurry." She turned away and slipped back into the main hall.

Antonia obeyed, rushing toward the stairwell just as the heavy bronze knocker sounded on the front door of the château. Reaching the top of the staircase, she stopped and listened as Mathilde greeted the visitor.

"Good evening, Herr Baron. May I take your coat? Madame Toussaint is in the sitting room."

Baron? Baron who? She didn't dare linger on the landing, but crept silently back to her room. She perched on the bed, nervous and idle, then began to shiver from the cold. With the bed quilt draped over her shoulders she leaned against the wall, drawing up her knees. The house was curiously silent, and she heard nothing but the call of a crow outside her window. Then, still sitting, she fell asleep.

CHAPTER TWENTY-THREE

December 1942

Nick wiped up the last of his gravy with his bread and smiled toward Mathilde. The bandage over his shrapnel wound was reduced to a small patch now, and his handsome face was visible. "Please tell her how much I enjoyed the dinner, would you?" he said to Sandrine.

She translated the compliment, and Mathilde nodded her appreciation of it.

"You don't know any French at all?" she asked.

"I know some, ma'am," Ian announced. *"Parlay voo anglay, mad mohselle?"* His accent was atrocious.

Sandrine shook her head. "Oh, dear. Well, that won't do at all. Fortunately, we foresaw that problem and your identification papers will show that you're both from the Brussels Institute for the Deaf and that you can't speak."

"So the papers have finally come?" Nick asked. "Jolly good."

"Yes, they arrived at the café just a short while ago. Gaston, would you fetch them from the sitting-room desk?"

"You'll both have Belgian names, which you should learn, but be careful not to react if someone speaks to you. I'll do all the talking for you. You'll have to work on your demeanor too. You pilots have a way of walking, a bit self-important, with big strides like you're used to people getting out of your way. Practice walking with a slight slouch, like tired workers, slightly afraid of strangers."

Gaston returned with a gray cardboard envelope. "Thank you, Gaston. All right, you'll be Henri Wouters." She handed one set of papers to Nick. "And Ian, you're Bernard Maes. Check the year of your birth and learn it. We'll leave tomorrow evening, so you should pack your things carefully tonight. I don't want you to be carrying *anything* that marks you as foreign. No coins, foreign cigarettes, insignia rings. Check all your pockets for anything that doesn't belong to a deaf man from Brussels."

"And we have to watch out for anyone in uniform," Nick said.

"But how will we know who's who?" Ian asked.

"It doesn't make any difference. Belgian police, German gendarmes, French Milice, Spanish carabineros. Some are military and some civilian, but they're all police, and they're all dangerous. You need to be deaf and mute in front of all of them."

"What about our guns, ma'am?" Ian asked.

"I'll carry them. If I expect a confrontation that requires shooting, I'll give them back to you."

Nick frowned in consternation. "I don't like the idea of being unarmed. Why are you less likely to be searched than us?"

"Because I have special permission," she answered softly, ending the discussion. Antonia glanced over at Mathilde, who lowered her eyes.

"If you'll excuse me, I have work to do now." Sandrine seemed to lose interest in the conversation and stood up. "When you've finished your coffee, gentlemen, please return to your room downstairs and extinguish the lights. I'll see you tomorrow."

She turned away from the group and marched from the kitchen, leaving a vacuum of silence behind her.

While Gaston loaded the four rucksacks, two of them deliberately shabby, into the trunk of the Mercedes, the pilots appeared in their workers' clothing and climbed into the rear. Gaston was the driver, and Sandrine sat next to him in the front. Antonia squeezed herself in next to the two men in the rear. Their clothing was rancid with male sweat, and it was unpleasant to sit crammed together with them. After a moment's reflection, she realized that was probably the reason for issuing them soiled clothing. No one would want to have much to do with them and would let them pass in a crowd.

"Why are we leaving so late?" Ian asked. "There's got to be an earlier train to Paris."

Sandrine looked over her shoulder. "Yes, there is a direct connection, but it's too carefully patrolled. We'll travel to Mons and switch to a local train that's full of farmers and then cross the border by foot at Quiévrain."

Nick leaned back against the soft leather seat. "Nice car. Warm too. What a pity you can't drive us all the way in this."

"A pity, indeed. We're lucky to have it to get to the Gare de Midi. Otherwise you'd have to take several trams and pass dozens of police. Even if I had enough petrol, my permit extends only to Brussels."

They rode in near silence the rest of the way, with both Gaston and Sandrine watching the streets for checkpoints.

"Here we are," Gaston said, pulling up in front of the station. "Go with God," he added, making the sign of the cross on his head and shoulders.

Sandrine surveyed the street as Antonia and the pilots squeezed out of their cramped space and fetched their respective rucksacks from the trunk. Gaston drove away at normal speed, as if dropping passengers at the train station were an everyday duty.

The timing was perfect. With their prepurchased tickets, they boarded the train without incident, three minutes before departure time. To Antonia's relief, the only other passengers in the compartment were an elderly couple, people she would expect to have the least sympathy with the occupiers and the most willingness to ignore suspicious behavior.

The train ride from Brussels to Mons took less than three hours, but it seemed endless. Unable to talk, the two pilots fidgeted until the old man smiled and handed one of them his newspaper. Sandrine's expression hinted at reproach toward the pilots, then gratitude toward the old man. Ian smiled weakly and pretended to read.

The couple commented briefly on the weather, and Sandrine, the veteran, engaged them skillfully in small talk, carefully avoiding any compromising subject, but then she too fell silent. Finally they pulled into the station at Mons.

The connecting train arrived only moments later on the opposite track, and Antonia saw the wisdom of using a local train. The wooden seats were uncomfortable, farmers had crates of chickens at their feet, and children whined or sat sullen at their side, sucking their fingers.

The car was full of smoke from homemade ersatz-tobacco cigarettes. Border police would find the cars as disagreeable as she did and certainly wouldn't waste time investigating them. But scarcely had she become accustomed to the air and the jostling, when the train pulled into Quiévrain and they had to exit.

The entire passenger load of the train descended and lined up before the French customs station, staffed by both French agents and German gendarmes.

At the front of the group, Sandrine was stopped, and Antonia felt a rush of fear. She carried their guns. But Sandrine smiled affably and engaged the customs man, making direct eye contact and complimenting him on his efficiency.

He perused her identification papers, then passed her through without baggage inspection. Antonia came next, weaponless, but with out-of-season winter clothing and a very large envelope of money, which she couldn't explain. Her training kept her outwardly calm, indifferent, her glance brief and casual as she handed over her carefully forged papers. The officer frowned for a moment, and Antonia's heart raced, but the frown disappeared and he passed her through.

The two pilots were next. Ian had mastered the look of an innocent dullard, though Nick was still nervous. "What happened to your face?" the customs officer asked him. Nick gawked stupidly at him. "They're deaf," Sandrine said. She signaled to both men to empty their pockets and they obeyed, pulling out the lining. The customs officer winced at the contents, which were not quite clean, and waved them through.

The feeling of victory was short-lived, for they had to catch more trains and endure untold more scrutiny, and when they stepped off the last train, it was night. Sandrine collected them outside the station. "I hope you enjoyed all that sitting, because here's where we walk, and it's a long way. To start, we have to cross the Somme."

"Don't people build bridges for that?" Ian wisecracked.

Sandrine was not amused. "This close to the border, they'll all be patrolled. The only way to avoid them is to cross far away from any bridge."

"Sounds reasonable," Antonia said. "So what are we waiting for?"

"For him." Sandrine brushed past her toward a man she obviously recognized. He was stocky, dark skinned, with well-muscled forearms, like a man used to hard physical labor.

"Arnaud, good evening. I've got two pilots and a colleague tonight. How are the conditions?"

"Good, I think. No patrols. No rain. Should be all right." He nodded a perfunctory greeting at the newcomers and strode away. They hurried to catch up with him, and after an hour, they were beyond the light of the town. Arnaud withdrew a small torch from his pack, and they continued the march across field and through woodland.

For the next two hours they heard only the night sounds of the field and forest: soft rustling in the tops of the trees, the deep coo of an owl, a twittering that might have been bats, the clicking of crickets or frogs, and the constant snapping of twigs as they hiked off-path. If they hadn't been fleeing for their lives, it would have been a pleasure to hike through the winter forest.

Then she saw it, a dull glow in the distance where one shouldn't be. Arnaud saw it too and brought them to a halt. "Wait here," he whispered, and they all dropped down to a crouch. He forged ahead, soundlessly. In a few minutes he was back, obviously agitated. He crouched next to Sandrine and whispered.

She turned and translated to the pilots. "Campers with a bonfire. We can't get to the boat. We'll have to swim across. Fortunately, this time of year the current is slow."

"Um. I can't swim," Ian announced, glumly.

Sandrine translated to Arnaud, who raised a hand signaling he had a solution. He drew a coil of rope and tied one end of it to a sturdy tree close to the water's edge. After testing the knot, he bent over and drew off his trousers and rolled them up. "I'll tie the line when I get to the other side," he said to Sandrine. "When it goes taut, you'll know it's safe to come across."

Sandrine translated the instructions to the Brits, and they grunted reluctant agreement. "What about our packs?" Nick asked.

Glancing around at the underbrush, Sandrine said, "Raft. I'll go last, and the rest of you can pull it and me across." She explained the plan to the guide, and, without further discussion, he rolled his clothing up into a ball and shoved it into his pack. Holding one end of the rope, he plowed forward through the reeds, visible by the moonlight until he dropped into the black water and disappeared. Only the snaking of the rope showed he was swimming.

Sandrine was in charge again. "All right everyone. Get busy. We don't want to leave Arnaud shivering in his underwear too long."

All four of them set about gathering branches with a minimum of noise, and Nick, as it turned out, was adept at raft building, even by torchlight. With two deft cuts of the rope, he connected the branches in all the strategic places. The final product was primitive but seemingly adequate to support the weight of five backpacks.

"I'll be next man in, if nobody minds. I want to get this over with," Nick said, stripping as well. He crammed his clothes into his kit and a moment later was in the water, pulling himself along, and Ian stoically followed.

"You ready?" Sandrine asked. "If the boys can do it, the girls can too."

"Sure, as soon as we slide the raft into the water." The bulky apparatus with its several backpacks floated satisfactorily at the water's edge, and so Antonia stripped down to bra and pants. Already shivering, she forced her clothes into the last space in her rucksack. "Wish me luck," she whispered, and on a sudden whim, she leaned forward and pressed a brief kiss on Sandrine's lips, then slipped into the reeds.

The frigid water was a shock, as she feared, but the painful cold itself was an incentive to get across quickly, and after a dozen tugs on the overhead line, she was on the other side. Ian and Nick waded out to haul her up on the shore.

While she stood drenched and quaking, Arnaud reeled in the rope, bringing the raft and Sandrine to the shoreline. They must have made a ridiculous sight all hunched together in their underwear, Antonia thought, but she was far too cold to draw any humor from it.

Antonia hurriedly dressed, her teeth chattering, and though her trousers dampened quickly against her skin, they blocked the breeze and reduced the cold from intolerable to merely uncomfortable.

With their packs hoisted onto their backs, they trudged on, following Arnaud the last half kilometer to the farmhouse. After a brief introduction to the farmer and his wife, she went to the fireplace and stood as close as she dared, warming the damp front of her clothing. The feeling was exquisite.

The rest of the evening was a blur. Chill turned to warmth, hunger to satiety. Constant translation for the Brits made conversation awkward, so soon the only language was French. When dinner was over, Sandrine drew the farmer aside to make discreet payment for this and previous dinners. Then, after a few more courtesies and the use of the outhouse, he led the four of them to the barn, where blankets were already laid out. Sheer physical exhaustion and a full stomach were enough to bring immediate sleep, even on piles of prickly straw.

The respite was short, for the next morning, after a quick breakfast of bread and cheese, they were hustled into the farmer's coal-burning truck and chugging south to Paris.

When he deposited them at the outskirts and they began the hour-long march to Gare d'Austerlitz, Nick gazed around him. "Crikey. My first time in Paris, and I had to fight my way through the wilderness to get here. A pity we can't do any sightseeing."

"Not if you want to get back to England alive." Sandrine pointed with her head toward German soldiers at a café across the street.

The crowd inside the Gare d'Austerlitz gave them the illusion of safety, but the train to Bayonne wasn't at the scheduled track. "What's the problem?" Sandrine asked at the ticket window.

"I don't know, madam." He shrugged. "Watch the board. They'll post the track when the train comes in."

"Let's keep moving. We'll be less conspicuous," Sandrine suggested. They wove their way in and out of the clusters of people who were smoking, sitting on their luggage, waiting. They turned a corner and found themselves on the auxiliary tracks. Sandrine stopped abruptly.

"What are cattle cars doing here? They don't load livestock from this station."

"Nobody's permitted here," a voice behind them said. Alarmed, Antonia pivoted, her hand already reaching for her papers. But it was only a railroad man and not a Milice. "These tracks are closed," he said, and his somber tone told them something more than inconvenience was at stake.

"Sorry, we didn't know," Sandrine replied, and tugged Ian by the arm back in the direction they'd come. Antonia followed, glancing once behind her. The empty cattle cars seemed ominous, malevolent.

"What the hell was that all about?" Nick asked sotto voce, as they moved away.

"He didn't say," Sandrine said. "Just keep walking."

They strolled for the next twenty minutes, back and forth through the crowds, not speaking or making eye contact with other passengers.

Finally the announcement came—"Train to Bayonne on Track 5"—and they crowded in among hundreds of others. Good, Antonia thought. The more crowded the train, the harder it would be to patrol.

❖

BAYONNE. The station sign slid by the train window. They lifted their rucksacks from the floor of the packed corridor and shuffled behind the other passengers to the exit.

Ahead of them Germans manned the border station. Where were the French?

"It's all right," Sandrine murmured reassuringly. "Philippe warned me this might happen. We'll do the same thing he did."

She led the others away from the line. "Sophie, you go first. Down that corridor leading to the toilets. At the end is a door to the street. If all goes well, Fernand will have already been here to unlock it and will be waiting just across the street. He's tall, with a moustache."

And if he's not there? Antonia refrained from asking. She followed the directions toward the tiny toilet, the odor of which discouraged use. At the end of the corridor, behind a pile of crates, was the door, and she tried the handle. It was unlocked so she edged the crates away from the door and slipped through, closing it quietly behind her.

A tall, swarthy man waited across the street, reading a newspaper. As she approached, he looked up and revealed, to her relief, a moustache.

"Fernand?"

"Yes," he answered, folding the paper.

"The others are directly behind me, I hope," she added. But he was already glancing past her, and his smile told her the next person was out.

When Sandrine emerged last, he shook hands with everyone. "Just let me lock up again so the stationmaster doesn't suspect anything. My truck's over there."

He pointed toward a ramshackle farm vehicle with a closed two-person cabin and an open wagon in the rear. It carried the usual piles of hay to conceal them. When would the Gestapo finally catch on that hay was one of their enemy's best weapons?

❖

The truck halted with a slight shudder. At the sound of Sandrine's voice, Antonia threw back the cover of hay and surveyed the new environment. Behind them was a stand of pine trees and, in front of them, open fields and a large stone house. Though it had a yard with chickens, it was more villa than farmhouse, and Antonia recalled Sandrine telling her that Fernand earned a living as an interpreter at the German headquarters in Anglet. An excellent cover for a smuggler of men.

She climbed out and caught up with Sandrine at the door, where a slight, round-faced woman awaited them.

"Come on in, all of you," the woman said in French. I know you're hungry so dinner's ready."

Nick hadn't understood, but as he stepped in the entryway, he exclaimed, "Crikey. I smell beef! Real beef." He stared up into the air as if he could see the clouds of aroma.

"Even I understood that." The woman laughed, glancing at Sandrine. "Courtesy of the local black market."

"Ah, so you've been up to your old tricks then. Business must be good." Sandrine slipped off her rucksack and let it drop to the floor.

"This week, yes. You keep supplying me with funds, and I'll keep finding the smugglers."

"Don't worry, Elvire," Sandrine said. "We've come bearing cash."

"Good to know. Now put your things in the living room, and go wash up. Then the lads can help me set the table. We want to get you all filled up for your big climb."

Dinner-table conversation had been cheerful, as between old friends, and even though the airmen scarcely took part, they laughed when the others laughed, and Sandrine, with her dark-blond hair tied up in a bandanna, looked radiant. Antonia tried not to glance too often at her.

Afterward, Fernand escorted the men to the room that had belonged to the couple's children. Sandrine and Antonia had the privilege of the living room, where a fire had been set.

"We've put the sofa cushions on the floor along with some blankets," Elvire explained. "You'll have to sleep like Persians, but at least you won't get cold." She added another log and wiped her hands on her apron.

"Good night, my dears." With quick cheek kisses to both of them, she padded off in thick slippers to her bedroom.

Sandrine dropped down onto one of the cushions and unlaced her shoes. She drew them off with a sigh of pleasure. "Oh, that feels good."

"I've been waiting all evening to do that." Antonia pulled her heavy boots off as well and rubbed her toes. "The fire's nice too," she added, suddenly shy. It would be the first time she would sleep near a woman since Dora. She blushed at the comparison. "They're lovely people, Fernand and Elvire. Have you always stopped here?"

"Yes, always. Andrée met them back when she formed the line. They put their lives at risk each time, and the only money they ask for is to cover the black-market food. They think it's important for everyone to get a big healthy meal before crossing the mountains."

"It's really going to be that bad?"

"I'm afraid so. You'll be hiking for twenty-four hours—cold, exhausted, and footsore. Patrols comb both sides of the mountain, and you might have to run for your life—if not from the French Milice, then from the Spanish carabineros. Police are police, and they have orders to stop you."

"But other than that, it'll be fun, eh?"

"Yes, heaps of fun. Anyhow, that part of the route isn't fixed. A Basque guide named Florentino will pick us up tomorrow. He knows the mountains better than just about everyone."

"Have you ever lost anyone?"

"Yes." Sandrine let the answer sink in. "But there's no point in talking about it. Go to sleep now." She pulled Antonia's blanket up over her shoulder with parental concern.

Antonia gazed up at the half-lit face, warmly delineated by the firelight on one side and obscure on the other. "I haven't had anyone tuck me in for decades. Do you also tell stories?"

Sandrine lay on her side, facing her. "*You* should be telling the stories. You're the one who jumped back into Belgium. That took courage."

"Less courage than what you do, over and over again. You seem utterly fearless."

"I do my best." She brushed her fingertips along Antonia's cheek.

Her entire body heated at the touch. Surely it was an invitation. She rose on one elbow, gathering courage for the kiss. Any kind of kiss.

"Good night, dear," Sandrine said suddenly, and turned away from her.

Antonia lay back down again, her mind reeling. What had just happened? Had she misinterpreted a simple gesture? The uncertainty was excruciating. She shrank down closer to the fire at her feet, pulled the blanket halfway over her head, and tried to think of nothing.

It was no good. She was too much aware of Sandrine, lying next to her. The drowsiness she'd felt after dinner had vanished, and now she lay with her head buzzing. Sandrine's short breaths made it clear she didn't sleep either. It felt like they were two filaments in a lightbulb, with an electric current vibrating between them.

"Sandrine, I'm cold. Really. Can I lie against you to get warm?" *God, that sounded pathetic.*

"Yes, I'm cold too. But we have to go to sleep, all right?"

Antonia slid up against the warm back and shuddered with pleasure at the touch. She dared not curl her arm around Sandrine's waist, so she folded it up against her own chest.

"Is that better?" Sandrine's voice was soft.

"Yes, much better."

It *was* better. Arousal came and went, replaced by an enormous comfort, something short of romance but beyond friendship. In the dead of winter and in war, and for that night, it seemed enough.

Antonia awoke alone, wrapped in both blankets. Gradually her sleep-befuddled mind made sense of the sounds of Sandrine and Elvire in the kitchen and of the smell of cooked beans. She drew on her shoes and laced them, hearing the two pilots also emerge from their room. Embarrassed to be the last one, she struggled to her feet and folded the blankets. She longed for a bath, but a quick wash of her face in the basin next to the WC would have to do.

The others were already seated at the table scooping eggs and beans onto their plates. In spite of the ample dinner the night before, the aviators were ravenous, finishing their meals while Antonia had just begun.

Sandrine spoke little and, after eating, busied herself with inspecting her rucksack.

"I don't suppose there's any point in my carrying these any more." She held up one of the .38 Enfields before handing them back to their owners. "Though I can't imagine their doing much good if we meet a patrol with rifles."

The sound of someone arriving by bicycle outside ended the conversation, and a few moments later Florentino stepped into the kitchen.

He was huge. Antonia recalled that Basques were supposed to be short, but this one was certainly not. He looked like he could carry a man across his broad shoulders. His features were rugged but not brutish. He spoke only Basque, which worried Antonia slightly, though less than the fact that he smelled faintly of alcohol.

He carried four walking sticks and presented them without commentary to each of them. Was it a way to warn them of the difficulties ahead?

After a round of embraces, good wishes, and pats on the back, they set off southwestward. The sky was clear, the winter air was bracing, and Antonia felt travel-hardened. She no longer had the child-voice in her head that kept asking how much longer it would take. She simply hiked, stoically, one step after the other, as if the walking itself were their entire purpose in spite of the dull ache in her hips and thighs.

Scarcely had they started out when they turned off the road and began to follow a narrow shepherd's path, where her constant tripping over rocks and roots redirected her pain to her ankles and feet. She began to see the wisdom in Florentino's occasional nipping from a small bottle of spirits.

He allowed them to stop every two hours, but the ten-minute respite was almost more cruel than kind. Then, six hours into the hike, he called a halt for lunch, and Antonia dropped down where she stood. Nick and Ian stretched out flat on the ground, and Sandrine rubbed her calf muscles. Only Florentino, whose large paws dwarfed the bread in his hand, seemed indifferent.

Half an hour for bread, cheese, and water, and they started again, with Antonia's every muscle screaming protest. And now it had begun to snow.

Soon it began to fall in thick flakes. A small part of her mind took pleasure at the beauty of snowfall on the tree-studded hills, but keeping an eye on the man in front of her and watching the slippery ground occupied the rest of it. She stumbled repeatedly, each mishap sending a bright wave of pain up her leg.

When night fell, she felt as if she were wandering in another world—cold, damp, slippery, and infernal. Finally Florentino stopped, and behind him, the others bumped against each other.

She puzzled as Florentino knelt before a double tree trunk with a circle of rocks at its base, then snorted quietly in amusement when he uncovered a pair of unworn espadrilles and another bottle of cognac. "The man knows what's important, doesn't he?" she said to Sandrine.

"Amazing, isn't it? It doesn't seem to affect his ability to guide us, does it?"

"That remains to be seen. For all we know, we might be somewhere in Switzerland."

Florentino got to his feet, stared up through the snow, and frowned. "Cold," he said, in one of his few words of French, and unstoppered the new bottle. Yes, the wind was obviously bringing a new drop in temperature. Then, to her surprise, he offered the cognac to her.

She hesitated only a moment, then gratefully accepted it, tipped it back, and let the scorching liquid burn its way down her throat. She wheezed for a moment, then felt the pleasant warmth flow into her chest. She passed the bottle to Sandrine, who repeated the gesture and handed it on to the men.

It was a good move, Antonia decided. Though the whisky probably had no actual beneficial effect, the act of sharing gave them all a boost of courage to get over the mountain.

Trudging forward, she sank into her own thoughts, and the events leading up to her plight passed through her mind's eye. Dunkirk, the hospital at Orpington, her training at Beaulieu, the dreary room in the Rue Marché au Charbon, the sobbing Rywka surrendering her child, the fireplace at the Château Malou. Where would she be in a year?

"I know where we are now," Sandrine announced, as if in answer. "Just a few kilometers from Spain."

Spain, Antonia thought. What a beautiful word.

❖

Soon even Florentino had a lighter, quicker step, and when he passed around the bottle with the last few drops of his cognac, she knew that the end of his "fuel" meant the end of the trip.

And finally, when they forced their aching legs over one more hill and looked down, there it was, the third of their refuges, in the Promised Land. This one was the most ramshackle of all, a stone farmhouse with a barn that looked like it had stood there for centuries. The smoke that rose from the chimney was the sweetest sight Antonia could imagine, signaling life and warmth against the hard, cold landscape.

One hearty rap on the farmhouse door and it opened immediately to a swarthy, bearded man and a rush of warm fragrant air. "Jaime!" Florentino greeted him enthusiastically.

"Florentino, amigo!" Jaime exclaimed, clapping him on the shoulder, then stepped aside to admit them. The door opened to a short corridor, and Antonia inhaled the smell of wood smoke, onions frying in a pan, and, curiously, cinnamon.

A robust woman emerged from the kitchen room, said something to her husband, then pointed to their shoes. Antonia grasped that they should remove them and obliged happily, as did the others, and they all lined up their footwear along the corridor wall.

Colombina, that seemed to be her name, directed them into the kitchen, where Jaime seated them around a long wooden table, speaking in a stream of Spanish that only his wife understood. Sustaining her side of the conversation, she laid out tortillas and beans and an omelet filled with olives. Antonia waited for their hostess to sit down before eating, but Colombina still bustled about the kitchen. Finally she returned to the table with a pitcher of hot wine and a single candle, which she set down at the center.

"Feliz Navidad," she said, beaming.

"Christmas? It's Christmas?" Ian expressed Antonia's amazement as well as his own. They'd been on the road so long, she'd forgotten the calendar.

"Si, Si. Creeseemas." Colombina parroted him playfully and poured out the steaming liquid into seven cups.

"Feliz Navidad," they all said as a toast, and Antonia took the first swallow of the warm, celebratory wine. It went down more smoothly than Florentino's cognac had but filled her with the same euphoria. She glanced over at Sandrine, who smiled back, and she couldn't remember a more joyous Christmas dinner since childhood.

The simple fare became a feast, though lack of a common language among Spaniards, a Basque, a Belgian, and the three English inhibited conversation beyond the occasional exclamation of *"magnifico"* or *"delicioso."*

Afterward, they moved into a wide living room for another serving of hot sweet wine. They soon found other forms of communication— back-slapping, arm-squeezing, the chanting of "Jingle Bells" in three languages, and a sudden extemporaneous leaping dance by Jaime. Not to be outdone, his face ruddy from the alcohol, Ian attempted a jig to a tune he sang himself.

"Crikey, I didn't know ya had it in ya." Nick laughed.

"That's going to cost me, tomorrow," Ian answered, falling back next to him on the sofa.

Colombina looked at her watch and wagged a finger at the men, and it was clear the celebration was over. Jaime signaled them all to retrieve their boots and follow him outside.

The walk across the courtyard was frigid, and by comparison, the barn, warmed by the presence of two cows and a donkey, was welcoming. So also were the rough horse blankets that Jaime issued each of them.

Experienced now in camping etiquette, the three men broke off toward one side of the barn, leaving Antonia and Sandrine on the other. Having already stood before the men in her underwear, Antonia was little concerned with modesty, but she was grateful to have some distance from their snoring. She dropped down onto her blanket and lay back, light-headed.

"Christmas in a stable, how wonderful." She chortled. "All that's lacking is the baby."

Sandrine slid off her boots and lowered herself cautiously onto the straw, obviously attentive to sore muscles. *"Ufff.* I'm five seconds away from sleep. I'll wash tomorrow." Then she fell back onto her blanket and closed her eyes.

Antonia weighed the benefits of washing in icy water and found them wanting, and she focused instead on finding a comfortable sleeping position. Exhaustion, a full stomach, and hot, spiced wine were together the perfect soporific.

Did she dream a noise? In her sleep she seemed to hear the cry of an infant and some woman's voice murmuring comfort. She reached out her dream hand to caress its tiny head and grasped a wad of straw. She woke suddenly, her eyes focusing first on the empty space where Sandrine had slept and then on the open barn door.

Gathering her blanket around her shoulders, she crept outside. Sandrine leaned on the edge of the water trough huddled in her own blanket, gazing up at the midnight sky. Silently, Antonia went to join her and they sat together, their breaths giving off little clouds of steam.

She studied the clear sky. "Be nice to see a shooting star, wouldn't it? For good luck."

"You mean a meteorite," Sandrine replied dryly.

"Yes, of course a meteorite. But we can also take it as a sign that everything's going to be all right. For gosh sake, it's Christmas night. Have a little poetry in your soul."

Sandrine bumped shoulders with her. "You're right. It's a beautiful night. I can see a little magic in it. Keep an eye out for fancy men on camels. They might have gifts."

"Yes, I could use a gift. Gold would be good. Not sure about the frankincense and myrrh."

Sandrine shifted sideways to look directly at her, suddenly serious. "I don't need any gifts tonight, Sophie. Arriving here safe and with you is gift enough."

"Me?" Antonia's face warmed at the declaration of...of what? She wasn't sure, but she wanted to give something in return. "Yes, I feel the same. It's the best Christmas I can imagine." Then, impulsively, she reached for Sandrine's hand and brought it to her lips.

"My real name is Antonia. I want you to know."

"Antonia. It's a beautiful name. Thank you for that trust. I'll try to live up to it." Sandrine caressed her cheek, then suddenly leaned across her and pressed warm lips on her mouth. The kiss lasted scarcely more than a second, but it wasn't a friendship kiss. It had crossed a line toward...whatever the next thing was. It stood out from the rest of the evening like the ringing of a bell, and the silence after it was full and rich. Green eyes held her glance for just a moment.

"Merry Christmas, Antonia," Sandrine murmured, then stood up and marched back into the barn, her horse blanket trailing behind her like a robe.

❖

As always, Antonia was the last to wake. Sandrine and the three men were already up and about, and she hastened to wash at the trough and join them in the kitchen. A sense of cheer was in the air, a nervous anticipation of the end of the journey planned for that day.

Sandrine settled financial obligations to the hosts and to the departing Florentino, and after a bracing coffee and a thick slice of bread, the four of them set out alone.

Two hours brought them to a slope dotted with brush and a few low trees. They descended, zigzagging behind the cover of brush whenever possible until halfway down, when Sandrine drew a pair of field glasses from her pack and scanned the terrain.

With naked eyes, Antonia could see a few farmhouses spotting the landscape. In the far distance, a church spire marked a town. "San Sebastian," Sandrine announced, "the town before Bilbao." Nothing seemed to be moving, but on the road winding toward the base of the hill, a single stationary object stood on the side of the road.

"Ah, good. That must be them," Sandrine said.

"Them? Who?" Antonia took the binoculars from her hand and peered through them.

"From the British Consulate. I called them from the farmhouse and asked them if they could meet us closer—as a special favor today."

"You're sure it's them?" Antonia still squinted through the glasses.

"Yes, I'm sure. Can you see the tiny blue spot on the fender? That's the Union Jack. They agreed to meet us at the bridge on the other side of the gully."

"Well, I'm off, then." Nick got to his feet and began a headlong rush down the slope. Ian took off after him, ignoring Sandrine's calls to stay under cover.

"Damned fools," she muttered. "They're not out of danger yet."

The two men had made it to the bridge when a shot rang out and they dropped to the ground, taking cover in the gully.

Still high on the slope next to Sandrine, Antonia could now see the military vehicle that had been concealed behind a rocky formation. Spanish carabineros, who were only too happy to assist in the roundup of escapees and deposit them in their own concentration camps. Two of them leapt from the vehicle with rifles and fired into the gully.

Presumably tempted by the proximity of the rescue car, Ian broke cover and sprinted toward it while bullets pinged off the stones on both sides of him. The carabineros seemed extraordinarily bad shots. Finally the car door opened and hands reached out to pull him inside.

Emboldened, Nick tried to follow, springing from stone to bush to hillock and then across the gully. Little puffs of dust erupted on both sides of him. Just as he scrambled out of the gully, a bullet struck him in the leg, and he tumbled backward scarcely three meters from the car.

"Damn!" Sandrine swore. "He's so close. Why doesn't someone come and help him? I bet if we draw their fire…" She took off in a running crouch toward the bridge. With grave misgivings as to the wisdom of "drawing fire," Antonia hesitated, then followed.

There was a long silence. Sandrine had taken cover and was momentarily out of sight, but the carabineros too had moved and were invisible again. Until they fired, it was impossible to locate their position. Antonia threw herself on the ground, waiting for a sound or signal from anywhere. It seemed a stalemate, both ridiculous and terrifying.

Suddenly something sharp pressed into her back. A bayonet blade kept her in place, while a booted foot pinned her gun hand in the dirt. A dark and hairy hand crossed her limited field of vision and snatched the pistol away. She was helpless.

Fury and sorrow at once rushed through her mind, that she'd let down her guard and was going to be killed at the very end of the long trek. All their labor had been in vain.

The blade rose from between her shoulders, and she twisted over onto her back to look at her assailant. He was almost comical, a caricature of the Spaniard. Fair skinned, but with a drooping moustache and a leer.

He glanced at both of his hands, seemed to decide that two guns were more than he needed, and tossed his rifle behind him well beyond her reach. Then, straddling her, he knelt down and pointed his pistol at her face. His breath was sour with both tobacco and alcohol, and his wide grin revealed mottled teeth.

Her hands open helplessly by her shoulders, she tried to recall the self-defense tricks she'd learned in training, but her own gun was aimed at her head, rendering them all useless. He seemed in no hurry, and the fly buzzing around his head seemed to underline the vast stretch of time in which he decided what to do with her.

Then, a sudden twist of his mouth suggested he'd decided to be done with it, and he pressed the nozzle of his pistol under her chin.

The fly returned, landing on his face, and he twitched sideways, his gun hand moving slightly away from her throat. She seized the moment and threw out her right hand, knocking the gun muzzle to the left, but the shock of her blow caused him to pull the trigger. The gunshot so close to her ear deafened her, but immediately with the sound came a horrendous jolt of pain as a bullet tore through her left hand.

Drunk as he was, the gunshot also seemed to shock him, and he swayed, apparently befuddled, for a moment, until another gunshot rang out. She flinched, waiting for another jolt of pain to erupt somewhere, but nothing happened.

Instead, his face relaxed and he toppled sideways onto the ground.

She struggled to sit up, pressing her profusely bleeding left hand against her chest, and a figure rose over the body of the carabinero.

"Sandrine! What a relief! Where's the other guy?"

Sandrine knelt down next to her. "My God, you're covered with blood. Where did he shoot you?" She cradled Antonia in her arms.

"It's my hand. Where's the other Spaniard!?" she repeated.

"I don't know. I saw him run toward the car trying to shoot Nick, but he was too drunk. Nick made it into the car and they took off. Then I ran back here. Just in time, obviously."

She ripped the blue bandana from her head and wrapped it tightly around the bleeding hand, tying it at the wrist. Renewed gunfire urged them into motion. "Can you walk? I don't want a gun battle with number-two man."

Antonia grunted. "Yes, just help me up."

Standing behind her, Sandrine gripped her under her arms and hauled her to her feet. Antonia tottered for a moment, a rush of pain scalding her hand.

Sandrine snatched up the pistol from the dead carabinero's hand and tucked it into her belt. Slinging the Spanish rifle over her shoulder, she slipped an arm around Antonia's back. "Come on. Think about God, England, and Saint George." She pulled her forward and they began an awkward jog back toward safety.

Gunshots continued to ring out, but with no signs of anything being hit, and the sounds became ever more distant.

When they were once again among the trees, with only silence below them, they halted and Sandrine rummaged through her kit.

Antonia grunted. "I'm pretty sure the slug went through my hand, but we should try to clean it. I have a little sulfa powder with the bandages in my pack. Ex-nurse, you know."

"Good. We'll fix you up and take you back to the farm." Sandrine swabbed down the oozing palm and pressed gently, until Antonia cried out. "Aieeee! Broken bone, broken bone!"

"Yeah, it looks like it, but you're also damned lucky. You've got a big artery in the hand that goes down and curves back, and the bullet just missed it. So you won't bleed to death while we hike." Sandrine wrapped a long strip of sterile bandage around the hand, tying it in a knot at the uninjured thumb.

Antonia gritted her teeth against the pain, which now pulsed as far as her elbow. "*Ooof.* Let's get going before I start to cry."

Sandrine helped her to her feet again. "Cry all you want, dear. I'll never tell a soul. After you've had a little rest at Anglet, we'll return to Brussels. Now that our 'parcels' are delivered, we can train the rest of the way home." Sandrine led her back up into the foothills of the Pyrenees.

"It's just that it's still Christmas day." Antonia couldn't stop whining. "Where are the goddamn kings? There are supposed to be kings."

CHAPTER TWENTY-FOUR

Brussels, December 31, 1942

Antonia checked her watch on her still heavily bandaged wrist. Midnight. The Gestapo would be celebrating New Year's Eve, just like everyone else, and no one would bother to send a direction-finder vehicle through the Malou woods. The perfect time to transmit.

She climbed the stairs to the new attic "radio room" that Mathilde and Gaston had created during her long hike into Spain. Gaston had built a false wall at one end of the attic with an entryway made of a panel that looked just like the rest of the wall. Mathilde had wiped down the oppressive dust and added cushions to make the cubicle comfortable.

Laborious and clumsy as it had been using her "wrong" right hand, she'd already apprised London of the successful mission to Spain, and now she merely waited for instructions for the next one. What pilots had been lost in the interim, and where had they gone down? She set her headphones on.

Sandrine startled her as she stepped inside the cubicle holding two glasses of champagne. "Happy New Year, Antonia. Let's hope 1943 sees the end of the war."

"Happy New Year to you." They tapped glasses and Antonia drank, letting her glance linger for a moment on the shine of Sandrine's hair under the overhead lamp. She averted her eyes, annoyed at herself for her constant craving. Nothing had come of the Christmas kiss, and she sensed no sign of one being offered for New Year's. She had already fully exploited her crippled hand for tenderness and sympathy.

"Any messages come in yet?"

"No. I was just tuning in." She looked at her watch again. "They should be sending just about now." The first ping sounded. "Yes, it's starting."

She scribbled rapidly as the dots and dashes poured through, nodding mechanically along with the rhythm. Then the transmission ended. She bent over the notepad of scrawl from her right hand and, comparing the letters with her poem code chart, began to decipher the gibberish into English words.

"The first part of the message is for you, it seems." She read out loud from the slip of paper.

No Arthur Talbot in RAF stop. Only Reginald Talbot stop. Squadron 52 is maintenance squadron in Iraq stop. No engagement in European theater.

Sandrine threw her head back. "Oh, thank God."

"Why thank God?"

"Because I killed him. I can't tell you how much that's been on my conscience."

"Oh. But…he doesn't exist."

"I mean I executed a Gestapo agent who called himself Arthur Talbot. He gave his squadron as the 52nd and it's tormented me for weeks. The bastard even carried a picture of a woman and baby. I wonder who they were."

Antonia didn't reply and mulled over the fact that Sandrine had killed at least two men point-blank. Would she herself have the courage to do so?

"Listen, I've been thinking." Sandrine broke into her thoughts. "We need another radio operator."

"What? You want to replace me? Just because of my hand?"

"No, of course not. But what would have happened if we'd been caught in Spain? Who would have notified London? No, we need a backup or an assistant who can send messages when you can't. I think you should train one of us in Morse, on your wireless."

"Where will I find the time?"

"You've got nothing *but* time. I'm going to be running around with Christine setting up new safe houses and collecting the new pilots. You've got to interrogate them, but other than that, you have no duties."

"I suppose you have a point." Antonia dropped her headphones onto her neck, grasping the earpieces as if asserting ownership. "Who do you have in mind? Philippe?"

Sandrine shook her head. "I don't think so. He has his farm to run, and he doesn't know English."

"What about Francis or Laura?"

"They have to be at the café all the time. They'd be missed if they came out here for training. And we certainly can't move the wireless back there."

"So who's left that we trust? And knows English?"

"Fortunately, I gave the problem a lot of thought, and I've already found someone perfect for the job. Celine Collin. She's from the Ardenne but seems to be staying permanently in Brussels now. She wants to be involved."

"Celine? Laura's sister? She's awfully young. And will she even want to do it?"

Sandrine smiled, with only the faintest hint of smugness.

"She's already agreed. Do you want to talk to her? She's in the kitchen with Mathilde."

"You scoundrel. You had this whole conversation planned! What if I'd said no?"

"I knew you wouldn't." Sandrine leaned in and pecked her on the cheek before heading toward the stairs.

Ah, so that was going to be the New Year's kiss.

Celine Collin's long, narrow face was pretty in an ordinary way, and her slight overbite and taciturn manner did little to dispel the impression of simplicity. But when she spoke about strategies to defeat the Germans, her close-set eyes blazed and a bright, analytical mind revealed itself.

Antonia pulled up a stool next to her in the château kitchen, while behind them, Mathilde chopped vegetables for dinner.

"Why did you come back to Brussels? You're certainly much safer with your family in the Ardenne."

"I was working sometimes as a courier for the evaders hiding in the hills near my village, but those are mostly guys who ran away from the forced-labor roundups. Not much going on there. When Laura told me about the Comet Line, that sounded more important. Since she's my sister, it was easy to get a permit to change residence to Brussels."

Antonia studied the pale face, with its superficial mask of innocence and the hint of a hardened veteran behind it. "Where did you learn English?"

"At school before the war. I speak Flemish too, even a little German. When the Nazis came, I started listening to the BBC, first to Radio Londres in French and then to the English broadcasts too. I learned a lot more that way."

"Listening to the BBC is illegal. You should be careful." As soon as she'd made the remark, she realized how condescending it was.

Celine snorted. "I think everyone in my town listens to the BBC. In the Ardenne the Nazis don't check so carefully."

"In any case, it's not so important to know perfect English to send messages. You just have to make short sentences and put them into our code and then into Morse. The briefer the better."

"Yes, I know that."

Antonia was beginning to appreciate the quality of mind she was dealing with. "All right, then. We'll give you a try. But first, you'll have to learn the alphabet in Morse. That shouldn't be so difficult."

"It's not. I've already started, and I know them up to the letter N. A is *dot dash*. B is *dash dot dot dot*. C is *dash dot dash dot*. E is—"

"Stop, please. I believe you. But we don't say 'dot' and 'dash.' We call the sounds *dah* and *di*, with the *di* at the end of a letter called *dit*. So C, for example, is *dah di dah dit*. And I can teach you some good memory tricks. For example, you can associate the letter V, as in victory, with the opening notes of Beethoven's *Fifth Symphony*, that is, *di-di-di-dah*. You can even use that letter in isolation for 'victory' so you don't have to spell out the whole word."

"Oh, I like that." Celine tapped it out a few times on the table.

"Excellent. So here's your assignment for now. First, finish learning the alphabet. Practice it day and night, and when you've got it down, start spelling out names and words. I want you to think in Morse and dream in Morse. Then I want you to come back in five days' time with a message that you can give me in Morse. One long sentence will do, anything you want."

"I can do it, I'm sure."

"I want you to say it to me without stopping, using only *dah* and *di* and *dit*. If you get everything right, we'll move on to the next stage, where you 'send' it to me on the handset. That way I can see how steady your hand is."

"You're going to trust me with the radio?"

"Disconnected, of course. But that's only half the job. You have to be able to put the message into our own code system, and that will take a little longer to teach you."

"I'll learn it. You'll see. I really want to do this." The simple, small-town face took on an intensity that rendered her beautiful, and Antonia felt a sudden affection for her. She was going to break hearts with that passion one day.

Antonia accompanied Celine upstairs and to the door of the château, where she'd parked her bicycle. "Five days, the whole alphabet."

Celine threw a leg over her bicycle, and leaned sideways to kiss Antonia quickly on the cheek. *"Di di di dah,"* she called out as she rode off.

Waving at the departing figure, Antonia smiled at the word *Victory*, Celine's first communication in Morse.

The February afternoon after her third lesson was brisk, and as Celine pedaled away bundled in headscarf and mittens, Suzi galloping after her, Gaston was collecting firewood in a wheelbarrow. She waved to him and sped past the carriage house onto the road back to Brussels center.

Satisfied also with the improvement in her own wounded hand, which now could send almost normally, Antonia returned to the sitting room where Sandrine had a fire going.

Sandrine glanced up from her book, pedagogic in her reading glasses. "How's she doing?" Antonia stood with her back to the fire, enjoying the spread of heat up her legs. It was so peaceful, so domestic, both of them there together by the fire, Mathilde downstairs preparing dinner, Gaston bringing in wood, and their "little sister" riding off on her bicycle.

"She's very talented. She'll be sending in no time. Then you won't need me any longer. Promise me you won't throw me out?"

Sandrine laughed, the firelight twinkling in her spectacles. "I'll never throw you out. You're much too valuable to me."

"Valuable. Really?" She fished for some sort of declaration.

Before Sandrine could answer, the sound of a car arriving in front of the château drew their attention. A moment later, Gaston stuck his head through the doorway without knocking.

"Excuse me, madam. It's Monsieur le Baron. Perhaps Madame Forrester should…"

Sandrine jumped up from the sofa. "Yes. Antonia, I'm sorry. You have to go upstairs, right away. Stay in your room until Mathilde calls you, please."

Antonia obeyed, rushing into the stairwell.

She slipped into her room and sat on the edge of her bed, then paced, then sat down again. Who was the visitor? Monsieur le Baron, Mathilde had said. How many barons were there in Brussels? She knew of only one.

The realization caused many pieces to fall into place. Not only was the visitor not supposed to see her, the unexplained stranger in the house, but she herself was not supposed to see him, the man who dispensed favors. Like an unrequisitioned car and a petrol ration.

The vague suspicion that she'd harbored but been able to thrust to the back of her mind now emerged as ugly certainty, and it sickened her.

Shivering, she drew the quilt from the bed and wrapped it around her shoulders. A moment later she heard a soft tap on the door. It creaked open and Mathilde stepped halfway in.

"Is he gone?" she asked with childish hopefulness.

"He usually stays for an hour or two." Mathilde stared at the floor and her glance said everything. Then, with cool objectivity, she said, "Dinner will be delayed."

"I see. All right. Thank you, Mathilde." She retreated to the bed, cocooned in her quilt, and laid her head on the pillow. Her mind roiled with impotent disgust. In the cold silence of the room, she fell asleep again and dreamt of standing in the snow before a cozy cottage. Through the open door she could see a fire burning, and she sensed Sandrine waiting someplace within. But when she stepped through the doorway toward the hearth, she found herself surrounded by wounded soldiers on a burning deck. She turned to flee and the floor gave way. Flailing as the flames caught her hair, she sank into the icy water.

❖

The dinner conversation was minimal and curt. Though the early evening visit of the governor general hung in the air like a bad odor, no one spoke of it. Antonia herself could scarcely order her thoughts. Politically, she understood that it gained them all protection, but the idea of what had happened, and would happen again, repelled her.

Sandrine herself was taciturn, but the faint blush on her face all evening suggested she knew she was tainted, and Antonia felt guilty for reproaching her, even if only in her own mind.

Finally Sandrine broke the silence. "Christine has four men ready for a trip down the line. Two of them are the pilots you interrogated. She also has a friend who wants to join the Free Belgian army in England and an ex-city councilman who's wanted by the Gestapo. I'll be taking them down along with Philippe. It's time for him to learn the line so I don't always have to be the one. It's going to be harder with four 'passengers,' especially when one of them is elderly, but that's what we've got this time."

"Uh-huh," Antonia mumbled, chewing.

An uncomfortable silence followed, and Sandrine spoke again. "To make matters worse, Florentino is wearing out. We can't keep sending him over week after week. We need another guide, a second man who can alternate with him."

Antonia nodded indifferent agreement.

"And we'll need more funds soon too. Another drop from London." Sandrine looked directly at her. "Can you arrange that for next week?"

"Yes, of course," Antonia replied woodenly. "I'll ask for it in my next transmission."

"I should be back in about a week, and the money will be gone then. It would be most welcome if new funds were waiting."

"Yes, it would." Antonia finished her meal without further remark and excused herself from the table. Once back in her room she stared glumly out the window again. Night had fallen completely, and no moonlight shone through the leaden night sky. The pond was a wide black spot, icy and grim, a metaphor for what was inside her.

Through her closed door, she heard Sandrine come up the stairs and go to her own room. Antonia pressed her ear against the door that separated them. The wood was cold against her cheek, and she felt suddenly craven. She heard very little in any case, though a few dull sounds suggested Sandrine was making a fire to take off the chill of the empty room. Once she was warm, she would probably undress and wash from the pitcher and bowl on her table. Antonia imagined her standing in front of the fire, wiping down her body with the wet rag. Wiping away the baron's touch.

Antonia pushed herself angrily away from the wall, at once repulsed and aroused. But the thought returned of Sandrine's thighs, wet with soapy water. Thighs that the violator had touched at will.

She rubbed her face and returned to the window, her chest pounding with outrage that ruthless power could snatch away what she had honestly labored for.

Yes, she thought in the curious internal dialogue with herself. She had earned Sandrine's love, during a week of dangerous trekking through three countries, swimming across icy rivers, sleeping in filthy barns, hiding from the police, catching a bullet in her hand. They had risked their lives together, had huddled in each other's arms against the cold. And yet, while she edged into Sandrine's affections, tracing their closing proximity by millimeters, the most powerful Nazi in Belgium had simply shown up and taken possession of her.

Antonia paced again and heard her own angry breathing. On an impulse, she marched toward the door between their rooms and knocked.

"Yes?" the voice on the other side said.

"I'd like to come in. To talk," Antonia said. She was careful not to make it a question for fear of an answer of "no."

There was a long silence. Agonizingly long. Then the door opened. Sandrine stood in front of her in a white satin nightgown that reached to her ankles. The top of the nightgown was divided into panels of lacework, one covering each breast with a deep décolleté. Over that, she had put on a peignoir of the same material. The fabric was gathered at the shoulder and stood up slightly, and the long sleeves had lace at the cuffs. What a difference from the rough clothing of their trip down the line.

Antonia, still dressed, felt like an oaf. "May I come in?" she repeated.

Sandrine's look was unreadable. "Come in by the fire. It must be cold in your room."

An opening. "Yes, it is. Very cold."

They stood before the crackling fire. "About your visitor this evening. Baron von Falkenhausen."

"What about him?"

Antonia glanced around, searching for the right words. She had no right words. "It's true, then. He…what's the charming euphemism? He has his way with you."

"Of course it's true. How else do you think you're able to live here without being arrested? How else do you suppose I can harbor a parade of British aviators without constant scrutiny?"

She stopped for a breath, her ire obviously growing. "At last count, I've saved forty-six people, you included." She retreated to a red upholstered armchair and crossed her legs angrily.

"Is there no other way?"

"No other way to keep a powerful man sexually beholden to me?" Sandrine's voice rose in pitch. "You think if I just cooked him a nice dinner every week, he'd let me keep my house and car? A car that transports contraband and Allied pilots? Did you join your spy organization directly from the convent?"

That stung. "You've got it wrong. I'm not puritanical. I don't care who you've had sex with. No." She corrected herself. "I do care. Do you enjoy it?"

Sandrine's eyes blazed. "What sort of question is that? Of course I don't enjoy it. You have such a low opinion of me that you think I fuck Nazis for pleasure? How dare you talk to me like that? I surrender to his abuse and then have to endure this sanctimony from you? Get out of my room."

"No, you don't understand." Antonia refused to move. "It wasn't an accusation. I'm sorry if it sounded like one. It's anger partly on your behalf, and also…" She took a breath. "It's jealousy."

"What?" Now it was Sandrine who was puzzled.

"We've been through so much together, going down the line. You even kissed me, on Christmas Eve, and I haven't ever dared to touch you. Not in the way I want. I just keep waiting for you to care for me and let me come close." She felt her lips press together in her own suppressed rage. "And then this vile man arrives and puts his hands on you and touches you in a way I never could, and I can't bear the thought of it."

Sandrine frowned into the fire but said nothing.

Terrified of the silence, Antonia rambled on. "I don't know, I can't know, how you feel about me. Or if you ever thought of…that. A woman, I mean. Who loved you and wanted you. I have. I do." Antonia held her forehead, hearing her voice tighten. "And it's tearing my heart out to know I can't have you but he can, any time he wants, as often as he wants."

Sandrine still sat. With her legs crossed under her long silk gown and her hands hanging loosely from each armrest, she looked almost regal. Like the Marschallin in *Rosenkavalier*, the tiny, still-lucid part of Antonia's brain thought. And she herself stood there in slacks, a desperate Octavian.

But the Marschallin remained silent.

"Say something, for God's sake," she implored.

"I don't know what to say. You're valuable to me, and I'm sorry if I snapped at you. It's just that…well, no woman has ever said those things to me. It's confusing. I don't…I can't…"

"You're not angry?"

"No, I'm not. And I understand that you don't condemn me. So we're even, I suppose. But I can't deal with this subject right now. I have to meet Philippe very early at the train station, and I have a lot on my mind. I think…I think maybe it's best if you go back to your own room now." She stood up, in an apparently gentle way of urging Antonia back toward the door.

Antonia retreated. "If you wish. Good night, then." She stood in the open doorway.

Sandrine stood for a long moment studying her, with neither love nor pity in her expression. Only a sort of helplessness.

"Good night, Antonia," she said softly.

"Good night," she replied, and the door closed slowly, inexorably, in front of her.

CHAPTER TWENTY-FIVE

Heinz Büttner was a proud man. At least that was how he explained his tendency to hold a grudge almost indefinitely. Browbeaten his entire youth by an overbearing father, he wouldn't stand for another to demean him, no matter how slight the offense. And for some damned woman to call him a coward? That shit was going to cost her.

He watched the café for weeks, both on and off duty, but could find no sign of criminal behavior. In desperation, he followed the older woman home, hoping she'd violate some order or other and he could catch her out. If he did, he'd surely be reinstated and perhaps even get a crack at joining the prestigious Security Service. But best of all, he'd enjoy seeing the expression on the slut's face.

The surprises piled up. The woman in question owned a château, with a pond and woods. And she was indeed guilty of a crime, though he hadn't reckoned with the size of it. She was fucking the governor general. Not only could he not use that against her, but her status as whore was also going to make entrapping her all the more difficult.

But Heinz Büttner was a proud man, he reminded himself. And a persistent one.

His duty hours were long, and it was not easy to stalk this Belgian collaborator, but he was determined to discredit the slut in the eyes of her master and then, with a little luck, to have her arrested. The bitch had no idea who she was dealing with.

He was the cold-eyed hunter and she the prey, so he congratulated himself when his doggedness brought him finally to the Château Malou woods just as she was leaving in her fancy car. With four suspicious men.

Four combat-age men, who should have been in the forced-labor details, or on the farms, or anywhere but there, and slipping away at dusk. They were clearly up to something, and this was his chance.

He watched them load up, wave good-bye to someone at the doorway, and drive away. As soon as the château door was closed, he stepped out of the bushes and peered down the road, trying to determine the direction they'd gone. He'd need that information for his report. Then, realizing he'd been careless, he withdrew again and began the way back to where he'd parked his bicycle.

He'd almost reached it when he heard the snapping of twigs behind him and turned.

Gaston was discreet. He took pains to not pry into or even speculate about the personal aspects of his employer's life. But he had known Sandrine Toussaint since she was a child, having been hired on when she reached school age, and so he knew her moods. He had sensed immediately her servitude to the governor general and hated it, but he also understood her—and his—helplessness to change it. His role was simply to maintain and provision the house and allow her to carry out the mission that they all supported.

But something had happened the evening before between Mme Toussaint and her guest, and the almost unbearable tension between them didn't dissipate until Mme Forrester telephoned the young Celine Collin and summoned her for wireless instruction. When the young lady arrived in all her exuberance, the atmosphere immediately brightened and he was relieved.

The departure for the trip down the line was scheduled for five in the evening, and the number of passengers in the car this time prevented him from acting as chauffeur. Instead, Mme Toussaint would drive herself, with her four escapees occupying the other seats, and she would hand the car over at the station to Christine Mathys, who would return it before curfew.

Not to be left idle, he tested the car motor and found it working, determined that the tank had enough petrol for the trip, repaired the garage-door hinge, and brought in more firewood.

At four o'clock, while the travelers brought their rucksacks to the entry hall and enjoyed a final supper prepared by Mathilde, he did a leisurely walk-about along the road and through the surrounding woods to ensure that no visitors, by coincidence or by stealth, were there to witness the event. Veteran of the Great War that he was, he took his role of protector seriously enough to carry his old hunting rifle with him.

And so, at exactly five o'clock, he stood concealed among the trees at the northern edge of the gravel circle at the front of the château and observed the packing and then the departure of the automobile. He considered stepping out to say good-bye but changed his mind at the last moment.

Perhaps melancholy kept him in the shadows, the waterless fountain blocking him from visibility. Sullen, he watched Mathilde wave them off and the car start down the slowly darkening path. The great oak door to the château shut, and he shouldered his rifle, preparing to go back inside when something caught his eye.

On the other side of the gravel court, a man stepped out briefly from the bush and peered after the retreating car. Then, as if realizing he was exposed, he dropped back behind the trees.

Gaston was off immediately and silently. He circled around the court, keeping out of sight, until he was near the road. He feared for a moment he'd lost sight of the intruder in the dusk, but the darkness itself came to his aid. The intruder turned on a light to illuminate his way through the unfamiliar woods, and Gaston, who knew every bush, easily followed the spot of light moving among the trees.

When the stranger came to a halt and bent to attach his light to the front of a bicycle, Gaston stepped out behind him.

"What are you doing here?" he demanded.

The intruder spun around and reached instinctively for his sidearm, but the rifle bore aimed precisely at his forehead stopped his hand in mid-air.

Gaston could not make out his uniform in the dark but did not need to. It was one of the half-dozen policing entities that kept all Belgium under control, and he had seen the departing escapees. He had to be removed. Still, he might be allowed a few words to explain himself.

"Don't point that rifle at me, you idiot. If something happens to me, you'll pay with your life."

"Wrong answer," Gaston said, and fired. The intruder dropped to the ground without a sound.

Gaston lifted the light from the bicycle and did an about-face, lighting his way along the path back to the house.

❖

Twenty minutes later he stood in the circle of women and dogs around the dead man.

"A gendarme," Antonia said. "I wonder why he was so stupid as to patrol these woods alone."

"He wasn't patrolling," Celine said, watching, amused, as her dog sniffed the corpse. "I recognize him. It's Heinz Büttner, and he was here on his own, spying on Sandrine."

"Well, here is where he'll stay," Gaston muttered as he plunged his shovel into the ground. "This is as good a place as any to bury him. It's off the path."

"Do you think anyone will come looking for him?" Mathilde asked.

"Only if he told people where he was going," Antonia responded, shoveling out more of the moist dirt. "He seemed to have a personal grudge, so it's possible he didn't. In any case, we have to warn Sandrine, as soon as she reaches a place where we can call her."

"But even if they do suspect Sandrine, how will they know where she is?" Celine idly nudged the dead man's boot with her foot.

"I suppose they won't," Antonia replied, grunting with the effort of lifting the damp soil. "But they'll be on the lookout for her, both here and at Belgian border crossings. We have to warn her." She plunged the shovel back into the ground, pressing it deeper with her foot.

Conversation stopped for a moment as they dug a hole of a suitable size. Finally Gaston stopped and righted himself, rubbing his back. "That seems enough."

"The gun." Antonia pointed down at the holster still at the side of the cadaver. "We can always use another gun."

"Boots, too, come to think of it. In these hard times." Gaston knelt and yanked them off, one by one. By the light of the dead man's own torch, they slid him shoeless into his grave and shoveled loose soil over it. They tamped it down with their feet and scattered leaves and branches over the mound.

"Let's go back now. I'll telephone our people at the first way station and warn Sandrine that someone may be looking for her," Antonia said. "Unfortunately, she won't get the message until she's already over the border and in France."

"This could all blow over if Büttner is simply listed as missing," Gaston said hopefully. "But if he's traced here, anything could happen, to her and to us. I think we all have to be ready to run."

Antonia looked down at the camouflaged grave at their feet. "Bastard. All because he thought it was okay to shoot a dog."

They started back, the two elkhounds bounding ahead of them, but Celine held back for a moment. "Wait," she called out. "One last thing." She lifted her dog from the ground and set her in the midst of the camouflaged grave. "Make poo poo, Suzi," she cooed.

Antonia waited a few moments in bemused silence, as the dachshund looked up, confused. Then she scratched a few times in the freshly turned dirt and obliged.

Celine patted her on the head. "Good dog."

Chapter Twenty-six

February 1943

Sandrine stood at the end of a long line at the Spanish border, crossing into France. She was exhausted, but it was the comforting fatigue of another completed delivery. Four more good men were on their way to freedom. And one of them even reminded her of Laurent.

Antonia had told her at the beginning of the trip about the discovery of Büttner's spying and warned her that she might be under scrutiny, but she hadn't seen any sign of it along the way. Her luck was holding up.

The recent BBC news, which she'd heard the day before at Jaime and Colombina's farmhouse, was also uplifting. Not only had the German advance stalled in Russia, but Rommel was being driven back out of Tunisia.

Strange, to personally know the man in the news, who stood for Germany's military might in Africa. She rejoiced at his every defeat but couldn't help but feel a twinge for the cultured man she'd shared a concert with. Strange, too, that a person could play a violin one year and kill another country's soldiers the next. Though that was more or less what Laurent had done too. Did Frau Rommel also keep his violin on the mantelpiece?

She leapt by free association to her own mantelpiece and Antonia standing by it admiring her photos. Unfortunate that she'd had to leave before the tension of their late-night confrontation had dissipated. It was unfinished business that she didn't know how to finish, and the weeklong trip down the line had merely postponed doing so.

Antonia. The lovely name that was a gift. So much richer than Sophie. She couldn't remember ever caring for someone so much. But she could sense Antonia's desire radiating from her, and it terrified her, like having a tiger in the house that she wanted to caress but dared not for fear of being devoured.

Leaning to the side, she counted off the remaining people. Philippe was already safely through. Good. Only four others remained. She did a mental inventory of the contents of her rucksack, in the event of a search. Antonia's rucksack. So much more efficient than her own, with zippered compartments. It even smelled like her a bit.

"Your papers, madam." A man's voice startled her, and it took a moment for her to recognize the danger she was in. It was not a customs officer but a French Milice.

She smiled as amiably as possible without appearing to flirt and handed over her counterfeit identification. He peered at it, examined her other papers, peered at it again, scratching at the glue that held the photo on it. It was a new product, but a well-made one, on an authentic form. She had even carefully smudged it to make it look worn. But the glue behind the photo was new.

"Open your bag, madam," he ordered her, and she obeyed, holding the smile. He fished out all its contents, including her underwear, and laid them out on his table. Nothing that could have aroused suspicion.

"Why were you in Spain?"

"I was visiting a friend."

He scrutinized her entry stamp. "For just one day?" Your address is in Belgium, and you came all the way in winter to Spain for one day?"

"Yes. That's all the time I could spare. I have a family to care for."

"Who did you visit?" His eyes bored into hers.

"An old friend." She made up a name.

"In what city?"

"Bilbao," she answered immediately. "On the Ronda Kalea, in case you care."

He continued to stare, as if he could read her deepest thoughts. "I don't care." He turned to the Milice standing beside him. "Take her for interrogation. I don't like this woman."

❖

Antonia tacked up the antenna around two sides of the attic cubicle. Her chagrin after the late-night scene with Sandrine had ebbed over the following week as she occupied herself with daily hardships and tasks. She even felt a certain relief after Sandrine had departed, for no other reason than that her absence meant Alexander von Falkenhausen would have no access to her. The Büttner incident seemed to have no consequences, and now she was carrying out the most pleasant of her duties, teaching Celine Collin how to be a radio operator.

She had grown very fond of the girl. Celine had the strong character of her sister Laura but was uncompromised by the demands of marriage and a business. In peacetime, she might have been called a "handful," but in the Resistance, that rebelliousness manifested as courage. Unfortunately, she inclined toward recklessness, and Antonia felt protective of her.

They sat together in front of the transmitter and she handed over the earphones "You've already shown me how adept you are at handling all the dials and switches, so I'm going to let you start it up today and then sit in on a real transmission."

Celine executed the required tasks with aplomb. When the signal light glowed with satisfying brightness, she handed back the earphones. "I know all this by heart. And I've memorized the SOE code you use too. That is, if I have the poem, I can do the encryption."

"We'll find out how good you are today. You're going to sit here next to me and listen with one earphone while I use the other. I have to send a few coded lines to my supervisor. I'd like you to follow the Morse and then transcribe it as you hear it."

"Great challenge. Let me just get some paper ready." Celine took a comfortable position with pencil in one hand and the single earphone in the other. "Okay, let's go."

Antonia held the one earphone up to her ear and, with her free hand, tuned to the appropriate frequency and began to tap. The message was encrypted, but her mind registered each coded word in its original meaning.

Pilots adrian briggs stp allen meriweather stp dick wheatley waiting for clearance stp please provide schools and commanders names for interrogation stp note am training new operator for future communications code name angel end.

She gave her personal code reference and terminated the transmission.

"How'd you do?"

Celine laid down her pencil. "I got it, but I think I spelled some of the men's names wrong." She slid the paper over for Antonia's perusal.

"Actually, it's quite good. You got everything but Wheatley and Meriweather, and they're close enough. I'm very pleased. The next time the SOE transmits, you can listen in directly and see if you get the same message I do."

"I wish you'd let me transmit something. Maybe a—"

A rap at the door of their cubicle interrupted them, and Mathilde came in without waiting for a reply. Even in the dim light Antonia could see she was shaken.

"What is it?"

"Philippe Ledoux called from Bayonne. The Gestapo has arrested Madame Toussaint."

Antonia grew cold. "What happened?"

"On the return. She delivered the men, but Milice stopped her at the border crossing." Mathilde spoke calmly but clutched her apron. "You have to leave. Both of you. The police will find out who she is, if they don't know already, and they'll come back here."

Mastering her own panic and despair, Antonia did a rundown of dangers, strategies. "The new-pilot rescues should stay at the fish market, and Celine can go back to Laura. But what will happen to you and Gaston?"

"We'll stay with the house. We can pretend to be stupid servants, who knew nothing. And even if they arrest us, they have no proof we were ever involved, not if you take the radio. But they'll probably confiscate the house," she added sorrowfully.

"What about the dogs?"

"I don't think they'll hurt them. Even the Gestapo likes dogs. But Philippe Ledoux will also come looking for them. Don't worry about us. Just go and save yourself. Belgium needs you both."

"Yes, you're right." She hurriedly disconnected the antenna and stowed all the components in the radio valise. "Celine, go on back to Laura's. You should be safe there until we can decide on the next step."

"Where will you go?" Celine asked.

"Back to where I was before, at Christine's. Come on, we have to pack up everything here so the Gestapo doesn't find anything."

Mathilde disconnected the lamp and removed paper, pencils, maps. "I'll send Gaston up here to make the place look like storage again. Just be on the alert yourself now."

They descended together, Celine to her bicycle, Mathilde to locate Gaston, and Antonia to her room. Sandrine had her good rucksack, so she took an old one, and in a matter of minutes, she'd packed a change of clothes, counterfeit identity papers, money, and pistol. She was in the doorway when she had a second thought and returned to the wardrobe. Still clean and ironed, Laurent's blue shirt hung innocently, waiting to be worn. She snatched it from its hanger, rolled it up, and stuffed it into her rucksack.

Then she was at the entryway before the house, where Gaston held her bicycle. "Where can we reach you if we have to?" he asked, then shook his head. "No, it's better we don't know. I'm an old man. I don't know how strong I can be."

"Thank you for everything, Gaston, Mathilde," Antonia blurted out, and embraced them both. "You've been like family." She strapped her two bundles to the back of her bicycle. "I'll see you after the war," she called out over her shoulder, and started for the woods.

Heavily encumbered, she pedaled awkwardly for a few hundred meters along the path before she stopped. From the shelter of the trees, she gazed back at the Château Malou and felt a pang of longing. Huge and empty as it was, it was the closest thing to a home she'd known in many years. And it belonged to Sandrine.

While she watched, the long black limousine of the Gestapo drew up in front of the portal. It wasn't the Baron von Falkenhausen this time, but four SS men.

The Milice had found out who their prisoner was.

❖

She rode eastward, then northward, making a wide circle back toward central Brussels. It was after curfew now, and patrols were on the lookout. With her rucksack and valise, she would immediately attract attention. Her nerves were on edge and her mind raced, trying to sort out the next few steps. She suppressed the sorrow and sickening dread of Sandrine's arrest. First, she had to get to safety.

But was the Gestapo looking for her anyhow? Only if Sandrine had talked, and surely she wouldn't have. Not yet, at least. They would torture her and…Antonia brushed the awful image from her mind. She had to keep her head clear.

The attic room on the Rue Marché au Charbon was almost certainly empty. And with a little luck, she could make contact with Moishe again. Christine would hide her, and she would be within walking distance of the café.

It was dark now, and that made it easier for her to stay in the shadows. She circumvented Marie-Louise Square, avoided the larger streets, and ducked into dark corners at the sight of automobile headlights, all of which, at that hour, would be German.

Crossing the Rue de Vallon, she heard laughter and threw herself into an alley, just as a two-man patrol rounded a corner and marched past her. She waited until she could no longer hear them, then continued, taking detours whenever the streets were too wide or too bright. She passed through the district of the central railroad station, where it was impossible to remain out of sight, but made it to the darkness of the Grasmarkt. She was almost there.

The Rue Marché au Charbon was just ahead and…an electric torch shone suddenly in her face. She froze. Behind the light she could just make out the silhouette of a man.

"Stop! Show your papers." Belgian gendarmes.

She halted, straddling her bicycle, forcing herself to relax, to take on the demeanor of the person she was on her identification papers. Sophie Lejeune, nurse's aid, rushing to a patient. She handed over her papers with one hand, shielding her eyes against the torch's glare with the other.

One of them shone his torch beam on her identification, then on the radio valise, and Antonia caught her breath silently. In thirty seconds she would be arrested for espionage. But her rucksack seemed to interest him more. "Let's see what you've got in there." He handed his torch to his partner and helped her slide the rucksack off her shoulders. "Medicines? Bandages? A thermometer?"

A reply would have been useless. He was about to find her gun. She wondered if she could tip the bike over on them and escape by running. Senseless.

Dry-mouthed, she watched him unbuckle the top of the rucksack and slide one hand inside halfway up his arm. He groped around for a moment, then stopped abruptly. His eyes met hers, and she knew he had his hand on the gun. She stared back, it seemed, for a lifetime.

He pressed his lips together as if in thought, then withdrew his arm slowly from the rucksack. Without taking his eyes from her, he buckled the top closed again and handed the sack back to her.

"Be more careful in the future, mademoiselle," he said in the impassive voice of an official. "The next time, you may not be so lucky." And he waved her on.

"Thank you, monsieur," she said, subdued. Then, quietly, "Perhaps we'll see each other again after the war."

"With a little luck," he said, and strode away. Her heart still pounding, she rode off in the direction of the Rue Marché au Charbon.

She hammered on the door of Christine's shop until the door opened. Without asking questions Christine helped her in with her bicycle and locked the door behind them. She led her toward the rear of the dark shop, where she clicked on a small lamp.

"What's happened?"

Antonia pressed her fingers to her lips, trying to keep them from trembling. But now, in the safety of Christine's shop, she could no longer hold her feelings back and broke into tears. "Sandrine, they've got Sandrine."

"Dear God." Christine took the bicycle from her and pointed with her chin toward a chair. "Sit down. Did anyone follow you here?" She wheeled the bicycle into a narrow storeroom behind the stairs. A moment later she was back.

"No, I don't think so. The street was empty." She took a few breaths. "The Gestapo arrived to raid the house just after I escaped. I can't go back, and I don't know what will happen to Gaston and Mathilde."

She glanced up at Christine, whose face, even in the dim light, seemed drawn, and the realization hit home. "But we're all in danger, aren't we? If they can make her talk, they'll come for us all."

"Yes. They will. But when I signed on to this, I knew it was life-and-death. I've already lost my husband and my son to the Germans. Then we lost Andrée and Frédéric, and two of our couriers. And yesterday the Jews under my care were arrested."

"What? Aisik and Rywka taken?"

"Yes, in a street roundup. To Mechelen, I'm sure."

"What about Moishe? They were staying with him."

"Also captured. During an action. I don't know where he is, or if he's even alive."

"Oh, God. The whole family." Overwhelmed, she slumped, laying her face in her hands.

"Except the baby. The baby will live."

"That's something, I suppose," she answered, monotone. She was limp, indecisive. "Oh, Christine. I was so brave and hopeful when I left England. But now it seems like everything's lost. What are we doing this for if everyone we care for is gone?"

"Is that why you're doing this? For a handful of people? You give up too easily. I've lost everyone too. I have no joy in my life except in the thought that we might defeat these monsters. I don't believe in God, but I do believe in conscience, and in my final hour—even if it's in a Nazi cell—I'll be able to answer to it."

"You're right. They haven't arrested us yet, and until they do, we can keep on trying to free Sandrine. Better to fall in a rescue attempt than cornered in a shop, eh?"

Christine squeezed her shoulder. "Exactly. Let's talk to the others at the café tomorrow. I'll also contact our partisan friends. They'll have some ideas about what to do."

Antonia nodded glumly. "I need to contact the SOE and let them know what's happened, but of course you're right. Tomorrow we'll have clear heads."

"In the meantime, it's the hour for the BBC report. Come on in and have a listen. Maybe we'll hear something encouraging." Christine opened the door at the far end of the shop, and Antonia stepped through it for the first time.

She puzzled for a moment until she realized she was looking at an apartment that consisted of two stories. The lower part, behind the ground floor storefront where they stood, was a kitchen-and-bathroom combination. Useful for keeping an eye on the shop.

"Come upstairs, where the radio is," Christine said, starting up the tiny spiral staircase. The upper floor consisted of a bedroom and sitting room rather like the Goldman apartment, with a cushion-covered bed that served as a sofa.

"Make yourself comfortable, dear," Christine said, pulling two chairs over to the cupboard where the radio sat. "Lately, the news has been good, and the Germans seem to be on the back foot. She switched on the radio but didn't touch the dial. Obviously, it was set permanently to the critical station.

After an initial buzzing and crackling, the always-thrilling *da-da-da-DUM* of Beethoven's *Fifth Symphony* sounded, Morse code for the letter V. Then the familiar upper-class voice began.

This is London calling, the European News Service of the British Broadcasting Corporation. Here is the news: Americans have begun independent air raids on German soil, beginning with the German naval base at Wilhelmshaven. Meanwhile, the RAF continues its heavy bombing of Berlin. In the Pacific theater, the American heavy cruiser USS Chicago *has been sunk by Japanese aerial torpedoes in the Solomon Islands.*

The Casablanca Conference between President Roosevelt, Prime Minister Churchill, and General Charles de Gaulle, representing the Free French Forces, has ended with the demand for Germany's unconditional surrender. Premier Joseph Stalin declined to attend, citing the Stalingrad crisis. In Stalingrad, however, Field Marshal Friedrich Paulus has just surrendered the German Sixth army to Soviet troops. In the wake of this victory, Chairman Stalin insists that the Western Allies establish a second front to alleviate pressure on the Red Army.

And now here are our personal messages.

Christine turned down the volume. "Stalingrad fallen. I think that's the death knell for the fascists. There *will* be a second front sooner or later, and the Germans will lose this war."

"I'm sure you're right, but it won't be in time to save Sandrine or Moishe, or the others."

Christine stood up. "Then *we* have to do it. For now, your room is empty and the bed is made up. Go ahead and send your report to

London, and I'll contact Kuba. Then, instead of lamenting, we should both get a good night's sleep. I'll wake you at seven thirty."

Antonia grunted dull agreement and took up her radio and rucksack. Following Christine to the first-story landing, she began composing her SOE report in her head. She would tell them the ominous truth, that while the battlefront war might be progressing, the resistance they had planned on seemed to be crumbling.

She began the long plod up the stairs.

Chapter Twenty-seven

Sandrine sat shackled with eight others, thrown back and forth in the rear of the van, uncertain of her destination. Since the Milice in Bayonne had determined her true identity—she'd never learned how—she assumed she would go to one of the prisons in Brussels. Not until the doors of the van opened and she looked out toward the gate of a stone fortress did she realize she'd been brought to Breendonk, Belgium's concentration camp.

She hadn't been shot, she suspected, because Alexander von Falkenhausen had learned of her capture and intervened. Had he felt a faint pang of conscience? Nostalgia? Loyalty? Shame?

But no one had officially interrogated her yet, and, given what usually happened to resistants who withheld information, she wasn't sure that was an improvement.

She knew as much about Breendonk as most people outside the collaborating government did—that it was a massive stone fortress from an earlier century that served as a collection camp for resistants, Communists, black marketers, and Jews in preparation for deportation.

But the chilling stone portal and long cobblestone corridor was medieval and correspondingly terrifying. Heavy steel doors opened and closed behind the parade of new prisoners, and shouts of the guards echoed against the stone surfaces.

At the end of the corridor was the reception area. She received prison clothing and learned she was Prisoner Nr. 925, but while the other new arrivals were then shunted off down one corridor, the guards prodded her down another toward a section marked Special Prisoners.

Heavy keys opened the half-wood, half-iron door, and with her hands still cuffed behind her back, she was shoved into a cell too small to lie down in. A hinged wooden bench locked upright on the wall rendered sitting impossible as well.

"Don't move," the guard snarled, locking the heavy door in front of her. The grillwork at the top enabled him to monitor her every move, so she obeyed and waited patiently. But after an hour of standing motionless, she began to sway. Her sense of balance failed, and she began to rock. Her legs and back ached, and so she shuffled slowly back to support herself against the rear wall.

"The order was not to move," the guard shouted as he yanked opened the cell door. He smashed his truncheon against her head and shoulder, causing her to fall to her knees. With her hands behind her back, she couldn't fend off his blows, and he continued to beat her. Finally he stood back and shouted, "Stand up. The order was to stand up!"

She struggled to her feet, bleeding from her nose and with her head ringing, and tried to brace herself by spreading her feet. "At attention. You'll learn respect if I have to break every bone." The guard struck her legs from both sides, forcing her feet together. When she finally stood upright again, he stopped beating her and stepped back out of the cell, slamming the door in front of him.

How long would she have to stand that way? She could feel her face begin to swell, and the ache all along her back and legs grew in intensity. But they hadn't shackled her feet for some reason, and since the guard couldn't see them, she edged them apart centimeter by centimeter, increasing her ability to balance and shift her weight subtly from side to side. It gave her something to think about in the long, torturous hours.

How long had it been anyhow? There was no window in the corridor, and the light from the overhead bulb outside her door was constant. A change of guard told her that some meaningful unit of time had passed.

"Please, can I have some water? I'm so thirsty," she called out to the new man, but he ignored her.

The hours passed, and the tormenting dryness in her mouth compounded her misery. Finally, when she feared going mad, the door creaked open again.

"Dinnertime, kids." The guard laughed. "And then beddie-bye." He elbowed her aside and released the hinged plank that had been hooked to the wall. It fell with a loud clatter, taking up half the width of the cell at the height of her knee. The guard pivoted her around, reshackled her hands in front of her, and pushed her onto the bench.

"Here you go, Princess. *Bon appétit*," he said, and presented her with a canister of water.

She drank greedily, the lukewarm water flowing exquisitely down her throat, soothing her. She barely paused for breath, afraid the guard would seize the canister before she'd emptied it, but he was occupied in the next cell, tormenting the prisoner with the same sort of derision. She wondered faintly who the man was.

She was permitted to lie down during the night, but with her hands once again shackled behind her, she found little relief. She dozed for a few minutes at a time, then jerked awake when the pain in her shoulder became too sharp, and she labored to sit up and then lie down on her other side. A bucket was provided for urination, but it was just another form of torment to have to pull apart her prison clothing with shackled hands and then pull it together again. By morning, she was dazed and deranged. Concerns about Antonia, and the others on the line, and even about her own likely death, faded before the physical suffering of the moment.

Still, she consoled herself, hearing the man in the cell next to her being beaten, that such numbness of spirit had its advantages. The pain became duller too, more absorbed into a permanent state of being. If that was the only torment, she could perhaps remain silent.

The malevolence on the face of the new guard who hauled her to her feet in the morning quickly disabused her of that hope. "Time for interrogation," he said, pulling a wool hood over her head. As if she wasn't already helpless, she was now completely at his mercy.

He prodded her to make a right turn, and with repeated jabs to her back, he forced her down a long corridor. After a series of turns, the guard shoved her against the wall, telling her to wait, and then yanked off the hood. She blinked in the bright light, finding herself in a curious curved hallway.

A moment later, another prisoner was led into the same hallway and placed alongside her. The guard jerked off his hood and she stepped back, startled.

Moishe. His face was a mass of bruises with one eye swollen shut.

She was about to greet him by name but caught herself. He also turned away from her toward the guard. Of course. Acknowledging each other would only provide more information to their captors.

They stood in obedient silence for a few moments until the guard prodded her around the last corner into the interrogation room and she balked, nauseous with fear. Now she grasped why they had brought two prisoners to be interrogated at once. She was going to be tortured, and he would hear her screams.

The chamber was large and sordid, with soiled cement walls and the smell of sweat and urine. On the floor to the left stood a steel object made up of two large wedges, which she could make no sense of. But the purpose of the pulley on the ceiling and the rope that hung from it was obvious.

More terrifying was the rough wooden table on the right with shackles on both sides. A wire sheathed in rubber lay at one end of the table, next to a pair of heavy rubber gloves. The wall that the table abutted held an electric socket.

Her legs were like gelatin and scarcely held her as he dragged her to the table, and while he uncuffed her hands from behind her and reshackled her to the table, she panted with terror. Could she make herself die? When someone taped a length of exposed wire to one of her palms, she began to tremble all over.

The head of an officer looked down at her, filling her field of vision. "I have a few questions for you," he said without any preliminaries. "As long as you answer truthfully, all will be well. But at the first lie, it will become very unpleasant."

How much did he already know?

"I will start with a little truth on my side. I know your name. Sandrine Toussaint. So, now you will reciprocate with some truth of your own. What were you doing in Spain with false papers? We know you are part of a network that smuggles criminals and enemy soldiers across the border into Spain. How long have you been doing this?"

She was anxious to give him an answer that would satisfy him. "Not long. It was my first trip," she said weakly, and held her breath. Was that a good answer? It must have been, for nothing happened.

He looked into the air over her head as he formulated his next question. "So, you are new at this. Who gave you the order and determined the route? Who is your supervisor?"

What could she tell him without incriminating someone? "I have no supervisor. I was acting completely alone."

He shook his head sorrowfully. "That can't possibly be true," he said, and signaled someone she couldn't see.

A jolt of electricity shot through her right arm, causing the muscles to spasm violently and her body to jerk to the side. The current seemed to go on and on, a hot underground stream, cooking her from the inside.

Then it stopped. Her heart pounded as if it would burst from her chest.

He held another wire to her throat. "Just so that you know, I have started out rather gently. In fact, we can send the current through any part of your body we wish. And all of it will be quite nasty. So, let's start again. We know that someone is transporting enemy soldiers to Spain. We thought we'd put an end to that when we arrested the de Jonghs, but now we find there are others. You can save yourself a great deal of suffering if you give us the name of your commander."

"I have none. I swear. I was on my own."

With a look of exasperation, he gave the signal and the torment began again. This time her entire upper body convulsed and her heart fluttered wildly. She called out a low, hoarse moan that strangled in her throat, and she clenched her teeth until it seemed they would crack. She started to black out, and he signaled for the current to stop.

She panted in shallow breaths through clenched jaws.

"You are wasting my time and putting me in a very bad mood. Shall I force your legs apart and place the electrodes inside of you? That is the next step, you know. It leaves quite a mess on our table."

"I was on my own, I swear it!"

"Enough. Heinrich!" He called another man over. "Spread her legs."

"No. I'll tell you…what you want," she rasped. He had broken her.

"Very good." His tone became gentle. "Now, who was your commander?"

She searched her memory for someone, anyone, far away, someone who might still escape, or whose death she could live with. None came to her. She had only seconds to come up with a name. Christine? No, never. Colombina, a Basque? No, he'd never believe her. C…C…A name with C?

"Corot," she forced out in a croak, then struggled with the rest of the memory. "Jean Corot."

"C…O…R…O…T? Is that how you spell it? Your damned French names."

"Yes, that's right." She panted, plunging into memory trying to reconstruct, or invent, something convincing. If he jolted her again, she would confess everything.

"That's not enough. We need an address. Give me an address."

"Wolvengracht, I think. Yes, that's where I met him once. After that couriers brought the orders. Never knew their names."

"Well, now we're moving along. A street number would be helpful." He waved over a guard with a pad and pencil.

"Not sure. A round number. One hundred, two hundred. Something like that."

"Since we're doing so well, perhaps you can give me another name, eh?" He grinned down at her, almost amiable.

"She shook her head weakly. "The others are all dead. You caught them. You've won. No one's left."

He raised his hand again, and she went rigid with fear for the next jolt, but it was merely a signal for the guard to unshackle her. "This will do for now. But if no such person as Jean Corot exists, you will be on this table again, my dear, and it will not go nearly so well." He tilted his head toward the two guards standing by. "Take her back."

When the guards pulled her off the table, she could no longer stand. They half walked her, half dragged her toward the corridor. At the entranceway, they passed Moishe, who gawked at her, wide-eyed, ashen.

"Corot," she groaned at him. "I gave them Jean Corot. I'm sorry."

"Shut up, bitch!" The guard's truncheon came down on her shoulder, but not before she caught Moishe's faint nod as he seemed to grasp the strategy.

Dear God, she hoped so. Moishe was as fallible as she was, and under the horrendous torture, he could give up an authentic name. A name the Gestapo would love to have. Sophie Lejeune. Her beloved Antonia.

Chapter Twenty-eight

A ntonia was awake by seven. She had packed a supply of underwear and a change of clothes, along with her service revolver, and so dressed in clean clothing. Having no food in her room for breakfast, she was leaving her apartment by seven thirty.

Christine met her at the foot of the stairs with a cup of ersatz coffee and some buttered bread. "Here, much easier to think with a little food in your stomach." Antonia ate gratefully but declined to sit down. On that morning, she didn't want to be comfortable.

"I've contacted Kuba, and he thinks he can get together some people in a couple of days. We'll suggest that to Francis and Laura. The café doesn't open until ten, but they're both usually there by eight o'clock."

On the lookout for gendarmes of any sort, they moved quickly along the streets and across the Grand Place. The majestic square of medieval guild houses and opulent residences, splendid in the morning sunlight, seemed callously indifferent to their agony.

At the Rue des Bouchers, they slipped into the alley behind the Café Suèdoise and rapped on the door. Laura opened it.

"They've arrested Sandrine," Antonia announced, stepping inside. Uttering the words caused her chest to tighten again in sorrow.

Francis pulled out chairs for her and Christine. "Yes, we know. Philippe called us yesterday. He thinks someone along the route denounced her, perhaps a black marketer who wasn't paid enough, and that they simply posted a description of her at the border stations."

"So, what can we do? We have to save her somehow."

"What do you suggest we do?" Francis asked coldly.

"Help her escape, for God's sake." Exasperation sounded through the sorrow. "Isn't that what we do? Help people escape?"

"She's right, Francis. We can't just leave her in Gestapo hands." Laura thought for a moment. "Besides, they're bound to torture her, so we're all in mortal danger."

Francis shook his head. "But we're not a group of storm troopers. The only firepower we have is those two Sten guns you gave us and a few pistols. At most, we could attack a truck or a car if they were moving her some place, but we don't even know where she is."

"That's true," Laura said glumly. "We tried to rescue Andrée and Frédéric from several prisons each time they were moved, but it all came to nothing. We just don't have the resources to attack the Gestapo."

Antonia looked to Christine for support, but she leaned on her fist and stared into empty space. "I'm appalled you're giving up on her so quickly. We should at least find out where she is."

"We can do that if she's in Brussels," Francis said, giving her an iota of hope. "We have contacts at Saint-Gilles prison, in Mechelen, and at Breendonk. Someone will be sure to know something." He nodded at himself, apparently relieved to have something purposeful to do.

"But then what?" Laura held up empty hands. "As you said, we don't have the firepower. We have counterfeiters, smugglers, patriots willing to provide information or food, or hide our airmen. But I don't know anyone, really, who could mount a rescue operation."

"I do," Christine said, raising her head. "The Jewish partisans."

Antonia nodded energetically. "I worked with them for two months before Sandrine accepted me into the Comet Line, and I can tell you, they're tough as nails. They rescued one of their men from a hospital and aren't afraid to go anywhere."

Francis winced slightly. "I met your friend Moishe, and he seemed all right, but we don't know the others. Do we want to get involved with a lot of Communists and bandits? Their strategies aren't the same as ours."

Antonia stifled her anger. "They're stalwart men, fighting for a country that isn't even theirs. They're used to confrontation, and now they have a lot of guns from London."

Laura spoke up. "Even if we do decide to 'get involved,' why would they want to help us? Don't they have their own battles to fight?"

"Some of those battles are the same as ours. Their own people are being rounded up daily, alongside resisters like us. My neighbors, who were partisans, were arrested too." She took a deep breath.

"It seems to me you have this choice—to abandon Sandrine to her fate with the Gestapo or appeal to the partisans for help. I'm telling you now that I'll contact them with or without your approval."

Laura glanced over at her husband. "She's right, you know. Aren't my enemy's enemies my friends? I think this is a chance we have to take. Sandrine is very valuable to us."

Antonia looked off into the distance. "Yeah, to me too."

On the following Sunday, when the café was closed, four swarthy men crept into its back room: Kuba and three men Antonia had never seen before. She wished they'd all been familiar faces, but feared the ones she missed had all been captured or killed.

On the other side of the room, as if hesitant to engage too closely with the foreigners, members of the Comet Line sat: Christine, Francis, Laura, young Celine, and the newly returned Philippe.

Antonia introduced only Kuba, and he in turn introduced his men by their first names—Youra, Robert, and Jean—all of them young, and none of them inspiring much confidence.

She addressed the Comet Line side of the room. "I've already explained that we've lost someone critical to our group and need any help we can get to save her. But Kuba has news of his own."

The partisan leader glanced around at the circle of Belgians. "These are terrible times, and we also have lost some of our own recently." He directed his remark to Antonia. "You know that Aisik and Rywka were taken in a raid, along with two others of our group. Our friend Moishe was also arrested last week, but we don't know where the Gestapo took him. We usually hear about the executions, so we think he is alive."

He spoke tolerable French, but hearing him alongside the Belgians of the Comet Line, Antonia realized how thick his accent was. She hoped it wouldn't put the others off. They needed him too much.

To her surprise, Francis raised a hand and spoke directly to Kuba. "He *is* alive. We have a contact at Breendonk, the chaplain, Monsignor Gramann. He's Austrian, but a good man, and smuggles out messages all the time. We just got this one." He held up a tiny piece of rag. From where Antonia sat, it looked like someone had scribbled something on it with charcoal.

"It says, *Sandrine Toussaint, Moishe Goldman. Alive, silent, on way to Dossin.*"

"Ah, that's a relief," Kuba said. We have people inside the Dossin barracks at Mechelen. They're prisoners, but they can also smuggle information in and out. We can get a message to them."

"Can't we radio London for help?" Young Celine looked around at the skeptical faces.

"What good will that do?" Francis scoffed. "They can't do anything except drop supplies and guns. And besides, it's not like one of their own has been captured."

"I'm surprised they're both still alive," Kuba said. "But if they're going to Dossin, that means deportation. That's the collecting point."

"Deportation to where?" Celine asked.

"The Germans keep insisting it's to work camps in the East, but no one falls for that anymore. Too many reports have come back that there's no trace of the people from the earlier convoys. If they're working, it's inside a concentration camp, and the biggest camp is Auschwitz."

Christine spoke up for the first time. "The fact that four days after their arrest, they're both still alive and the Gestapo hasn't raided us, tells me they haven't talked. They both must have come up with good stories, though I can't imagine what that could be."

Antonia nodded, half in her own thoughts. "I think von Falkenhausen saved her from death. Or at least postponed it."

"With Moishe, I don't think the Gestapo know who they've got," Kuba added. "He's very good at lying with sincerity. He'll convince them he's just another pathetic Yid running errands for someone else."

Antonia moved on to strategy. "Either way, the question remains, where do we intercept them—at Breendonk or at Dossin?"

"Can we break into Breendonk?" Laura asked.

Francis gave a bitter laugh. "Have you ever seen that place? It's a fortress, surrounded by a moat. Impossible to break in or out of."

Kuba scratched his beard stubble. "Dossin isn't much better. There's security everywhere."

Youra spoke up solemnly. "We can break them out during the deportation."

Francis looked over at the stranger and frowned. "You want to raid a train? Like crazy bandits?"

"Why not?" Youra replied. "The Germans aren't almighty. And unless they have guards in every railcar, the trains are much more vulnerable than a fortress or a barracks."

Laura's expression brightened slightly. "Can we get information about the deportation train, like when it's scheduled to leave?"

Jean joined the conversation. "It's possible they haven't scheduled departure yet, but when they do, we can find out."

Kuba scratched the back of his fist while he thought. "Our most important task now is getting information. We'll need to know first whether Moishe and your friend will be on that transport, and if so, the day and time of departure. And, ideally, in which car."

"Frankly, it sounds awfully risky to me, not to say plain crazy, stopping a train like so many bandits. But if you think you can do it, we'll work on getting some of that information for you," Francis said.

"Good. In the meantime, Youra, Jean, and Robert will look at the weak spots along the route, *how* to get the train to stop, and where the security is sparse. We don't want to dash off to the rescue like dogs after a car."

"My thought, exactly," Françis muttered. "While you set up your attack, Laura and I will hold down the Café Suèdoise and look after our hidden airmen."

"I'm going along," Antonia said. "This rescue was my idea in the first place, and if you think you can stop a train, I want to be one of the 'crazy bandits' doing it with you."

"Can I go too?" Celine asked, looking at both Laura and Youra. "I'm not afraid of danger."

"I'm sure you're not," Antonia said. "But we need you here. If something happens to me, you're the only other person who can use the wireless to send a message to London."

"Then please come back. I don't want my first message to London to be *So sorry. Sophie Lejeune is dead.*"

❖

When the guards opened the door of her solitary cell two days later and handed her the clothes she had worn at her arrest, Sandrine had no idea what it meant. And when they did the same with Moishe in the cell next to hers, she feared the worst. Did it mean they were going to be executed and their prison clothing spared the damage?

But as they were marched in single file away from the punitive cells, she was relieved, for the execution yard, she knew, was to the left, and the guards led them down a corridor to the right.

More bewildering, they joined a line of some dozen men and two women prisoners already standing in the main corridor. As soon as they arrived, someone at the front called out "March," and the line moved forward. In just a few moments, they were at the entry portal.

Intent on trying to guess where they were being taken, she almost missed seeing the new captive the guards were dragging past them into the prison.

SS men held him on both sides, and a third followed. He staggered, his head lowered, and he had clearly been beaten up before he arrived. It wasn't until he lifted his head to look around that she saw the red birthmark covering the upper left side of his face.

Jean Corot. She stifled the urge to smile. The strategy had worked, and now he almost certainly would face the same sort of interrogation she and Moishe had endured. A sort of justice, for a man who had made a living following Jews home and denouncing them to the Gestapo.

Moishe noticed him too and glanced back quickly at her, but the barked command of their own guard caused him to look away.

On the landing outside the portal, an open truck waited, and they were prodded to climb into the back. Unfortunately, they were seated too far apart to talk.

Where were they going? To labor, another prison, or to execution? Whatever lay ahead of them couldn't be as terrible as the torture table in Breendonk.

CHAPTER TWENTY-NINE

The Dossin military casern was part of Belgium's military history. Like Breendonk, it was imposing, even formidable, but not in itself malevolent. It took the hand of the conqueror to turn it into a purgatory.

The transport truck passed through the portal into the courtyard at the center of the building complex. Obeying the shouted commands, Sandrine climbed down from the truck bed and lined up with the other prisoners before a clerk at a table. The clerk had a ledger open before him, and as each person stepped up and gave his name, he checked it against the manifest that arrived with the truck.

"Sandrine Toussaint," she said, dutifully, and the clerk wrote her name into the ledger before passing her on to another line to enter the building. She had to surrender her identification papers but could keep any personal luggage, though, as a Breendonk prisoner, she had neither one. Like the others, she received a card on a string to wear around her neck. It listed name, date of birth, prisoner registration number, and number of the convoy to which she was assigned. She was number 983, she noted, and she was to be on the twentieth convoy.

The regimentation was meticulous, and in the line that shuffled along the corridor, she found herself once again two prisoners behind Moishe. A guard prodded them both into a barracks room on the right and counted off thirty people.

Her assigned room held rows of bunk beds along two walls, and she understood now why the guard had counted. Exactly thirty bunks filled the room, each with a straw mattress and a blanket. Filthy as they seemed, they were vastly better than a short wooden bench.

Mothers and children were among the thirty people in her barracks room, obviously brought in from a street raid rather than a prison. She thought of Rywka. Was she still somewhere in the casern?

The room buzzed with conversation, but the noise faded when a guard called them to attention and directed them to file into the north end of the court, which now functioned as a dining area. Supper was soup and bread and, compared to the swill she'd eaten at Breendonk, was actually tolerable. She looked for Moishe, but he'd left his place in the line and she lost sight of him.

After the allotted hour, they returned to the barracks room, and as soon as they were in their bunks, the lights went off. The door was shut, but a light burning in the corridor shone through the overhead windows on the inside wall and cast the room in a sort of purgatorial semi-darkness. A figure approached, and Sandrine recoiled, drawing up her knees.

"Ssshh, it's all right," the form hissed. "It's Moishe. I want to talk." He bent down to crouch on the floor at the side of her bed, only his head visible at her feet.

"What's wrong?" She realized the absurdity of her question. Everything was wrong. "What do you want to talk about?"

"Thank you for the name Corot. I 'confessed' it after the first jolt, and it probably saved my life."

"I'm glad. Then they didn't have to torture you long?"

"No. I mean yes. They tortured me a long time. They wanted more."

"Dear God. Could you hold out?"

"Yes and no. I did give them another name. Yours."

"Mine?" She was aghast. "You betrayed *me*?"

"I knew they'd gotten a confession from you, about Corot, so I said we both worked for him but were new at it, and that was as much as I could tell them. They seemed proud of themselves to have gotten two names. In any case, they stopped. If they'd gone on much longer, I'd have broken."

"I would have too. That was smart, to simply confirm what they'd already gotten from us. We saved a few of our friends. I'm glad." She shrugged, though she knew he couldn't see her. "It was a good, brave run, but I think it's over for us now."

He exhaled slowly. "I used to feel sorry for myself, you know? Always alone, while Aisik had a nice family. I had no idea how rich I was. And now it's all gone."

She was silent, for he could have been speaking for her too. How incredibly lucky and self-indulgent she'd been, cultivating her money and her estate yet lamenting her loneliness. When her arrest swept it away, both the indulgence and the self-pity seemed ridiculous. "So, where does it go from here?"

"Deportation. To a camp called Auschwitz, someone said."

"Not much better than execution. Everything I love and care about is left behind."

"Lucky you. I have nothing left behind now at all." He struggled to his feet and shuffled back to his own bunk.

For her part, she uncurled and dropped down onto her mattress, the first one she'd lain on in four days, and fell asleep immediately.

The guard shouting from the doorway awakened her, and the reaction of the entire barrack room was immediate. Through the barred window, she could see that it was barely dawn. She was already dressed, having no other clothes, so simply slipped on her shoes and filed out of the room. After the regulation three minutes in the public toilet, she rejoined the line going into the courtyard. Roll call was by room and assigned number, and when she heard Moishe's voice call out after 980, she felt a great comfort knowing he was there, like a brother. A moment later she heard her own number and called out "Present!" The line then filed past a camp table where someone handed them a cup of ersatz coffee and a slice of gritty bread.

She had scarcely finished her sparse meal when the order came, to march back indoors. Once inside, to Sandrine's surprise, the prisoners could mingle and talk to one another, though everyone spoke softly, as if fearing to be caught. She caught Moishe's eye and waved him over.

She looked around glumly. "I wonder how long we'll be here. And do you suppose our people know where we are?"

"I'm not sure. Even if our comrades track us down, they can't do much to break us out. Some Resistance people are supposedly in here, and I'm looking for them, but I think we're on our own."

A prisoner came into the barracks with a mop and bucket. Sandrine watched him, and though he seemed sullen, she noticed that he stopped at certain bunks and mopped more thoroughly than at others.

When he reached Moishe, she understood why. "The convoy is in two days," he said under his breath. "Collect anything sharp you can. Saws, knives, hammers, anything. If you want to get a message out, give it to me tomorrow." Then he moved several bunks down the row and muttered the same message.

"But how do we get our hands on tools?" she asked.

The man from the nearest bunk overheard and approached. Gaunt and intense, his large eyes bright with desperation, he nodded nervously. "They do repairs here, and they don't watch utensils during the meals. I plan to grab anything I can."

"To do what with? What good will a knife do you? They all have guns."

He kept nodding, and she could feel his determination like a heat rising from him. "Yeah, but they won't be anywhere near us. Haven't you heard? This time, they're putting us in freight cars. I don't know what's gonna happen, but I tell you, I'm not going to sit and do nothing between here and Germany."

Sandrine remembered the freight cars they'd seen at the Gare d'Austerlitz in Paris. Windowless cars that stank of livestock. If that was the case, she wasn't going to sit and do nothing either. She approached the guard in the corridor.

"Is there a workshop? Carpentry? Sewing? I'd like to work. It's better than staring at the wall all day."

He looked at her as if she were insane but then said, "I'll tell them. Go back to your bunk."

She was amazed at how easy it was to obtain work. The Flemish SS troops that managed the barracks seemed obsessed with keeping good military order, and if anyone actually volunteered for work, that was a plus. She was assigned the same evening to the workshop on a lower floor. A senior prisoner handed her a roll of burlap and instructed her on how to fill it with straw and sew it shut. She worked, surveying the workshop, studying where each object was stowed or hung, in particular the scissors, and when the work period ended, she snatched a pair of them and slid it inside her prison dress.

Once back in the barracks, she hid it inside her own mattress. That evening, they were summoned for supper again, her second at Dossin. While she ate her soup, she watched Moishe slide a butter knife under his prison jacket. Then he wandered off.

When he returned to the barracks at the end of the meal, he was flushed with excitement. "Aisik is here. Rywka too. I caught sight of them on the other side of the casern. I've got to find a way to get to them." He fretted awhile. "Rywka looked terrible. Bent over like she's sick."

"Can you talk to them tomorrow at breakfast?"

"They're on a different roll call and go out before us. But I'll figure something out." He went back to his bunk, brooding, and she knew not to try to talk to him. In any case, half an hour later, the lights went out and it was time to sleep.

The next morning at the breakfast line he took his ersatz coffee and bread and threaded his way through the milling prisoners toward the other side of the casern. Though she waited, staring in the direction he'd gone, he didn't return. When her group filed back into their barracks, she saw with a shock that prisoner number 980, three persons ahead of her in line, was a complete stranger.

It took her a moment to reconstruct what had happened. Moishe must have located his brother and negotiated an exchange of numbers. The guards didn't seem to care, as long as there was a person for every number. She dropped down onto her bunk, desolate. She understood that his family took priority, but she felt abandoned.

Her only solace was the scissors she could feel under her back in her mattress.

A guard appeared at the door. "Line up, everyone!"

"The trucks are here to take us to the trains," the man on the next bunk said. "I hope you have something. I've got this." He lifted his shirt just enough for her to see a small saw blade.

"How did you get that?"

"Same as you. Volunteered for work. Carpenter's shop. They don't count their tools."

"You, quiet there. Everyone in line by number."

She found her place again behind number 982.

Four trucks waited in the courtyard, and two were already loaded. As she stood in line for her own truck, she saw them—Aisik, Rywka, and Moishe. She couldn't tell if Moishe had spotted her, though she raised her hand in a small wave. Then his truck pulled out of the casern and onto the street.

A guard barked out an order, and her own line moved toward the third truck.

❖

Her last hope was that the prisoners in all four trucks would be housed in the same railcar. At the substation, they were unloaded in a line and counted off once again into each car, and it was like a knife in her heart when she saw Moishe and his family climbing up the ramp into the car ahead of her. She would be alone, her only companion the stranger with the saw blade.

The railcar's fetid odor made her catch her breath. Was it worth being near the only sanitary facility—the empty bucket in one of the corners? No. It would soon be full and vile.

All four corners had ventilation openings high overhead, with wooden slats that admitted air but no light. If she could escape, it would have to be through the door or one of those vents. She took hold of the wiry arm of the "saw" man and tugged him toward the corner farthest from the bucket.

He grasped her intent and joined her, squatting in the corner, claiming space for them both as all the others from their barracks clambered in. Behind them came another group, which they didn't know, all carrying baggage, and then the car was full.

Someone shouted in German on the platform and the door slid shut. A moment later something metallic clattered faintly, as if someone was attaching it to the door handle. The air was stifling, and during the hour the car sat motionless in the station, she withdrew into herself.

From the time she was captured, she'd never stopped being afraid. But now, regret diluted her fear. Closing her eyes, she called up the inventory of her heart and fondled each memory like a jewel. Guy, a decent husband, in spite of his politics. He'd certainly have regretted them, if he'd lived. Sweet, handsome Laurent, who'd fallen defending his homeland. If only she could spend a single hour with him again, chasing the ducks and splashing in the pond below their château. Laura and Francis, stalwart souls who would mourn her but carry on because they knew she'd want them to. Gaston and Mathilde, as brave as any frontline soldiers; Christine, maternal in spite of herself; and Celine, in the flower of her youth. Then the sharpest pang of all struck her. Antonia.

Antonia, who had offered her love. Antonia, whom she cherished in return. Even loved, perhaps. Yes, the pleasure she felt being near her, studying her intelligent, earnest face, what was that but love? Why did she fear her touch then? Fool. Fool! She wanted to bang her head against the wooden wall behind her. She'd thrown away a chance at happiness and now was going into the unknown, possibly to her death, guarding a ridiculous, pathetic chastity.

The train began to move, and the jolt roused her. The others in the car began to moan and complain, and scuffle with their neighbor for space, but she leapt to her feet.

The ventilator was above her head, and she could only just reach it with the scissor blade. To her dismay, the angle was too high for her to cut effectively into the wood. Next to her, the stranger, who was taller, had slightly better luck with his saw blade. After ten minutes of hacking, he'd split one of the twelve horizontal slats while she was only beginning to cut into hers. Her arm and shoulder were already aching.

"Stupid people, you're wasting your time," someone behind her muttered. But some other person said, "Leave them alone. At least they're not going along like sheep." The remark gave her the encouragement to keep hacking.

The man who defended them spoke up again, right at her shoulder. "Maybe this will help, madam." In the dark, she could barely make him out. A corpulent man, in a suit, of all things, holding a small suitcase. "Stand on this." He set it at her feet against the wooden wall and helped her climb onto it.

The added height made a significant difference, and before long she'd broken the slat, just as her neighbor's bony hand split his second one. Three out of twelve.

The train picked up speed and the car began to rock slightly, rendering the cutting more difficult, but she changed hands and managed to keep going, in spite of the pain.

They were getting the hang of it now. While he finished off one slat, she began to cut into the next one, giving him a notch from which to begin. Four slats, then five, then six.

Finally, out of a sort of desperation, they found that they needed only to cut three-quarters through the slat before the stranger could break it by sheer force. Seven, eight, ten.

"Fools. What good will it do you?" the cynic on the floor of the car groused. "Hardly anyone can fit through that hole. And even if you do squeeze yourself through, we're going too fast. You'll be killed."

Sandrine leaned against the wall, fingers swollen and every muscle aching, refusing to let her labor be in vain. There had to be a way. Perhaps it was possible to hang from the roof of the car and wait for a village crossing, or a curve. There had to be some of those along the way. But how long could she hang outside a train car and not fall, or be spotted by the guard?

Then, miraculously, with a screeching of brakes, the train not only slowed but came to a full stop. It could have meant anything, but it made no difference anyhow. "Will you help me up?" she asked the corpulent shape that still stood behind her.

"Yes, madam. God help you be free for both of us." He cupped his hands in front of him, allowing her to step up into them, and, gripping his shoulder with one hand, she launched herself upward to seize the frame of the ventilator window with the other.

The space was small, barely wide enough for her shoulders, but terror and excitement gave her strength to force them through in spite of the bruises. She gripped the roof of the car and heard the ripping of her dress as she pumped her hips centimeter by centimeter through the opening.

Gunshots rang out, and voices sounded from the rear of the train. Something was happening but she couldn't tell what. Her legs were through now, though her shoulders, back, and hips were covered with abrasions, and she hung for a moment from the roof before dropping onto the gravel by the tracks. Breathless, she crouched for a moment, in time to see the saw-man force his shoulders through the opening as well, and then she fled.

She could see others running, from a railcar at the rear of the train, and she flung herself headlong after them into the woods.

More gunshots. Shouting in German. A burst of machine-gun fire. Some of the escapees fell. She looked toward the densest part of the woods and forced her aching legs to carry her farther. She stumbled, staggered to her feet. Ping. A bullet passed her and struck a tree. Don't stop. Don't stop, her mind screamed, and she threw herself forward wildly, blindly, her muscles on fire.

A ditch engulfed her, and she fell flat amidst dry brush. Spent, she reached for the nearest dead foliage and pulled it over her. She heard two of them, shouting orders, curses, in German, but the crunching of their boots told her they'd passed by.

She stayed still, forcing silence on her panting, ready to spend the night in the dirt if necessary. She waited, and waited, became one with the ground. Finally, she heard the chuffing of the steam locomotive as it started up again.

Only then did she recall that Aisik, Rywka, and Moishe were still aboard the train, hurtling east with only a butter knife.

CHAPTER THIRTY

At the outskirts of Mechelen, Antonia straddled her bicycle next to Youra, Robert, and Jean, still incredulous at the entire undertaking. She'd feared from the beginning they had more bravado than reason, and now she was sure of it.

Youra was obviously in charge. "Our informants report that the train carries a special railcar at the end for troublemakers, known resisters, and people who've escaped from other convoys. We're assuming that's where they'll be, so that's the one we're aiming for."

"I was wondering how we'd find 'our' people," Antonia said. "But where are your guns? You'll need guns for this."

Youra looked puzzled. "We're not going to attack anyone, and besides, the guards are usually at the front of the train and we're tackling the cars at the end. We're counting on the distance and the surprise effect to make guns unnecessary."

She stifled her shock at his naiveté. "I...uh...think you should have guns."

"We don't expect to fight. The plan is to simply run out and open the railcar and let people get away. Besides, we don't have any guns."

"Well, I've got one. I wouldn't think of confronting a guarded deportation train without one."

"Um. I'll be the one going first to the train. Can I borrow it?"

Antonia grimaced at the thought of surrendering her pistol, but it was true. Youra would be at the forefront, and any shooting would be at him. Filled with misgivings, she withdrew the holster and lanyard from under her jacket and handed it to him.

Looping the lanyard over his head and tucking the holster under his own coat, he continued explaining the evening's plan. Antonia listened intently. Insane or not, it was the last hope for rescue.

"We've passed the word to our people in Dossin to tell the deportees to be ready for escape and to try to procure tools from the barracks if possible. But we have no idea how far that information got, or what good it will do. The security police lost a lot of prisoners from previous convoys, and I think that's why they've replaced the third-class cars with freight cars. Still, they're made out of wood, so escape possibilities do exist, however slim."

Antonia's heart sank. All these obstacles and uncertainties. So much depended on chance, on the distribution of guards, on the initiative of the deportees themselves, on the accuracy of the information they were getting.

Youra glanced at his watch. "It's nine o'clock. The convoy's scheduled to leave at ten, like all the others. I've identified an optimum spot for the stoppage. On the track at Mechelen-Leuven, between Haacht and Boortmeerbeek."

"Why there?"

"First, because the train has to slow down for a curve. Then, the forest all around will provide us cover. Even better, it's within running distance to a tramline back to Brussels. Anyone getting out and away from the guards just has to lie low for a while and then filter back among the people on the tram."

"Almost seems too good to be true," Robert remarked.

"Well, it's not *that* good," Jean added. "We still have to worry about the security police chasing people down. The woods start twenty meters from the track, and in that space you're a clear target."

"Yes, but a moving target," Youra said. "Anyhow, we should start now, to make sure we have plenty of time to set up the lantern."

"The lantern." Antonia stared glumly down at the object he held in his hand, a hurricane lantern with red tissue paper glued around it. It looked like a Halloween toy, and an amateurishly made one at that. "You're going to pull this whole thing off with a red lantern?"

"No, of course not. We also have these three wire cutters."

"And your gun," Robert said, though without much conviction.

She nodded slowly, dread lying like cement on her chest. At Youra's signal, they began pedaling toward Haacht.

They finally arrived at the chosen spot, which would indeed require the train to slow. Antonia had to give him that. But the moonlight was so bright she could read her watch without shining her torch on it. They would be sitting ducks. The escapees too.

She didn't have time to agonize, for as soon as Youra had placed the red lantern on the track and they'd taken up their positions, the whistle of the steam locomotive sounded in the distance. Three minutes later, the train appeared, hurtling toward them.

Oh, no! She realized their error too late. The lantern was placed on the far end of the curve! The conductor wouldn't see it until the last minute and would simply run over it. What a disaster.

But the ear-splitting shriek of the braking train told Antonia otherwise. The locomotive had run over the lantern but was still trying to stop. Finally it shuddered to a standstill, fifty meters farther along the track than they'd planned. The car at the end was far up ahead of them.

Cursing at the time they lost running, Antonia saw Robert leap out of the bushes and dash toward the last car, and she followed him.

She shone her torch up on the bolt that held the sliding door in place. Heavy wire secured it. Robert placed his wire cutter over it and tried to cut. It was too thick. He nipped from different directions, trying to gain purchase, to get in position to use all his strength to force the handles together. Seconds ticked by.

Farther along the train Youra was firing the pistol. Her pathetic little Enfield .38 going *pop pop pop*. With half her attention on the slowly separating wire, she finally heard the barrage of return fire and felt a rush of panic.

Finally, the wire broke. Thank God. She and Robert grabbed hold of the bar and slid open the freight car door, then shone their lights inside.

Frightened, ghostlike faces looked out at them, apparently paralyzed by the light. "Get out! Get out!" Robert shouted, but no one reacted. He tried German. *"Schnell, schnell! Fliehen Sie, doch."*

People slowly began to grasp the order to flee and leapt out past her, brushing against her shoulder.

None of them was Sandrine.

She jumped back onto the ground and ran toward the next car, where Jean was struggling with another wire. But now the security guards were closing in, firing wildly, and time had run out. The moonlight made them perfect targets, and the only thing that prevented their being shot was distance. They abandoned the train and crashed into the bushes.

Antonia hit the ground, then scrambled away from the embankment. Through the foliage she could still see the train. Guards, a dozen of them, had fanned out along the route shooting into the bushes, but before she fled, she saw people popping out of the ventilators from some of the other railcars.

The Dossin prisoners seemed to have heard the partisans' warning to steal cutting tools. A few, heartbreakingly few, were managing to escape on their own. But none of them looked like Sandrine. She wanted to drop onto the ground and cry.

Bullets crashing against a branch over her head sent her lurching farther away from the embankment into the woods. The shouting faded, and a few minutes later the security detachment fell silent and the steam locomotive started up again.

Resigned, she stumbled into the woods.

She understood the meaning of loss now. And of love. They'd never been intimate, yet she was certain in every cell of her body of her love for Sandrine. This must have been what Rywka felt.

In a small clearing, she came upon a cluster of people. At their center, Jean was handing out Belgian franc notes so that the escapees could take the tram. She would have laughed at the banality of it, had she not been so close to tears at her own failure.

She looked among the faces—the men, women, even of one child, standing around Robert—and she knew none of them. She made an about-face and began the mournful trek back to her bicycle. What would she tell Laura and Christine and Francis, and all the others on the line? She was too spent to cry.

She stumbled past another group and halted, confused. Exhaustion and sorrow were taking their toll. She was imagining things. But then the specter moved, rushed toward her, and they embraced. Antonia held the warm body for a long moment, wracked by sobs.

"You stopped the train," Sandrine murmured into her neck. "You stopped the goddamn train. For me."

Antonia grasped Sandrine's face and kissed her wetly, first on the cheek, then on the lips, and embraced her again tightly. "For you *and* Moishe."

She released her grip. "The three men who thought this up are from his group. But we only had time to open the last car, and neither of you was there. Was he with you?"

Sandrine shook her head mournfully. "He was supposed to be. But at Dossin, he spotted his brother and sister-in-law and went to join them. We were in different railcars somewhere in the middle."

"Is it possible they got out?"

"I doubt it. His sister-in-law was sick. They wouldn't have left her. I think they're on their way now to Germany."

"To Auschwitz." Antonia felt wooden. "That's where this convoy is going."

She took Sandrine's hand and led her back to the railroad embankment and to her bike. In the distance, a train whistle sounded mournfully.

Chapter Thirty-one

A ntonia helped Sandrine onto the rear of her bike and tried to pedal along the footpath that paralleled the rail line.

"It's no use. The road is too rough and we can't make any speed. We'll have to look for shelter for the rest of the night and make our way back to Brussels in the morning." She dismounted and leaned toward Sandrine, trying to read her expression. "How are you holding up? Are you in pain?" She caressed her cheek. "Your poor face is all swollen."

"They beat me a lot at Breendonk, but when they transferred me to Dossin, I could rest for a day. The food was even tolerable. So I'm sore everywhere, but I'm all right." She slid off the rear of the bike and glanced around. "Do you know where we are?"

"Somewhere near Haacht. Surely someone around here will take in two women."

"Then let's try. I can't walk much farther." Sandrine grasped one of the handlebars and half-pushed, half-leaned on it for support.

As they emerged from the woods, they saw half-a-dozen houses on the outskirts of a village and marched to the closest one that had some outbuildings. Though the lights were out, their persistent knocking brought a man to the door.

"What do you want?" he asked in Flemish, his tone aggressive.

Sandrine answered in Flemish as well, though Antonia could hear her French accent. "We've escaped from a German convoy. May we stay in one of your sheds, just until morning? We won't be any bother."

"Escapees, ah! By the love of Jesus, of course you can. The Boches killed my wife's brother. Come on, you can stay in our barn."

He stepped back from the door for a moment and called out over his shoulder, "Escapees from the train. Bring some blankets for them, please." When he emerged again, he held a kerosene lantern.

"Sorry it's not better, but it's not so cold tonight," he said, sliding open the door to a small barn. In the corner, a mule shuffled nervously as they entered. "Don't worry, old girl. It's just a couple of ladies for the night," he called out, and untied one of the rolls of straw, spreading it into two heaps on the floor.

At that moment, his wife came in, hauling a bucket of steaming water and two folded blankets. Behind her, a small boy carried a clay pitcher.

"Poor things," she said. "I brought you some fresh milk from the neighbor. It's all we have at the moment. But the water's hot. I was just about to bathe the boy, but it's better you have it. If you've been in one of those trains, you'll need it." She set down the bucket at their feet and draped a folded rag over the side.

Antonia thanked their benefactors, using one of the few Flemish expressions she knew, and accepted the pitcher of milk from the child.

"Our neighbor drives into Brussels sometimes with his van to sell eggs and meat," the man said. "I'll ask him to drive you tomorrow. He's a good man, a patriot."

"You're very kind. What a relief to know so many good Belgians are willing to help."

"Not so many, and not good enough. We're all afraid," he said wistfully. "But my neighbor, he's a good man. I'm sure I can convince him."

He set the lantern down next to the blankets. "I'll also leave this with you, but be sure to put it out before you sleep." The farmer led his family out, sliding the barn door closed.

In the tiny sphere of lantern light, Antonia reached for the pitcher and passed it to Sandrine. "Here, take it. I'm sure you need it more than I do."

Sandrine swallowed half of the milk and handed back the pitcher. "Yes, that helps a lot, but you can have the rest. It's really all I can stomach right now."

"If you're sure." Antonia finished off the farmer's gift and set the empty container aside. She slid closer to Sandrine and touched her swollen face. "Poor creature. You must be in pain."

"Not so much. I'm just so relieved to be safe, and with you. I feel like I'm filthy, though. I tried to wash at Dossin, but all we had was cold water at a sink." She slid her fingers down a strand of hair and winced.

"Let me wash you. The water will help warm you too." Antonia dragged over the bucket and helped remove the torn and clammy clothing from Sandrine's back.

"Oh, my God. You're covered with bruises and scratches."

"Yes, they beat me for the slightest reason. But the scratches are from climbing out of the train. I'd love it if you could wash them. You, a battlefield nurse. I couldn't ask for anything better." She slipped off the rest of her rancid clothing and sat exposed, vulnerable, allowing the intimate touch of the washrag.

Antonia swept the warm cloth lightly down Sandrine's back and along each arm, then moved around in front of her to wash her throat and breasts. Sandrine closed her eyes, accepting the tender care without embarrassment.

"I wish I could wash all the horror and the fear off you too." She rinsed the rag and washed the same places again, each stroke a damp caress, then she leaned in to kiss her throat. "You can't know how shattered I was thinking I'd lost you."

Sandrine gazed mournfully at her. "I thought of you all the time, you know. I was certain I was going to my death, and my one regret was that I'd pushed you away."

"It's all right. We're together now."

"They tortured me," Sandrine said starkly. "And I surrendered." She grimaced, and her voice became raw as tears pooled in her eyes. "I thought I could be strong, but they broke me. I gave them a false name, but if it had lasted a minute longer, I'd have given them *all* the names." She laid her head on Antonia's shoulder. "I failed you. I failed everyone, and in the train I was sure my punishment was to die without ever having loved you."

"Loved me? How…do you mean?" Antonia dipped the rag again into the water and wiped the tears and dirt from Sandrine's face.

"I mean loved your body. The way you wanted. I had to stare into the abyss to grasp what you meant to me and what I'd thrown away out of fear."

"You never had anything to be afraid of. What I offered took nothing away from you."

"I know that now." She laid her hand on Antonia's and guided the warm rag over her breasts and belly and thighs, washing away not just the insult of captivity but also her foolish fears. She closed her eyes at the warmth and the insinuating touch, then turned on one hip and draped an arm around Antonia's neck.

Against the warm ear she murmured, "On the train, to block out the squalor and the dread, I imagined making love to you."

Antonia's hand went still, lying across the naked thigh. "I imagined making love to you every day."

Sandrine kissed her softly on the lips. "I consent, I agree, I surrender. I want to know you completely and to belong to you. Only not tonight, my darling. I'm too battered, too anguished to feel pleasure. And I can't forget our friends still on that train, rolling on toward some kind of hell."

"I can't forget them either, and I wouldn't think of expecting desire from someone who's injured. But you're part of me now, and I'll never leave you. If someone takes you away, I'll follow until I'm dead, and I'll haunt anyone who harms you." Antonia pulled the farmer's blanket up over the naked shoulders.

Sandrine stroked her face. "I have so many beautiful rings at home. I wish I could give you one now, to mark my pledge."

"Some day…" Antonia absentmindedly rolled the edge of the old blanket between her fingers, until one of the long coarse threads pulled loose. She unraveled it further and tore it from the end of the blanket. "Will you accept a temporary substitute?"

Sandrine watched Antonia's hands work, measuring the thread into segments of several inches. "What are you up to?"

Without replying, she bit the thread apart with her teeth. "Give me your hand."

Sandrine obeyed, slightly amused, as Antonia wrapped the thread twice around her ring finger. They had been speaking French, but Antonia reverted now to her most formal English. "With this ring I thee wed, with my body I thee worship, and with all my worldly goods I thee endow," she said, and tied a tiny knot.

Beaming, Sandrine took up the other half of the thread and wound it around Antonia's finger. "I ask you, Antonia, to be my beloved, and I pledge…" she began in English. But a vow of such magnitude seemed to require her own language, so she added, *"Mon amitié et mon amour les plus profonds jusqu'à ce que la mort nous sépare.* This is our marriage vow, that pledges my deepest love until death." She knotted the ends together.

"Yes, till death do us part," Antonia repeated, and embraced the one who was now her other self. Their kiss was long and deep, each one affirming the pledge with the heat of her body, and though both of them became aroused, they withdrew and let their passion ebb again, for that one night, mindful of the others who plunged into the darkness.

❖

It was dusk when the van with VANDENHOVEN PRODUKTIE painted on its side backed into the alley behind the Café Suèdoise. Francis opened the van door and helped Sandrine to the ground. She stood for a moment, staring at the wall behind him, while Antonia wheeled out her bicycle.

"What's that?" she asked, pointing to a large but obviously hastily scribbled V on the alley wall almost a meter in height.

"Patriotic graffiti, the newest thing," he said, less grumpy than usual.

Celine's glee was more evident. "Isn't it wonderful? V for victory. People started scribbling them just a couple of days ago, and now they're all over town. The Boches hate it, of course, but so far they haven't caught anyone."

Laura appeared from the storeroom, and as the driver of the van started his motor, she stepped up to the truck window. "Thank you for your help," she said, and presented him with a bottle of wine.

All of them then hurried into the storeroom, and when everyone had taken a seat around the service table, Francis fetched another bottle and opened it with an air of ceremony.

"I still can't quite believe you pulled it off, Antonia, but here you both are." He poured the wine into their various glasses and held up his own. "To you, Sandrine, for coming back to us, and to you, Antonia for doing the impossible."

The Comet Line team raised their glasses and drank, but when Laura set hers down, she was somber. "How are you, my dear? Did they hurt you terribly?"

"I'm managing, thank you. And I don't want to think about the pain. Just about the future."

"The future, yes." Laura looked despondent. "I'm glad you're recovering, but you're a fugitive, now. That means we've lost you anyhow, doesn't it?"

Sandrine nodded. "Yes, that's what it means. I have no home to hide the pilots or myself in, no car to transport them, and I don't even dare show my face in Brussels. I'm useless to you now."

"I suppose that's true," Francis said. "I'm grateful you're alive, but keeping the line going will be doubly difficult now."

"You still have Philippe and Christine, not to mention the counterfeiters, the photographers, the medics, and the guides in the mountains. Christine knows the line now, although it remains to be seen if any of our safe houses are compromised."

"I don't think so," Laura said. "We contacted everyone along the line and no one has been arrested. Philippe also knows the route and we can teach others. We'll keep going, the same as we did after we lost Andrée."

Francis turned toward Antonia. "What will you do now? Can you ask London to send a plane to pick you up?"

Sandrine looked slightly alarmed at the suggestion, but Antonia glanced reassuringly at her. "I'm not running away. I'll contact London with an update and ask them to send another agent for your interrogations. Another wireless too. But I won't leave Belgium."

"Where will you go?" Laura asked.

"I'm not sure. Into hiding for a while, with Sandrine. Someplace far away from Brussels. Any ideas?"

At the other end of the table, absentmindedly twirling one of her blond curls, Celine spoke up. "Stopping a train in full charge, what a coup. The maquis in the Ardenne could use someone like you."

She leaned forward, elbows on the table, as if suddenly hearing her own idea. "I mean seriously. They really could. Especially if you bring guns and a wireless. Why not come back with me to the Ardenne? You'd be out of sight and at the same time still working."

Antonia stared, not seeing her, weighing the suggestion. "Maquis? Yes, that *is* the sort of thing they do, isn't it? Stop trains, I mean. But do you know how to link up with them? It's not like we can simply hike into the woods and offer our services."

Laura laughed. "Actually, you can."

"My cousin Raymond is already with them," Celine explained. "And my grandparents own one of the farms that provision them. I carried messages for the maquis a few times before I came here to be with Laura. Young girls with cute doggies make very good couriers. No one ever suspects us."

"Cyprian, the head of the maquis around Marcouray, is an old friend from school," Laura added. "The bravest person I know."

"You think he's brave? Myself, I think he's a little crazy," Francis scoffed. "But I suppose there's a place in wartime for people like him."

Laura ignored him. "You should join them. Both of you would still be 'in the family' fighting the Germans, but more out of reach."

Sandrine caught Antonia's eye. "I like the idea, don't you? After what they put me through, I don't want to just hide. I want to blow things up."

"And live off the land?"

"Yes, even that. After Breendonk, a tent and bonfire in the woods seems idyllic." She frowned with a sudden reservation and added, "But how would that affect your responsibilities to London?"

Antonia pondered for a moment. "Well, I have to check in with SOE, of course, to tell them my Brussels cover is lost. But I doubt they'll be keen to bring me back if they can use me on another mission, and if I point out that the Ardenne is a zone of resistance, they should approve. I rather like the idea of being Robin Hood."

"Who's Robin Hood?" Celine asked.

"A twelfth-century English outlaw who lived with his band in the woods and fought the local tyrants."

"Ah, English maquisards. You see? It's in your blood," Celine declared. "You'll be great."

Chapter Thirty-two

March 1943

Antonia stood awkwardly in the kitchen of the Delcour farmhouse, while Celine made introductions. "Grandmother, Grandfather, these are my friends from Brussels—Madame Toussaint, head of the Comet Line, and Madame Forrester, our Englishwoman and my wireless teacher."

She paused for breath. "Antonia, Sandrine, these are my grandparents. Oh, and that's my cousin Raymond." She pointed toward a boy of about twenty, with the same sort of war-aged youth that shone in her own face.

"A pleasure to meet you," Antonia said, shaking hands with all three.

"Thank you for your hospitality and protection," Sandrine added.

Monsieur Delcour beamed. "Oh, we're honored to have two people from the Comet Line with us. I understand you'll be going up to the camp soon."

"Yes, that's the plan. We have to discuss all that with Cyprian when he arrives."

"Oh, he's already here, in the basement, sharpening some tools. The grindstone is too heavy to drag to the camp. Please sit down while you wait." He gestured toward an oak table with half a dozen chairs.

Just then, the basement door opened and a tall, angular man of about forty emerged, wearing a generic military tunic. A pistol hung in a holster at his side, and he cradled an axe and a saw blade in his elbow. "Ah, our comrades from Brussels have arrived."

Antonia was taken aback. She'd somehow expected a more heroic-looking man, or at least a more robust one. But Cyprian was the antithesis of robust. Wiry and gaunt, he had a sharply carved face, his features delicate. His gray eyes were hooded, as if his mind was elsewhere, and, most shocking of all, he was balding.

Ridiculous, that she associated physical courage with a full head of hair. She was embarrassed to have thought so.

She shook his hand, which was sinewy, like that of a carpenter or laborer, and the grime under his nails marked a man who worked on the land. "Nice to meet you," she said blandly.

"Celine has told us about you and that you're now fugitives. Well, a loss to the Comet Line is a gain to us."

"I hope we'll be a gain," Sandrine said. "Antonia was a nurse and also has a radio transmitter. As for me, I'm a quick study."

"I believe you, madam, and I'm sure you'll be quite valuable once we teach you how to plant explosives."

He turned to Antonia. "So tell me more about this wireless. You can transmit to London, to ask for arms?" Laying his heavy tools on the floor, he sat down at the table with them.

"We can ask for anything you want. Weapons, ammunition, explosives, though occasionally London can spare a few special items that are severely rationed here. You just need to give me the coordinates of a good drop site. I assume I can transmit from this house?" She directed the question toward Monsieur Delcour.

"Yes, of course you can, dear. We have a room upstairs where you'll get better reception. I'll bring up a map of the area," he said, and disappeared down the stairwell from which Cyprian had just appeared.

"That's wonderful," Cyprian said. "But let me tell you about our little band of maquisards that you'll be joining. We're currently at about forty, though we have a second camp not far away of about thirty escapees and aviators from another escape line."

"Another escape line?" Sandrine was intrigued. "Where are they going?"

"To Switzerland, by way of Bastogne and Luxembourg. Of course it never goes smoothly, and some of the men have been camped out for weeks. Our camp is less transitive. It's mostly made up of men who fled the labor conscriptions and turned partisans, a couple of escaped soviets, and Tunisian prisoners of war. We even have a deserter, an Austrian."

"Any women?" Antonia asked.

"Well, Celine and a few others like her in the town act as our couriers. In the camp, we have only one, Tineke, and I'm sure she'll be glad to have company. Don't worry. The men are all well behaved. More seriously, we're short of arms. We have only a few pistols, light rifles, grenades, and some mines. We won't be able to issue you a gun."

"No need to worry. First of all, I have my own sidearm, and secondly, we should be able to increase your arms' supply right away by contacting London."

"Here we are." Monsieur arrived at the top of the basement stairs somewhat out of breath with a map in his hand. He laid it out on the table and slid it toward Cyprian.

After studying it a moment he tapped one spot with a finger. "We can reach this valley here fairly easily with a couple of mules. The bottom is nice and flat, and the towns just south of it could act as a landmark."

Antonia took note of the geographical coordinates. "I'll radio a request tonight. It has to be approved, but I should think in a few days we'd have a delivery. Of Sten guns, at least."

"That sounds fine. If you can transmit the request this evening, I'll come by tomorrow morning and escort you up to the camp."

"We'll be happy to accommodate you both overnight," Monsieur Delcour said. "You're practically family."

The attic of the Delcour house was much less spacious than that of the Château Malou, but in the end, it was warmer and significantly closer to the kitchen and fireplace. With the speed of long practice, Antonia set up the wireless antenna, and with a linen chest acting as a desk, she squatted with Celine before the wireless kit.

"I'm going to send the message, but I want you to listen." She detached one of the earpieces from her headset and handed it to Celine.

"Afterward, I'll leave the set here, so you'll be able to send on it whenever I can't. This way, I—or even Cyprian—can send down a message to you, and you can transmit it."

"I like it," Celine said. "More responsibility than delivering eggs and mail." She pressed the earpiece against her ear. "Okay, go ahead. I'm ready."

Antonia tuned the transmitter to the correct frequency and began the coded message, "hearing" the original words through each group of scrambled letters.

Made contact with ardenne partisans called maquisards stp mix of escapees pows evaders and misc illegals all combat ready stp need arms and money stp request drop at lat forty-nine degrees pt seven six two four six and long four degrees pt six two eight five one stp village of marcoury on south border stp wait for yr confirmation with message the dog is sleeping in the sun stp sophie end.

"So that's done. Now it'll be your job to check the BBC messages every evening and turn on the receiver regularly to look for London's response. As soon as you report their reply to me and Cyprian in the camp, we'll go out with a team to receive the drop."

"I won't let you down," Celine said.

Sandrine came into the room just as she turned off all the switches and laid down the headset. "If you're done with that, Madame Delcour has announced dinner. She's also made up the three beds for us in the guest room."

Antonia exchanged glances with her over Celine's head, certain they both thought the same thing. *Three beds in the guest room. Another night kept apart. Oh joy.*

The three-hour hike to the campsite was probably longer than it would have been under ideal conditions, Antonia thought. But rain made the ground slippery, and everyone was heavily burdened. Along with their own packs, Cyprian and Raymond carried tools, and she and Sandrine bore three-dozen eggs packed in straw, a kilo of butter, ten kilos of potatoes, and six loaves of fresh bread, wrapped in paper.

"Here we are, the heart of the Siroux Forest," Cyprian said, parting the low-hanging branches of two pine trees.

In the morning light, the campsite looked welcoming and peaceful, in spite of the rain. She surveyed the motley collection of shelters, from parachute-silk tents and dugouts to wooden huts. Some dozen men were busy in the vicinity.

She had no way of knowing what they'd been before they fled to the woods. Some still wore the wooden sabots of the peasants or battered field boots, and a few sported the high black boots of the Germans. She smiled internally, imagining how they'd procured them.

Two of them, sawing wood under a tarp, had military tunics of some sort. But the others she could see, carrying jerricans of water or hammering planks or standing about smoking, wore drab shirts and loose trousers tucked into their socks. Almost all had dark berets hanging carelessly on the side of their heads, which seemed to be the sign of the maquisard. That and the pistol handles peeking out from above some of their belts.

Antonia's rumpled shirt, that once belonged to Laurent Toussaint, the sweater and slacks she'd picked up at Christine's, and the jacket she'd been wearing since she'd parachuted in, fit well into the motley maquis fashion. All they lacked were berets.

"You'll be sharing quarters with Tineke," Cyprian said, directing them to a shed with a corrugated roof covered with branches. Antonia perused it, grateful they had a roof rather than one of the tents spotting the hillside, yet faintly perturbed that they would once again—in fact, permanently—be deprived of intimacy. They would have to be inventive.

They stepped inside the roughly ten-foot-square wooden structure to the sight of two sets of bunk beds, only one of which showed any sign of use. The other three had a simple blanket rolled up at the foot of a bare mattress. The space between them was barely wide enough for someone to turn around in, and the absence of other furniture made it clear that they would spend most of their time outdoors.

"Set the food down here under the bed," Cyprian directed them. "Tineke will be back this afternoon to make a meal out of it."

Antonia's ears picked up. *This afternoon*, he'd said. "That's fine. In the meantime, may Sandrine and I have some time off from duties? She's only just recovering from a week imprisoned at Breendonk." She neglected to mention that Sandrine had rested quite well for a week in Brussels. "And I..." She thought fast. "I've been up all night repairing the wireless."

"That's fine. We'll find some jobs for you around the camp this afternoon, after you've rested. I thought we could set up a little clinic where you could take a look at some of the men who have an ailment or injury."

He stepped out of the shed and spoke to them from the ground outside. "No one expects major surgery up here, but it'll reassure the men to know we have a medic on site."

"Of course. That sounds like a great idea." Antonia smiled and nodded, and when he was out of sight, she barred the door. With her back against it, she surveyed their new home. Solo sleeping. Well, she was used to that. The light came from a single opening over the door, its hatch propped open with a stick. Crates along one end of the shed were obviously intended to hold their private possessions. Fortunately, they had very little. She would miss having a flush toilet, though.

Perched on the edge of one of the lower bunks, Sandrine looked around as well. "Basic, very basic. But with you, it'll be cozy." She smiled up at Antonia. "Romantic even, with the rain. Don't you think?"

"Very romantic. In fact, I believe we have an opportunity to seize." She sidled over to the bunk bed and sat down. A gust of wind drove a splatter of rain against the wall behind them, confirming her observation. "I never thought a rainstorm could be so…stimulating."

"It is, isn't it?" Without preliminaries, Sandrine slid a hand under Antonia's shirt and caressed her breast while covering her mouth with her kiss. Sudden as it was, the kiss enflamed her, and she gave it back while undoing Sandrine's shirt and pulling it down from her shoulders.

"Damn. I've waited so long for this. If I were a man, I'd have a great big bulge in my pants."

"Mmm." Sandrine slid her hand down to Antonia's crotch. "I don't feel any bulge, but it's nice and warm down there."

"I bet it's nice and warm here too." She slid a hand down inside Sandrine's trousers over the skin of her belly, her fingertips just brushing the edge of wiry hair. It was all they needed. With a flurry of hands and arms, and discarded clothing, both of them were soon nude and lying side by side on the single bunk.

Her long abstinence had caused desire to build so that the first touch of Sandrine's palm between her thighs and the hard nipple in her mouth brought Antonia instantly to high arousal.

They had little time for foreplay, and she didn't need it. Sandrine's pliant opening of her legs and the wetness between them suggested she didn't either. "Show me I belong to you," she said, pulling Antonia's mouth from her breast and bringing her head up to kiss.

It wasn't a gentle kiss; they were long past that. It was hard and wet and penetrating, their tongues hungry for each other. They strained against each other, and if Antonia was not so feverish with passion, she might have laughed at how quickly two women in their thirties could turn into adolescent boys, turgid and hot.

She found Sandrine's sex moist and waiting, and laid claim to it. The hard swelling beneath her fingertips told her she had no need to be coy, so she began the intrusion. Moaning, Sandrine threaded her fingers into Antonia's hair.

"Yes," Sandrine moaned. "Yes, oh yes, do *that*."

Antonia entered and withdrew mercilessly, forcing the legs apart with her knee.

Panting surrender, Sandrine pressed toward her with each thrust. Each moan grew louder and more urgent. But when Antonia hushed her, the danger and secrecy of their lovemaking merely fanned the flame toward ecstasy. At the last moment, she covered Sandrine's mouth with her own, smothering her cry of climax.

Sandrine's head dropped back onto the mattress, her chest rising and falling as she gasped in air. Antonia lay beside her and chuckled softly in her ear. "Imagine how much nicer it will be when we have a real bed together and a nice hot bath," she murmured, and drew the blanket up over both of them.

❖

A pounding on the flimsy door awakened them, and Antonia lurched out of Sandrine's sleepy embrace. "Just a moment," she called, pulling on her trousers and then throwing back the door latch.

"Oh, you must be Tineke. Sorry, we locked the door instinctively. Cyprian said you wouldn't be back before the afternoon."

"It *is* afternoon." The portly white-haired woman stepped inside and tossed a large sack of apples onto one of the upper bunks. "Anyhow, it's nice to meet you. Antonia and Sandrine, is it?" She nodded amiably toward them as she pulled off her wet coat and hung it on one of the hooks on the hut wall.

She sat down on the edge of what was clearly her bunk and drew off her boots. "I hear tell you're going to be the camp medic," she said to Antonia.

"So I'm told. Well, I suppose that's as good a use of me as any."

The unlatched door had fallen open, and Cyprian now stood framed in the doorway. "Yes, I've decided that's what we need. We're always having our little accidents, and we can't take people back down to Marcouray. We'll set you up in one of the tents."

"That's fine. But you know, I'll need medical materials. Here, I'll draw up a list."

She tore off a piece of brown paper from the bread package and located a pencil in her rucksack. "I don't know how many of these are available, but they're pretty basic for any kind of first aid." She spoke out loud as she wrote each one down. "Alcohol, rolled gauze, adhesive tape, surgical needle and sutures, splint material, sulfa powder, aspirin, tincture of iodine, safety pins, scissors and tweezers, thermometer, bulb suction device, syringe, calamine lotion."

"I'll send Raymond back down tomorrow morning with the list, and Celine can collect whatever's available for you. In the meantime, we'll locate a tent for your clinic. As for you," he turned toward Sandrine, "how well do you handle explosives?"

"Explosives?" she asked in a small voice.

"Good. We're putting you on sabotage duty. You'll report to Antoine and he'll incorporate you into the team."

"Uh, yes sir." She glanced sideways toward Antonia, who only shrugged.

"Oh, and by the way," he added, tossing two small dark bundles at them. "Here are your uniforms."

"Uniforms?" Antonia caught them in midair and handed one over to Sandrine. A Basque beret, navy blue, obviously well worn, with a badge of the cross of Lorraine on one side. "I guess this means we're 'one of the boys.'"

❖

The July night was crystal clear. Stepping out from their hut, Antonia halted for a moment and stared up at the stars. They filled all the sky that she could see between the trees, so dense that she couldn't make out any constellations, only the sparkling of an unfathomable number of lights.

Behind her, Sandrine laid a hand on her back. "Comforting, aren't they? They almost make you forget the war."

They watched for a moment together, then Antonia's attention was drawn to the cooking fire at the center of the camp, set in an earthen fire pit to minimize the exposure of light.

"Tineke's made rabbit stew," Sandrine added. "Be nice to have meat for a change." Brushing against each other as they walked, for the sheer pleasure of touch, they joined the group already eating.

Cyprian had already finished and he waved them over. They filled their tin plates and dropped onto the ground on both sides of him.

"How's your tent clinic coming along?" Cyprian leaned back on one elbow. By firelight, his delicate face was rather handsome. All but for the lack of hair. "Do you have everything you need?"

Antonia finished chewing a mouthful of stew. "Fine, so far. But no one's needed medical attention. Maybe you should give me some other job as well. I don't want Laura to regret sending us down here."

"Don't worry, you're both valuable to us. By the way, how is she? Laura, I mean. Does she seem happy?"

Antonia thought for a moment. "As happy as anyone can be risking her life every day for the Resistance. She's pretty busy with the café, too."

"Did she…um…ever mention me?"

"Yes, of course. She spoke very highly of you."

"Really?" He stared for a moment into the bonfire. "I'm glad."

"I take it you cared for her at one time." Sandrine's remark amounted to a question.

"I was crazy about her at school. But so was every other guy. She was a beauty. She was always nice to me, and I thought I had a chance with her. Then, one of the boys challenged me to a fight in front of her. I thought fistfighting was primitive and stupid, and refused. I just walked away. The whole school called me a coward after that, and Laura seemed to lose interest too."

"That doesn't sound like Laura," Antonia said.

"I never got a chance to find out what she thought. About that time, Francis showed up. He was a little older than the rest of us, came down from Brussels, and had this mane of hair. Amazing how many people think hair's a sign of bravery, eh? In any case, she left Marcouray with him, and I've always wondered if she still thinks I'm a coward."

"Of course she doesn't. Besides, here you are, leading a band of maquisards. It's not the sort of thing cowardly men do, is it?"

Cyprian chuckled. "It doesn't take courage. Just the ability to organize things and have good ideas about where to camp, hide, get food."

Tineke the cook arrived just then, overhearing him. She sat down next to them and lit a tiny pipe. "Maybe you can organize another shipment of food from Marcouray. You're eating the last of our supplies." She glanced at their empty plates. "Ate."

"I'll go down tomorrow," Antonia said. "I want to check for messages from London."

Cyprian became businesslike. "Please ask London for more ammunition and explosives. The drop they made last week was a good start, but it was too small."

"I'm sure London will be happy to oblige."

Cyprian wasn't listening. "Ignore what I just said. I'm going down with you, to get information and more carpenters' tools. We've been engaging in small harassment in the local area, but I think it is time we got more serious." He got to his feet and stalked away.

"More serious?" Sandrine looked puzzled. "I wonder what that means."

CHAPTER THIRTY-THREE

May 1944

We've finally gotten good at this, Sandrine thought as she watched the track below, barely visible in the darkness. They'd made several pathetic attempts to destroy rails on straight-line tracks and ended up watching the trains plow right on over the damaged sections by sheer momentum. Antonia's brief SOE lessons in rail-crippling were useful only if they had access to the stationary locomotive, which they never did. A serious reassessment of the physics involved had resulted in Plan C, derailment on a curve, where the train's momentum was a liability rather than an asset.

They'd gradually gotten better tools too, over the year. The claylike green Nobel 808, which the SOE now supplied them in quantity, was easy to transport in backpacks without danger, although inhaling its almond-like odor too long gave her a headache. The new cupric-chloride timing "pencils" were an added advantage, which removed the need to string out long fuses or detonating wires and thus remain dangerously close to the explosion.

She herself had packed the series of plasticine globs along both the outer and inner track, each one with two brass detonators set at five minutes. When they'd all run for cover, she savored the pleasing sound of eight nearly simultaneous detonations blasting a wide gap in the rail lines. Then it was the men's turn, to use their sledgehammers to knock the rails off at a tangent to the curve.

They'd timed it well, working at night by torchlight, and now she crouched with Raymond and three other maquisards a safe distance up the slope, both the trap and those who set it well hidden in the darkness.

The train was late, and she fretted, though by that time, few trains ran on schedule. "Small" sabotage at the front end, by Belgian railroad personnel "losing" orders or turning off track switches, created delays that tormented the occupiers without endangering themselves.

She was chilled to the bone when, two hours later, they finally heard the distant chugging of the steam engine. The men fell silent, as if the driver or the armed detachment on the train could hear them. Finally it wafted toward them, the sweet sound of the screeching brakes as, far too late, the driver saw the damaged tracks.

Then the pilot wheels of the locomotive reached the gap, and the driving wheels behind them, forced by the enormous momentum of the tender and line of cars, drove the locomotive toward the right, away from the curve. But it had no tracks to roll on, and, for a second, she imagined the locomotive itself choking out a "Huh?"

As if in slow motion, the huge black engine, still belching columns of gray steam, plowed forward on the tangent, churning up a thick spray of dirt and gravel. The sudden loss of movement caused the cars behind it to accordion off the tracks, and two of them in the middle toppled over entirely.

Soldiers poured out of two of the railcars and began shooting wildly.

"Take that, you stinking bastards," Raymond called out as they all clambered up the rest of the slope, carrying their sledgehammers and tool sack.

"Keep down, Raymond," Sandrine barked at him, but he was too excited by the huge success to forego enjoying it. He turned around once again and waved, jeering at the pursuers far below them.

"Unnhh!" He grunted suddenly and dropped to his knees, clutching his shoulder, obviously struck.

"Idiot," one of the other men said, snatching him up under his good arm and dragging him farther up the slope. Keeping alongside the injured man and his helper, she swept the ground with her torch beam, illuminating any obstacles, and they managed to continue running until they were out of sight of their pursuers. When it was obvious they were out of reach, they sat down to rest and Sandrine pulled off Raymond's jacket.

"Shit. I'm sorry about that, guys," he said. "I just couldn't resist."

"Yeah, well, you got what you deserved." One of the men snorted. "You had to jump out in front of that bullet, and now we've got to carry you back."

"I'll be all right. Really. Just give me something for the bleeding. I can make it back by myself."

"Here, take this." Someone handed over a not-too-clean bandanna, and Sandrine stuffed it under his jacket. "Can you walk?"

"Yeah, sure. I'll be fine. Let's just get going. I missed dinner."

The group continued into the Siroux Forest along the winding and almost invisible trails they'd carefully marked, removing the signal ribbons as they passed.

Two hours later, they were at the encampment and the men took Raymond directly to the medical tent. Antonia was ready, as she always was after a raid, and helped remove Raymond's jacket. She washed the wound and turned him around to examine his back.

"Ah, there's an exit wound. Bigger and messier. But at least we won't have to pry out the bullet. You were lucky it passed under the shoulder blade without hitting an artery. Does it hurt?"

"Actually, yes. Like hell. So you'll have to take very good care of me. Bring me my food, wash my laundry."

"Don't push it, my boy. To qualify for that you'd need at least a head wound." She frowned concern as she began to carefully wash the exit wound. It seeped blood, but she staunched the flow with a wad of bandage soaked in Mercurochrome. She wrapped sterile cotton bandaging around the shoulder and anchored his arm across his chest to prevent movement.

The flap at the front of the tent opened and Cyprian stooped inside. "I hear we've got a wounded warrior here." He inspected the newly bandaged shoulder without comment. "How did the derailment go, by the way?"

"Magnificent!" Raymond exclaimed. "Best job we've done ever."

"Except you forgot to run away. You're not supposed to wave 'bye-bye' at them, you know."

"I'd like to take him down to the doctor at Marcouray," Antonia said. "I'm out of sulfa powder and don't want to risk his getting an infection."

Cyprian sighed. "Well, if you have to, go ahead."

"We can start out early tomorrow morning and get there by midday. I'd like Sandrine to come with me, to help carry back supplies."

He scratched his cheek. "Sure, that's fine. Put Raymond to work too. Teach him we're not playing football up here." He took a step toward the tent opening, then turned back for a moment. "Congratulations on the job, though, kid," he said, and returned to the cooking fire at the center of the camp.

❖

Antonia had given first aid for hundreds of battle wounds and then passed the patient on to some medical facility. She didn't like to treat a bullet wound in a forest and send the man back to his hut in his dirty clothes to sleep it off. At the very least, she needed sulfa.

The sleepy Ardenne town of Marcouray boasted of only one doctor, and he'd been spared labor conscription due to advanced age. His "surgery" was simply a room in his house, and his "pharmacy" a cabinet of jars and boxes that was only slightly superior to her own inventory.

"It looks good," he announced upon examining the wounded shoulder. "The bullet passed through, and both entry and exit wounds are clean. You're correct that a sprinkling of sulfanilamide will give him extra protection." He rebandaged the shoulder and patted the patient on the cheek. "You seem to otherwise be in excellent health, my boy. Be glad you're living in the fresh air of the forest and not in some cellar."

Raymond seemed perplexed. "Why would anyone live in a cellar?"

"I have several patients who live in hiding. The lack of sunlight is harmful, especially to the children."

Antonia knew what he meant. Jews were hiding in Marcouray. She thought of Jackie, the lovely child of Aisik and Rywka, who would be nearly five. She wondered where he was and if he'd already forgotten who his parents were.

The thought of the baby and the three adults she'd known brought a twinge of helpless sorrow, and she forced herself back to the present.

"Well, that's good news. Come on, you can rest a little at the Delcours'," she said, leading Raymond from the doctor's house. "I'll see what the war news is while Sandrine collects supplies, and then we can start back to the camp."

It had begun to rain again when they arrived at the farmhouse. Madame Delcour fussed maternally over her invalid grandson when Celine arrived in the kitchen with Suzi at her heels. She peered at her cousin's shoulder. "Well, that was dumb, wasn't it?"

"Don't be mean," Raymond said. "I can still wrestle you to the ground with one arm." It was clear the two cousins had a history of affectionate abuse, so Antonia merely changed the subject.

"Do you have any news from Brussels?"

"Lots. From Brussels and from the world. Both good and bad."

"Start with the good, please."

"Well," Laura said, "the atmosphere in Brussels has changed. Since Stalingrad, the people seem much more hostile to the occupation. Those Vs are scribbled now on the walls everywhere. And then there's the mystery of Von Falkenhausen."

Sandrine frowned. "What mystery? Has he caused any trouble for the café or for the line?"

"No. Nothing like that. He's still governor general, but he's in Berlin all the time now. Francis thinks something's going on. A power struggle or something. I've even heard rumors that he hates Hitler."

"Lot of good *that* will do him." Antonia sneered. "So what's the bad news?"

Celine sighed. "Arrests, all along the line. Florentino was captured. So were Fernand and Elvire."

"Dear God." Sandrine closed her eyes and shook her head faintly. "Those three were like a rock to us all. What about Mathilde and Gaston?"

"No word. Some German officers are quartered in the house now. The dogs are with Philippe."

"I don't suppose you've heard any news about the Jewish partisans," Antonia said.

"No, nothing. But Laura said she and Francis have stopped moving aviators and POWs. London wants them to either stay in hiding or for the rescuers to redirect them into the countryside to the maquis camps, where the Allied armies can repatriate them."

"Repatriate? The invasion must be close then," Antonia remarked.

"So, do you want to hear the world news? It's a little better."

"We listen to Radio London too, but what can you add?" Madame Delcour said.

Celine leaned back on the sofa, scratching Suzi's head and enjoying the role of reporter. "Well, the war news is good. They don't tell me that much over the wireless, but they did say the Italians have signed an armistice with the Allies, and Montgomery is working his way northward. Mussolini was imprisoned in the mountains, but Hitler's agents managed to spring him and appointed him head of 'The Italian Social Republic.' Whatever that is. Anyhow…" She drew a folded piece of paper from a shirt pocket and consulted it.

"In Germany it's a little more uncertain, with heavy losses of Allied bombers, but they've done a lot to cut back the Nazis' industry, plus they bombed Peenemünde, where the Germans are supposed to have their rockets. But the Red Army has liberated Kharkov and is now on a major offensive against Kiev."

Antonia glanced at her watch. "Oh, sorry. It's time. While you're all listening to Little Miss BBC, I've got to go up and transmit a message."

❖

Antonia withdrew to the attic where the radio was already set up, so she flicked on all its switches and fine-tuned the frequency. With mechanical efficiency, she set on the earphones and began to tap out the message:

Ardenne train derailment big success stp major attk on ardenne targets plannd bt need large quantity explosv stp pls drp same spot same hr stp if tuesday good pls confrm w mssage tulips r blooming in Holland end.

She dropped the earphones to her neck and was about to disconnect when she got a signal in return, and she flicked the connection over to the receiver. For some reason, London was breaking custom and initiating a direct message. Astonished, she set the earphones back on and reached for a pencil.

Will submit request for explosv undrstood and will snd code mssage upon officl approval stp lysander schedled for 1 may will pick up sophie for reassignmnt stp replace dora in france stp landing at same field same hour as before stp this time morse letter J stp end.

Aghast at the sudden news, Antonia switched back to the transmitter and tapped out *Why replace dora stp work here urgent and cannot leave end.*

The answer came back immediately.

Dora dead stp no alternativ stp nothing more urgent than this stp order comes frm highst quarters end.

The line went silent and Antonia sat twice stunned. Dora dead. Dora, who had given her an hour of unashamed pleasure, knowing they both were about to walk through the valley of death. And she had to leave Belgium.

Still dazed, she returned to the living room, where Celine and Sandrine sat in conversation with Monsieur Delcour.

"London is reassigning me. They'll pick me up in two days," she announced morosely.

"What? You can't go. We need you here," Celine said.

"I know. I don't want to. But something big must be about to happen."

"It must have to do with the invasion," Sandrine said solemnly, as if she weighed the importance of the war effort against her claim on Antonia.

"Yes," Antonia murmured, trying to think of what to say when Madame Delcour rushed into the room. "One of the children from Marcouray has just arrived. I think you should hear this." All three of them followed her into the kitchen.

A boy of about seven stood by the table, hunched over from the cold, his hair dripping wet.

"Tell the lady what you told me," Madame Delcour said softly, drawing off his sodden jacket and shirt and bringing him closer to the stove.

He drew in his breath with a mucous-filled sniff. "Trucks. The Boches," he said in a small soprano voice. "Papa said to tell you."

"How many trucks?" Madame Delcour draped a dry blanket over his naked shoulders.

"Three. And a big car. At the mayor's house."

"Did your papa say how many soldiers?"

He shook his head, staring at the floor.

"More than ten?"

"Yes." He nodded for emphasis.

"More than twenty?"

He frowned, trying to remember. "I don't know."

"We've got to take a look," Antonia said. "Can we get anywhere near the mayor's house?"

Celine was already pulling on her coat. "We know the baker, at the far end of the street."

A dash down through the field and onto the cow path behind the Marcouray houses brought them to the first shop on the main street.

A vigorous rap on the rear door brought the baker, who admitted them without hesitation. "Come upstairs. You can't see much. The officers are all inside, but it looks like they're preparing for a raid."

Antonia opened the attic window and leaned out as far as she could. In the gray drizzle, she could make out the three trucks and, as the boy had said, another vehicle, an armored personnel carrier. The sudden appearance of the force had no military reason, so the purpose was obvious. They were preparing an attack on the Siroux maquis encampment. Someone had denounced them, and even if the Germans didn't know the exact location of the camp, twenty or so men could filter through the woods and eventually find them, from the smoke of their cooking fire if nothing else.

"Looks like they're waiting for morning and a break in the weather before they advance. We've got to warn Cyprian so that he scatters the camp." She shook her head. "Except it's almost nighttime. How do we get back to the camp? I don't think we can find our way in the dark."

"I can," Celine announced. "I've been carrying messages and supplies through the Siroux woods all year. I know the route with my eyes shut."

Antonia stood up. "We'll go with you."

"No, out of the question. You'll just slow me down. Besides, what's the point of your coming back to camp when it's going to disperse anyhow? Stay here in hiding until you can break out and meet your plane. This is *my* job."

Taken aback by Celine's newfound authority, Antonia had to agree.

"All right. Do what you have to do. Godspeed," she added, kissing her on the cheek.

Buttoning up her coat and pulling her beret low on her forehead, Celine started out in the rain along the muddy path.

Thunder rolled in the distance as Antonia watched the young woman disappear into the obscure woods. They hadn't really said good-bye. Dread weighed in her chest like a rock.

❖

After an hour of trudging by flashlight along muddy ground that only she recognized as a path, Celine began to have doubts. She knew the route, of that she was confident, but the slippery climb was harder than she expected, and she was soaked through.

In one or two places, where the water-soaked branches hung low and slapped against her, she became afraid. Not of Germans, but of the other night creatures—wild boars that might leap out at her, a stag deer or even an owl roused from sleep that might flutter down at her. Worse, centuries of tales of phantoms and other forms of malevolence seemed to whisper at her from behind, and though she scoffed at them, she picked up her pace.

Finally, panting and dizzy with exhaustion, she came to the first sentry post and gave the password. "*Vive Belgique*, it's me. Celine."

A man stepped out from under a bush-covered tarp where he'd been squatting, half asleep on a crate. "What the hell are you doing here alone?"

She explained the emergency, dragging him with her back to the camp where they roused the others. Cyprian staggered from his hut.

"The Germans," she said. "In Marcouray. About twenty, maybe more. Looks like they're waiting for dawn for the raid."

"Damn. All right. We'll be ready for them." He turned to the man at his side. "Antoine, round up the new people and tell them to pack the tents and load them on the mules. Take only what tools they can carry on their backs. Disperse them in three groups to Cielle, Beffe, and Chavee, and make sure each group has a supply of guns and ammunition."

He peered through the rain at the men who were gathering around him. "Raymond, Georges, Nicolas, pick out three other men. You're all coming with me. We're going to knock off a few Boches."

"What? You're going to fight them?"

"Yes, the maquis will scatter and can re-form later, but me, I'm not going to run away. I'm not a coward."

"Of course you're not…but…" Celine stammered for a moment at the strange assertion. "Well, then, I'm going back with you. That's my family down there, and my village. I'm not going to run off while you fight."

Cyprian stared at her for a moment. "God, you're just as willful as Laura." He touched her cheek. "And just as beautiful too. All right. But first go to your hut and tell Tineke to give you a dry coat. And eat something. You're pale as a ghost."

Celine hurried to the hut that, with three good friends, had been as much a home as her mother's house. Tineke was already up.

"A coat. Of course. Here, take mine. I have a sweater and a waterproof for myself. Wait, we have cheese and bread left from supper." She uncovered a basket with assorted foodstuffs and made up a bundle with a piece of cloth.

"Thanks, Tineke. Take care of yourself. I'll see you again in a few days," She embraced her and headed out again. In the maquis, one never said good-bye.

CHAPTER THIRTY-FOUR

Dawn was faintly visible over the eastern mountains, and the rain had let up when Monsieur Delcour turned back from the window. "Someone's coming just now across the field. Eight people."

Antonia rushed to the window. It's Cyprian and some of the men. And Celine has come back with them. They're insane!"

Ten minutes later they walked through the door, and Mme Delcour met them with an offer of ersatz coffee. Cyprian accepted a cup but was otherwise all business. "How many are there?"

"About twenty men," Antonia replied. "They have two trucks and an armored car. When I checked about fifteen minutes ago, they hadn't mobilized yet. Presumably they're waiting for full daylight."

"Where are they positioned?"

"They seem to all be around the mayor's house. It looks like one or two officers have commandeered the house for the night. We got close enough to see there's one more truck than they need, so we're pretty sure the empty one is for us. As prisoners or cadavers."

"What are you planning to do?" Sandrine asked. "You can't expect to fight them."

"Oh yes, I can. They're here in our forest and it would be cowardly not to confront them. We have a few grenades. Enough to knock out the trucks. In any case, we need to hold them off for at least half a day to give our men time to move the camp."

"How do we get close to them, though?" Celine asked.

"What about the milk truck from the Soreil farm?" Raymond asked. "He usually makes the rounds just at this time. It'd be a good cover."

Cyprian peered through the window that looked toward the farm. "Soreil's probably wondering if he should make his rounds today or just wait until the Germans leave. Let's help him decide."

He was already out the door.

At the dairy farm, the farmer was willing to hand over his delivery truck but insisted on removing his valuable milk cans. While he hauled them out, Cyprian examined the vehicle.

"Here's what we'll do. We'll wait just outside the village, as if it were any other morning. The Germans will be coming out in single file, and it'll be easy to take them by surprise with the grenades. I'm guessing the armored car will come out first. Most of the men will still be in the street behind it where they can't reach us. That's where the rest of you'll come in."

He surveyed the nine fighters around him. "Nicolas, you come with me in the truck. The rest of you take up positions in the houses along both sides of the street. Don't fire until you hear the grenades, when they start to back up. They won't be prepared for fire from behind them."

Celine shook her head. "No. I'm staying with you and the truck. I made three trips through the forest in one night. I don't have a gun and I'm a lousy shot, but I'm throwing one of those grenades, so don't try to talk me out of it."

"Me too," Raymond announced. "I can't shoot the Sten gun with this bad shoulder, so I'm useless for that. But I can throw with my other hand. Besides, this is my village and these are my people. I want to be in the front."

"All right, all right." Cyprian conceded, though he shook his head. "You and Celine can carry the grenades and throw them along with the others when I give the signal. The rest of you scatter among the houses along the street wherever you can. I'll give you ten minutes and then we take off. You have to be in place by then."

"Here, you might as well be using this." Raymond pulled the strap of the Sten gun over his head and handed it to Antonia.

"Fine. Sandrine can use my pistol." She draped the lanyard over Sandrine's shoulder and they took off running toward the village.

At the first house, the baker admitted them without a word and followed them up to the attic room. The view of the street below was excellent, though Antonia was alarmed to see the detachment already lined up. She threw open the windows, and both of them knelt by the windowsill. Antonia aimed the Sten gun at the closest target.

But below them, the lineup wasn't as they expected. Leading the line of soldiers was a personnel carrier she hadn't seen before and that Cyprian hadn't reckoned with. Positioned between the two trucks, it was out of reach of lateral fire from her and the others in the houses, but worse, it carried two machine guns mounted on the front.

The line began to move, and when the first of the trucks reached the end of the street, she heard the grenades detonate. The first truck exploded, but the sickening sound of the machine guns told her the worst had happened.

The whole battle lasted scarcely three minutes, and then the convoy continued on out of the village. After an agonizing wait, until the soldiers were out of range, Antonia rushed downstairs and into the street.

Half a dozen other doors flew open and people emerged from their houses, dashing toward the bullet-ridden milk truck.

Cyprian lay facedown on the ground where he'd fallen from the driver's side. Someone turned him over, revealing a blood-drenched chest that contrasted hideously with his pale white face. The man who knelt over him closed the still-open eyes.

On the other side of the truck, Sandrine yanked open the door and Raymond toppled into her arms, bloody and no longer breathing. She pulled him away from the seat and Antonia clambered in.

Celine and Nicolas both lay crumpled on the floor in the back of the truck.

"Celine, Celine. Talk to me." Antonia took the young body into her arms and pressed her lips on the still-warm forehead. Gasping weakly for air, Celine moved her lips, trying to speak. Blood trickled from a hole in the side of her throat and it was clear that blood also flowed into her lungs, for she choked. She struggled to form a final word. "Please…Suzi…"

Antonia stroked her cheek. "Don't worry, darling. Suzi's safe. We'll take good care of her," she promised, but Celine's head lolled lifelessly against her shoulder.

Speechless with grief, she carried the body out of the truck. Sandrine came to her side, and together they laid the limp form on the ground next to Raymond and Cyprian. Behind her, someone else pulled

Nicolas from the truck and laid him out as well. Sandrine knelt beside the four bodies, fighting back tears.

The baker—Antonia had never learned his name—appeared. "We'll carry them back to their families," he said. "Don't stay here."

"Her dog. She has a dog."

"The Delcours have her, don't worry," the baker said. "But you, go back into the forest to some other camp. You can still fight." He gripped her by the shoulder with a mix of urging and paternal affection. "Go. Take care of yourselves."

"These are our friends, and we don't even have time to mourn them," Antonia said hoarsely.

Sandrine stroked a hair from Celine's still bright young face. "Too many to mourn." She stood up and wiped her face with her sleeve. "We have to go and meet your plane. It'll take us until nightfall to reach the landing site."

Antonia got to her feet, numb. "We're forever walking away from death." She laid the strap of her Sten gun over her shoulder. "When will it end?"

Sandrine took her arm. "Not for a while."

❖

They hiked all day and spoke little, saving their breath. Now and again, Antonia took Sandrine's hand, just to feel her warmth. But she couldn't bear to talk about the recent events. If she gave in to grief for Celine, she'd break down in anguish for all the others. Sandrine grieved as well, she knew, but lamenting would sap what little strength they had left for the escape.

When they reached the valley where the Lysander was to land, the sun was setting behind them. They crouched together partially hidden by growth, waiting. "Fleeing with the shirts on our backs again."

"No point in owning a suitcase, is there?" Sandrine took a long drink from their water bottle and handed it to Antonia. "God, I don't know what I'd do if that had been you killed back there in that truck." She shifted her position and took Antonia in her arms. "You're all I have left."

Antonia closed her eyes, feeling Sandrine's breath in her hair. "You too. You know, I thought I understood the sorrow of Dunkirk, seeing all those men hurt and dying. But that was sort of abstract. The real grief is losing someone you love."

Sandrine touched the back of one finger to the scar that rose from Antonia's shoulder blade to her neck. "If something had happened to me, at Breendonk or—"

"Shhhh," Antonia whispered suddenly, and pointed toward the hill opposite them.

A German personnel carrier was just visible at the top of the ridge. Three men leapt out of it and threaded their way down the hillside toward the landing area.

"Crap," Antonia muttered. How could they know? Had collaborators seen the previous landing and reported it? This was a disaster. Now the pickup would be impossible.

"They haven't caught sight of us," Sandrine whispered. "Otherwise they'd have started firing."

Antonia did the calculations. The plane wasn't due for a couple of hours, so they had time to ambush the men, assuming they could be silent. They were outnumbered, but they had the element of surprise. It seemed insane, but they had no choice.

"Our guns are no good for distance, Antonia whispered back. "We'll have to get closer, much closer. We'll let them settle in first and then work our way toward them."

They watched for over half an hour, keeping sight of where each of the three men meandered and stood. Finally, Antonia handed Sandrine the Sten gun and whispered "now," and they began to thread their way around the valley. They crept, excruciatingly slowly, in a wide circle, keeping to the underbrush. It seemed to take an hour, but finally they crouched within range of the first man. He sat, one knee drawn up, as if at a picnic, and smoked a cigarette.

Sandrine aimed the Sten gun, and holding her breath, she slowly caressed the trigger—until it erupted.

The man twisted sideways, hit in the shoulder and she let loose a volley of shots. He staggered to his feet but then dropped again onto his back.

The gunshot gave them away, but now the odds were even. The other two soldiers ran toward them firing wildly, and Antonia fired back whenever she caught sight of them between the trees. Sandrine fired twice, uselessly.

They both crouched quietly, waiting for the soldiers to take the initiative, but they remained silent. It was dark now, impossible to make out movement more than a few feet away. The men were obviously waiting for that.

Antonia moved ahead, in the direction she thought they'd be, needing to be close for the handgun. She saw something move in the brush and fired, threw herself to the side and fired again. The cracking of twigs told her he was untouched and had moved off to her side.

Behind her she heard another long volley. Sandrine was being profligate with the ammunition, and they had only that one magazine.

The twig cracking was closer, and she shot into the brush where the sound came from. He leaped again to the side and she fired again. She crouched near a tree, trying to stay behind it with respect to where her pursuer was, but he feinted again and she shot. Hell, he was playing cat and mouse, and meanwhile, Sandrine was peppering the darkness with the *rat-a-tat* of the Sten gun.

Something crashed at her side and she fired at it, only to realize he'd thrown a rock and she'd wasted another round on it. Did she have any left? She couldn't remember now how many times she'd fired.

He must have been counting too, for suddenly he loomed up in front of her laughing, with his rifle pointed at her. He'd miscounted. In reflex, she pulled her own trigger and it fired one final shot, hitting him pointblank in the chest.

Toppling forward, he discharged his own gun toward her legs, the slug cutting past her into the tree. His momentum caused him to crash against her, knocking her head against the tree before they both slid to the ground. She lay stunned, underneath his limp body, and Sandrine was still firing wildly. Then she stopped. She'd emptied the magazine.

Christ.

Pinned down by the weight of her assailant, Antonia felt a sudden heat on her chest. The soldier's blood was pouring over her.

She heard a thud, then nothing. Just the evening breeze. Then moaning, somewhere in front of her.

Sandrine was hurt.

Sandrine called her name, breaking her heart, but she resisted the urge to crash through the brush toward the sound. Then she made out the words. Mixed into what sounded like incoherent groans, Sandrine was warning her.

"He's waiting. Don't come," she sobbed, though it sounded for all the world like cries of pain.

Antonia was torn. Was the woman she loved being used as bait, or was she dying? Or both. It was excruciating. The cries became weaker. "He's waiting…waiting…waiting."

She remained silent, immobile, under the dead weight of the soldier. Then Sandrine stopped calling out. Mad with indecision, she still waited. She lay in a dark, silent hell struggling to breathe and she asked herself what she was waiting for. If Sandrine was dead, what was left to fight for? Or to fight with, for she had no ammunition. Then she remembered.

She heard a rustling in the bushes and sensed that the third man had come closer. She tried to imagine his thoughts. He had to be wondering if she was still alive and wouldn't stop until he'd assured himself she wasn't. She relaxed under the body of her attacker, her arms outstretched.

She heard him creep around the dead man and sensed the brightness of his torch beam on her closed eyes. With his foot, he shoved aside the body of his comrade and stood over her. Would he shoot her out of vengeance, or to be sure she was dead? Or would the wide patch of blood on her chest convince him? She held her breath and tried to remain motionless.

He kicked her once in the side. She stayed limp and he kicked her again. Surely he could hear the noise of her pounding heart.

But he stepped away and returned to his other prey. Sandrine called out again, "No…no…no." He laughed again and said something in German.

Once again in the dark and freed of the weight of the dead man, Antonia rose silently. Slowly, soundlessly, she unlaced her boot, then crawled forward, as if in a nightmare of paralysis, and a vast amount of time seemed to pass.

Then she saw him, a dark shape on top of Sandrine. She fought him, thrashed under him, and he grunted.

In a flash Antonia was on his back, looping the wire shoelace over his head and around his throat. She yanked him backward and pulled with all her strength. He rose, clutching at the wire, twisted from side to side, trying to throw her off, and then, trapped by his pants around his legs, fell to his knees. Panting through clenched teeth, she straddled him and rode him like a bull. She thought of Celine, of Sandrine's torture, of Rywka's sobs for her child, and her grip hardened to iron.

Finally he collapsed and she threw herself on the ground next to Sandrine. "Are you all right?"

Sandrine was already sitting up holding her head. "Yeah, I think so, though my head is pounding. He saw that I'd run out of bullets, and he hit me on the head. I guess when he figured out I was female, he didn't want to kill me right away. Or else he was using me as bait. When I came to, I realized I couldn't do anything except keep you away."

"How did you know I was still alive?"

"I could sense it. I was sure you were out there and that he was waiting for you to come to me."

Antonia took her by one arm and pulled her to her feet. "Bastards," she snarled. "If they're not killing us, they're trying to rape us."

"That's the least of it. Where are the torches?"

Antonia searched inside her jacket and came up with a small square pocket torch and clicked it on. "Whew. At least we have one. What happened to yours?"

"In my pack. Somewhere in the bushes. But we can use his." She unhooked the torch from the dead man's belt. Its beam was still strong.

"It'll do fine," Antonia said, glancing up at the sky. "The plane could arrive any time, so we should go down to the landing site and set up the beacons."

"Um, yes. The plane. That's expecting only you. This should be interesting."

Leaning together for support, they began the trudge down the slope. At the landing field, they tried to gauge the center, with maximum distance on all sides from the trees and bushes.

"How are we going to do this?" Sandrine asked. "We don't have the pickup team and we have only two lights. We need four plus the signaling torch."

"We can manage with bonfires for the three lights on the long side and use your light for the foot of the L. Plenty of dead wood around." She patted her pocket. "Finally, I'll get to use the matches they packed for me in my jump kit. Fancy carrying them around for two years."

"Let's hope it doesn't start to rain." Sandrine swept up handfuls of dead wood from the ground and they built the first pyre where they stood. Then, pacing out the first ninety meters of the "long" side of the L shape, Antonia gathered kindling for the second fire while Sandrine did the same for the next ninety meters and the third fire.

"The timing will be important. We can't light these until we hear the approach, and of course, if it's not *our* plane…Well, I don't want to think about it."

"Silly creature, you." Sandrine's mood was obviously improving. "We've survived two years of war, prison, and rape. Lighting bonfires is nothing." She snapped her fingers.

"Glad you think so", Antonia said, looking up at the night sky. "Because I hear a buzzing that could be our ride. I'll set up the lamp beacon if you can light the bonfires. They should have enough straw to catch right away." She slapped a tiny metal matchbox into Sandrine's hand and took off running.

Two hundred meters later she arrived, winded, at the first, still-dark woodpile and paced out fifty meters at right angles to the "line" of the other fires. The buzz was becoming louder, like a motorcycle approaching. She hurried to dig out a small hole and inserted one of the torches. It wobbled a bit, but when she clicked it on, she judged it as visible from above.

The clatter of the airplane motor was loud now, though she still couldn't make out the form of the aircraft.

She ran to the spot midway between the two beacons of the foot of the L and clicked on her torch. Tilting it to 45° upward, she began sending *Di dah dah dah*…pause…*di dah dah dah*…pause. To the side she could see Sandrine approaching, and in the distance all three beacon fires were burning. She kept flashing up at the sky: J…J…J… J…J. God, she hoped the aircraft wasn't German.

Finally it appeared, black against the ambient gray sky, heartbreakingly small and fragile. A Westland Lysander. Never had she loved a plane so much. It flashed its position lights in the assigned code: R…R…R…R. Then, with amazing agility, it descended at a sharp angle and landed close to the middle bonfire.

Success.

Antonia and Sandrine took off toward the plane. The plastic canopy slid open, and the pilot leaned out over the edge of the cockpit. "What's going on?" he shouted down at them. "I had orders to pick up one agent."

"Don't give me any flak, Captain," Antonia called up to him. "We've just been in a firefight with three Nazis, and more could come any time. My friend here has a concussion, and I'm not leaving without her."

The pilot blew out a stream of air as if weighing the danger. "I don't know…"

"Look, Captain. This woman is a major leader in the Resistance and has saved a few hundred pilots just like yourself, so let's not cause an international incident, shall we? We're taking her out of here." She pushed Sandrine toward the metal ladder at the side of the plane.

Antonia climbed into the passenger pit after her and sat down on one of the narrow benches, resting her back on the auxiliary fuel tank that separated them from the pilot. She pulled the canopy shut and the plane began rolling again. Obviously, the pilot had overcome his misgivings.

As soon as they gained altitude, Sandrine peered through the canopy down at the ground. "Two of our beacon fires are still burning. Will that give away the landing site?"

"It was already compromised, I'm sure. That patrol wasn't there by accident." Antonia glanced around the passenger pit, lit indirectly by the overhead reflection of the pilot's instrument panel and, beyond that, by the moon. The voice of the pilot startled her. "If you see an enemy plane, press the button to your left," he called back. "You can see to the rear and I can't."

"Righto. Happy to accommodate." She scanned the airspace behind them. "So far, so good." Then after a moment, "Sorry to be so brusque back there. You're right to be suspicious. But the SOE will know who this woman is."

Apparently placated, he answered, "There's a flask of hot coffee under the seat. And next to it is a bottle of whisky. Help yourself."

"Jolly good!" Antonia fetched up both containers and poured whiskey-enriched coffee into the flask lid. She took a sip, to test the mixture, and held it out to Sandrine. But Sandrine stared through the canopy as if hypnotized.

"Are you okay?"

"Yes, I think so. Just a little overwhelmed."

"Haven't you flown before?"

"No, never."

"Ah, then flying a Lysander at low altitude is probably not the best place to start. Here, try some of this. It'll warm you up."

Sandrine sipped it, smiled politely, and then returned to gazing down at the hills and valleys of the Ardenne that passed below them.

Antonia turned back to the pilot, "By the way, where are we going?" she shouted over the fuel tank.

"France," he called back, and it was obvious that was all she was going to get out of him. She turned her attention to Sandrine, lit both by reflected instrument lights and by the moon—and completely starstruck.

Antonia smiled. The passenger pit of the tiny plane, for all its rocking and freezing temperature, was their private place. Finally they had a room of their own, and yet Sandrine only had eyes for the land that passed below them, her homeland. Taking Sandrine's cold hand in hers, she understood.

CHAPTER THIRTY-FIVE

May 31, 1944

Behind her, Antonia could overhear the pilot talking on his radio, and receiving landing instructions. Surely the message wasn't coming from England, and if not, how did the local agents manage to transmit from the ground without danger?

A few minutes later, the Lysander rumbled to a landing on rough ground. "Here we are, ladies," the pilot said over his shoulder.

Antonia slid back the canopy and stood up, curious to learn where "here" was. She threw a slightly numb leg over the side of the fuselage and shivered at the touch of cold metal on her thigh. The landing beacons were too far away to give useful light, so as she climbed down the tiny steel ladder, she saw only the dull form of her welcoming committee of one. Some distance behind him, two other men stood together with a lantern.

Four steps and a slight leap, and as she touched ground she felt a hand on her shoulder. "Welcome to France, Toni," a familiar voice said. An impossible voice. She stared for a long moment, trying to make him out, incredulous.

"Lew? Lew Rhydderch? What the hell?! You went down in the crash." She could hear herself sputtering.

"Funny. I thought the same thing about you."

"But...how'd you make it out?"

"It weren't easy, old girl. I had the devil's own time until the people got me down to Switzerland."

She embraced him quickly, energetically. "Switzerland? You mean the Comet Line rescued you? Why didn't the SOE let me know?" Her astonishment ratcheted up a notch, toward indignation.

"It weren't the Comet Line, but a Dutch group that helped me. There's more than one line, though the Jerries keep killing them off."

"Excuse me! Could someone help me down this damned ladder?"

"Oh, sorry." Antonia turned around to offer a hand to Sandrine. Taller than she, Lew reached over her head to help Sandrine down the rest of the way. "Hey, who's your friend?"

"Didn't the SOE tell you who I was working with?"

"No, but you can tell me now. Come on, we'll talk inside." He turned to wave off the two men standing to the side. One of them wore a curious metal gadget on his chest and held a tall metal T-rod. "Thanks lads. We'll contact you for the next landing. Cheerio."

"Who are they?"

"Local men who provide the landing lights and S-phone to the pilot. Newest technology from London that lets us guide you in by radio. Worked like a charm."

The Lysander taxied back along the field and took off again while they scrambled toward a car that waited at the edge of the field.

Lew got in and started the motor, and once they were underway, he spoke to Antonia at his side. "So, tell me again who your friend is."

"Hey, don't talk about me like I'm dead" came from the backseat. She'd rarely heard Sandrine speak English and was amused by her accent. "I'm Sandrine Toussaint from the Comet Line, the escape line that your lot was so keen to organize a few years ago. I know Antonia's been sending SOE regular reports on the pilots we saved. She sent half of them from my house."

Lew reached a hand over his shoulder. "Well done to you, Sandrine! Pleased to meet you. I've heard of the Comet Line, but not of you, but I'm just another working sod at the bottom of the 'need to know' list."

Antonia turned toward him as if seeing him for the first time. "So you made it all the way home to old Blighty and all they did was send you back? Why didn't they post you to Belgium?"

"I was injured so it took me a month to get home, then another two months to get fit, and by that time, you obviously had your own business going. I guess they thought I'd have just been baggage. And I suppose they didn't tell you about me for the same reason they didn't tell me about you, because it would be just another fact the Gestapo could get out of us."

"So they assigned you to France, even though your French stank."

"Yeah, but Dora's French was pretty good. We worked together for almost two years until the Jerries got her. A week ago."

"Where is she?" Antonia remembered a lovely, innocent night. "Her body, I mean?"

"With the Germans. Whatever they do with the people they execute."

"Oh, I see."

"It's never a heroic end. Not for any of us," Lew replied. "Anyhow, when I asked for another agent, I didn't know who they were sending until this morning. I was just as surprised as you. By the way, you'll be needing this." He drew a large leather wallet out of a side pocket and handed it to her. Antonia opened it and flipped through the papers inside.

"Ah, so the SOE already has a new identity for me." She slid the wallet inside her jacket. "Can you get some papers for Sandrine?"

"I'll ask for them, but a lot's going on in Bayeux and that will have low priority."

"Bayeux. Is that where we are?" Sandrine asked.

"Yes. The SOE's been working with the local resistance groups, supplying munitions. In return, the local people pass back intelligence about troop numbers, facilities, anything London might need to know."

"What have you found out?"

"Well, the German forces here are under General Rommel. But they seem to have little motorized transport and are mostly older or foreign troops. No elite fighters."

"So, what was the rush to get me here?"

"Something big's going on. It even has a name. Operation Bodyguard."

"Is that the name of the invasion?"

"More like the preparation, but officially, we still don't know anything about that. And neither do the Jerries. 'Bodyguard' is one of several feint operations to convince German high command that the invasion is planned for next year, and that when it does come, it'll be at Pas de Calais. They're already bringing in inflatable tanks so German reconnaissance will photograph them and think a battalion's forming."

"Pretty clever. So where do I come in? And Sandrine, ideally."

"Someone's got to send out a lot of complicated messages, false information about fictional field armies, order of battle, and so forth. Someone who can transmit fast, for long periods, to give the impression we're commencing major operations elsewhere. You come in because the SOE obviously thinks you're better at that than I am."

"Won't they be able to pinpoint us? I mean if we're transmitting all the time?"

"Even if they do, they're not going to try to capture us. Not if they think they're tapping into critical intelligence. You'll be a gold mine for them, and they won't touch you."

"We'll be based in Bayeux?"

"For the moment. But you know the SOE. They could move us any time, possibly closer to the landing site. We always try to stay mobile."

Antonia snorted. "Mobility's the only thing I know, but each time we move, I lose more stuff. Can I get a change of underwear anywhere here?"

"You can change with me, if you like." Lew smirked.

She smirked back. "War and carnage hasn't mellowed you a bit, has it, Lew?"

❖

June 1, 1945

Antonia studied the walls of the tiny dark nook that was their radio room. When the war was over, if she survived it, she wanted a house with large rooms. And the radio would have to be a receiver only. Music, entertainment, and uplifting news, like the BBC messages they'd listened to the evening before.

Advances by the Russians in the Crimea and the Allies in Italy. Heavy Allied bombings of the continent, obviously as a softening up. Could they manage to create the illusion of a delayed invasion in light of all that?

Lew appeared in the doorway, and Sandrine was visible behind him holding cups of steaming tea.

"Tea break. Jolly good," Antonia said, sliding her chair back from the wireless table. "I've sent out the two messages you gave me about the fictional British Fourth Army based in Edinburgh, and the fictional First U.S. Army Group targeting Pas de Calais. I've put it in the old code, the one the SOE used only for weather and non-strategic information. I'm sure they've broken it by now since it's so simple. Let's hope they fall for it."

Lew pulled out two more folding chairs and sat down on one of them. "Or that they at least get a little nervous about it and keep a few divisions stationed in Norway just in case, and the rest of their forces around Calais."

Sandrine handed over one of the cups and took the other chair. "Won't they detect all the activity down here?"

Lew nodded. "Unavoidable. But the whole point is to keep them uncertain and buy time. Ideally, we want to convince them that what's happening here is diversionary. Once they set a strategy, there's always a delay before they can change it, even when they begin to suspect they were wrong. It has to go through a hierarchy of command."

"Ideally," Antonia repeated. "By the way, how will we know when and where the actual invasion *will* take place? Will the SOE send us a message?"

Lew tapped out a cigarette from a crumpled pack and lit it with a trench lighter. "I think London wants all the surrounding Resistance groups to spring into action in one large assault, even if they don't know the focus of the invasion. As I understand it, the BBC will transmit a variety of code signals to all the resisters at the same time, triggering a wave of sabotage against rail lines, power stations, communication networks. Anything to delay the sending of reinforcements."

Sandrine set down her cup. "Ambitious strategy. What will our code signal be?"

Lew smiled with a hint of smugness. "Some very nice French poetry, I believe."

❖

June 5, 1945

Antonia slept in short segments, rising every few hours to continue transmitting fictional strategic reports to fictional headquarters. Lew relieved her for brief periods but was otherwise occupied with gathering real intelligence from local sources.

The room where they all slept was adjacent to the room where they worked, and though Antonia appreciated the combat necessity of close quarters, she longed for the day when she and Sandrine could share a room alone. She also marveled that married women were able to sleep at all next to a snoring man.

For all his brusque machismo, Lew had cheerfully taken on the role of cook and provider from the limited supplies dropped the week before. While Sandrine acted as courier and interpreter with local resisters, and Antonia sat before the wireless, Lew would disappear for an hour or two and return with something to eat. Then, without comment, he'd warm it over the double-coil hot plate he'd managed to procure and serve it on fine china. He also had a respectable hoard of black English tea.

They'd just finished a tolerable stew of turnips and horsemeat when Lew set down his plate and held his watch under the light. "Almost time for the BBC news. C'mon, girls, gather 'round the campfire." He pulled his chair closer to the radio.

They joined him and waited for Edith Piaf to stop singing about her broken heart and for the news broadcast to come on. Finally, at 23:15 o'clock exactly, they heard the *di-di-di—dah*, the thrilling cadence that stirred the heart of every Frenchman and every Belgian.

Then the clipped tenor voice they all loved began his recitation.

June 5, 1944. This is London calling, the European News Service of the British Broadcasting Corporation. Here is the news. But first, here are some messages for our friends in occupied countries. The Trojan War will not be held. John is growing a very long beard this week. The long sighs of the violins of autumn. Les sanglots longs des violons d'automne. Wound my heart with a monotonous languor. And in the news: From the Italian Front the late bulletin reports that Allied armor and motorized infantry roared into Rome, across the Tiber and into the heart of the city...

Lew jumped up from his chair and snatched the air. "That's it! That's the signal."

"What? Which one of those was the signal?" Sandrine asked.

Lew turned down the volume of the radio as it droned on about Allied advances in Italy.

"The line of the Verlaine poem. *Les sanglots longs des violons d'autumne,*" he repeated with a Welsh accent. "That means they're coming! Operations will start within forty-eight hours. It's time for us to go into high speed and put things into motion from here."

"And what are those things?" Sandrine asked.

"Don't worry. I've got jobs for everyone. Toni, you and I'll move out today toward Arromanches. We've set up a safe house there, and I'm scheduled to meet with the Arromanches group to start defusing the mines on the beaches. You'll continue broadcasting from the house, repeating your fake strategies and messages nonstop, until the very last minute and beyond. As long as Rommel and his bosses think the Normandy activity is a feint, they won't budge from Calais, and every hour they hesitate is an hour gained."

"And me?" Sandrine asked.

"We need you to deliver plastic explosives to our French comrades here in Bayeux. Unless you can think of a way to keep Rommel from ordering more troops down from the North."

"Where is he? Rommel, I mean. Does anyone know?"

"Word is, he's based near Calais, but he has local headquarters in Bayeux too. Right at the beginning of the route de Caen. Why?" He laughed at the thought. "You think you can divert his attention for a couple of days?"

She seemed to stare into the middle distance for a moment. "Maybe."

Antonia shook her head. "I know what you're thinking, and please, don't attempt it. They'll arrest you the minute you get near the place. We don't need that. *I* don't need that at this late date."

Lew reached for something bulky under the table. "She's right. Technically, you're under my command, and I order you to stay away from them. Instead, I want you to deliver this package." He held out what looked like a baby wrapped in several blankets. A doll's head peeked out from the top of the bundle. "It's the explosive material they need to blow up the signal station. Go to 25 rue d'Olivet and ask for Emil Leblanc."

"Clever wrapping," Sandrine observed, allowing the subject to change.

"No one's going to stop a woman running with a baby." He placed the load in her arms, then spread a map of Bayeux out on the table.

"Leblanc's place is right here." He tapped on one of the small streets, which she noted wasn't far away from the route de Caen.

"When you finish the delivery, you'll have to make your way to Arromanches. We'll be at 200 avenue de Verdun. Remember that."

"25 rue d'Olivet and 200 avenue de Verdun," she repeated, memorizing the two addresses. With a quick, slightly anxious glance toward Antonia, she clutched the explosives-in-swaddling and hurried out onto the street.

❖

Antonia watched through the window, drumming her fingers on the glass as Sandrine turned a corner and disappeared from sight.

Behind her, Lew was dismantling the radio and packing it into its valise. "Don't be worrying yerself, Toni. She's a French speaker, in France, and she's been evading the Nazis longer than you."

She turned around. "She's also been captured and tortured by the Gestapo, so don't give me that 'she's a pro' fairy tale. Anything can happen to anyone." Busying herself, she collected their half-dozen code books and maps and dropped them into a crate, along with a Browning automatic and four cartridge boxes.

"True, that. But you have to let her do her job. We can't keep wringing our hands about each other."

"You've never wrung your hands about anyone. You just don't care about her." She added two flashlights and reached for their box of replacement crystals, tubes, wires, and spare radio parts.

"Not the way you do. I've seen the way you two are together. Like lovers."

She set down the box and slowly turned to face him. "What are you talking about?"

Lew crossed his arms and leered amiably. "Don't waste yer steam denying it now. Dora told me about yer little adventure before you left Ringway, so I know what you girls get up to sometimes."

"She told you about…?" Her face became hot. "That was indelicate of her."

Lew laughed out loud. "Oh, nothing was delicate about Dora, I can tell you. We were together for almost two years, and I knew her better than you. In the biblical sense too. Bit of a wild woman, that one.

Guess that makes you and me in-laws, sort of, eh?" He snickered. "Or outlaws. But she *did* like to talk. It's a wonder she didn't give away state secrets."

"What happened with Dora was meaningless and has nothing to do with Sandrine and me, so I would appreciate your not mentioning it ever again."

"I won't. Word of honor." He held up his right hand. "I just wanted to show you I'm not shocked. Actually, I think it's good for both of you, and you seem happy. A pity that you're both off the market, though. A fella gets lonely."

Shock and outright fear softened to annoyance. "Can we talk about something else now? How much of all this stuff are we going to take to Arromanches?"

"All of it. We want to eat and stay warm, don't we? So I'll pack the bedding and you box up our kitchen supplies. Start with the hot plate. Worth its weight in gold, that."

Calmed by his assurances, she set up another ordinance crate and laid the hot plate into it, along with their stew pot and kettle. After collecting their few towels, she began to pack the dishes. "These are beautiful." She held up one with a blue-willow pattern. "Where did you get fine china in the middle of a war zone?"

He joined her at the table. "The same place I got these." He lifted a towel covering their mismatched silverware. She'd noticed them at all the meals they'd eaten but never thought to ask about them.

"Nothing matches anything else, but I'm thinking sterling silver's never bad, eh?"

"Did you steal them? Or what?" She picked up what looked like an oyster fork.

"Nothing like that. They're from an antique shop in town where Dora made friends. They had a lot of things hidden so the Nazis wouldn't steal them, but they needed money. I gave them quite a lot, more than the Germans would have, plus a load of Spam and a carton of cigarettes. Much better than cash." He returned to the other room to roll up their field mattresses.

Antonia studied the tiny fork, turning it in the light. Although one of the two prongs was broken, the mix of sterling silver and gold plate, along with the silversmith's mark on the handle, told her it was old and valuable, even if damaged. The pattern was ornate, baroque curlicues of gold surrounding a wave pattern etched into the silver, and a line of gold ran the length of the handle.

"Do you have any tools?"

"Some. Hammer, pliers, wire cutter. Basic stuff. In the green metal case under the sink."

"Good," she said, then bundled up the silverware in a towel and tucked it in with the plates.

A bomb detonated somewhere in the distance. Then another one, and the packing became urgent. She forced herself not to think of Sandrine, running through the streets unarmed.

"Hurry up there, will ya?" came from the other room.

"I'm here." She crammed the tool case alongside the hot plate and kettle, then hefted both crates and followed him out to the car.

The rain that had been continuous most of the day discouraged street activity, and Sandrine completed the errand to the rue d'Olivet with relative ease. Within an hour of leaving Lew's Bayeux headquarters, she'd delivered the "baby" to the relevant hands with much thanks and the offer of cigarettes. She declined and simply asked the shortest way to the route de Caen.

Once on the street again, unburdened by the awkward bundle, she strode nervously toward a meeting that might be totally useless. Or suicidal. But fate had placed certain cards in her hand, and it would be a waste to not play them. She removed her beret, which, even without an insignia, hinted too much of the maquisard, and ran her fingers through her hair. Lew's little electric burner had allowed her to heat water to wash it, and now that it had grown long, she was conscious of how attractive it was. But was it attractive enough to flirt with a general preparing for battle?

Rommel's headquarters were unmistakable. A solid edifice, protected on one side by buildings and on the other by a wall of sandbags. Soldiers stood guard at the front.

She gathered her courage and marched up to one of them, her heart racing. "Could you please inform General Rommel that Sandrine Toussaint would like to speak with him?" she asked in halting German.

The guards looked flabbergasted, and although her knowledge of German slang was poor, she grasped that they discussed between them whether to shoo her away or shoot her. The obstacle seemed insurmountable until both guards suddenly stood at attention and delivered a crisp salute to someone behind her.

She pivoted around to face a wide chest covered with decorations and a familiar face.

"Ah, Madame Toussaint, what a surprise. To what do I owe this pleasure?"

Dear God, he even remembered her name.

"Good day, Herr General. Oh, but it's Generalfeldmarschall now, isn't it? Congratulations on your promotion."

"Yes, the titles they give us to keep us fighting. At least those of us in uniform. Our enemies in the Resistance have a different system." He smiled ironically, as if they shared a secret, then got to the point.

"So, Madame Toussaint, how can I be of service?"

She tilted her head just slightly, hoping her coyness was sufficiently subtle. "I knew you were in France, carrying out your duties, but when I learned you were in Bayeux I couldn't believe my good fortune. I wonder if you could spare a moment for me."

"Dear lady, I am…uh…fighting a war, as you can see." He swept his hand in an arc ending at the wall of sandbags. Then he seemed to reconsider. "But I always have a spare moment for an attractive woman." At his nod, one of the guards opened the door to the entryway of the building. Once inside, to the equal bafflement of the officers who awaited him, he leaned past her and opened a door to a private room. "Please, come in."

"Lieutenant, would you bring us some tea?" he said over his shoulder, then extended a hand toward the chair before his desk. "Please have a seat." Several maps were open on the desk, but he carefully folded them and set them aside.

"Madame Toussaint, this cannot be purely a social call," he said with an eyebrow slightly raised.

"Uh, no. You're quite right. In fact, it has to do with my…uh… delicate situation in Brussels." She studied his expression, looking for traces of suspicion. Everything depended on his not knowing she had been arrested and sent to Breendonk. Something a front-line soldier might not know, even if the Gestapo did.

They were interrupted by a quick rap and the entry of the adjutant with a tray of two steaming porcelain cups and a dish of sweets. He waited for her to take a cup and then reached for the other. "Yes, go on." He blew into his tea, the porcelain cup looking tiny and fragile in his meaty hand.

"I was, well, I suppose you could say, compromised. Perhaps you will recall the concert reception where we met, along with Baron von Falkenhausen. After that evening, he offered me his…protection. That was a great comfort. However, of late, he has been absent from Brussels a great deal and many Belgians view me as…Well, I have to come out and say it. As a collaborator."

He had begun to squint slightly, and she feared he'd seen through her lie. "I am aware of General von Falkenhausen's visits to Berlin. He's an important man and you must expect such back and forth. But it's a shame that he left you so vulnerable."

"Yes, without the Baron's protection, I was in great danger from the Resistance, so I fled here to France, where I have friends."

"A judicious move, and you were lucky—or very clever—to be able to travel so far without problems. So what do you need from me?"

"A permit to reside. Surely you have the authority to issue that, or to have the local administration issue it. This part of France is the only place that will be safe in the next few months." She sipped from her own tea, then set the cup down when she realized her hand was shaking. Did he notice?

"What makes you say that?" He gave her a penetrating look. It seemed that she had hooked him, if only lightly.

"I have friends who have friends who are informed. You know how it is. Most everyone agrees that all the fighting will be farther north. Plus, I confess, I listen to the BBC."

He chuckled. "I do too. So what did you hear?"

"Then you know about the attacks planned in Norway and at Calais. I want to stay where it's quiet and try to ride out this war. Can you help me? You're my last resort."

He turned his teacup on its saucer and smiled like a rich uncle about to make a gift. "The quiet in the midst of the storm, eh? I'll see what I can do. If you'll stop by here tomorrow afternoon, perhaps I'll have something for you."

She relaxed with an exaggerated sigh. "What a relief. I can't tell you how grateful I am."

He seemed to relax as well. "So, you remembered our reception in Brussels. A pleasant evening, wasn't it?"

"Yes, and the wonderful violin concerto. You confessed you played the violin. That was a surprise."

He laughed again. "So you remember that I played violin, not that I lead tanks. Ah, how I love the mind of a woman. Do you play violin yourself?"

"Uh…no. But my brother Laurent did. He carried the musical banner in the family and had visions of being a soloist."

"And he stopped playing because of the war?"

"He stopped playing because he was killed. Just before the Belgian surrender." For the briefest moment, her bitterness surfaced and she swallowed with a dry throat.

"By German fire, I assume."

"Yes."

He dropped his eyes and nodded gently. "I'm sorry to hear it," he said with apparent sincerity. "I also have a brother who 'carries the musical banner,' as you so beautifully put it. Gerhard. He aspires to be an opera singer. But of course he's in service now."

"A shame, isn't it? The war started and all the music stopped."

"It will start again. It always does." He emptied his cup.

"Can you imagine playing again after the war?" she asked. Was the question impertinent, or did he still imagine a German victory?

"Perhaps. If not, at least I'll go to another violin concert. My wife loves them. I do look forward to that time."

"We're all waiting for that time, aren't we?"

Something rumbled in the distance and they both glanced up. It was impossible to tell whether it was thunder or bombardment.

"True, but until then, one has one's duty."

The thunderclap came again.

"A storm seems to be coming up," he said. "Perhaps you can listen to your violins tonight on the radio."

"You too, Herr Feldmarschall. Surely with the storm, there won't be any activity along the coast either tonight or in the next days." She drank the last of the tea and set the cup down lightly on his desk. "A good night to visit your wife, even."

"She'd like that. It's her birthday tomorrow. Perhaps I'll surprise her."

"Women love being surprised," she said, and stood up to conclude the conversation.

He leapt up and drew the chair away from behind her, then helped her on with her coat. "Thank you for the pleasure of your company, Madame Toussaint. As for your permit, I will arrange for my adjutant to have it ready for you tomorrow evening, in my absence."

"You are very kind. Please give my felicitations to your wife. She's a lucky woman."

Once on the street again, she all but wiped her brow. Had she really convinced the field marshal of the western front to stand down for a day? And would that even be enough? Forty-eight hours, Lew had said.

A light drizzle still fell and, barring obstacles, she calculated arriving in Arromanches before dark, with plenty of time to find her way to 200 avenue de Verdun. At least she was safe from German soldiers near Bayeux. She smiled to herself. Collaboration, even the semblance of it, had obvious advantages.

Drawing up the collar of her coat, she set off at a good pace toward the main road leading northeast. It was early evening, but the heavy cloud cover made it seem like night. The road would be long, but at least it was direct, and she wouldn't have to look for directional signs.

As the darkness increased, more thunder rumbled in the distance, and she could hear now that it was bombardment. She glanced up, wondering if she could catch sight of the bombers.

At first she could see only the waves of wind-blown clouds, but then something caught her eye and she stopped. Gliders, black against the gray sky, dozens of them. No, hundreds. Like a vast flock of sleek birds, passing silently overhead toward some inland destination. Coming from the north, it could only be the Allied forces, embarked on a strategy she couldn't imagine. She wished them well, and hurried to reach her own destination.

It was almost two in the morning when she arrived in Arromanches, and it took her another half hour to find 200 rue de Verdun. The door opened immediately to her knock and Antonia embraced her tightly.

"Where were you? I was terrified something happened to you."

Lew appeared behind her, unemotional. "What took ya?"

"I stopped for a cup of tea with Rommel," she said.

"This is no time for wisecracks. Things are about to explode."

"Yes, I know. I saw hundreds of gliders arriving. By now they've landed south of here. I'm sure it's the first wave."

Antonia sent a final message reiterating the false information and then turned off the wireless. Exhausted, all three of them dropped onto their mattresses and slept fitfully.

Around five in the morning, sleep became impossible as the sound of bombardment became more pronounced. Instead of the intermittent thud, they heard a continuous rolling thunder of explosions.

Lew stood up, rubbing his face. "The bombers will be covering the beach areas now, trying to knock out the defenses."

Antonia was on her feet now too, pulling on a sweater. "You think they'll be landing this morning, then?"

Sandrine laced up her shoes. "I have to see that. Is there any place we can look out over the sea from here?"

"Yes, upstairs. The attic has a window facing the channel."

They filed up the stairs, and Antonia threw open the window so the two of them could stand shoulder to shoulder.

"There they are," Antonia said.

A dim gray dawn was just breaking, but against the dull morning light she could easily make out the swarm of aircraft edging toward them. Scores and hundreds and thousands. Her mind couldn't take it all in. She dropped her eyes to the steel-gray surface of the channel. There, more deadly still, the black line of an armada stretched across the horizon.

"It's the beginning of the end, isn't it?" Sandrine asked, rhetorically. "The Nazis are finished."

"Oh, I hope so. But listen. This may be a terrible time to do this. Or maybe it's the perfect time, before all hell breaks loose. I've been wanting to do this for a year but never came across any gold in the Siroux forest."

"What are you rambling on about, dear?" Sandrine asked.

"This." Antonia took hold of her right hand and slid the heavy object onto her ring finger.

"What? You've given me a wedding ring?" Sandrine held it up to the light and studied the wide band of etched silver with an irregular width and edges in a filigree of gold. Only the fact that its ends overlapped rather than joined revealed it was once something else.

"I made it myself, from an antique fork, just a couple of hours ago. It took my mind off worrying about you. It's not fine art, but the metal's precious, and it's better than string."

"Oh, it's gorgeous. Like something made for an ancient princess. I love it. But you'll have to wait a bit for a ring from me. I want to give you a family ring, but we'll have to see if it survives the war in a bank vault."

Antonia encircled her from behind, pressing her face into the amber hair. "Another reason to win this war and get back to the Château Malou."

They stood awhile in the embrace, while the wind lifted Sandrine's hair, and even the presentation of the ring could not dispel their trepidation.

"We've lost so many," Sandrine murmured. "Laurent, Andrée, Florentino. Celine. And in a little while, a lot more are going to die in front of us. If I close my eyes, I can see them down there on the beach already, falling in the thousands."

Antonia held her more tightly and let the ocean wind blow into the room, over both of them. She murmured her own litany of ghosts. "Aisik, Rywka, Moishe, all the others on that train. All the other trains."

They were silent for a while, speechless at the staggering truth as the sky overhead continued to darken. Sandrine swept her glance across the terrifying panorama and cupped her ears

"Listen to the sound. A sky full of droning. Heartbreaking."

Antonia nodded. "Yes. Like the sobs of violins."

POSTSCRIPT

The story of the French and Belgian Résistance during World War II is inspiring and tragic, and the sexual preferences of its heroes would have been irrelevant. Nonetheless, in this tale, which holds close to historical reality and uses real names, I have taken the liberty of highlighting a love that was surely present, even if invisible.

Occupied Belgium had no single entity called "the Resistance," but rather a tangle of organizations with various and sometimes contradictory goals that merged and separated continuously as the war went on. They fought as much against collaborationist fellow Belgians as against the Germans, and included Communist veterans of the Spanish civil war, soldiers who escaped and formed Free Belgian troops, Jewish groups, remnants of Belgian political parties, people fleeing labor conscription, and ordinary people who aided escapees and sheltered Jews or their children.

Three of those organizations were the Armed Jewish Partisans, the Comet Line, and the maquis of the Ardenne Forest. I have the honor of knowing descendants of resistants from two of these groups, who gave me permission to use the actual names and tales of their heroic relatives. Given that the events in question may be esoteric for some readers, I list here a few brief descriptions of the entities. In all cases, a trip to Google will give you much more information.

Armed Jewish Partisans (Partisans Armés Juifs) An association of mostly non-Belgian Jews who engaged in actions primarily against collaborationist Jews and Belgians and only secondarily against the

Germans. Most were Communist or leftist-identified. My source was *Temoinages*, a book of interviews of thirty-eight members, published by their descendants. A monument to one of them, Jakob Gutfrajnd (called Kuba in the novel), stands near my house.

Breendonk A concrete Belgian fortress built in 1909 between Brussels and Antwerp that the occupying Nazis expanded into a concentration camp. It is maintained today as a museum.

Café Suèdoise (La Cantine Suèdoise). A charitable canteen that neutral Sweden established in Brussels to provide food for children. Its local managers, who were active in the Comet Line, gradually made the canteen into their headquarters. In the same building, civilian clothing was collected and distributed to disguise escaping aviators. The constant activity in the canteen provided good coverage for the arrival and departure of strangers.

Château Malou An eighteenth-century château, currently owned by the Commune of Woluwe and within sight of my house. I found a lot of information regarding its pre-war history, but none regarding its status during the German occupation. Nothing suggests it was a safe house for British aviators or part of the Comet Line, but it was pleasing to imagine whenever I took my dog on "walkies" across the estate.

Collin Family The niece of Celine Collin, herself named after her heroic aunt, provided me with details about her aunt's involvement with the maquis of the Siroux forest. She also took me to see Celine's gravesite monument near the village of Marcouray, which tells of her death by German snipers in September 1944.

Comet Line *(Le Réseau Comète)* One of several organizations that helped downed aviators and others (Jews, anti-Nazi politicians, escaped POWS, forced-labor evaders) through France to either Spain or Switzerland. It was founded by Andrée de Jongh and her father Frédéric, both of whom were captured—she on her thirty-third journey to Spain. She was sent to Ravensbrück but survived the war, though Frédéric was executed, as well as twenty-three other leaders. In total, the Comet Line is credited with saving between seven and eight hundred Allied soldiers and civilians.

Dossin Military Barracks Located in the town of Mechelen (French-*Malines*), these were converted by the occupying Nazis into a collecting camp for Jews, resisters, and other undesirables in preparation for deportation to the East.

Dunkirk Evacuation (France) May 27-June 4, 1940 The initial defeat and retreat to the beaches of the British Expeditionary Force that was rescued by military vessels and a flotilla of small craft. The surviving forces made continuation of the war possible while the soldiers left behind and hidden by sympathizers led to the creation of the various "lines" that smuggled personnel out of the occupied countries.

Ersatz (German: "substitute") Now an English word for all food substitutes, the concept was introduced during the war years as coffee and tobacco became scarce and other plants were used, with varying success, as alternatives.

Alexander von Falkenhausen Nazi Governor General of Belgium (1940-1944) A Prussian aristocrat and close friend of Rommel and other anti-Hitler conspirators, he was suspected of supporting the assassination attempt in July 1944 and was imprisoned by Hitler. Nonetheless, having signed orders for the deportations of Jews and resisters from Belgium to Auschwitz, he was tried in Brussels in 1951 and sentenced to hard labor in Germany, though later pardoned by Chancellor Adenauer.

Goldman Family All the victims of the industrialized slaughter machine of the Third Reich have their tragic stories. I have chosen this one because I had the humbling experience of meeting the now-seventy-something "baby Jackie" of the novel. Jackie not only provided me with the details of the story of Aisik, Rywka (who died at Auschwitz), and Moishe (Michel, who survived), but guided me around Breendonk concentration camp where Moishe had been imprisoned.

Maquis /maquisards A general term applying to men (and a few women) who originally fled into their respective hills and forests to avoid labor conscription and later evolved into guerilla fighters that harassed the occupying Germans. Armed by the SOE through parachute drops of munitions, they provided significant assistance to the Allies during the invasion of Normandy and the liberation of Belgium and France.

Police Forces Under the general authority of the German military, Belgium was controlled overtly by German gendarmes (military police) and collaborationist Belgian police, and secretly by the Gestapo through their agents in the *Sicherheitsdienst* (security service) and *Sicherheitspolizei* (security police). In addition, many anonymous informers (*muchards*) were on the Gestapo payroll. While

German forces were ubiquitous, the evaders of the Comet Line were also subject to the scrutiny of the *Milice Française* in France and the Falangist forces in Spain.

Queen Alexandra's Royal Army Nursing Corps The nursing branch of the British Army. They played a significant role in the care of British soldiers, both in the war zone and at home. They were among those fleeing at Dunkirk.

Rexists (*Parti Rexiste*) An extreme right-wing nationalist Belgian party similar to the Italian Fascists and the Spanish Falangists, led by Léon Degrelle. Desiring a right-wing revolution with the dominance of the Catholic Church, they took their name from the Church social doctrine of *Christus Rex*, though the official Church disavowed them. They collaborated openly with the Nazi occupation and made up the Wallonie division of the Waffen SS, which fought in Russia. Flemish nationalists provided the same sort of right-wing support from the Flemish side.

Erwin Rommel German field marshal. One of the generals who tore through Belgium in May 1940, he helped create the Atlantic Wall against a feared Allied invasion. In June 1944, he was put in charge of coastal defense along with von Runstedt and believed that the main thrust of the invasion would be at Pas-de-Calais. Consequently, he left Normandy on June 6 for a family visit and a meeting with Hitler, and was absent when the Allied forces landed. He did play violin as a young man, and his younger brother was an opera singer.

Rue du Marché au Charbon A street in the old quarter of Brussels where Jews were hidden. The building described here is the current Maison Arc-en-ciel, the gay center of Brussels.

Special Operations Executive (SOE) Britain's wide-ranging espionage, sabotage, reconnaissance, and resistance-aiding organization in the occupied countries. The program lasted from 1940 to 1945 and employed or controlled some 13,000 people, of which about 3,200 were women. SOE refitted military aircraft to drop containers (of armaments, explosives, general war material, and money) and personnel into the occupied zone. Primary craft were Whitleys, Stirlings, Halifaxes, and the agents' favorite, since it could fetch them out from a small landing space, the tiny Westland Lysander.

Twentieth Convoy (from Belgium) The only deportation convoy successfully stopped on the ground. Youra Livchitz (of the *Partisans*

Armés Juifs) and two non-Jewish school friends, Robert Maistriau and Jean Franklemon, stopped the train with a simple red lantern and a single pistol. They were able to open only one carriage and free seventeen people, but during the course of the next hours, some two hundred escaped, about half of whom were killed or recaptured and deported later. Wikipedia gives the number of successful escapes at one hundred fifteen.

Wallonie/Flanders Wallonie, in the south of Belgium, is French-speaking while Flanders, in the north, uses Flemish, a variation of Dutch. Brussels, in the middle of Flanders, is considered bilingual, though the majority speaks French.

About the Author

A recovered academic, Justine Saracen started out producing dreary theses, dissertations, and articles for esoteric literary journals. Writing fiction, it turned out, was way more fun. With eight historical thrillers now under her literary belt, she has moved from Ancient Egyptian theology (*The 100th Generation*) to the Crusades (*Vulture's Kiss*) to the Roman Renaissance.

Sistine Heresy, which conjures up a thoroughly blasphemic backstory to Michelangelo's Sistine Chapel frescoes, won a 2009 Independent Publisher's Award (IPPY) and was a finalist in the ForeWord Book of the Year Award.

A few centuries further along, WWII thriller *Mephisto Aria*, was a finalist in the EPIC award competition, won Rainbow awards for Best Historical Novel and Best Writing Style, and took the 2011 Golden Crown first prize for best historical novel.

The Eddie Izzard-inspired novel, *Sarah, Son of God*, followed soon after. In the story within a story, a transgendered beauty takes us through Stonewall-rioting New York, Venice under the Inquisition, and Nero's Rome. The novel won the Rainbow First Prize for Best Transgendered Novel.

Her second WWII thriller, *Tyger, Tyger, Burning Bright*, which follows the lives of four homosexuals during the Third Reich, won the 2012 Rainbow First Prize for Historical Novel. Having lived in Germany and taught courses on 20th Century German history, Justine is deeply engaged in the moral issues of the "urge to war" and the ease with which it infects.

Beloved Gomorrah, appearing March 2013, marked a return to her critique of Bible myths—in this case an LGBT version of Sodom and Gomorrah—though it also involves a lot of Red Sea diving and the dangerous allure of a certain Hollywood actress.

Saracen lives on a "charming little winding street in Brussels." Being an adopted European has brought her close to the memories of WWII and engendered a sort of obsession with the war years. *The Witch of Stalingrad*, her work in progress, tells of the collaboration between an American journalist and an aviator in the Soviet Air Force in WWII. It is based on the true story of the female Russian pilots who fought on the Eastern Front and at Stalingrad, and whom the Germans called "the night witches."

When dwelling in reality, Justine's favorite pursuits are scuba diving and listening to opera.

Books Available from Bold Strokes Books

The Heat of Angels by Lisa Girolami. Fires burn in more than one place in Los Angeles. (978-1-62639-042-3)

Season of the Wolf by Robin Summers. Two women running from their pasts are thrust together by an unimaginable evil. Can they overcome the horrors that haunt them in time to save each other? (978-1-62639-043-0)

Desperate Measures by P. J. Trebelhorn. Homicide detective Kay Griffith and contractor Brenda Jansen meet amidst turmoil neither of them is aware of until murder suspect Tommy Rayne makes his move to exact revenge on Kay. (978-1-62639-044-7)

The Magic Hunt by L.L. Raand. With her Pack being hunted by human extremists and beset by enemies masquerading as friends, can Sylvan protect them and her mate, or will she succumb to the feral rage that threatens to turn her rogue, destroying them all? A Midnight Hunters novel. (978-1-62639-045-4)

Waiting for the Violins by Justine Saracen. After surviving Dunkirk, a scarred and embittered British nurse returns to Nazi-occupied Brussels to join the Resistance, and finds that nothing is fair in love and war. (978-1-62639-046-1)

Because of Her by KE Payne. When Tabby Morton is forced to move to London, she's convinced her life will never be the same again. But the beautiful and intriguing Eden Palmer is about to show her that this time, change is most definitely for the better. (978-1-62639-049-2)

Wingspan by Karis Walsh. Wildlife biologist Bailey Chase is content to live at the wild bird sanctuary she has created on Washington's Olympic Peninsula until she is lured beyond the safety of isolation by architect Kendall Pearson. (978-1-60282-983-1)

Night Bound by Winter Pennington. Kass struggles to keep her head, her heart, and her relationships in order. She's still having a difficult time accepting being an Alpha female. But her wolf is certain of what she wants and she's intent on securing her power. (978-1-60282-984-8)

Slash and Burn by Valerie Bronwen. The murder of a roundly despised author at a LGBT writer's conference in New Orleans turns Winter Lovelace's relaxing weekend hobnobbing with her peers into a nightmare of suspense—especially when her ex turns up. (978-1-60282-986-2)

The Blush Factor by Gun Brooke. Ice-cold business tycoon Eleanor Ashcroft only cares about the three P's—Power, Profit, and Prosperity—until young Addison Garr makes her doubt both that and the state of her frostbitten heart. (978-1-60282-985-5)

The Quickening: A Sisters of Spirits Novel by Yvonne Heidt. Ghosts, visions, and demons are all in a day's work for Tiffany. But when Kat asks for help on a serial killer case, life takes on another dimension altogether. (978-1-60282-975-6)

Windigo Thrall by Cate Culpepper. Six women trapped in a mountain cabin by a blizzard, stalked by an ancient cannibal demon bent on stealing their sanity—and their lives. (978-1-60282-950-3)

Smoke and Fire by Julie Cannon. Oil and water, passion and desire, a combustible combination. Can two women fight the fire that draws them together and threatens to keep them apart? (978-1-60282-977-0)

Asher's Fault by Elizabeth Wheeler. Fourteen-year-old Asher Price sees the world in black and white, much like the photos he takes, but when his little brother drowns at the same moment Asher experiences his first same-sex kiss, he can no longer hide behind the lens of his camera and eventually discovers he isn't the only one with a secret. (978-1-60282-982-4)

Love and Devotion by Jove Belle. KC Hall trips her way through life, stumbling into an affair with a married bombshell twice her age.

Thankfully, her best friend, Emma Reynolds, is there to show her the true meaning of Love and Devotion. (978-1-60282-965-7)

Rush by Carsen Taite. Murder, secrets, and romance combine to create the ultimate rush. (978-1-60282-966-4)

The Shoal of Time by J.M. Redmann. It sounded too easy. Micky Knight is reluctant to take the case because the easy ones often turn into the hard ones, and the hard ones turn into the dangerous ones. In this one, easy turns hard without warning. (978-1-60282-967-1)

In Between by Jane Hoppen. At the age of 14, Sophie Schmidt discovers that she was born an intersexual baby and sets off on a journey to find her place in a world that denies her true existence. (978-1-60282-968-8)

Secret Lies by Amy Dunne. While fleeing from her abuser, Nicola Jackson bumps into Jenny O'Connor, and their unlikely friendship quickly develops into a blossoming romance—but when it comes down to a matter of life or death, are they both willing to face their fears? (978-1-60282-970-1)

Under Her Spell by Maggie Morton. The magic of love brought Terra and Athene together, but now a magical quest stands between them—a quest for Athene's hand in marriage. Will their passion keep them together, or will stronger magic tear them apart? (978-1-60282-973-2)

Homestead by Radclyffe. R. Clayton Sutter figures getting NorthAm Fuel's newest refinery operational on a rolling tract of land in Upstate New York should take a month or two, but then, she hadn't counted on local resistance in the form of vandalism, petitions, and one furious farmer named Tess Rogers. (978-1-60282-956-5)

Battle of Forces: Sera Toujours by Ali Vali. Kendal and Piper return to New Orleans to start the rest of eternity together, but the return of an old enemy makes their peaceful reunion short-lived, especially when they join forces with the new queen of the vampires. (978-1-60282-957-2)

How Sweet It Is by Melissa Brayden. Some things are better than chocolate. Molly O'Brien enjoys her quiet life running the bakeshop in a small town. When the beautiful Jordan Tuscana returns home, Molly can't deny the attraction—or the stirrings of something more. (978-1-60282-958-9)

The Missing Juliet: A Fisher Key Adventure by Sam Cameron. A teenage detective and her friends search for a kidnapped Hollywood star in the Florida Keys. (978-1-60282-959-6)

Amor and More: Love Everafter edited by Radclyffe and Stacia Seaman. Rediscover favorite couples as Bold Strokes Books authors reveal glimpses of life and love beyond the honeymoon in short stories featuring main characters from favorite BSB novels. (978-1-60282-963-3)

First Love by CJ Harte. Finding true love is hard enough, but for Jordan Thompson, daughter of a conservative president, it's challenging, especially when that love is a female rodeo cowgirl. (978-1-60282-949-7)

Pale Wings Protecting by Lesley Davis. Posing as a couple to investigate the abduction of infants, Special Agent Blythe Kent and Detective Daryl Chandler find themselves drawn into a battle over the innocents, with demons on one side and the unlikeliest of protectors on the other. (978-1-60282-964-0)

Mounting Danger by Karis Walsh. Sergeant Rachel Bryce, an outcast on the police force, is put in charge of the department's newly formed mounted division. Can she and polo champion Callan Lanford resist their growing attraction as they struggle to safeguard the disaster-prone unit? (978-1-60282-951-0)

Meeting Chance by Jennifer Lavoie. When man's best friend turns on Aaron Cassidy, the teen keeps his distance until fate puts Chance in his hands. (978-1-60282-952-7)

At Her Feet by Rebekah Weatherspoon. Digital marketing producer Suzanne Kim knows she has found the perfect love in her new mistress Pilar, but before they can make the ultimate commitment, Suzanne's professional life threatens to disrupt their perfectly balanced bliss. (978-1-60282-948-0)

Show of Force by AJ Quinn. A chance meeting between navy pilot Evan Kane and correspondent Tate McKenna takes them on a roller-coaster ride where the stakes are high, but the reward is higher: a chance at love. (978-1-60282-942-8)

Clean Slate by Andrea Bramhall. Can Erin and Morgan work through their individual demons to rediscover their love for each other, or are the unexplainable wounds too deep to heal? (978-1-60282-943-5)

Hold Me Forever by D. Jackson Leigh. An investigation into illegal cloning in the quarter horse racing industry threatens to destroy the growing attraction between Georgia debutante Mae St. John and Louisiana horse trainer Whit Casey. (978-1-60282-944-2)

Trusting Tomorrow by PJ Trebelhorn. Funeral director Logan Swift thinks she's perfectly happy with her solitary life devoted to helping others cope with loss until Brooke Collier moves in next door to care for her elderly grandparents. (978-1-60282-891-9)

Forsaking All Others by Kathleen Knowles. What if what you think you want is the opposite of what makes you happy? (978-1-60282-892-6)

Exit Wounds by VK Powell. When Officer Loane Landry falls in love with ATF informant Abigail Mancuso, she realizes that nothing is as it seems—not the case, not her lover, not even the dead. (978-1-60282-893-3)

Dirty Power by Ashley Bartlett. Cooper's been through hell and back, and she's still broke and on the run. But at least she found the twins. They'll keep her alive. Right? (978-1-60282-896-4)

The Rarest Rose by I. Beacham. After a decade of living in her beloved house, Ele disturbs its past and finds her life being haunted by the presence of a ghost who will show her that true love never dies. (978-1-60282-884-1)

Code of Honor by Radclyffe. The face of terror is hard to recognize—especially when it's homegrown. The next book in the Honor series. (978-1-60282-885-8)

Does She Love You? by Rachel Spangler. When Annabelle and Davis find out they are both in a relationship with the same woman, it leaves them facing life-altering questions about trust, redemption, and the possibility of finding love in the wake of betrayal. (978-1-60282-886-5)

The Road to Her by KE Payne. Sparks fly when actress Holly Croft, star of UK soap Portobello Road, meets her new on-screen love interest, the enigmatic and sexy Elise Manford. (978-1-60282-887-2)